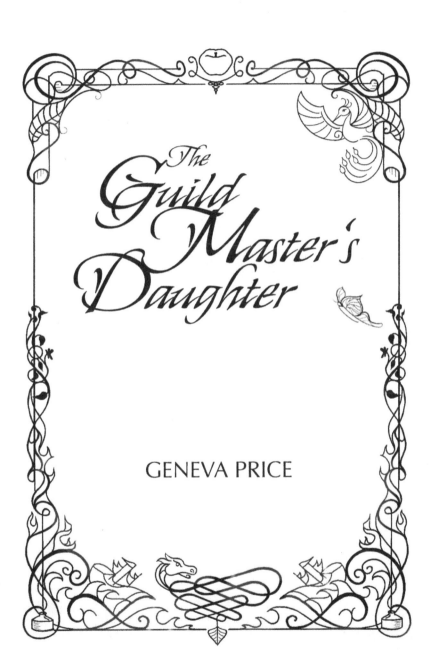

The Guild Master's Daughter

GENEVA PRICE

ISBN (paperback): 979-8-9883465-0-0
ISBN (eBook): 979-8-9883465-1-7
ISBN (hardback): 979-8-9883465-2-4

Cover Illustrations by Geneva Price

Phantasia Studio Production
Published by Geneva Price LLC
www.GenevaPrice.com

For FRC and ENC.
And for myself, to prove that it was possible.

About the Characters in this Book

When writing historical fantasy, an author must choose how much history and how much fantasy to employ, particularly when it comes to the characters. Should they be historical or should they be entirely made up, or a mix of the two? If one chooses to use historical figures, how much fiction should one use to fill in the inevitable gaps in factual knowledge? In this case, where the story is framed by the existence of a secret society of the world's greatest artists, it seemed absurd to reject the actual masters and their inspirational works of art in favor of entirely fictionalized artists and imaginary art which no reader can discover. Consequently, I decided to use real historical figures, and to do so almost exclusively. Every person in this book, save one (well, two if you count the Guild itself as character), were real people. However, someone had to be the villain.

I have attempted to adhere to verifiable historical facts. The names, positions, relationships, locations, works of art, etc., have been honored to the extent such information was readily available. However, this information served only as a naked mannequin on which each character was dressed. The personalities, motivations, attitudes, and actions of these characters are completely fictionalized to suit the story. In some cases these are flattering, in others, they are not, although no insult is intended to the figures themselves or their descendants in blood or heritage. Nothing about the representations of these characters should be taken as an accurate portrayal or likeness.

Deprived, on your very entrance into life, of an excellent Father, whose paternal care would have protected, and whose example would have enlightened you; there have doubtless been many times, when you have sighed to find yourself bereaved of that connexion enjoyed by your companions, and which it was impossible for any kindness or exertion on my part wholly to supply.

- Mrs. Barbara Hofland, The Son of a Genius

CHAPTER ONE

The Voyage

Faith was lost in a world of pure imagination.

In her mind she flew into a bonfire sunset that trailed to blue-purple dusk in her wake. Her body pulsed with the rhythmic beat of wings until they went still and soared effortlessly over deep, dark water. The sun drew Faith westward toward a strange new world that cast long, dark shadows before it.

The great bird on which Faith rode banked and circled lazily on a column of air. Tilting over the flat expanse of ocean far below, Faith tightened her grip on the smooth leather harness and flattened herself against the scarlet feathers. She urged the phoenix on with her knees and her thoughts. *Faster. Higher.* Ginger hair whipped across her face. She felt no fear of heights, only the sweet exhilaration of freedom and power.

Faith's only fear was the ocean. This high up it was rendered a featureless plain, but she sensed something primal and uncontrollable in its depths. Something there hunted her. She could feel it tracking her arc across the sky, waiting for the moment she would dip too low. Then it would strike.

The phoenix cried out defiantly.

"Faith!"

Faith started at the sound of her name so loud and near to her ear. Reality greeted her with a jolt. She was not soaring through the sky on a majestic firebird. Instead, she rode the roll and pitch of the *Illinois*, perched atop a storage locker with her back against the quarterdeck wall. Instead of riding britches, she wore a high waisted dress with a fitted bodice and full skirt under a coat that pulled uncomfortably across her shoulders. Her hair was a tight knot beneath her bonnet, the only loose part of it the fugitive tendrils torn free by the wind. The only leather in her hands was the soft-covered sketchbook she had been drawing in.

Her step-father stood in front of her with an impatient expression.

"Yes, Colonel!" She said, quickly sitting upright.

"I've been calling you." He scowled down at her.

It was hard to hear anything over the sound of the water, wind, creak of the ship, snapping sails, and calls of seabirds, but Faith knew he would not appreciate excuses.

"I'm sorry, Colonel," Faith said, lowering her eyes. This drew the Colonel's attention to the sketchbook on her lap and his scowl deepened. The corner of her drawing curled and danced as though clambering for attention. Too late, Faith snapped the book shut.

"What have you been sketching?" the Colonel asked, holding out his hand. Faith's stomach knotted but she obediently handed the book to him. He held it open at arm's length, closing and re-opening his left eye.

"A bird," he pronounced when he had succeeded in focusing. "Nothing like any seabird I've seen. In fact, there could be no bird like this. The tail is far too long and elaborate to allow for flight under any conditions. Preposterous, really. And the lines here are weak," he said, tapping his finger on an outstretched wing and smudging the graphite. "You must make a more careful study of reality. You will have better results than indulging wild flights of fancy."

Faith looked away and bit the inside of her cheek. She knew she was not a master artist like he, but she had thought the drawing a good one. Shame heated her already wind-burned cheeks and she scolded herself for her vanity.

"Thank you, Colonel. I will try to do better."

The Colonel nodded, his expression easing. "That is all we can do."

He paged backward in her book, squinting at other drawings until he came to one that made him stop. His brows climbed and his thin lips compressed to almost nothing.

"Sirens? What is in your head, Faith Trumbull? Vulgar and disgraceful!"

Faith winced as he tore the offending page from her sketchbook as though he had torn it from her own body. He crumpled the paper in his fist and stepped to the railing to throw it over. The bent and creased sirens spiraled in an eddy of wind before dropping out of sight. For a heartbeat, Faith thought he might throw the whole sketchbook over. Her eyes pricked with tears but she bit down against the protest that rose in her throat.

When the Colonel turned back to her he still held her book in his hand but Faith would not breathe easier until it was back in hers.

"On a voyage of this length, it is unavoidable that you have been exposed to sailors' stories, but an educated lady as yourself should recognize them for the ignorant superstitions that they are!"

A loud bang interrupted the Colonel. As he turned with a glare, Faith snuck a glance at the sailors near them on the deck. Eyes on their work, none gave obvious offense. Still, the Colonel continued more quietly, "They should be dismissed as one would the rantings of the fevered, not multiplied with graphic illustration!"

In truth, Faith *was* enthralled with the marvelous tales the sailors told of strange events and stranger creatures. Hearing about krakens and kelpies had certainly done nothing to alleviate her fear of the sea- she could hardly venture closer than two paces to the railing- but she had been spellbound nonetheless. Their world was one of adventure and mystery, danger and beauty, altogether unlike her ordered and predictable one. Even if their stories had been less thrilling, after more than a month on board, they were nearly the only distraction left to her. She was bored *and* wicked.

"Yes, Colonel," she said, acknowledging his rebuke. Afraid to meet his eyes, she spoke to the buttons of his coat. "I admit that I have paid more heed than I should have but only for want of other occupations. I have read all of the books we brought, some of them more than twice. There is no more embroidery to be done without more thread. Besides, I didn't think their stories so different from the Classics or the poets." With morbid fascination, Faith had read the Rime of the Ancient Mariner at least a dozen times with hardly a cross look from the Colonel. "Why is the one acceptable to illustrate and the other not?"

"All art, indeed all thought, should be devoted to that which instructs in virtue and uplifts the spirit. Some myths and poetry are worthy to this task. Sordid and salacious tales of lustful waterborne demons, however, are not! Understanding this distinction is why these things are the province of men, particularly the masters among them. Ladies should confine themselves to fruits and flowers and the occasional modest portrait."

"Yes, Colonel, I will remember that," Faith answered, although where she would find fruits or flowers at sea was beyond her. She had traded a drawing to the Captain's cook for the last mealy apple several days ago. As for portraits...she had drawn nearly every face on board, but she wondered how modest he would find some of the sailor's countenances. To her they were pirates and explorers, star crossed lovers and tragic heroes, Byronic privateers and ancient mariners. She'd even drawn an albatross around the neck of a grizzled old sailor who looked the part. Faith eyed the sketchbook in the Colonel's hand, the knot in her stomach tightening at the thought of him looking through it further.

"Good. I suppose it is to be expected. Idle hands were ever the devil's tools," he said in a consoling tone, apparently appeased. "Consequently, you will be especially glad to hear what I came to tell you. I have spoken with Captain Noyes and it seems we have reached Montauk. We should be in port within a day, overmorrow at the most."

"That's wonderful news!"

A wave of joy to match the swells beneath the hull lifted Faith's spirits. When they had first sighted land, she had known there would soon be an end to the tedious boredom, turning food, and terrible smells. The excitement had faded as the far off shoreline slipped by day after day, never closer. With this news though, Faith could dare to believe the ordeal was near its end. She would have a proper bath and put on a fresh dress and feel truly clean for the first time in many weeks. More appealing than anything was the prospect of solid ground beneath her feet.

"Go below and tell your mother. I am certain she will be relieved as well, perhaps enough to join us for dinner. As for this" he said, holding up her sketchbook, "I will hold it for now. I suggest these last hours be spent in prayerful contemplation. There is one book you should never tire of reading."

"Yes, Colonel," Faith said, biting again at the inside of her cheek.

He responded with a curt nod that was as much approval as dismissal. He turned up the quarterdeck stairs, stride crisp and bearing upright in spite of the tilting deck.

Faith watched him for a moment. Even in his early sixties, Colonel John Trumbull was a formidable man. His hair was gray but full, his features still sharp and distinguished. He carried himself with self assurance and a noble bearing befitting his political and artistic fame. Revolutionary War hero, political prisoner, diplomat, internationally renowned artist, he counted presidents and statesmen among his regular correspondents. He filled many important roles, but doting father was not among them.

Faith often wondered what her real father had been like. Her mother refused to speak of him, whether out of pain of loss or respect for the Colonel, Faith did not know. Would he have been as handsome and well respected? Would he have been more loving and less reserved? Would he have praised her simple drawings and let her call him Father, or even Papa, like other girls did?

She sighed and turned her gaze to the horizon. The sky had been strangely hazy since early summer, as though a gauzy veil had been drawn over the firmament, but the sunsets were dazzling. The sun was now a golden puddle beneath an explosion of carmine, vermillion, and magenta. A seagull flew past, its silhouette consumed by the bright center of the sinking sun before reemerging as a dark chevron on a flaming sky. Like a phoenix in fire.

Faith sighed again and shook her head, ridding it of unproductive thoughts. Wondering how her life might have been different was as useful as daydreaming about mythical birds. And utterly ungrateful. A man of the Colonel's stature must maintain his dignity, both in his affections and in those who shared his name. She supposed it was a mark of his esteem that he expected so much of her, and gave so little praise for it. Faith reminded herself that she was fortunate and should be proud to consider a man like him her father. If she worked harder to school her wild and wicked heart, and if he didn't look too carefully at her sketchbook, she was sure she could one day make him proud in return.

With fresh resolve and the happy prospect of an end to their voyage, Faith made her unsteady way to the stairs, grabbing in turn onto each rope, stanchion, and box that lined her path. The ocean had grown more fitful as the afternoon had passed and she could not rid herself of the image of losing her balance and tumbling overboard. At the top of the steps she paused and took one last gulp of fresh air before heading below deck.

She held her breath while her eyes adjusted to the sudden darkness. Sadly, there was no adjusting to the smell that rose up from the 'tween deck hatch down to steerage. It had not been long after they set sail before unwashed bodies, mildewed bedding, human waste, and sickness had formed a noxious miasma that was no match for the meager air from a few portholes. The fumes rose up through the hatch like a creature trying to escape its own stench.

Of course, the Colonel would never have demeaned himself to travel in such conditions and had secured them a room. Faith walked as quickly as decorum allowed down the common space between the staterooms, not daring to draw breath again until she was at her own cabin door. She stepped into the cramped room and wrinkled her nose. It did not smell good in the cabin either. Her mother had suffered seasickness the whole voyage and the bedding was musty with constant damp. But the porthole was open, moving the stale smell of vomit and mold, and compared to the stench from steerage, it was tolerable.

Her mother raised her head as the door scraped shut, then fell again when she saw it was Faith.

"Good news, Mama! The Colonel says we will reach port in a day or two!"

Her mother groaned. "Bloody hell child! Must you shout so?" Her Scots tinged English accent was raspy with sleep. Her mother turned on her side and covered her head with a pillow. Her next words came out muffled. "I don't know why you are so excited. There are as many sharks in New York as there are in the water. We'd find a warmer welcome at the bottom of the sea."

The idea made Faith shiver, although she did share some of her mother's worry about what waited for them on shore. Faith was, like her mother, born in England - hardly an endearing trait to the Americans following two wars now. It did not help that her mother, an orphan raised far from high society, lacked the refined manners that were so valued on both sides of the Atlantic. Her accent and her language were coarse. Her efforts to imitate the graceful courtesies were forced and exaggerated. It was a trait that vexed the Colonel in private but one he never failed to defend in public.

They had gone to America once before, when Faith was very little. At the outset, their ship had been caught in a terrible gale and the reception by the Colonel's family had not been gentler. When her mother was tipsy, she would start to complain of some unforgivable Incident, but the Colonel would not tolerate the topic. Faith could not specifically recall the ship's dangerous passage nor any part of the Incident, but both had left a mark in her mind. Whatever had happened, the Colonel had severed most of his family connections and they'd hardly had a letter since.

Fortunately though, none of his family lived in New York and visitors were unlikely. There was little to dim Faith's excitement about leaving the ship beyond her mother's melancholy. Still, she did speak more quietly.

"Will you come to dinner at least?" Faith asked as she went to the small dresser secured to the wall. She poured water from the pitcher into its chipped basin, careful not to splash lest the Colonel scold her for being sloppy. In the black splotched mirror, she watched her mother rise up on one elbow to consider Faith's request. Usually a great beauty, Sarah Trumbull's face was gaunt and pale with dark rings beneath her eyes. "You might feel better if you eat."

"No, I will stay abed," Sarah said, sinking back down.

Faith found herself frowning as she directed her attention to her own reflection. She removed her bonnet to find a sunburnt nose and chin and a frizzy halo about her head. She splashed some water on her face and used wet fingers to coax the curls back into place. She was only partly successful, but it would have to do. Having washed off the salt air and neatened herself as well as she could, she turned back to her mother.

"Can I bring you something, at least?"

"Wine, dear. Bring me some wine. It settles my nerves."

"Yes, Mama," Faith said as she slipped quietly out the cabin door.

Is there a thing of which it is said, "See, this is new?"
It has already been in the ages before us.
The people of long ago are not remembered,
nor will there be any remembrance of people yet to come
by those who come after them.

Ecclesiastes 1:10

CHAPTER TWO

The Last Campaign

The Colonel lingered in the common area for a while after dinner, but soon excused himself to pace the deck. The night was unusually balmy with a strong wind driving broad bands of clouds across the sky. The waning gibbous moon gave them a silver aura and made the white-capped waves glow. Squinting, the Colonel could make out the black silhouette of land. He regarded it with both eagerness and apprehension, as though on the eve of battle.

He had only ever wanted one thing in life: a legacy. From the time he had learned of Phidias and Praxiteles, Zeuxis and Apelles, names celebrated for their art more than two thousand years after their deaths, he too had dreamt of such immortal fame. He had been certain and determined that he too would create such works of enduring art that his name would live on, remembered long after those associated with the baser affairs of war and politics had been lost to the tides of history. A rueful smile turned the corners of his lips as he remembered the look on his father's face when he had asked to study under Mr. Copley rather than take the place his father had procured for him at Harvard.

"This isn't Athens," his father had said.

Hindsight turned the Colonel's smile into a frown. His father had been too right.

It had not been until after the first war that an introduction by Dr. Franklin had connected him with Benjamin West, the gifted American expatriot who had risen to become royal painter to the British king. It was from West that he had learned what it truly meant to have Talent. From the moment he had learned of the Guild, it was no longer enough to be considered a master by common men. After all, what was the approbation of the blind and uncultured compared to those who knew the real power of the pencil? From that day he had determined to become a Guild Master himself, a legend among legends.

Thirty years later, he had thought his dues overpaid. He had thought it was his time. The Colonel had sailed to England with two purposes. One, to benefit from the eminent physicians who, he had been assured, could both alleviate the pain and further deterioration of his ever-useless left eye and stop the spread of its affliction to the right. The greater mission had been to visit Guild Master West and secure his endorsement for the foundation of an American Guild with himself at its head. He had failed at both purposes.

The deck rocked sharply, forcing the Colonel to steady himself at the rail. He held it white knuckled as he remembered the interview with Mr. West. The Colonel had been received in Mr. West's studio where he was at work on an enormous canvas. Mr. West had been refining the musculature of a pale horse at the center of a tumultuous scene.

The Colonel had delivered his proposal to the man's back, the motion of Guild Master West's brush the only clue to his thoughts. When the Colonel had finished, there had been a silence as the brush moved undisturbed from palette to canvas.

"Will you endorse my bid?" the Colonel had asked.

The brush wavered ever so slightly. "No."

"That is your answer? How can you object to an American Guild? Surely you recognize that we are no longer the artistic wasteland you left so long ago. The constant stream of American Talent which has come to you here and the strength of their product is enough to demonstrate that we merit a chapter of our own."

"I do recognize the American Talent. I have had the pleasure of initiating a great many of them and seeing them rise to the level of Master. Yourself included." His tone had been infuriatingly mild. Patronizing.

"Then you must also realize how dangerous it is that, with the difficulty of travel and inconstant politics, so many of them never complete the training. There are far more Journeymen and fewer Masters than there should be. Some could even be considered rogues." Mr. West had not answered him. The Colonel had grown heated at West's apparent indifference to this threat. "Or is the problem that you are an old man desperately clinging to his former glory, unwilling to pass the torch to a worthy heir?"

This time the brush stopped. Mr. West laid it on the edge of his palette and turned to face the Colonel. He regarded the Colonel for several moments with a somber expression before speaking.

"John. After all these years, do you think so ill of me? I do not oppose the formation of an American Guild. In fact, I think it is long overdue."

"Then it is me whom you find objectionable?"

"I have reservations on two counts. I have already been approached by Mr. Vanderlyn seeking the same position."

"Vanderlyn! Stop your jest. I'll grant he has Talent enough, but that upstart lacks any notion of the classical ideals, the sacred traditions that the Guild is duty bound to protect! Just look at his body of work. My work, and the esteem in which it is held, speaks for me."

"Perhaps, but consider that the American Academy commissioned Vanderlyn to expand its collection. He had their confidence."

"The Academy is run by doctors and merchants. They know nothing about art, and certainly not the Guild. Besides, he did nothing with the opportunity."

"We both know that is because they became insolvent. You were its most recent vice-president. What have you done with the position?" Mr. West did not pause to let the Colonel answer. "My point is that Vanderlyn would not have received that commission if he were not highly regarded by your brethren, and his work is popular with the educated laymen. The High Council will consider that a referendum on his fitness for the honor of Guild Master as much as for you. I will also tell you this, and hope you will take the breach of confidence as a sign of my esteem for you: Vanderlyn has plans to establish his own art academy, and to house the American Guild within that. That is why he sought me out."

"And you have endorsed him?"

Mr. West shrugged. "John, I have lived in England for so long and owe so much of my career to her, I can no longer consider myself an American. If a new chapter is to be founded, it must be at the discretion of those who will be governed by it. It is not my place to nominate or endorse. As a member of the High Council I will only vote what is before me."

The Colonel nodded, crossing his arms over his chest. "What is your second reservation, then?"

"You will not like it but I urge you to consider it. Perhaps Vanderlyn is the better candidate."

The Colonel sputtered in indignation but Mr. West held up a hand.

"You and I are old, John. Neither of us is as skilled as we once were. As we age, our vision dims."

"You are blaming this on my eyesight? I'll remind you that I have never had good use of my left eye, and earned my Mastery with ease!"

Mr. West shook his head. "I meant our imaginations as much as our eyesight. Look at this painting. Do you think it as good or better than my older ones?" He gestured to a tall, narrow painting leaning in the corner. A woman surrounded by divine light and with a dragon at her heels was being lifted by angels toward heaven. It was inspired work. "Do your recent works compare favorably to your past? Since your return, what has been the demand for your art?"

"Negligible, but that is entirely explained by the tensions between our countries. Even with an English wife and child and a son in the British Army, it is apparently too much for a prominent American patriot such as myself to ask for British patronage."

"Are you sure that is the reason? I wonder if your countrymen who are also in England now face the same obstacle?" Mr. West waved away his incendiary question. "That is of no matter. Perhaps you are right. Maybe I am reluctant to give up the helm. Maybe it is vanity, or maybe I, like you, am protective of those ideals you mention. But you and I must both consider that those ideals change, have changed, over the centuries. Perhaps it is time to let the new Talent take over while we gracefully fade into obscurity."

"I have no intention of fading away, gracefully or otherwise. I assure you I am in my prime and I will achieve my purpose with or without you. Know that I consider your lack of support a grave offense. I bid you good-day, sir!" the Colonel had said, turning on his heel to leave.

It had been the Colonel's intention to leave England as abruptly as he had left West's studio, but the outbreak of the second war had trapped him there before he could wrap up his affairs. Now, seven years later, he was finally ending his last- and he was certain it was his last- dismal sojourn in England with nothing to show for it but a mountain of debt. As it was, the stateroom below his feet represented nearly the last of his dwindling credit, this voyage one final, desperate campaign. If he did not succeed now, when?

The thought of lost time propelled the Colonel away from the ship's railing to pace the deck once again, heels knocking loudly on the planks. He clasped a fist behind his back, remembering how many times capricious fate had turned him aside in pursuit of his life's goal. Wars. Illness. Duty, both moral and to his country. *Betrayal*. With his connections and a few carefully worded letters, he had derailed Vanderlyn's ambitions and bought himself a little time, but he could not afford to be turned aside again.

And yet, all of those past hindrances paled in comparison to the one that loomed before him tonight. What he had seen in Faith's sketchbook had shaken him to the core.

Even with his impaired sight he could see the genius in her work. For pencil drawings in a pocket size sketchbook, done on the rolling deck of a ship in a strong swell, they were nothing short of incredible. The compositions were well balanced, the lines sure and elegant. Undoubtedly, the exposure to his own skill had contributed to hers, but it was far more than that. He could see the movement of the ocean and hear the call of the sirens. He had seen the unmistakable shimmer of inspiration. When he had warned Guild Master West of rogues, he had never thought to find one in his own household. Such innate Talent was rarely seen, and never in a woman. It was a perversion, a crime against nature.

Her very existence had already cost him much. To think that some ill-begotten fetch from an utterly visionless woman could threaten to undermine the Colonel's overdue legacy, or worse, threaten to expose the power that the Guild had long safeguarded, was too much to be borne.

But what was he to do about it? As a matter of strict propriety, he should notify his Guild Master. Until an American Guild had been established, however, that was Mr. West. The Colonel refused to entertain the thought. Of course, once an American Guild had been established, the Colonel would, God willing, be the master of it, and the dilemma she posed would be entirely at his discretion. He would have to keep her Talent suppressed until then. And after? She could not possibly be trained within the Guild; women had no place there. Yet, he could not dismiss her either. Ignorant and unchecked, she would be dangerous.

The Colonel stopped, grasping a stay that twitched in a fierce gust of wind. Lost in thought, he barely noticed the flapping of his coat tails or the spatter of rain on his face. Faith was the fulcrum, he realized, the point about which his fortunes pivoted. Allowed to develop her Talent, she would be his ruin, but put to good use she could be an asset. She and her abilities would need to be carefully controlled.

"Evening, Mr. Trumbull. Was it you wearing a hole in my deck a moment ago?" Captain Noyes startled the Colonel out of his thoughts.

"Yes, Captain, but it's Colonel if you please." The Colonel's hand went instinctively to the hilt of his Hessian sword, only to remember he had left it on the dresser, along with the Bible and Faith's sketchbook. "My apologies for your deck but I have many pressing affairs waiting for me in New York and I am eager to dock."

"Me too," the Captain said, looking at the sails and the sky. The Colonel noticed that he could no longer see the shore, nor the moon. The sky was thick with scudding cloud. "Storm coming. Hoping we can land ahead of it."

"Indeed," the Colonel replied.

Can you draw out Leviathan with a fishhook?
...will it speak soft words to you?
...will you play with it as with a bird or
will you put it on a leash for your girls?

- Job 41:1

CHAPTER THREE

The Great Gale

The thickness of the hull that surrounded Faith below deck was only a trifle more reassuring than the railing above. She had no fear of washing overboard, but she was acutely aware of the sea pressing in on all sides. When they had sailed in its gently cupped palm, Faith's anxiety was an ever present but manageable knot in the back of her mind. Tonight however, they were squeezed by a querulous fist. Cradle-like lulls were punctuated by dramatic rises and falls, creaks and moans, that made Faith's heart pound and pushed all sensible thoughts from her mind. One angry spasm too many and the ship would surely splinter.

Between her nervousness about both the Colonel's and the ocean's temper, and her excitement that she would soon be beyond at least the ocean's grasp, Faith had hardly been able to eat. Now, her stomach twisted around the bits of biscuit, stringy vegetables, and stale water that she had managed. An answering groan from without conjured a vivid image of their ship tumbling within the belly of an enormous beast.

Faith squeezed her eyes against the vision and shrank deeper into the niche that was her bunk. As the swell subsided, she opened her eyes and scanned the walls for signs of leaks. Finding none, her gaze fell on the bed. Her mother snored undisturbed, the empty carafe of wine sliding on the railed table beside her. The Colonel had not yet retired.

In need of distraction, Faith had resolutely followed his advice and reached for the worn leather Bible, ignoring her sketchbook which the

Colonel had left next to it with his sword. The Bible lay heavy in her lap atop the blanket that was pulled up under her arms. Faith opened it to the page marked by its ribbon and found herself in the Book of Job. Having no particular purpose, she began where the Colonel had left off.

She read with fleeting attention about the righteous man from whom God had stripped everything as a test of his faith. The print was cramped and hard to read in the oscillating light of the swaying oil lamp. Her eyes followed the words as best they could until, realizing her mind had not followed the argument, she would go back a few verses and start again. As Job argued with his friends about the nature of a god who would torment a subject so, Faith marked only the occasional philosophy or curious image. It was not until God himself answered Job, speaking from out of the whirlwind, that the words and images ensnared her imagination.

She leaned over the book, her shadow darkening the page, as visions of God stopping up the sea with bars and doors and draping it in a garment of cloud and darkness formed in her head. What would it be like to command the rain and the path of lightning, to order the stars themselves and to make them sing? How was it to fashion a world of your own design and to populate it? To craft the horse and the hawk, imbuing each with its beauty and virtue, or to devise, as on a whim, something new and exquisite and wholly unknown to man?

And then she read of Leviathan. She saw it as though it swam in the air before her, its infinite coils trailing a shining wake in the sea of her mind. Flame shot from its mouth as smoke poured from its nostrils and curled before its glowing eyes. Its teeth were a murderous portcullis raised above the gate of a black and sulfurous void. An un-restrainable beast of the sea with a heart as hard as millstone, clothed in a double coat of scales so tight that no air could come between, it feared no bronze or iron blade. On earth, it was a creature without fear; in heaven, the gods feared Leviathan.

Faith glanced at her sketchbook. Her fingers twitched with the desire to draw, to let loose the visions that howled at the gates of her mind. She tried to look away. The Colonel had been clear that he did not want her to draw. Had he left it out to test her? To take it back without permission would not only fail his test, it would be stealing. The sketchbook called to her, as though the sirens still lived within it. Faith did not know what she would do if she were caught, but the temptation was too great.

Faith shoved the Bible and blanket aside. She fumbled in her pockets hanging with her dress until she found her pencil. Trembling with both terror and excitement, Faith snatched up the sketchbook. She scrambled back into bed and pulled the blanket up. The pencil was dull but she could not pause to find the pen knife to sharpen it. Spreading the book upon her bent knees, she took a single breath and began to draw.

The pencil whispered over the paper and the graphite glittered in the lamplight as she sketched the vision in her head. So consumed was she that Faith no longer felt the movement of the ship or flinched at its creaks and cracks. Those things were now a part of the world that came to life beneath her pencil, a world of her own making.

As the image in her mind leached onto the paper, her heart slowed its frantic pace and her muscles stopped their tremors. She drew quickly, feeling less like she was creating the image so much as revealing it. Faith had just turned to the details- a sharper line here, a darker shadow there- marveling that she had lead left to do them, when she became aware of footsteps in the hall outside the cabin door. Her heart skipped a beat and her face tingled as blood rushed from it. How quickly Faith had already forgotten her promise to do better! The Colonel would be furious.

She did not have time to put the sketchbook back. His hand was on the door.

Faith shoved the sketchbook and pencil beneath her pillow and fell upon it. She closed her eyes.

She heard the Colonel enter. The effort to slow her panting breath in mimicry of sleep made her chest ache as though she were suffocating. He crossed the room toward her until his shadow darkened the light behind her eyelids. Faith felt him lift the Bible, still open on the bed, and heard it close with a soft thump. Through her lashes she saw him turn away. The shadows swung crazily as he lifted the lamp down. A moment later all was dark. Faith breathed a long, open-mouthed and silent, sigh of relief.

* * *

Faith awoke to a crash in the dark cabin. The bunk lurched violently beneath her, throwing her against the wall. She could see nothing, but a roar filled her ears. Far off, a bell clanged madly. Nearer, a man's voice shouted "Douse the lamps! Douse all the lamps!"

"Mama? Colonel?" she called out, her voice wavering.

"I'm here," her mother replied, her voice equally small. "The Colonel has gone above."

Faith half slid, half fell out of bed as the ship dove and plunged. She groped her way to her mother's bed, finding her hand in the darkness. It felt thin and cold and weak in Faith's grasp. They huddled together, shuddering with the ship as waves pounded against it. Faith felt the ocean's angry fist closing about them. The darkness itself pressed in on her until she thought, if she reached out, she could touch it. She choked for air against the tightness in her chest. Her mother sobbed and shook next to her.

They both gasped as the ship pitched and a deafening crack tore through the roar of the wind and thunder. Her mother's sobs turned to retching and the smell of sour wine and bile filled Faith's nose. Faith crawled away, her own stomach twisting. She stifled a gag.

An eerie moan echoed through the water and Faith's heart stopped in her chest. She could feel it coming, that thing that hunted her. A moment later, something slammed into the hull outside their cabin. The ship shivered.

Panic exploded in Faith's mind. She had to get out of the cabin.

Faith leapt from the end of the bed, gaining the door in a single footfall. She fell against the jamb and groped for the latch. Her fingers brushed the fabric of her coat. She tore it from its hook and shrugged into it before bursting into the pitch black hall. Her mother shouted, "Faith! Come back!" her words ending in a wet gurgle.

Back pressed to the wall, Faith felt her way to the deck stairs. Loose things scraped and slid across the floor. Her eyes were locked on the rectangle of lighter darkness that marked the opening to the deck as though it were a pole star.

As she passed the hatch to the 'tween deck she retched. Fear and overturned chamber pots had intensified the smell. She could hear people crying out from below. Water spilled from above, cascading down the stairs and over her feet. Faith grasped the railing and pulled herself to the upper deck.

She emerged into a nightmare. Menacing black clouds swirled overhead and reached down to meet the heaving sea. All boundaries between sea and sky were gone, converging into a roiling mass of wind and water. A flash of lightning revealed the rocky coast, ominously close. The wind was driving them towards it. Faith covered her ears at the clap of thunder that followed.

A fierce gust of warm, moist air, like the breath of a giant beast, slammed into her. Stinging rain flew horizontally. Shielding her eyes, Faith scanned the deck for the Colonel. All around, the crew worked frantically to secure the ship, while the Captain barked orders from the quarterdeck. "Cut it free!" she heard him yell, before the wind reduced his command to urgent pantomime. The helmsman stood his post, a look of grim determination on his face.

Another flash of lightning brought Faith's eyes skyward to where the splintered remains of the upper mainmast stabbed the sky like a broken sword. Stays and tangled rigging draped across the deck and over the railing, sailors scrambling among the lines. The ship rode up an enormous swell, bow pointed to heaven, and hovered weightless at the top. Faith had the giddy sense that the ship was flying, until it tipped down the back of the wave and crashed into a black valley in the sea. Faith was thrown from her feet. Water washed over her. She clutched at a stanchion as a thundering boom reverberated through the ship.

Beyond where the sailors worked to cut the dragging lines, a line of windblown foam described another rising swell. Faith watched in horror as it grew, a great wall of water higher than the deck. The ship listed into the trough that opened before it, the deck slanting away from Faith until she felt like she was hanging over the abyss.

She saw a shadow in its depths, thick and serpentine. Her eyes followed it up into the gathering wave. Lightning arced through the clouds above, turning the water translucent. In its obsidian wall she saw a horned head, the white cap of the wave above it like a crown. Glowing eyes fixed on her.

Leviathan.

The beast lunged toward her like a striking snake, carrying the crest of the wave with it. Faith tried to scream but no sound came out. Saltwater filled her mouth and eyes as the wave threatened to scour her from the deck. Faith wrapped herself tighter around the stanchion, pressing her face to the wet wood, panting in fear.

Water pelted her from above and below for what seemed like a lifetime. It was all she could remember and all she could think forward to. And then, through the roar of the wind and water, she heard her name.

"Faith!" the Colonel yelled. "What are you doing up—"

Another tremendous boom like a battering ram on a fortress gate sent the Colonel stumbling. Another shock wave ran through the ship. When Faith screamed this time, it was sharp and full of terror.

"Mr. Trumbull!" The Captain shouted into a lull, "Get below deck this instance." Turning to a nearby sailor he yelled, "Seal those hatches!"

The Colonel tore Faith from her stanchion and carried her down the stairs with an arm around her waist. Overhead, a sailor closed the hatch like an undertaker lowering the lid of a coffin. Faith's strength left her and she sagged in the Colonel's grip. In a daze she heard him muttering, "*Colonel* Trumbull. It's Colonel Trumbull, *Captain*."

The Colonel dropped Faith on her bed and latched the door to the cabin. Faith put a foot to the floor, but recoiled when it touched pooling water. She huddled against the wall of her bunk, her hands brushing against something in the tangled linens. Her sketchbook. She closed her eyes and clutched it to her chest. She did not pray to God for salvation. She prayed for a phoenix.

Every period of life has amusements that are natural and proper to it. You may indulge the variety of your taste in these, while you keep within the bounds of that propriety which is suitable to your sex. Some amusements are conducive to health;... there are a variety of others, which are neither useful nor ornamental;

- Dr. John Gregory, A Father's Legacy to his Daughters

CHAPTER FOUR

The Academy

Faith got on her hands and knees, feeling about blindly in the dark for her trunk. She let out a satisfied grunt when she felt its smooth hard top. Grabbing a handle, she slid it out of the deep recess beneath the closet shelves and into the light of the hall. Flipping open the latches, she raised the top to reveal a folded length of white cloth.

"I found it!" she shouted with triumph to Katherine, her mother's maid, who was interrogating another closet at the base of the stairs. Faith could hear her muttering in her coarse Irish accent as she came up the stairs.

"I'm glad I'll not be havin' to hear about this n'more," she said as she came up behind Faith. The missing set of linens had been a much lamented mystery since they had last been seen in April. With a dinner party on the horizon, the burden of solving it had fallen to Katherine. "But what coof put table linens up here?"

Faith shrugged with a small smile. "The porters must have thought they were bedsheets." After they had landed in New York last September, they had moved into a house on Broadway. It seemed they had only just settled in when the landlord sold the property and they had been forced to move in May. Faith much preferred the new house on Hudson Square that fronted a charming park with a view of the Hudson River. However, the move had not been an orderly process and table linens were not the only things that had been misplaced.

Faith started to pull the cloth out, but felt something bulky shift within its folds. She found two candlesticks swaddled in the matching napkins. She held them out to Katherine.

"I don't know if anyone's thought to miss these yet, but you'd better take them down before they do." Faith gathered the linens into her arms, a whiff of mildew wrinkling her nose. "These will have to be washed first," she said handing the bundle to Kathleen.

"They will!" the woman agreed, turning her head away.

Katherine headed back down the stairs and Faith kneeled again in front of the chest to see what other misplaced treasures might be in there. She found dresses that she and her mother had worn in the spring, along with the pins that had held them on the line to dry. No doubt they had been hanging next to the linens and all were placed in a convenient, half empty trunk.

Pushing those aside, she found a stack of books in a corner of the trunk. She took them out one by one, reading each title with a sentimental smile. A well-worn copy of *Paradise Lost. Mansfield Park. Corsair.* How many times had she read and re-read these on the ship? *The Son of a Genius. A Father's Legacy to his Daughters.* Her smile faded somewhat at this last, recalling how its instruction on etiquette and living had always made her skin feel too tight, but brightened again when she picked up *Lyrical Ballads.* She flipped through its rippled pages, quickly discovering the source of the mildew smell.

Faith reached for the last book in the trunk, stopping when she saw the cover. Her hand hovered over her sketchbook. She had not seen it since after the storm.

Suppressing the shiver that went down her spine, Faith picked it up, cradling it on the palm of one hand as she ran the fingertips of the other across its cover. Like the other books, it was swollen and puffy. It had been closed with a piece of twine to press its covers together. Or perhaps to imprison whatever demon lived within it. Holding it again, the memory of the storm came back to her.

For an eternity, Faith had braced herself in the corner of her bunk, clutching her sketchbook like a talisman against evil as the wet of her clothes had soaked it through. At first, fear had overwhelmed her, believing each terrible concussion to be Leviathan pummeling the ship. She had waited for the hull to break, for the water to rush in, and for the beast to wrap her in its mighty coils. She had tried to cry out but it was as though it already squeezed her chest. All she had managed was an insignificant whimper against the raging gale as she saw herself, muted and restrained, drowning in the cold, crushing depths.

And then a will to live so fierce that it would have taken her breath if she had any to give, sparked an ember of hope. Instead of sinking, she had envisaged herself as a phoenix rising. With the brightness of the sun, she saw herself rise beyond the grasp of Leviathan's jaws, immune to its flaming breath. Somewhere in that span of hope, the banging had stopped and the ship had settled.

Eventually, she had stood, legs cramped and trembling, and made her way cautiously to the upper deck. The ship was a battered mess, the broken mast like frayed yarn. The sky was broken too, strewn with choppy masses of dark clouds, low hanging drifts of white mist, and shifting rays of sunlight. The clouds overhead had suddenly parted, bathing the ship in a beam of golden light. The warmth on Faith's face had felt like the rainbow after the flood. Then the sky shifted again and the light faded.

It was in the aftermath that Faith learned it was the broken mast top, trailing by the rigging, that had pounded the ship with each surge. During the two days it took for them to limp into harbor, there was talk of nothing but the danger they had been in as it threatened to punch a hole in the side, while the wind had pushed them ever closer to shore. Just as the crew had cut the lines and freed them of the battering ram, the winds had suddenly turned and they were saved.

And yet Faith could not forget what she had seen and felt and heard as the storm raged. She could still see the horned head and its glowing eyes and hear its growls and searching calls. It did not help that, among the excited chatter, she had overheard some sailors' whispered argument about whether it was a kraken or a serpent that had beset the ship. She had to bite her cheek to keep from chiming in. The Colonel would have scolded her for indulging rank superstition. Still, she could not convince herself it wasn't real, nor could she escape the feeling that she had called it from the depths herself.

What of the phoenix though? If she had somehow invoked the demon, had she also manifested her salvation? There was less evidence for that. No hushed tales of firebirds passed between deckhands. While she had felt the fear and the exaltation in equal measure, the latter proved more ephemeral.

It was far easier to believe, if she had any power at all, that she had created a monster. Her fears had set up housekeeping at the gatehouse of her imagination, warning all thoughts that passed by about the dangers that might lie beyond. She had thought the sketchbook lost in the confusion of disembarking and, for a time, had not missed it.

With the rationality of intervening months, the notion that her drawings could have been responsible for any of the harrowing experience, good or bad, had begun to feel ridiculous. It could all be put down to an overwrought imagination trying to make sense of a truly terrifying situation. When she dared give her imagination freer rein again, Faith had lost the habit of drawing. There were times when some vision would come to her so intensely it was as if her soul itched, but whenever she found herself looking for pencil and paper to relieve it, she would focus on some menial task until the urge faded away. Industriousness had two rewards: keeping her distractibility in check and pleasing the Colonel. It had made for a placid, if dull, existence with one particular misgiving. It irked Faith that those who preached hard work as the way to peace might have been right.

But now, to see her sketchbook again after so long, she felt a shiver of excitement mingled with fear. Faith laughed inwardly at herself for being such a sentimental fool and began to untie the knotted twine. Something stayed her hand.

It was all nonsense, she assured herself. There was nothing to be afraid of; Faith simply had no need to revisit the feeble doodles of a bored, and consequently impressionable, child. Surely she had better things to do with her time.

Faith tossed the unopened sketchbook into the trunk and piled the books back atop it. Faith snapped the trunk lid shut and pushed it far back into the closet where it disappeared into the shadows again. Gathering up the dresses, she headed down the stairs to put them in the laundry.

Faith had just dropped them on the pile with the other washing when the distinctive rattle of the front door's transom announced that the Colonel had come home. He hung his coat on the tree by the door as the cold blast of air that had followed him in raced ahead down the hall. Faith tightened the shawl around her shoulders with a frown for the weather. It made England's oft-maligned climate seem downright temperate by comparison.

Their first winter had been predictably cold and dreary, but when spring had tried to come the winds and snow had refused to concede. A few balmy days had coaxed the trees to blossom, but then a sudden storm covered the delicate buds in glistening shrouds of ice. It had been quite beautiful until the next warm spell melted the ice and the flowers hung black and blighted. It had continued, the promise of spring repeatedly broken by unrepentant winter, as March turned to April and April to May.

Summer had proved no hardier a foe, only adding fluctuations of torrential rain and devastating drought to the inconstancy of temperature. In the past few weeks it seemed that summer had won some ground in the battle of the seasons. Faith had finally been able to go outside without coat and gloves, to feel on her skin the alternating warm and cool of sunlight and shade beneath the beleaguered trees. She had wanted to run and dance, to indulge the bacchanalian high spirits that only a bright day after such a long dark winter could inspire. Instead she had contented herself with a daily, decorous walk through the park to the riverside to watch the sloops and the ferry that ran upriver to Albany, trailing a frothy cloud of steam against a brilliant blue sky. And then, this morning, they had awoken to a frost utterly unheard of in the last week of August. Her jailor had returned and the house was once again her chill prison.

The Colonel's step was quick down the hall. Faith nearly collided with him on her way to greet him.

"Excuse me, Colonel!" she said, shrinking aside to let him pass. Instead he stopped in front of her, his face animated.

"Faith! Is your mother about? I have excellent news to share with you both!"

"The weather has turned her spirits, but I can get her if it is important."

Faith hesitated ever so slightly in reporting her mother's condition. Today it was too dark, tomorrow it might be too bright, another day the idea of company too hateful. It seemed she was ever indisposed. That in itself was not the worst thing, but the amounts of wine her mother drank to fortify herself against it were not only ineffective but irritated the Colonel to no end. This time, only the briefest furrow creased his brow. It must be great news indeed.

"No matter, I will tell her later when she is feeling better. Come with me!" the Colonel ordered, leading the way to his study.

Intrigued by the atypical bounce in his step, Faith followed and took up her usual seat at a small writing desk across from his larger one. As his eyesight had diminished, the Colonel had relied on Faith's mother more and more for the mundane and repetitive tasks of business such as keeping certain accounts and copying letters. As her mother's capacity had also diminished, those tasks had fallen to Faith. Back straight, hands folded in her lap, Faith waited to hear his news.

"As you know from the letters which you have so diligently copied for me, I have expended every effort to assist in the revitalization of the American Academy of Fine Art. You may have wondered why I have devoted so much of my time to it, in neglect of my own art and every other pursuit."

In truth, Faith had not wondered. She assumed he had chosen to focus on the Academy precisely because there was no other work to be done. In their brief time on Broadway, they had been in the heart of town with a veritable parade of distinguished gentlemen coming to call and commissioning portraits for themselves, their ladies, or dear, dear friends. Faith had assisted in the studio, grinding pigments, cleaning brushes, and setting out his tools like the assistant to a surgeon. He had entrusted her with recording the color keys for each portrait and filling in the backgrounds. Faith had enjoyed the busyness and the winter had passed quickly.

The Colonel, on the other hand, considered portrait work the lowest form of artistic drudgery that was still respectable. However, when they had moved to Hudson Square, he had loudly marked its absence. Here, they were too far out of town to be of much notice to any but the politicians who frequented City Hall a few blocks away, where his portraits of the best of them already hung. It was then that he had turned his attention to the Academy.

"I owe the Academy a great debt. I was one of its earliest officers, vice president, in fact, when we last left for England. Sadly, it was during this tenure that the Academy faltered and almost failed. Of course, it was never my intention to be gone so long, and I thought it left in competent hands, but I must share some of the blame. Although I have always championed the Academy's ideals, I did not give its matters the attention they required. Looking back, I should have realized that it could not succeed without my dedicated stewardship. This is, however, a mistake I have happily been able to rectify. Not only have we secured a location and the funds to renovate it, but I have just come from a meeting of the directors in which we have set a date in late October for the official reopening of the Academy."

"That's wonderful news! Does that mean you will be teaching classes there?" Faith asked. She was surprised how the idea that she might join them sprang to mind.

An oddly vague look flashed across the Colonel's face. "There will be some students. Mr. Smith will surely take on a few drawing pupils, but not principally, no." Faith cringed internally at the mention of Mr. Smith, an odious man, but the only expression she allowed to reach her face was one of mild confusion.

"Isn't the purpose of an Academy to teach?"

Again the Colonel seemed to equivocate. "Academies exist to instruct, yes. But that can be accomplished in many ways. It is not my intention to take on every lad who ever scribbled on a wall and fancies himself an artist. If any pupils are admitted, they will be of *particular* merit." He paused a moment, as if following some internal thought, before continuing with more typical assurance. "The primary purpose of this Academy will be to instruct and uplift the citizenry with a collection of the most refined and virtuous art to be found in America. To this end, naturally, the directors have expressed their desire that I contribute a substantial number of my paintings to anchor the opening exhibit. Not only that, but the directors were most effusive in their thanks for my guidance and begged me to continue at their head to ensure that this new life for the Academy be a long and prosperous one. On both counts, I humbly agreed and Mr. Clinton, the current president, has instructed that he would formally and happily cede the position to me at the next director's election."

The Colonel concluded his speech in such a way that demanded awed congratulations. Faith obliged, legitimately glad for him, and for herself if his current good spirits carried forward. She clapped her hands beneath her chin. "President of the Academy! My excitement is dulled only by the obviousness of the position. No one else could have been a better candidate. And, to have your paintings finally on display again rather than hidden away in crates! Have you given any thought to which ones?"

"As it happens, I have begun a list." The Colonel produced a folded paper from his pocket and handed it to Faith. Hands clasped behind his back, he proceeded to speak to the upper registers of the walls as he paced before his desk.

"Although it is the modern custom for Academies to show only contemporary work, our goal is to demonstrate how favorably our American arts compare to the venerated masters. You will see that I started with the Old Masters' which are still in my possession. From my own work though, I should think a mix of historical- Bunker Hill for certain- and spiritual. Perhaps the Madonna and Child... but it is after Raphael's, so I might include that as an Old Master. Portraits, of course, but only those which set the proper tone. I have already included General Washington and decided against Jefferson, but I will have to give some thought to Hamilton and whether I should include anyone still living lest it be thought I am currying favor... Are you getting this down?"

Startled to realize he had meant for her to act as secretary to his rambling thoughts, Faith spun in her chair. The Colonel waited on the balls of his feet as she readied her pen and ink. When she was set to begin recording, the Colonel resumed his monologue. Faith took diligent notes, her mind wandering only occasionally to the small book tied with twine that called to her from somewhere overhead.

A fine woman, like other fine things in nature, has her proper
point of view, from which she may be seen to most advantage.
- Dr. John Gregory, A Father's Legacy to his Daughters

CHAPTER FIVE
The Seal

Faith cupped her frozen fingers to her mouth and tried to breathe life back into them. Her moist breath lingered for a moment but quickly disappeared. The weather had not thawed in the last two weeks and the small stove in the corner was no match to the chill. She stood in the middle of the carriage house, which was behind and separated from the main house by a small courtyard, surveying the organized disarray around her.

Since they had not had a carriage of their own since leaving London, it had seemed expedient to store the crates of artwork that had been brought back from England in the unoccupied building. At the moment however, Faith wished that they had put them somewhere warmer.

The Colonel had been helping her, or rather she had been helping him, unpack and sort the paintings for those that were destined for the Academy exhibit. They had hardly started when Mr. Murray had called and the Colonel had left her with the list and instructions. As requested, she had divided the pictures into groups according to their needs. Against one wall were those that showed some damage, while on another were those that simply required a good cleaning. Making a table out of an emptied crate, she had carefully laid out the rolled canvases that would need stretching and framing. She had accounted for all of the paintings on the list but a few.

Faith scanned the remaining pictures distributed around the crates. Lips quirked in consternation, her eyes landed on a door at the other end of the room. Her father had intended to make the little office his new studio before being distracted by Academy business. Perhaps he had stored some paintings in there.

Faith tried the door and found it unlocked. Peering in she saw the easel and her father's collection of brushes. On a table was the scale for measuring pigments with a case full of the necessary jars on the floor beneath it. There were a few canvases next to the easel but no sign of finished work. She was just pulling the door shut, with one last glance around, when she noticed a large canvas covered in a white sheet leaning on the wall behind the door. Curious, she stepped around and lifted the sheet.

It was immediately clear that it was not on her list, but something about it excited Faith's interest and she turned the sheet back all the way. In some respects, she could tell it was the Colonel's work, but in others it was hard to believe that it might be his. For one, he rarely painted landscapes other than backgrounds for his historical pieces and this was too romantic by far for those. Beyond the rather dark and looming rocks and trees that crowded the foreground, there was an idyllic valley with a curving stream. To one side stretched lush rolling hills dotted with grazing sheep. On the other rose wooded slopes where a break in the trees revealed the roof of a country manor. The sky sparkled and the clouds were opalescent.

Just as Faith was wondering how she had never seen this painting before, she realized that she had. The memory of it was like a dream, variously in and out of focus. Faith could remember sitting on the floor before it, the chubby, dimpled hands of a child reaching toward the picture. She felt that she had sat there for a long time, entranced by the tranquil scene until the study door had been thrown open and milling feet had broken the spell. "There you are! Where were you hiding?" her mother had cried, sweeping Faith up into her arms and pressing her tightly against her shoulder.

Even now, as Faith's gaze rested on the rocks and trees in the foreground, she felt the half-remembered pull. The space between them seemed to stretch and deepen as though inviting her to step into the charming space. The leaves fluttered as a warm breeze caressed Faith's cold cheeks. Bells tinkled in the distance.

Her eyes traveled to the rooftop in the trees. The face of a pale woman with soft blond curls and empty eyes flashed into her mind as her lavender perfume filled Faith's nose. She felt a chill wash over her and tried to rub the scent away.

A knock made Faith jump.

"Miss? Are you in here?"

Faith pressed a hand to her hammering heart as Katherine poked her head in the carriage house door.

"Yes, I'm here." Faith moved into Katherine's line of sight, trying to keep the breathlessness and startled irritation out of her voice.

"There's a gentleman here to see the Colonel."

"Did you take his card to the Colonel?"

"Not for anything, Miss. He's still meeting with the other gentleman."

Katherine was terrified of the Colonel and used every excuse to avoid him. His being in a meeting was one of many. Exasperation shortened Faith's tone.

"Fine, I'll take care of it. Just tell whoever it is I'll be a moment."

"Yes, Miss," Katherine said ducking her head, and disappeared.

Faith returned to the painting, which at this moment presented nothing odd. The brushstrokes and texture of the canvas conveyed no special sense of depth. It did not move and she smelled nothing but the dust that covered everything, including herself. Would she ever master her unruly imagination? With a perturbed frown, Faith rearranged the sheet over the painting, careful to leave it exactly as she found it. She had a distinct feeling that the Colonel would be unhappy to know that she had uncovered it.

Faith walked briskly back to the house, untying her dusty apron as she went. She brushed at her hair and skirts before going inside and left her apron on the hook just inside the door. Hands tingling with the relative warmth of the house, she made her way to the foyer and tried to smooth the annoyance from her face.

She must not have been entirely successful judging by the furrow that appeared in the waiting gentleman's brow. This was a shame because otherwise Faith could find no fault in his features. His face was youthful and strong with each element- jaw, cheekbones, nose, and brow- all clearly defined but none overbearing. The only muted aspect were eyes of an indistinct hazel and the laugh lines at their corners. He spoke before Faith had fully reached him.

"I beg your pardon, miss. I did not mean to disturb the household so. I've a letter of introduction to Mr. Trumbull and meant only to inquire about his availability. If he is not at his leisure, I would be happy to leave it and come back another time."

Where Katherine's Irish accent was rough as burlap, the gentleman's was as lilting as silk in a breeze. As Faith came to a stop in front of him, she noted he was tall and slim, well built and well dressed. Her irritation had vanished. Nervous self-consciousness had replaced it.

"Not at all, sir. I must apologize to you for such a confused reception. I assure you, your visit is no trouble at all."

"Are you certain? It would seem both you and Mr. Trumbull are already occupied." His eye's fell to Faith's sleeves which she discovered were marred by dirty swipes. She brushed at one of them but stopped when she saw the cloud of dust her action created. "If I may," he continued, pulling a handkerchief from a pocket and offering it to her. "You have a smudge at your nose."

"Oh!" Faith's hand flew up to hide the mark, flushing with embarrassment. There was a handkerchief in her own pocket, but Faith took his in her haste. It was warm from his body. She scrubbed at her upper lip and nose as he politely admired the parquet. When she thought she had rubbed as much as she dared before making herself even redder, Faith timidly presented her face for inspection.

The gentleman looked her over before tapping a spot next to his own nose. "Just here."

Faith folded the cloth to a clean spot and gave the area one more swipe. She forced herself to meet his eyes.

"That's it. Clean as spring rain," he said with a wink that made Faith's heart trip.

"Thank you, sir." Faith said, letting her eyes fall away to the side. She held out her hand for his letter. "Who should I tell the Colonel is calling?" As handsome as he was, she was eager to get this interview over before she died of mortification.

"Charles Ingham, miss."

Faith took the folded letter and knocked on her father's study door. She turned the letter over as she waited for the rumble of voices on the other side to stop. The handwriting on the front was simple but elegant. On the back there were two seals where ordinarily there would be one. An elaborate letter C in the gothic style was stamped in red wax. The other, in dark purple wax, was an owl taking flight with a starburst above its head. A little thrill of recognition went through Faith's mind. The same device was carved into the lid of one of the Colonel's writing boxes. How curious that Mr. Ingham should carry a letter with a seal of the same design. She was about to knock again when the Colonel called her in. Faith gave Mr. Ingham a small smile as she ducked into the study.

Faith curtsied to Mr. Murray, apologizing to him for the interruption, and then turned to the Colonel who was looking at her with a slight frown. Under the Colonel's gaze, she was even more aware of her disheveled appearance.

"A Mr. Ingham is here to see you." Faith crossed the short distance and placed the letter in the Colonel's hand. As he turned the letter over surprise flashed across his face but vanished in an instant.

"Mr. Murray and I were just about finished." A tilt of Mr. Murray's head seemed to indicate this was news to him. "Have a seat Faith. I would like to look over this letter before you bring him in."

Faith took her seat at the little desk and thought of disappearing into the woodwork while the two men concluded their business. The Colonel continued where he had apparently left off.

"Dr. Hosack has written to Fulton's widow about her lending pieces from his collection to the exhibition and I already have it on good authority that the Philadelphia Academy will not object. That will account for the pieces from West that the directors wanted without having to approach him directly. And as I was saying earlier, I have selected about twenty paintings from my collection-" he broke off and looked at Faith. "Are they all accounted for?"

"Nearly all." Faith handed him the list.

He waved a dismissive hand over it. "The rest are in your storehouse Murray. Some of them will require stretchers and cleaning, but I should have them ready by the time the sculpture casts are being moved out of storage and we can have the whole lot transported together."

"The casts will need cleaning too," Mr. Murray noted.

"Yes. And fig leaves on the nudes. Talk to Dixey about that. I believe he is up to the task. With my work, Fulton's collection, and the casts, we have a sound foundation. For the rest, we should put out a general appeal to other collectors to turn out the pockets of their drawing rooms, so to speak. I know you and Dr. Hosack have some work which you might contribute. A letter to Mr. Astor or Mr. Graham, for example, might result in a few worthwhile additions. We could also solicit contributions directly from some of our younger artists, but with the stipulation that inclusion in the exhibit is entirely within our discretion. I'm thinking Waldo, of course.

Jarvis is unorthodox but one of the favored portraitists. Sully, Allston..."
The Colonel trailed off in thought. He picked up Mr. Ingham's letter and
turned it absentmindedly.

"What about Vanderlyn? He already has an exhibit of his own in two
rooms of the hall. He secured them and fixed them up before we had any
notion that the Academy would be revived so quickly. "

"What does he pay in rent?"

Mr. Murray shrugged. "Nothing. But, he is charging one dollar for
admission."

"One dollar?! And he pays nothing in rent? Well that is why the
Academy has been on such poor footing. No longer! We will need his
rooms for the exhibition and he can hardly have a claim to that which he is
not paying for. Since I am not officially an officer yet, will you write to him
that he will have to vacate the space in the next two weeks?"

"He is in Jamaica. I will write to him, but it will take longer than two
weeks to get a response."

The Colonel shook his head. "Then we will have no choice but to move
them for him," he said as though he deeply regretted being in such a
position.

"We could include the pieces in the exhibition. Many of the other
directors appreciate his work."

The Colonel raised one eyebrow. "With every passing day I am more and
more relieved that I have returned my attention to the Academy.
Vanderlyn's work, while technically skilled, panders to the common
interest. It is too vulgar to promote the lofty goals our institution has set
out. If the directors insist on using his pieces, it will be against my advice
and better judgment."

Mr. Murray nodded his agreement. "I will write to him then. I daresay it
is not the first time a letter from me has brought him frustrating news." Mr.
Murray chuckled conspiratorially until, with a sidelong glance at Faith, he
remembered she was in the room. "Shall I also write to the others you
mentioned?"

"Only those collectors with whom you have influence. Dr. Hosack and I
will split the rest," the Colonel said rising from his seat. "I will extend the
invitations to the artists myself, but first we will have to establish guidelines
for their submissions. Thank you for your time, Mr. Murray. A pleasure as
always."

Mr. Murray rose and allowed himself to be escorted to the study door where he took his leave. The door had barely clicked shut behind him when the Colonel slit open the wax seals on Mr. Ingham's letter. The Colonel's writing box with the matching owl device on its lid was visible on the bookshelf beside the Colonel's desk. Faith wanted to ask about the connection but held her tongue. Instead she watched his face to see if its expression revealed any clues to the mystery. It was too difficult to tell whether his squinting eyes and knitted brow were caused by his impression of the letter or his efforts to focus on the handwriting. Ultimately, he must have found the letter favorable. He instructed her to show Mr. Ingham in.

Faith went back out into the foyer to find Mr. Ingham studying the portrait of her mother petting a small spaniel. She was elegantly dressed in a white turban and necklace of garnet beads, but the eyes were sad, almost pleading. Faith sometimes imagined she could hear the painting sigh.

"Who is this beautiful woman?" Mr. Ingham asked without turning around.

"My mother, Mrs. Sarah Trumbull."

Mr. Ingham turned to Faith, but only a quarter turn so that he could glance between her and the portrait. "Of course. Just as beautiful, but stronger and less tragic I think."

Faith blushed, not knowing how to respond to such a forward comment, particularly one that seemed both compliment and insult. She stood in uncertain silence until a noise from the study reminded her why she was here.

"The *Colonel* will be happy to see you now." She put a slight emphasis on Colonel, hoping he would get the hint. As flustered as he made her, she did not want Mr. Ingham to get off on the wrong foot with her step-father.

"The *Colonel* is too kind. As are you," he replied with matching emphasis and a playful grin. Faith found herself smiling openly in return as she led him into the study.

The two men exchanged their greetings and the Colonel formally introduced Faith to Mr. Ingham. Faith could not help but notice that the writing box now sat upon the Colonel's desk, unlocked and open. From where she stood, she could see nothing particularly unusual about its contents- a leather folio for paper and copies of letters, a stick of dark sealing wax that might or might not have been purple, and the handle of a stamp which may or may not depict the same owl as Mr. Ingham's seal.

Reluctant to leave with her curiosity so piqued, Faith lingered as long as she dare without inspiring the Colonel's ire. Only after she left did she realize she was still clutching Mr. Ingham's handkerchief.

While Mr. Ingham and the Colonel met, Faith found herself engaged in a succession of menial occupations that kept her within earshot of the foyer. She alternately scolded herself for letting her imagination get the better of her, as thoughts of secret societies like the Illuminati and the pagan rituals they were rumored to perform swirled in her thoughts, and rationalized that if she were purposefully loitering near the study, it was simply to catch Mr. Ingham and return his handkerchief. It was quite impossible that the Colonel would be involved in anything so profane as a secret society.

She was just out of sight at the top of the stairs when the Colonel and Mr. Ingham left the study. She knew it was wrong to listen at doors, but surely she could not be blamed for hearing what echoed through the open spaces of the house, particularly if she did not stop specifically to listen. Although her hands stayed occupied, her whole awareness was centered on her ears.

"The painting you won a premium for in Dublin," she heard the Colonel saying, his words just barely discernible over their footsteps, "the Cleopatra. Was that your Masterpiece?"

"It is, sir."

"Did you bring it with you to the States?"

"I did."

"Good. The Academy is having an opening exhibition and will be taking submissions the first week of October. I would encourage you to enter it, and whatever else you have brought that you think would make a good showing."

"Thank you, Colonel. I will be sure to do so."

Whatever else they said was lost to the rustle of fabric and the scrape and rattle of the front door as Mr. Ingham donned his coat and departed. For the rest of the day, visions conjured by masterpieces, Egyptian queens, secret fraternities and their arcane and mystic rites tumbled in Faith's mind like performers at a street fair. It wasn't until much later that evening that she again remembered Mr. Ingham's handkerchief in her pocket.

*And the woman said to the serpent, "We may eat the fruit of
the trees of the garden; but of the fruit of the tree which is in the
midst of the garden, God has said, 'You shall not eat it, nor shall
you touch it, lest you die."*

-Genesis 3:2

CHAPTER SIX

The Apple

The ticking of a clock, the crackling of a fire, and the scritching of nibs on
paper were the only sounds in the study. Faith and the Colonel had spent
the better part of the afternoon at their respective desks, he writing letters
and she copying them. She had heard of an invention called a polygraph
that Mr. Jefferson had at Monticello. By way of two connected pens, it
made a duplicate at the same time as the original. While that did not make
much allowance for correcting mistakes, Faith wished very much that one
were available to her.

Following the Colonel's meeting with Mr. Murray, there had been other
meetings, particularly a long one with Mr. Smith, Mr. Robertson, and Mr.
Dunlap setting out the guidelines for unsolicited submissions to the
exhibition, with each meeting generating a new list of letters and
documents to be produced that was tacked onto the end of the previous
list. Faith had been disappointed to see Mr. Smith, who always seemed to
be looking down his rather large, bent nose at everyone and everything,
several times while Mr. Ingham had not returned once. She was also
disappointed not to have seen any other letters with the owl seal, nor had
the special writing box left her father's bookcase once he had replaced it.

She would not have missed these things for lack of attention, except that
Faith had been kept tremendously busy. At first, the Colonel had put her to
repairing the damaged canvases by filling in nicks and scratches or, in one
extreme case, patching a slit that had been punched into the fabric. But

then the demands of correspondence had been too much. He had pressed her into service in his study. She had spent so much time at her writing desk that she wondered if her fingers would be black forever after.

Today, Faith had copied letters directed to a diverse audience of politicians, professionals, and wealthy businessmen, all with the same announcement about the impending Academy exhibition and the carefully worded solicitation to become an esteemed patron or contributor. Her father would keep the original draft in his letter book while Faith's neat and corrected copy would be mailed. The Colonel himself had written to the artists about submissions. Faith was both thankful, and found it a bit odd, that he never asked her to copy those letters, nor had she seen any of them in the outgoing post.

Now, Faith was nearing the end of her third copy of the submission guidelines, along with the end of her pen nib and, if she were honest, her wits. She no longer registered the words as she copied them. Her mind was as numb as her toes. Her desk was farthest from the fire and nearest the windows. As the autumn sun had set, it had taken every drop of warmth with it. The windows were now black mirrors, coldly reflecting the light of the fire and the candles on their desks without magnifying any of their heat.

The long case clock in the hall whirred and struck the hour just as she signed the Colonel's name to the document before her. She stretched back in her chair trying to relieve the burning ache in her right shoulder as she opened and closed her fists to relieve the cramping in her fingers. Her stomach rumbled. The teacup on her desk had not enough left to tell a fortune. The small plate next to it was similarly empty.

Faith could not bear to write another word, particularly if it meant trimming a new nib. She rose to stand by the fire and warm her feet. Faith glanced at the Colonel. He had not seemed to register the time, nor did he show any signs of stopping for dinner. He was bent to his task, left eye closed as he focused solely with the right. She could not see what he was working on, hidden as it was behind a low folding mirror that he said magnified the light precisely where he needed it. All she could see was the top of his pen dancing in tight little circles.

Only it was not a pen, she realized slowly, at least not a quill. It looked like polished wood, as might encase a custom made pencil. As particular as he was about his artist's tools, she had thought the Colonel too practical to spend the money on such a precious thing. Faith also noted that he never stopped to dip his pen. It must be a pencil, but who would write letters in pencil?

The little spark of interest Faith felt at this puzzle suddenly flared to excitement, driving away all remnants of the fog that had clouded her mind a moment before. The special writing box was open on his desk. Faith had not seen him take it out, nor could she see the owl and starburst with the lid opened away from her, but she knew it by its wood. The tight grain was nothing more than fine black lines between bands that glowed burgundy and purple in the firelight. She inched a step closer. The cover of the folio was turned back, revealing a stack of opened letters. The stick of sealing wax was still in its band in the lid, but the stamp was gone. She thought she saw its handle near his elbow.

Faith watched the pencil end twitch and spin until the Colonel came to the end of the letter. He folded it without blotting it and reached for the stamp. Without benefit of any wax, she saw him bring the stamp down on the letter.

Faith may have gasped inadvertently. She turned her face back to the fire lest he catch her staring. Out of the corner of her eye, he looked up, searching for her at her desk before finding her at the fireplace. He seemed to be in a stupor of his own.

"Have you finished? What time is it?" the Colonel asked.

"It is time for dinner, Colonel. Do you plan on stopping or would you like for me to bring you a tray?" Faith asked. She did not think she had a preference until his answer added fuel to her burning curiosity. If she returned with the tray quickly enough, she might get a better view of the writing box and his unaccountable actions.

Faith kept her steps measured until she was across the hard floored foyer. From there she fairly flew to the kitchen. She danced impatiently from one foot to the other as the cook assembled the tray, shooting skeptical looks at Faith all the while. Faith stuffed a roll in her mouth to appease her own stomach, earning another look. Just as she was thinking the cook was moving slowly just to spite her obvious impatience, the red cheeked woman handed her the tray. Faith walked back to the study as quickly as she could without spilling and pushed open the door that she had left ajar.

With relief she saw that he was still writing and with enough focus that he did not take notice of her in the doorway. She paused to settle herself into a more disinterested attitude and carried the tray to his desk.

All pretense at composure was lost when Faith saw what had been hidden behind the folding mirror.

In a single moment Faith took in several details. The instrument in his hand was indeed like a polished pencil at the top end, but the end beneath his grasp was a quill nib. The ink that filled it, although the inkwell on his desk was firmly capped, was peculiarly pearlescent while the letters that it scratched upon the page were instantly absorbed, matte black and dry. And then there were the letters, if they could be called letters. The Colonel was writing from right to left in some bizarre cipher.

Faith gasped in shock. In turn, the Colonel started as someone woken from a dream. His shoulder hit the tray. The tea splashed, overtaking the saucer, and dripped upon the nearest letter. With rising horror, Faith anticipated a black pool of fresh ink where the strange marks had been. Instead, the marks stayed fixed while the tea darkened the paper in an expanding stain, the edge of which seemed to scintillate with all the colors of the rainbow. She gaped in astonishment.

The Colonel turned on her, his face twisted with anger, his eyes bright with fury. Faith shrank away, cowering behind the raised tray as behind a shield. The tea splashed again. The Colonel's arm pulled back. For a moment she thought he might strike her. Instead he pointed to the study door and roared "*Get out!*"

Faith crouched and set the tray on the floor, the half empty teacup rattling with the trembling of her hands. She offered the Colonel the napkin from the tray.

"I'm sorry, sir. I was just startled... the writing... the pen..." her voice wavered and died. He ripped the napkin from her and ordered her out once again. Faith muttered another apology as tears sprang to her eyes. She ducked her head and ran to the door. Her hand had just touched the handle when the Colonel said, "Wait."

Faith stopped and turned slowly, hand still on the door handle. The Colonel was looking down at his desk as he pressed the napkin to the puddle of tea. A muscle moved in his jaw as he visibly gathered his temper. He seemed to be considering something. At last, he decided. He let out a breath and his fist unclenched.

"Come back. I have something to show you."

Faith took a few tentative steps towards the desk. She clasped her hands in front of her and kept her head low, afraid to look in the direction of the box or the strange letters. Or to let him see the tears brimming on her lashes.

"It is as much my fault as yours that you have seen what you have seen. Since that can't be undone, I will explain in order to set your mind at ease," he began. "You are familiar with the artistic guilds of the Renaissance?"

"Yes," Faith answered hesitantly. After days of wild speculation about what the seal could be, guilds had been top of her mind. She had also spent days admonishing herself that there was no such thing any longer. To have him mention it right off was either a triumph or a trap. She was caught between wanting to impress him with her knowledge and not wanting to appear to have considered it at all, unsure which was more likely to stoke his anger. Faith tried to walk a middle path. "My understanding is that the guilds controlled the training and employment of artists in order to protect the integrity of the craft."

"Exactly so. They guarded the secrets of the trade and controlled who could practice it, which, in turn, protected the prestige and the value of the artists' work. What you have seen here are the trappings of its last and most powerful guild, the Guild of Athena."

Athena. That explained the owl, but little else. "I thought the Freemasons were the only remaining guild. I've never heard of a Guild of Athena."

The Colonel snorted.

"That is intentional. The Guild of Athena's power, indeed its very purpose, is founded on its secrecy. It is also still a true art guild. The Freemasons may have begun as a craft guild but is now just a social fraternity," the Colonel said with a hint of disdain, though he hastened to add, "Don't misunderstand, there are a great number of honorable men who are Freemasons- General Washington, Dr. Franklin of course, I have painted a great many of them!- but there is hardly a one of them that could lay a brick wall if called upon to do so. The Masters of the Guild of Athena remain the top of their craft. Only a select few are ever apprenticed and fewer still become Masters like myself. And unlike the Freemasons, none would even know of the Guild's existence until they had received an invitation."

"I don't understand. You say the Guild is so selective, and yet it seems there are a great many artists who are practicing." Faith ventured. Timid at first, her voice grew bolder as the questions mounted one behind the other.

"Are they working outside of it? If so, what would keep patrons from employing them, particularly if the Guild is so secretive? How would patrons know whom to patronize?"

"You are right that the vast majority of artists today practice outside of and in ignorance of the Guild, but again, that is by design. The Guild has never concerned itself with the banality of art intended for commerce. Indeed, the work of most self-proclaimed artists is below the Guild's notice, just as the work of the Masters is above the appreciation of the common man. The common artist may serve the common interest, but the Masters of the Guild are dedicated to art that transcends the ordinary man's comprehension. We have inherited the secrets of the Old Masters. Protecting those secrets is the single-minded focus of the Guild."

The Colonel's great grandfather, John Robinson, had been a famous clergyman. Faith could not imagine that man's sermons were preached with more reverent intensity than the Colonel speaking of the Guild. But for all of his lofty speech, Faith had far more questions than answers about what she had seen. The commitment to secrecy explained the cipher and the seals, the invocation of Athena explained the owl, but why Athena? And why such secrecy? Faith could not imagine what artistic secret could be so important, or so well hidden. She had seen lesser artists draw and paint employing exactly those techniques which she had seen the Colonel use. The only difference in the outcome, she had thought, came down to skill.

Was there more to it? Was there some special weave of canvas or formula for pigment? Perhaps there was some way of applying the paint, some brushstroke or type of bristle. Maybe it was a trick of perspective. She had often heard geometry elevated to a sacred plane. Faith scanned the oddities on his desk. Her gaze stopped upon the chimera of a pencil. Did the secret have something to do with that?

Faith had little hope that he would answer, but burning curiosity made her bold enough to ask. "What kind of secrets?"

The Colonel followed her gaze to the half pen, half pencil lying on his desk. He was silent for a long moment. Sap in the logs popped and cracked. The clock ticked softly from the hall.

"I will show you if- look at me." Faith raised her eyes to meet his. "If you swear upon pain of death and eternal damnation that you will not speak of this to anyone."

Faith recoiled under the fierceness of his gaze but managed to whisper, "I swear."

The Colonel pulled a clean piece of paper to the center of his desk and took his chair. He picked up the strange pen which, as it hovered above the page had become entirely a pencil. The dark polished wood now extended from top to writing tip, except where the graphite core was exposed. It was finely sharpened even without knife or sandpaper. Faith pressed her fingers to her temples. She wondered if she were quite sane.

The Colonel began to draw. It was a simple round shape that was quickly recognizable as an apple. When the contour was complete, he began to fill it in. Instead of shades of graphite, the strokes were suddenly burgundy red. Faith covered a gasp with her palm. As he worked his way from shadow to highlight, the pen or pencil, or maybe now it was a brush, laid down ever lighter and warmer colors of red upon the cheeks of the apple. It changed to green-tinged yellows at the base of the stem.

Faith's hand fell to her throat "How is this possible?" she whispered.

The Colonel did not answer. When he was done drawing, he sat back and pushed the page toward Faith. As she stepped forward to look straight down on it, the apple seemed simultaneously flat and rounded. For a moment the two images battled and Faith felt a wave of dizziness. A heartbeat later, they resolved into one that looked as though a real apple sat upon the page.

"Go ahead, touch it."

Faith looked at him, then back at the apple. Tentatively, she reached out a finger, expecting her hand to pass through what must be an illusion. To her astonishment, her fingers met a solid object. A jolt of electricity tingled up her arm. She recoiled, but only for a second. Faith reached out again and stroked the fruit with her fingers, feeling its smooth hard surface.

"You can pick it up," he said.

Glancing at him questioningly, Faith cupped the apple with both hands. Gently, she lifted it. Without a flutter, it separated from its page. Faith found herself holding an apple that moments before had been nothing but a drawing. And before that, nothing at all. She put it to her nose. It even smelled like an apple. She dug a fingernail into its skin, which burst with a satisfying pop. Clear juice swelled and trickled down the apple's cheek.

"It's perfect!" Faith exclaimed. The Colonel looked pleased. "It looks good enough to eat!"

"No! You may not eat it!" he said with startling force. His next words were softer, if enigmatic. "As convincing as it is, one should never feast on illusions. You never know what they disguise."

"Even so, it is extraordinary!" Faith said breathlessly.

"Now, let it go," he instructed her.

"You mean, just drop it?"

He nodded.

Faith held the apple in front of her and reluctantly released her hold. Just as she expected it to hit the floor with a dull thud, it winked out of existence.

"Where did it go?"

The Colonel tapped the page on his desk. The apple, looking solid and real, sat upon the page as though she had never moved it. Faith felt giddy and insubstantial by comparison.

"Is it magic?" she asked, wide-eyed.

The Colonel shook his head. "Nothing so vulgar as magic. The Ink is a miracle. One that was discovered by the great daVinci himself."

"The Ink? Your inkwell is capped! I thought it was the pen."

"No, it is the Ink that contains the power, but only a few can use it. For those with the Talent, the Ink responds to the thoughts and the intentions of the artist."

"That is how it is a pencil one moment and a brush the next? Red one moment and green the next?"

"Exactly so, but more than that. The Ink captures and conveys every aspect of the artist's imagination, rendering sound and smell as much as color and form. When you look upon the Old Masters and hear the waves crash and smell the salt of the sea, or feel the hot breath of a vanquished dragon, that is the Ink."

"Whatever you draw becomes real?"

The Colonel glanced to the side. "After a fashion. It brings the imagination to life in a way that engages all of a viewer's senses, such that he can see and hear and feel what the artist feels. And yet, it is no substitute for reality. It has its limitations. Not only do few have the Talent to use it, and fewer still have the self discipline to control it, but not everyone can appreciate it. There are some who seem utterly immune to the Ink's power. They would see nothing but a drawing of an apple on that page and know nothing more about it."

"If that's the case, why hide it? If so few have the Talent, wouldn't it be better to let them all use it?"

"Certainly not!" The Colonel jerked upright. The apple wobbled on its page. "Just because a man has the Talent, does not mean that he can be trusted with its power. While the Ink can elevate and instruct when put to its proper use, it can be dangerous in the hands of the morally bankrupt. Imagine what would happen if they were allowed to infect people with their dark and horrible thoughts! DaVinci understood this from the moment he made his discovery. That is why he created the Guild of Athena to safeguard the Ink. It's purpose is to identify those with the Talent who merit training. And those who do not."

The Colonel said this last like a judge issuing a death penalty. Faith asked with a hint of dread, "What happens to those who aren't worthy?"

"In most cases, they are discouraged from any form of artistic expression, lest they stumble upon some awareness of their ability accidentally. It is because the Ink is kept secret that anything more is rarely needed. They are not even aware of what they are missing."

"Oh." Faith said, feeling that this was rather anti-climactic. "And what about the ones who are worthy?"

"They are invited to apprentice."

"With whom? With you?" The barest glimmer of a hope sat on the horizon of Faith's mind like pre-dawn light. She could see and touch and smell the apple. Did that mean she possessed the Talent? Could she learn to make paintings live and breath?

The Colonel shifted in his seat. "At present, no, but soon I hope. Currently, there is no American chapter of the Guild. All of the Masters here have had to train in England. These letters," he said, gesturing to the scattered papers on his desk, "the revival of the Academy, is my effort to end our dependence on the British Guild so that training can be done here."

"The Academy is the Guild?"

"No. The Academy is a facade behind which the American Guild will shelter. On its public face, it will encourage patronage and interest in the arts. At the same time, it justifies the congregation of great works and great artists in one space, allowing the Guild to operate secretly in plain sight. It is of critical importance that the Academy be reborn. Without it, the American Guild may not be born at all. When, however, our Guild is established, I will be its Master and I will be the one to approve who apprentices and who doesn't. I will appreciate your help in making that happen."

"Of course I will be happy to help." Then Faith hesitated, afraid to ask the question that danced at the fore of her thoughts. She glanced up, catching sight of the Trumbull family seal mounted on the wall: a shield with three black bulls' heads on a silver field. Beneath it on a scrolling pennant: *Fortuna favit audaci*. Fortune favors the bold.

"Do you think I have the Talent? Would I be able to apprentice?" Faith asked.

The Colonel laughed. Faith's glimmer of hope was a false dawn.

"Utterly impossible. Even if you had the Talent, which is something women rarely possess, women simply can not use it."

Faith tried to hide the disappointment that blew through her like an icy wind. The Colonel must have noticed some effect of it upon her face. His smile faded and he gave her a sympathetic look. "I know it seems unfair that such a miracle should be withheld. Console yourself with this thought. We all have a role to play in God's design. Art requires not only artists but a receptive audience. The latter is your role to play."

If a snake bites before it is charmed
There is no advantage in a charmer

- Ecclesiastes 10:11

CHAPTER SEVEN

The Strategem

The Colonel waited for Faith to leave before pressing the napkin to his eyes. They had been taxed enough with the letter writing; drawing the apple had made them burn intolerably. It had been a long time since he had used the Ink that way. He could feel the strain in more than just his eyes. Once he became Guild Master, his pen would be renewed with fresh Ink and the inspiration would flow again as it once had, he promised himself.

As he sat with his head cradled in linen-shrouded hands, the Colonel wondered if he had done the right thing by bringing Faith into his confidence about the Guild. Really, he had had no choice once she had seen the pen. He had to tell her something. He could have explained away the coded writing, letting her believe it was just a quaint convention of a secretive fraternity. But the pen... He cursed himself for having allowed it to happen. He had become so accustomed to his visionless wife from whom he never had to hide. He had been complacent and distracted.

The Colonel knew from his own experience how the pen's first introduction inflamed one's imagination. It was more seductive and consuming than any human object of lust. Once he knew of it, as superficial as that knowledge was, he had been able to think of nothing else but the wonders he might create with pen and Ink.

Demonstrating its power, even such a small sliver of its power, had been a dangerous gamble. He had needed to show Faith enough to justify the strangeness of what she had seen, to impress upon her its significance and, consequently, the need for strict secrecy. Anything less and she would have wondered what he was hiding. Or she might have dismissed his warnings as too much ado about nothing. Even a casual mention of the Ink in the wrong company could upend all of his carefully laid plans.

No, he could not have shown her less. But had he shown Faith too much? Would the thrill of possibility, the sense of magic and wonder, eat at her until she could think of nothing else? He had seen the hope light up her face and he had also seen it crumble. It had pained him, as it did putting a dog or horse out of its misery. Hard, but necessary for their own good. How much happier she would be if she had never known anything at all and how much more traumatic would it be to know the full extent of what she could never have? The Colonel shivered at the thought of being cut off from the Ink.

While he could hope that her disappointment was such that she would recover quickly and come to view the Ink as a charming curiosity, he was not such a fool as to think his prohibition was the end of the matter. Every masterpiece she saw from now on would goad her. For now, Faith was timorous enough to be biddable. He knew she would earnestly try to refrain, but could Talent like hers resist the call of the Ink? If she became bolder, if she were determined enough, there were ways around the Guild. The right inquiry to the wrong rogue...

The only thing worse than her Talent being openly known was to have her develop it in secret.

If only she were like the woman for whom she had been named! The Colonel's mother had been a paragon of feminine restraint. Faith, by contrast had always been impulsive and distractible. A sardonic smile twisted the Colonel's lips as he realized that he should have recognized these as the side effects of her Talent rather than the inherent giddiness of childhood. He had been far too indulgent. If he had caught it early, he might have stamped out her Talent entirely.

Now it was too late for that. Even if she were blind, as he nearly was, she would feel its pull. The best he could do was to dissuade her from it. But how?

The Colonel leaned back in his chair. Faith had asked what happened to those who did not merit training. He had answered thinking only of those whose poor character was known from the start. However, there had been occasions when a young man had been brought on as an apprentice, only to discover after the fact that his character was unsuitable for the honor. In those cases, he was denied further access to and training with the Ink, to the point of having all creative prospects stealthily and untraceably ruined by the Guild, and strongly encouraged, sometimes through fortuitous and anonymous funding, in a new and tedious endeavor that was sure to strangle the imagination. Faith could not, of course, be settled in a trade, become a shopkeeper or accountant, nor could she be sent to war.

The Colonel's eye swept over his desk, as though some answer might be found amongst the papers, or written in the grain of the wood itself. It landed on a small stack of letters that had arrived by ordinary post and been neglected on the corner of his desk. With a sigh of frustration, he sorted through them until a particular hand made him stop and drop the rest with a scowl.

Would he never see the end of trouble caused by base-born children? He had not heard from Ray in over a year, and only then to ask for money. Although some claimed to see the resemblance, the Colonel doubted such an imprudent and unmotivated wretch could possibly have been his son. Still, he had been the one charged with it and his dear wife had insisted when they were married that he see to Ray's future as to Faith's. The Colonel had already regretted the one promise and was increasingly regretting the other.

The contents of Ray's letter did nothing to sweeten the Colonel's sour mood. Predictably, he was writing to ask for money, this time on the occasion of Ray's marriage to a widow, a woman whom he could not possibly support on his half pay from the military. What was the boy thinking? After all the Colonel had spent on his education and care and now he would ruin himself with marriage without even a by-your-leave? Was she that beautiful? Maliciously, the Colonel wondered how well the wedding frock had hid the woman's belly. He would not be surprised if the next letter arrived to announce a child. If Ray had thought to ask, the Colonel could have told him how this marriage would work out, how every time he looked at his wife and child he would see the cause of all his misfortune. He would not give Ray money even if he had it. He threw the letter down in disgust and stared at it balefully.

As the Colonel ruminated on the outsized payments that had been exacted for his sins, an idea came to him. If his experience had taught him anything, there was one particularly powerful antidote to imagination. Marriage.

The Colonel sat up straighter. An advantageous marriage had always been his plan for Faith. The right match for her could right so many of the wrongs of his own ill-conceived one. He had not pursued it yet due to the objections of her mother who felt she was too young. It was time to override those objections.

If she had been of better English birth, she would have been presented to the Queen already and begun the cycle of courtship that was coming out. While things were different in the States, Faith was young but old enough. Faith was not quite the beauty that her mother had been before she had turned to drink, but she was pleasing enough with her gray-blue eyes, soft complexion, and cupid's bow mouth. Her only faults were a dimpled chin that the Colonel found too masculine and a nose which sat a bit heavily upon her face. Still, he doubted anyone other than a portraitist like himself would quibble, particularly the right suitor. He would have to find one with a good family, and without an ounce of imagination.

Thinking about prospective bachelors, the Colonel rose with the drawing of an apple in his hand. As he stood before the fire mulling his plan, he felt easier in his mind than he had in more than a year. The exhibition plans were coming together nicely, the success of the Academy's launch, and with it the American Guild with himself as its Master, were almost assured. If he could get Faith safely sequestered in a dull but profitable marriage, there would be nothing else in his way.

If that didn't work, he thought as he fed the apple to the fire, he would have to take more drastic measures.

The Colonel returned to his desk as the page turned black and crumpled in the heat. The apple shriveled and burst into multihued flames, bathing the room in a kaleidoscope of colors and filling the air with the acrid smell of burning sugar and something much more sinister.

The Colonel hardly noticed as he picked up his pen and began a letter to Mr. Smith. The only thing left was to deal with Vanderlyn. It was a shame, the Colonel mused, that he could not marry Vanderlyn off as well and be rid of him that way.

But heaven forbid you should ever relinquish the ease and independence of a single life, to become the slaves of a fool or a tyrant's caprice.
- Dr. John Gregory, A Father's Legacy to his Daughters

CHAPTER EIGHT
The Prospect

Faith's fingers were black again, this time with silver tarnish rather than ink. She tried to keep her mind on the polishing, admiring the emerging gleam as she buffed away the brownish haze from a large spoon, but was soon contemplating the inverted reflection in its bowl and wondering if perhaps there were a little upside down world sheltering within it. From there her thoughts strayed down other paths until, once again, she was thinking about the Ink.

When Faith had left the study that first night, the miracle of a medium that could bring all of the senses to life, and all of the questions it engendered, had filled her mind like a crowded ballroom. She had spun dizzily among them as she sat for dinner and began to eat. What was the Ink made of? Where had it come from? The Colonel had said it was discovered by daVinci, but did that mean he had found it or made it? More immediately, with what and how did the Colonel load his pen? How did it replenish itself?

What would it be like to try the Ink herself? With this question, Faith's mouth went dry and her throat thick, preventing any more food from passing. She had winced at the Colonel's laughter and felt the sting of his words when he had said women couldn't use it, but their true impact did not hit her until this moment. With the realization that she may never know what it was like to use the Ink, Faith's astonishment and delight, along with all of her questions, departed the floor and the band ceased to play.

She had cried that night and for several more after. After a while the tears had stopped, but not her restless thoughts. Her soul began to itch again, like it had when she had stopped drawing. Even when her body was still, she squirmed and shifted within her skin.

When she passed her mother's portrait in the entry hall and heard it sigh, she knew it must have been done with the Ink. She remembered every painting that she had seen move or had moved her and wondered if they had been done with the Ink as well. Of course, she also thought about the Colonel's landscape in the carriage house. It too must have been done with the Ink. How else had she felt the breeze and heard the sheep's bells? But what about the blond woman? Who was she and why was she a part of that picture?

One afternoon, while the Colonel was out, Faith had walked to the carriage house to look at it again. Her hand had been on the handle of the outer door when she had stopped, head bent against a cold wind. She stood there debating with herself until she shivered beneath her coat. Although the Colonel had said she was a viewer not a creator, she somehow knew he would not want her viewing that piece. To seek out what he had hidden would violate his trust. She thought better of it and went back to the house, coat flapping behind her in the wind.

After that, Faith resolved to accept her fate, to resign herself to the Ink being ever before her eyes but never within her grasp. It was not a happy decision but she found some peace in making it. The only way she knew to quell her wild thoughts was to feed them with blander food. When she wasn't copying letters or assisting the Colonel, Faith had ironed, organized, canned, prayed, and read- but only dreary, moralizing books. When she had business in the upstairs closet, she studiously ignored the call of her sketchbook in its leather and metal tomb. She mended every bit of fabric in the house that showed even the slightest inclination to fray or tear within the next two years. She had tried embroidery but abandoned that when she found herself stitching little butterflies that looked far too much like pixies.

And so this morning she found herself at one end of the dining table with the contents of the sideboard disgorged before her, polishing the silver. Her mother sat at the other end propped over a cup of tea, one hand massaging her forehead. Her breakfast dishes sat by her elbow. The Colonel had skipped breakfast in favor of an early morning meeting, allowing them to linger at the table longer than he would have approved.

Faith was scrubbing the crevices of a grape and vine motif on a chafing dish when she heard the Colonel return. Her mother bolted from her seat, cursing at the effect on her head, and scurried off to the kitchen with the dishes in her hand. The Colonel seemed pleased to find Faith industriously occupied and sat down at the table. Faith's mother came back in and greeted him.

"Good morning. If it is still morning. We cleaned up after breakfast some time ago," Sarah said, the white lie slipping easily from her lips, "but if you are hungry I will ask Cook to put something together for you."

"Just some tea, thank you."

Faith's mother had just turned to leave again when he stopped her. "On second thought, I have just remembered we received a crate of the sparkling water with the last post. Please bring me some of that and some for yourself and Faith as well. And a syrup if we have any."

Faith raised a surprised eyebrow and caught a matching glance from her mother. Other than a single nightly glass, the Colonel did not often drink alcohol. He treated the bubbly water he had imported from France much the same as others would treat champagne.

"How was your meeting this morning?" Faith asked when her mother left to get it.

"Extremely productive, thank you. For one, the jury finished making its selections from the unsolicited submissions and we can now get on with hanging everything."

"How did you find the class of submissions? Was it hard to choose among them?"

"I was favorably impressed with some. There was at least one who should abandon all artistic efforts and become a cobbler, but there were some promising entries."

Faith thought of Mr. Ingham as she dipped the corner of her rag into the paste and attacked a stubborn black spot. She asked without thinking, "And what of Mr. Ingham's submission. Did his Cleopatra make the cut?"

Faith felt as much as saw the Colonel's suspicious glare.

"What do you know about Mr. Ingham's work?"

Faith's underarms pricked with sweat. She wasn't supposed to have been listening at corners and now she'd given herself away. Faith cursed herself for a fool as she tried to think up an explanation.

"You told me about it. Remember the other day, after Mr. Smith had left, we were discussing the submissions."

Faith sent up a silent prayer that he had been as distracted and tired as he had looked and would not remember what he had told her. He was thinking on it when her mother came back into the room, three glasses of sparkling water on an unsteady tray. Whether he remembered or not, the interruption derailed his suspicions. At least, he continued talking as if the matter were resolved.

"Yes, well, we did accept it. Thank you, Mrs. Trumbull," he said, accepting his glass. "It is an exceptional picture for a man of his age. Of course, he is older than he looks. Would you believe he is twenty? He looks barely more than sixteen." The Colonel paused to take a drink as Faith remembered Mr. Ingham's features with pleasure. "He has an interesting technique for the skin. The result is too feminine for male portraits but I dare say he will be popular with the ladies. Perhaps he can do something with that sallow old witch, Mrs. Bier."

The Colonel raised his glass slightly as though to toast that idea before taking another sip. Faith took a drink as well, the bubbles tickling her nose and throat in a pleasant, scratchy way.

"You mentioned my meeting with Mr. Smith," The Colonel said after a brief silence. His face was more somber than a moment before and Faith's heart tumbled over itself. Had he realized he had not mentioned Mr. Ingham's picture? "As of this morning, Mr. Smith has resigned."

"Resigned?!" Faith's relief that he had not seen through her ruse gave her voice a breathy quality that exaggerated her apparent shock at the news.

"Surprising, isn't it? In fact, I think Mr. Smith was as surprised as anyone."

"How can that be? Did he not intend to resign?"

"I don't think so, no. As you know, the directors have repeatedly requested that Mr. Vanderlyn vacate his rooms at the Academy or contribute his paintings to the exhibition. Mr. Vanderlyn had refused to do either."

"Why wouldn't he agree to show his paintings?" Faith asked, legitimately puzzled. She found his Marius rather frightening- the Roman general's gaze had a murderous intensity - but his Ariadne, on the other hand, was beautiful and romantic. Faith's hand stopped scrubbing. Had they been made with the Ink? Faith pushed the question aside, re-focusing on the Colonel and the silver.

"He feels slighted because we were forced to move some of his paintings while he was out of the country. Most recently he informed the directors that he would commit his paintings in exchange for a portion of the entrance fees. As though his work would be the main draw! Can you believe it?"

"At least he has some business sense!" Faith's mother said. "I told you, you should have asked the same instead of giving them for free. With the weather this summer, the price of everything is up and you haven't collected a penny!"

The Colonel's voice was patronizingly calm. "We have discussed this. The loan of my paintings is just that, a loan. And an investment. They will know the worth of my pictures when they see the exhibition's success. They will be far more inclined to offer a portion of the proceeds after the fact, when it is they who are moved by gratitude than in response to what would seem a self-important demand before hand. Their refusal of Vanderlyn's offer proves the point. However, when I go to reclaim my pictures, their dependency on them will be very plain and I will be able to ask a fine sum for their permanent sale."

Faith's mother did not look satisfied with this explanation but she directed her frown toward the bottom of her glass and said nothing further.

"What does Mr. Vanderlyn's paintings have to do with Mr. Smith's resignation?" Faith asked, eager to get back to the story.

"Mr. Smith holds Mr. Vanderlyn's work in very low regard. He has often complained to me of the embarrassment he suffers that his pupils should have to pass such lascivious nudes on their way to his drawing classes. Perhaps he was concerned that the directors would accept Vanderlyn's offer, or had simply become frustrated by the refusal of the man to move them out. In any event, he demanded that Vanderlyn's pornography be removed immediately or he would resign. While I sympathize with his position, he overplayed his hand. They gave him no answer about Vanderlyn, but accepted Mr. Smith's resignation."

"That's terrible!" Faith said. She did not much like Mr. Smith but the result seemed unfair. "If the directors were already trying to evict Mr. Vanderlyn, why would they not appease Mr. Smith?"

"People do not like being told how to conduct their business," the Colonel said with a pointed look at Faith's mother before turning back to Faith. He did not see the sarcastic face her mother gave in return. "Mr. Smith pushed them too hard. It was his fit of temper, not his position, that put them off. He should never have made a threat he did not want to carry out. Let it be a lesson to you. Of course, if Mr. Smith leaves his rooms, I might like to take them over for an office and a studio when I am president."

"That sounds convenient," Faith said. The Colonel's tone had shifted so rapidly, she wondered if Mr. Smith's dismissal had troubled him at all. Perhaps he did not like Mr. Smith any more than Faith did.

The Colonel took another drink, his eyes lighting up mid sip.

"I've almost forgotten the most exciting news! When the Academy first opened under Mr. Livingston, it was supposed to have been a grand affair with a band and such. Unfortunately, an epidemic put those plans off. The idea came to me the other evening that we should honor the late Mr. Livingston- after all, he did found the Academy- and bring his original vision to life. I proposed that we should host a ball in conjunction with the opening. The directors thought this an excellent idea."

"A Ball! How wonderful!" Faith said. They hadn't attended anything more elaborate than a dinner party since the Fourth of July. Music and dancing and laughter would be a welcome respite from the dreary weather and the endless chores.

"They can't pay you for the paintings but they can hire a band?" her mother grumbled.

"Thanks to some generous patrons, yes."

"That's all very well then, but what are we to wear? And how will we get there? We have no carriage and it will be snowing, like as not."

"We will hire a carriage and you and Faith will have new dresses made," the Colonel answered patiently. Faith's mother detested large gatherings. Like Katherine avoiding the Colonel, Faith's mother would make up any excuse to avoid something like a ball.

"With what money, I should ask? I was unaware we had any generous patrons." Faith's eyes darted from her mother to the Colonel; Sarah's comment was a sharp jab at the Colonel's lack of commissions. A muscle in his temple twitched and his voice was tight but he kept his composure.

"We have some credit left and it will be well worth the expenditure. Consider it another investment."

Faith's mother narrowed her eyes. "What kind of investment?"

The Colonel turned to Faith instead of her mother. Faith felt a trickle of dread run down her spine.

"We've had a letter from your cousin Ray to announce that he has gotten married. It put me in mind that it is time we found a match for you."

Faith's stomach suddenly became cold and heavy, her mind blank. She heard her mother and the Colonel begin to argue, their voices distant in her spinning mind, as if they were in another room.

"She is too young! You agreed!"

"And I have changed my mind. If we were still in England she would have been out and settled a year ago."

"Who would have sponsored her? We were practically under house arrest!"

"That is entirely beside the point of her age."

"You were the enemy in England and I'm the enemy here. They act like I fired on Bunker Hill myself-"

"Perhaps if you would refrain from-"

"They wouldn't have me as a citizen-"

"That is precisely why-"

"You think one of these so-called patriots will want a British wife?"

"Enough woman!" The Colonel brought his fist down on the table making the silver jump with a loud jangle.

Faith's heart pounded in the following silence. The Colonel turned to Faith once more. He was calm and composed when he spoke.

"As we discussed the other day, we all have our roles to play in life. A woman's duty, your duty to this family, is to marry well." Faith's mother snorted. The Colonel shot her a withering look. "The time has come for you to see to that duty. Pay no heed to your mother's objections. They are only the sentimental expression of her reluctance to part from her daughter. You are a mature and modest young woman from one of the most well respected families in this country. I am confident that we will have no trouble finding a man of good standing with whom you will be very happy. Will you help me in this?"

Faith's thoughts were a tumultuous jumble of warm pride and cold dread. Had the Colonel ever complimented her before? Was she ready to be married? She was sure the answer to both questions was no. And yet, under the insistence of his stare, she found herself nodding. Her throat was too dry to speak.

"Excellent." The Colonel turned back to Faith's mother who was glaring at the middle of the table, two bright red spots on her otherwise pale cheeks. "Mrs. Trumbull, please see to the dresses right away. Once the word is out, the dressmakers will be busy. And, Faith, next time you polish silver, please wear gloves. We don't want any potential suitors to think you are a drudge."

* * *

Faith stood on the dressmaker's stool and looked at her reflection in the long mirror. The sturdy fabric of her usual house dresses had been traded for slippery satin and filmy lace. The cold, blue slip felt like water on her skin. The gauze overskirt was like mist clinging to a winter pond. Faith could not decide if the weightless sense of wearing nothing was exhilarating or embarrassing.

The dressmaker bobbed and hovered around Faith, folding and pinching, poking and pinning.

"How would you like the hem? Would you like it rucked in the Eastern style?" the dressmaker asked, drawing up the overskirt at Faith's left knee, "or would you like it scalloped?"

"I think I like the Eastern," Faith said, looking at her mother in the mirror. Sarah was reclined on a chaise, the feathered headpiece she had selected to complement her own dress sitting next to her. The dressmaker volunteered that the Eastern style was considered quite daring and was in high demand.

"Then the Colonel will surely object, at least to the daring part." Faith's mother said. "Since he is not here, I say do what you want. God knows you'll have few enough choices once you are married."

Faith worried the inside of her cheek as the dressmaker went back to work. Her mother's sourness on all points related to marriage aggravated Faith's own fears.

Faith met her mother's reflected gaze. "Were you ever happy married?" Faith asked softly.

Her mother snorted. "With the Colonel? I suppose I must have loved him in the beginning. He was so confident and worldly. And passionate, I thought at the time. When I would sit for a painting, he made me feel like whatever I was modeling. For a time it made me happy to feel like someone, anyone, else. I was happy to have you taken care of. Before we came to this bloody country. Before I realized he was no better than this ruddy bird," she said holding up her headdress. The peacock feathers bobbed violently.

Faith glanced at the dressmaker, expecting her to be aghast at such a comment. The woman kept her head bent studiously to her task, but Faith thought she was more flushed than before. Faith was sure it was not the first bit of domestic gossip the woman had heard.

"What about before the Colonel?" Faith pressed.

There was a long silence. Faith did not think her mother would answer. When she did speak, it was in a quiet wistful voice.

"I was very happy then. He loved me for what I was and didn't resent me for what I was not..." Her next words were hard and bitter again. "It seems there is only so much happiness allotted to a life and I spent mine in one go. My hope for you is that you are wiser and more fortunate."

Faith hoped so too.

Like all young girls who would inevitably marry, Faith had thought often of what she would wish for in a husband. Until recently, her vision had been as hazy as any object on a far horizon. Now though, the urgent proximity of being married had forced her to consider the issue with far more precision. Time spent clarifying her ideal match had easily overtaken thoughts about the Ink.

He would be indulgent and loving, thoughtful and kind, laugh when she did something frivolous and console her when things were hard. He would not mind if she took walks in the rain or stood, hair unbound, in the wind of a coming storm. They would picnic barefoot in the grass and read poetry from the obliging branches of a tree. He would let her draw and paint and tell her she was good, even if she were awful, and hang her pictures in the parlor and point them out with pride.

She knew these were not the traits the Colonel would seek out. Was it possible to find a man who suited the Colonel in both wealth and standing but who was not also his equal in reserve and unbending propriety, who would love her for who she was and not resent her for what she was not?

Did such a man exist? Could she find a Colonel Brandon or a Mr. Darcy, or were men like that all works of fiction?

Faith looked again at her mother's face, a pale, care-worn reflection of her own. If such a man were to be found, Faith would not settle for less.

But if you happen to have any learning, keep it a profound secret, especially from the men, who generally look with a jealous and malignant eye on a woman of great parts and a cultivated understanding.

- Dr. John Gregory, A Father's Legacy to his Daughters

CHAPTER NINE

The Ball

The butterflies in Faith's stomach fluttered with every bump and lurch of the carriage. She smoothed her skirt for what seemed the hundredth time, even though the trip was not much more than a mile. Her mother sat next to her, in a dark blue dress adorned with frothy lace that reminded Faith of breaking waves. Her face, beneath her peacock plumed headpiece, was unhappily resigned as she looked out the window. Before they left, the Colonel had reminded Faith's mother how important it was that they make a good impression tonight of all nights. He would not tolerate a repeat of the scandal last February when Sarah had to be carried home intoxicated from Mrs. Primes' even if they did have a carriage this time. The Colonel, in high contrast, sat determined and confident across from Faith with the Hessian sword he had taken during the Revolution balanced across a knee.

In the mirror before they left, Faith had looked mature and elegant. The only sign of the awkward, trembling child within was the twist of her lips as she bit the inside of her cheek. Katherine had done her hair up, strawberry ringlets framing her face. Faith wore the string of garnets and the drop earrings her mother had worn in the hall portrait. She had been surprised at how cold they were when they first touched her skin.

Faith twisted a bead of the necklace between gloved fingers. She was proud to wear the family jewelry and such a beautiful dress. That and the prospect of dancing, the one activity where it was acceptable to jump and spin and laugh until she was breathless and a little dizzy, should have made

Faith giddy with excitement. Tonight though she was weighed down by anticipation of a different sort. Faith's thoughts bounced restlessly between wondering what would happen if she failed to impress a suitor and what would happen if she succeeded.

She shivered when the carriage stopped, before the door had even opened. The night was bitingly cold and clear. She clutched her cloak about her like a cocoon as she stepped down, but the cold stones stole the heat through the soles of her thin evening slippers. She waited for her mother and the Colonel to step down behind her. Her mother's headdress snagged on the carriage doorway, breaking the ribs of two of the peacock feathers. The broken ends swung pathetically from the break. The Colonel snapped them off with a swift twist that made Sarah gasp, followed by a sound of dismay when he dropped the once majestic eyes on the ground and strode over them.

In contrast to the dark, fall night outside, the Academy foyer was bright and festive, awash in mirrored candle light that gleamed on freshly whitewashed walls and polished floors. The candles alone must have cost a fortune. Not only were there hundreds of them, but the faint scent of honey and lack of smoke said they were beeswax rather than tallow. Faith marveled at the kaleidoscope of brightly dressed women, punctuated by the dark coats of their escorts. A happy cacophony of greetings, laughter, clicking footsteps, and the strains of music echoed throughout the space. Although the room was warm enough, Faith reluctantly shed her cloak. She felt exposed and vulnerable without it. Faith took a deep breath, put on a smile, and tried to imagine that she was the poised young woman she had seen in the mirror.

They made the rounds. Faith's apprehension ebbed and flowed with each new greeting. She was almost at ease when they met familiar faces, such as Dr. Hosack and Mr. Murray. In the absence of bachelor sons, she found Governor Tompkins, Representative Townsend, and Mayor Ferguson less intimidating than their positions might suggest. When she was introduced, however, to the likes of Mr. Lawrence, Mr. Graham, and Mr. Gracie, along with the younger Messrs. Lawrence, Graham, and Gracie, she tensed as though she might be called into single combat. She found it hard to make eye contact. She stole surreptitious glances to take their measure and to see if they were taking hers. Some rational part of Faith's mind knew it was silly to feel as though she were being evaluated. It wasn't as though they had taken out an advert to say she was looking for a husband. Still, she thought she knew what a horse felt like being examined for sale. Only she envied the horse that could not know it was being judged.

After about a dozen or so such introductions that did not, in fact, result in anyone examining her canons or drawn pistols, Faith's jitters began to subside. She realized that other than curtsies, how-do-you-dos, and blushing gratefully at compliments, she had very little else to do. No one was interested in her opinions on the presidential election, the price of wheat, or how to retire the war debt while also rebuilding the nation's capitol after its destruction by the British, all of which she felt qualified to speak to after copying the Colonel's correspondence. Clearly her role was to stand about with what she hoped was a charming, interested smile, while the Colonel graciously accepted the accolades for the exhibition, which everyone was sure would thoroughly astonish them once they'd had the chance to see it all, and his many pictures, without which it would surely have been half as astonishing. The Colonel's evident gratification eased Faith's worries slightly. If he were in a good mood, he would not be as quick to find fault with her. Or with her mother whose half-frown was far from charming or interested.

His ebullient mood was tested when a shrill voice issued from an incongruously masculine face at the head of a small cadre of lavishly dressed women and one elderly gentleman.

"My dear Colonel Trumbull! I am most impressed by this affair and everywhere I have inquired, I have been told it is you we have to thank for it. It is exactly as Robert would have done and I so wish he were here to see it."

"Thank you, Mrs. Armstrong. I am glad to have done your brother's vision some measure of justice. My only regret is that it has taken us this long to honor his memory in a suitable fashion. I am very happy you are here tonight. Miss Margaret you look lovely as always. I hope that John and your son Robert have also come?"

"Oh, they are off arguing politics somewhere."

"I will seek them out. Edward! How do you do?" He said to the older gentleman, whose white hair twisted wildly around a balding crown, before turning to the woman at his side. "How are you this evening Mrs. Livingston? I'm sure you remember my wife, Mrs. Trumbull, but let me introduce my daughter. Faith Trumbull, this is Madame Marie Louise Magdaleine Valentine de Castera Moreau de Lassy ... Livingston."

The lady in question was younger than Mr. Livingston by at least half. She was devastatingly beautiful. As Faith bobbed politely, she saw her mother give an exaggerated curtsy that made Faith cringe.

"How do you do, Miss Trumbull? What a beautiful dress. It suits your pretty eyes," Mrs. Livingston said in a warm, Spanish accented voice, her eyes sweeping Faith up and down. Faith had to stifle an absurd urge to open her mouth and let the woman count her teeth.

"And you, Mrs. Trumbull, you look lovely this evening. I love your... feathers." Mrs. Livingston said with a smirk at the two beheaded quills that stuck out stiffly amongst the whole ones that remained.

"A true compliment coming from one so *young*," Faith's mother replied with patent civility and latent sarcasm.

With twin nods, Mrs. Livingston and Mrs. Armstrong moved off arm in arm with Mr. Livingston trailing behind. Mrs. Armstrong leaned in to whisper something to Mrs. Livingston, who glanced back at Faith's mother and covered a giggle with a gloved hand. Faith grew hot in the face and clenched her skirt in a satin fist.

"Are they serving the champagne yet, do you think?" Faith's mother asked of no one in particular.

The Colonel's face darkened. "Mind your tongue and your manners, my dear," the Colonel hissed. "The Livingstons are the most powerful family in the state. They may be Republicans but I'll not have you ruining Faith's chances with one of their few sons."

Faith's mother turned her head away and muttered something about strangling peacocks.

The Colonel was about to answer when something caught his eye that eased his scowl. Faith unclenched her fist when she saw Mr. and Mrs. King. Mrs. King, the epitome of quiet grace, was one of the few women that Sarah genuinely liked. Faith's mother visibly relaxed as they moved into Mrs. King's soothing orbit. The two women talked about the weather, the room, and the ladies' fashions while the Colonel and Mr. King discussed his presidential bid. As a fellow Federalist, the Colonel supported him whole heartedly, but the former Senator was modest about his chances. Faith observed to herself that Mr. King's curling hair below a bald pate looked like a laurel wreath on a Roman bust.

Lost in this thought, Faith was surprised when the Colonel excused them both from the group, leaving her mother under Mrs. King's care.

"There are some people I would like you to meet," the Colonel said. Faith's stomach tensed as she trailed the Colonel through the room. The press of people was warm and humid like a jungle, the ladies, with their frills and perfumes, its tropical flowers. Faith imagined herself an explorer pushing through thick overgrowth and wondered what man-eating beast she might encounter.

When she emerged into a clearing behind the Colonel, Faith was confronted by a rather large cluster of people at its center. She recognized DeWitt Clinton, the former mayor, and his wife. There was another couple, of whom the gentleman looked vaguely familiar. There was one young woman, about Faith's age, in a fur trimmed dress, and no fewer than four young men about her. Faith felt a little dizzy.

The Colonel greeted Mr. and Mrs. Clinton and introduced Faith to the other couple. Faith recognized the Astors' names from the many letters she had copied. Mr. Astor was a thick bear of a man with black hair and sun darkened face, except where paler skin marked a freshly shorn beard. Mrs. Astor was softly rounded all over except for dark eyes which held a keen edge. Her manner was kind and gracious but efficient, not a word or gesture wasted beyond those necessitated by custom or desired effect.

What Mrs. Astor kept in reserve was expended freely by her daughter, Eliza, the young woman about whom the young gentlemen fanned. She was smiling and bubbly. The glossy dark curls piled atop her head bounced gaily with every giggle and exclamation, enhancing the impression of effervescence. When she and Faith were introduced, a shadow of her mother's shrewdness passed over her face. Whether Faith was found to be acceptable or no social threat, the look was immediately replaced by an apparently genuine smile. Eliza crossed the group and took Faith's arm in hers.

"Let me introduce you to the boys," Eliza said, somehow remaining the center of attention even as she put Faith forward. For her part, Faith was happy to let her take command. Not only was Faith nervous under the Colonel's gaze, but Eliza's easy companionability had her flustered. Faith had never had a close friend. Eliza's ready acceptance and physical proximity made Faith feel warmed and uncomfortable simultaneously.

"These are my brothers. John, Jr. and William," Eliza said with a dismissive flick of her folded fan at each respectively.

John, Jr. was pale and thin with deep circles beneath eyes that wandered restlessly. His younger brother William was handsome enough with a strong jaw and cleft chin. His brow was heavy, casting dark eyes in contemplative shade. Together with thin, downturned lips, he had a serious, brooding expression.

"And these handsome young men are Charles and James Clinton." Eliza's voice was dramatically warmer than it had been for her brothers' introduction. Even without the disdain of sibling familiarity, Faith felt the same. Mr. Clinton's sons were far more compelling, both in looks and openness of expression. James in particular had a friendly smile and a dashing air, bending a kiss over Faith's hand. Faith was just happy that she managed to curtsy without falling over given that her knees felt capriciously weak.

"Watch that one. He's an incorrigible flirt," Eliza said, her eyes and her hand on Faith's forearm tightening faintly. The teasing smile she gave James told Faith that Eliza did not disapprove of him flirting, so long as it was directed at her.

Faith and the Colonel had interrupted a lively discussion about the terrible weather of the past year, its likely cause, and whether it would continue. Behind Faith's and Eliza's heads, Mr. Clinton's booming voice attempted to draw the Colonel into it.

"According to more than one cleric, this miserable weather is the result of God's wrath for our ill-conceived war against Britain. What do you think of this?"

"I agree that the war was the result of the grossest ignorance and misconduct, and worthy of punishment, but I believe it has already been meted out. We lost many great men, not to mention our general prosperity. I don't see why He would add to what we brought upon ourselves."

"I agree! While I supported our troops, the impact on trade has been a curse." Mr. Astor said. "If this cold were punishment, I can assure you that the other side is feeling it equally."

"All this cold weather can't have been bad for your fur trade!" Mr. Clinton said with a chuckle.

"The cold has been good for demand, but it presents other problems. My ships' captains have never seen so much ice in the Atlantic."

"I've heard it's all that ice that's causing the cold winds," Charles Clinton said, bringing the younger group back to the topic.

"That can't be. It isn't logical," William Astor said, his brow furrowed. He was neither argumentative nor condescending in his disagreement. It was as though he spoke to himself. "It is the cold that causes the ice, not the ice that causes the cold."

Eliza rolled her eyes at her brother. "You and your logic. On the contrary, I think Mr. Clinton's theory is a good one. If you put ice in an ice house, it makes it cold where it was warm before."

"Yes, but the winds in the Atlantic blow to the east. If they carried the cold wind off the ice, only Europe would be feeling it."

James Clinton laughed. "William has already disproved, on account of timing, the theory that Dr. Franklin's lightning rods have stirred up the weather patterns, and now he has disproven the ice theory. What do *you* think has caused the cold, William?"

William was unfazed by this challenge. "The sun is failing."

Everyone but Eliza looked as surprised by this announcement as Faith felt. Eliza spread her fan and shook her head.

"Extraordinary! Explain!" James said with a smile.

"The haze in the air has made it such that a man can look straight at the sun and hardly blink. This has revealed dark spots which, in turn, suggest that the sun is fading. The haze itself is proof. The sun is no longer able to burn off the vapors." As astonishing as this explanation was, William spoke with no more emotion than if he were reporting that water is wet.

"And what do you think of all this, Miss Trumbull? Tell us which theory is best and we shall abide by your decision," James said.

Faith's eyes bulged at the shock of being asked her opinion. She quickly replaced the undignified expression with a thoughtful one. By her own experience, she felt the misty sky was somehow involved, but was it a cause or a result? The idea that the sun was failing was outlandish, and suitably chilling, but William had explained it in such a doggedly logical way she could not think of a way to counter it without sounding empty headed or belligerent. Thankfully, she was spared the effort by an announcement that they were all to assemble in the sculpture gallery.

Mr. Clinton excused himself to make his speech and hurried off. The rest followed more leisurely, pressing ever closer together as the throng squeezed into the long, high-ceilinged space that had been transformed into a ballroom for the evening. The casts of Greek and Roman sculpture had been lined up on either side of the room like so many dancers in a set. The far end of the room held a temporary stage for the musicians and a podium. A hush fell over the crowd as Mr. Clinton began to speak.

Faith soon wondered if he would ever stop. As his speech rambled through a eulogy for the late Chancellor Livingston and what seemed an exhaustive recapitulation of the history of Greek and Roman arts, Faith stopped listening. Instead she was aware that she had somehow ended up between Eliza Astor and her brother William. Eliza was whispering comments to James Clinton on her other side while William stared unwaveringly at Mr. Clinton on his podium. The Colonel and the rest of the parents had become separated and stood several rows back. Faith fanned herself and let her eyes and thoughts wander over the sculpture casts that loomed over the crowd.

They stopped at the Laocoon, a stunning depiction of the Trojan priest who had warned his people not to accept the Greek's horse at Troy. It captured the terrifying moments of the hero and his two sons being devoured by the serpents that the Greek gods had sent to punish him. The coils of the snakes curling around the powerful men and the look of anguish on Laocoon's face made Faith turn cold in the hot room. A flicker of lamplight flashed in the eye of the serpent, mouth open, about to bite the priest. Faith felt the blood drain from her face. Her breathing quickened.

She jumped as the room rumbled like thunder.

It was applause. The speech was over.

"Miss Trumbull, you look pale. Are you well?" James asked

Faith was lightheaded and her mouth was dry. "I will be all right. I could use something to drink, I think."

The group made their way to the refreshments as quickly as the like-minded throng would allow, James supporting Faith's elbow solicitously while Charles walked on her other side. Eliza took note with an even expression which, for her, expressed displeasure.

Faith accepted a glass of punch gratefully and drank as much of it as she dared without looking gluttonous. A few moments later, Faith's mother and the Kings joined them. Her mother downed the punch in one draught and asked a liveried server if the champagne had been uncorked yet. Before he could answer, Mrs. King glided between them.

"It's earlier yet than it seems. We will come back in a bit and see if they have put it out. Have you seen the pictures yet?" Mrs. King asked, guiding Sarah away from the refreshments toward the Colonel.

"I'd like to see the pictures," Faith volunteered. There was one entry she was particularly curious to see. Her eyes swept quickly over the crowd hoping to spot a tall Irishman.

"I'd like to dance," Eliza answered as the band began to play again.

"William," Mrs. Astor said, "escort Miss Trumbull and your sister around the exhibits. After all, they are the reason for the occasion. There will be plenty of time for dancing," she finished with a firm look at Eliza.

"Yes, Mama. Would you like to join us?" Eliza directed an inviting smile at Charles and James Clinton.

"Of course," James answered and the troupe set off for the first painting gallery.

Faith saw the Colonel watching them go with a calculating expression.

As they made their way around, Eliza kept up a steady chatter with the Clinton brothers, positioning herself between them. Faith fell back and walked next to William.

"It's hard to believe this was once an alms house. The renovations were excellent, don't you think?" Faith asked.

"I had not seen it before," was all William responded.

Trying to engage in conversation, Faith remarked on the artwork, the compositions, the colors, the quality of line. William's comments were constrained to whether he found each one pleasing or not, sometimes going so far as to estimate its financial value. He paused at each painting, regarding it for a predictable length of time before moving on, as though fulfilling some minimum requirement. As it didn't seem to bother William whether she spoke or not, or walked with him or not, Faith gave up both.

Freed to devote her attention to the paintings, Faith trailed behind the others as they entered another gallery. A large seascape of ships in a violent storm caught her eye. She approached it with a mixed tingling of fear and excitement. Before she had even stopped, she could see the movement of the waves and the boiling of the dark clouds. Three ships tilted and creaked, bells sounding faintly over the roar of surf and sky, while the mast and spars of a fourth were caught on a rocky shelf. Faith wrapped her arms around herself as a gust of salty air seemed to blow against her. A wave crashed on the rocks. She felt the spray hit her face.

Faith stepped back with a gasp, hand to her cheek. She met with something solid that grunted in return.

Faith wheeled around to find Mr. Ingham looking down at her.

"Oh my! Oh! I'm terribly sorry." Faith said, steadying herself with her hands against his chest.

"I'm all right. Are you? You seem to have been very affected by the picture," he said with a nod at the seascape. A small smile played about his lips. The amusement twinkled in his eyes.

"Yes, of course," Faith said, pulling her hands away with a nervous laugh. "It's just that, um... I thought, um... It reminded me of a storm we were caught in when we sailed here last year. It was as though..." Faith trailed off and took a steadying breath. "You must think me very silly to startle at paintings."

"On the contrary! Few have ever rivaled the Dutch Masters for impact, and Backhuysen's seascapes are some of the most powerful among them. It's as though the waves are crashing right out of the frame," Mr. Ingham said, the corners of his eyes crinkling. In this light they were the same gray green as the stormy surf.

"You see it too?" Faith asked in astonishment before the realization hit her. The Ink. The Guild. The seal on Ingham's letter. It wasn't just her. Of course he could see the effects of the Ink as well as she. The unexpected thrill of connection, a secret shared, made her insides flutter. But Mr. Ingham couldn't just see what she saw. He could create it too.

"Mr. Ingham, Colonel Trumbull tells me you have a *masterpiece* here tonight," Faith said with a boldness that surprised her. Mr. Ingham raised an eyebrow in response. "Will you show it to me?"

The creases at the corners of his eyes deepened. "Happy to."

When they arrived at his painting, it was blocked by a small group admiring it. Once they had stepped away, Mr. Ingham positioned Faith in front of it and introduced her to its subject as though the Egyptian queen was a real woman.

"Miss Trumbull, I present the great lady, Cleopatra. You will forgive her if she is not much into conversation at the moment. She has had a hard turn of things and is quite distraught."

Faith gave Charles an amused smile before directing her attention to the painting. The queen reclined on a chaise, wearing a slim white dress and a golden winged crown upon lustrous black hair. Her eyes were tilted and dark, full of sadness, but also determination. Her face was exquisitely painted, brow furrowed with pain, lips slightly parted in a sigh. Her skin looked warm, soft, and glowing, poignantly alive for a woman who was about to die.

It was the asp, though, that commanded Faith's attention. The black snake hovered before the queen's bare shoulder, its body a twisting vine of powerful loops. Every scale was picked out with precision, glittering in the light. Faith's eye met that of the snake. It glinted black, cold, and hard.

Faith gave her senses over to the power of the painting. She drank in the queen's exotic perfume along with the heartbreak and unyielding dignity that had driven her to this moment. Facing a life worse than death, she would sacrifice her body rather than her soul. She looked to the asp with reverence rather than fear; she would die by the emblem of her own power. The scales whispered faintly over skin as the snake coiled to strike. She reached out to it.

Faith was jolted out of her trance by Mr. Ingham's hand closing gently down on hers, pulling it away from the painting. He held it for just a moment and then let go. Faith's cheeks flushed as she looked about in confusion to find herself back in the gallery. She felt as though she had awakened from a dream, but could not be sure which was dream and which reality.

"I'm sorry. I know better than to touch a painting," she offered weakly.

Mr. Ingham gave her a knowing smile. "Of course, but the serpent can be most beguiling. At least, that's what a woman named Eve once told me."

Faith put a hand to her forehead, feeling a little dizzy.

"Shall we get you some air?" Charles asked.

Faith nodded and they moved to the end of the gallery. Their way out was blocked by a cluster of viewers who were muttering appreciatively over two small watercolor landscapes. Faith was about to step around them when she recognized the paintings. She stopped dead, her head spinning even harder.

"Those are exceptional, aren't they?" Mr. Ingham remarked as the others dispersed, affording him a view. He leaned forward to read the label. "I didn't know the Colonel did watercolors like that. He is more versatile than I thought."

"Yes," Faith agreed absently, "I didn't know he had put them up." Mr. Ingham was right that the Colonel rarely painted in watercolor. They were

Faith's paintings. She shook her head, unable to make sense of it, and motioned that they should continue on.

The groggy, dream-like feeling faded as they walked. When they encountered the Astors and the Clintons again, Faith was feeling much better, at least physically. She made the introductions, noting with unexpected irritation the appreciative look Eliza gave Mr. Ingham.

They were headed to join the dancing at last but there was some confusion about who might dance with whom. Faith worried that she would be paired with William since he could not dance with his sister. She did not think that his plodding step and brooding countenance would make a very interesting partner and after all the strain of the evening thus far, she was determined to enjoy some aspect of the ball. She was relieved when Eliza informed her that William never danced. Charles bowed out as well and sent his brother James to the dance floor with Eliza on his arm. Faith was happily left to Mr. Ingham.

Faith danced the rest of the evening, a whirlwind of thoughts about suitors and storms and ships and serpents and Ink pushed to the edges of her mind as though by the spinning of her body. She stopped only once, when the band played a waltz. She had seen it danced in England and secretly learned the steps, but the Colonel found it indecent and had forbidden her to join. Instead she watched jealously as Eliza danced with Mr. Ingham in the shadow of Laocoon and his murderous serpents.

*What is commonly called love among you, is rather
gratitude, and a partiality to the man who prefers you to the rest
of your sex: and such a man you often marry with little of either
personal esteem or affection. Indeed, without any unusual share
of natural sensibility, and very peculiar good fortune, a woman
in this country has very little probability of marrying for love.*
- Dr. John Gregory, A Father's Legacy to his Daughters

CHAPTER TEN
The Still Life

That night Faith had vivid dreams of snakes, storms, and sinking ships. She ran from shadow beasts that hissed and snapped behind her, tripping and stumbling as her feet sank in wet sand. Glowing eyes and brimstone breath chased her through a dark, barren landscape. Ahead was a pool that shimmered like sunlight on dew. No rain marred its mirror-like surface even as it pelted the dusty earth all around. If she could reach the pool, she knew she would be safe. With frantic, clumsy movements Faith gained its shore only to be driven back by violet flames that flared upon the water. Faith stood paralyzed, trapped between the fire and the demons until Leviathan raised its fearsome head out of the stormy darkness. The glow of fire lit its gaping maw. Faith stepped back in fear, violet flames licking painlessly at her ankles. The mirror of the pool shattered into a thousand scintillating shards that fell through velvet blackness like a crystal rain.

Faith woke with a heaving breath, the tinkling of broken glass still in her ears. Her bed was damp with sweat, the sheets sticky and twisted about her. She thrashed her legs to kick them off and laid there looking at the ceiling, waiting for the air to cool her skin and for her breath to calm.

Her mind continued to race.

Her memories of the ball, entwined with the images from her dreams, were like a briar patch. Merry lights and laughter, the feel of Mr. Ingham's hands on her waist as he lifted her through a turn, Eliza Astor's smug smile, asps and serpents, crashing waves, moving pictures, and a pair of watercolors with the Colonel's name on them, each thought ensnared her. She tore free only to get caught up on the next one.

She heard movement downstairs and forced herself to get up. Her feet were sore and her legs ached. She opened her curtains and blinked in the cold autumn light. Her head hurt. Faith slipped into a work dress with as much economy of effort as she could and headed downstairs. When she entered the dining room, the Colonel was at the table finishing up his breakfast. There was no sign of Faith's mother. The Colonel set his fork on his plate with a clink and watched Faith pour herself some tea. He waited until she had sat down with a plate and had begun to eat before he spoke.

"After you eat and finish your chores," he said, " put on a nice dress and have Katherine do your hair. The Astors will be in the city for a few more days and we will visit this afternoon."

"Do you have business with Mr. Astor?" Faith asked with unfounded hope that their visit had nothing to do with her.

"Only to thank him for his contribution to the exhibition last night, which was, by the way, a tremendous success. Our primary business is with William Astor. After observing you both last night, I think he is the perfect match for you."

"William? What about one of the Clinton brothers? Or, Mr. Ingham?" Faith asked, trying to keep the disappointment out of her voice.

The Colonel laughed. "Mr. Ingham? He seems to be an upstanding young man but he is merely an artist. Besides, he's Catholic. Charles Clinton, I have it on authority from his mother, has already formed an attachment to a lady who was not present last night. James Clinton is much too reckless. I also fear that DeWitt, though he is a dear friend, has spent too much of his real and political capital. William Astor is exactly the steady, respectable young man we are looking for. His father is a shrewd business man- already he has a great fortune and no doubt will amass more. William stands to inherit a good deal even though he is the second son. It seems that the Astors have already decided to bypass John, Jr. on account of his frailties. William, on the other hand, is in good health and has a sound mind on his shoulder. He does not seem inclined to squander his inheritance frivolously."

Faith had to agree to that. William seemed unlikely to do anything frivolous. Faith gulped some tea to wash down the food that was suddenly too dry to swallow.

* * *

The world outside was as dreary as Faith's mood as she trudged behind the Colonel on their way to the Astor's. Wet, black tree trunks stood against a flat, steely sky. She walked a charcoal road past dusky brick and gray stone buildings. It was as monotonous as William's voice, as somber as his expression. Faith's thoughts were an equally muddy smear of resentment, self pity, and bitter resignation.

Distracted and irritable, she nearly ran into the Colonel when he stopped much sooner than she had expected. The Astor's city house was barely a block from their own. No wonder Mr. Astor had looked familiar. She had probably seen him on the street.

They were shown into a rich parlor of polished wood and plush carpeting. The air smelled of flowers, but with an over sweetness that suggested the bouquet was past its prime. The walls were lined with pictures and the windows framed with silk-lined and tasseled drapes. Faith accepted a cup of tea and perched on the edge of a velvet settee.

Eliza sat on the other end, going on about the previous evening. At first her enthusiastic welcome and happy chatter had been infectious, almost lightening Faith's mood. When she had turned to the subject of Mr. Ingham and what a skillful dancer he was however, the sweetly delicate Chinese tea turned to acid in Faith's mouth. Faith glanced at William who sat stoically across from them. He listened intently, as though at a scientific lecture, but was no more conversational than the night before. Faith thought she might cry with frustration. It was only due to years of hiding her true feelings from the Colonel that Faith was able to keep her face a placid and agreeable mask.

All in all, she wished she could join the Colonel and Mr. Astor as they discussed Mr. Clinton's canal project that everyone called Clinton's ditch. As Faith let her attention drift between the two conversations, the scent of flowers tickled her nose again. She also heard a faint buzzing sound somewhere across the room. She turned to look for the flowers but could find none.

Eliza noticed and gave her a quizzical look.

"I'm sorry. I keep smelling flowers but I don't see any in the room."

Eliza's lips curled in a self-satisfied smile. "You must be smelling my perfume. William brought it back for me when he came home from Germany. It's Parisian."

Faith hid a smile in her teacup. Either Eliza's Parisian perfume was going rancid or William had been swindled. When Faith's face was straight, she lowered her cup and changed the subject to the one thing about the ball that Eliza hadn't mentioned yet.

"What did you think of the paintings in the exhibition?"

Eliza frowned prettily. "I thought there were far too many portraits. Why would anyone want to look at pictures of people they don't know, and such ugly ones at that! And all the ones of battles and soldiers? Ghastly," Eliza said in a conspiratorial whisper with a glance at the Colonel.

"Surely you liked something!"

"I like romantic paintings. Heroes and fair maidens. Pretty landscapes you can get lost in. Most of them looked like Sunday sermons feel. Although your father had some charming watercolor landscapes that caught my eye."

Faith's teacup rattled. "You mean the ones of Prior Park and the Quarry at Bath?"

"I don't know what they were of, but they were pretty. What did you think William?"

William's brow furrowed as it seemed it must before issuing any answer. "I thought a few of the pictures would make a good investment."

"Don't be silly. We already own the best ones there. I'm just tired of looking at them," Eliza said.

"Which ones are those?" Faith asked.

"A few different things. Papa collects art when he goes to Europe. Some were Italian, one was Dutch."

"Dutch? The one of ships caught in a storm?" What had Mr. Ingham said the painter's name was?

Eliza supplied it. "Yes! The Backhuysen." Eliza gave a dramatic shiver. "It's beautiful but it gives me chills. We also offered to loan that one up there but they didn't want it."

Faith followed Eliza's gesture. A floral painting with sharply lit flowers against an ominously dark background hung above the mantel. The flowers, a season-defying mix of tulips, lilies, morning glories and roses, were so precisely rendered they looked more than life-like. The roses and tulips were blown out and about to drop their petals. With a sharp inhalation of surprise, Faith realized this was what she was smelling, lilies and overripe roses. A few moths and butterflies had settled on the blooms, their wings pulsing slowly. Faith heard the buzzing sound again.

"Did you hear that buzz?" she asked without thinking. A blur of motion caught her eye. A beetle chewing a painted leaf fluttered its wings with a bright whirr.

"Do you hear it too? John says he hears the painting buzz," Eliza asked with a concerned look. Faith's cheeks flushed.

"Of course it's not the painting! I'm sure it's just a fly in the window glass. Do you know who painted it?"

"Her name was Rachel Ruysch," William said.

"Her? Rachel?" Faith asked, unable to conceal her surprise.

"William would know," Eliza said with a dismissive wave of her hand. William nodded gravely. Faith glanced at the Colonel to see if he had taken note of the painting but he was deep in conversation.

Suddenly eager to change the subject away from paintings, Faith turned to William.

"Eliza mentioned you have been in Germany. Were you on holiday?"

Having finally found a topic that William was willing to cover at length, Faith listened to him speak about his schooling in Germany, his appreciation for their science and economics, his tolerance of their art and music, particularly the German and Austrian composers, and his distaste of poetry of any kind as being non-sensical. All the while the buzzing of the beetle's wings harmonized with the droning of his voice.

He whose face gives no light shall never become a star.
                    -William Blake, The Marriage of Heaven and Hell

CHAPTER ELEVEN

The Awakening

Faith's frame of mind when they left the Astor's was no better than when she had arrived. She was even more tired, her head still hurt, and she was distraught that, out of all the possible young bachelors in New York, the Colonel seemed quite set on marrying her to off to William Astor. Their visit had proven that he was no Colonel Brandon, staid on the outside, romantic at heart. William was utterly devoid of imagination.

Now, though, there was also the painting to consider. Clearly it had been done with the Ink, *by a woman*! Faith tried to remember what the Colonel had said the night he showed her the Ink. She had been overwhelmed with awe, but she was certain he had said women could be affected by the Ink but it was impossible for them to use it. In fact, it had been this very unattainability that had allowed Faith to temper her burning curiosity into a detached fascination. And yet, the floral still life with fluttering moths and buzzing beetles seemed to prove otherwise. Was William mistaken? Or was the Colonel?

Or perhaps, Faith had misunderstood. The Colonel had also said that women should confine themselves to fruits and flowers. Was it possible for women to use the Ink so long as they limited the subject matter? Had the Colonel been speaking only of the higher subjects, from his own frame of reference, when he had declared it impossible for women to use the Ink? If so, then the restriction was not one of ability so much as permission. This thought gave birth to a twisting, thorny kind of hope. If Faith swore to abide by the restrictions, could she use the Ink?

But could she really? Did she actually have the ability?

77

When they returned home, Faith went to her room seeking out her sketchbooks. There were more than just the one that had been banished to the depths of the hall closet. They lined her dresser drawer, hidden beneath her shifts. The earliest were filled with truly awkward efforts. Stiff, two-legged unicorns, misshapen gnomes and fairies and all the other blasphemously magical creatures of an English childhood, shared by her mother in secret. There were castles and treehouses and cottages, mysterious forests, deep valleys, lonely islands, and cities in the clouds. All the places she had run to in her mind to escape the tedium of reality.

She had gotten better over the years, but never enough to impress the Colonel. He had even criticized the watercolor landscapes that he had hung in the show. She wondered that he had displayed them at all, let alone set his name to them. Were they better than he had let on? Had he been purposefully harsh, perceiving in her a propensity for vanity?

Moments later, Faith found herself before the hall closet wrestling with indecision. Telling herself there was no harm in simply looking, Faith yanked the door open before she could change her mind. She dropped to her hands and knees, lifting the trunk as she slid it out to keep it from scraping on the floor. She pulled it only as far as necessary, keeping it hidden behind the door. She popped the latches, pushed the other books aside, and grabbed the sketchbook.

She had just pushed the trunk back when she heard footsteps in the hall. Muttering a curse she had learned from the sailors, Faith reached up and yanked a stack of blankets from the shelf above her. They fell atop the sketchbook in her hand.

Faith stood with the disheveled pile spilling over her arms as the Colonel appeared from around the closet door. "What are you doing?"

"Making a mess, it seems," Faith said with a self-deprecating laugh to hide the nervous waver in her voice. "I was cold last night and thought I would put another blanket on my bed, but I've accidentally brought the whole stack down. Now I will have to refold them all."

"Well, when you are done, please come to my study. I have letters for you to copy." The Colonel continued down the hall to his room.

Faith carried the linens into her bedroom and shut the door. Dropping the pile on her bed, she took the sketchbook to a chair by the window. Without hesitation she pulled the twine bow. The little book sprang open in greeting. Faith paged through with narrowed eyes, seeing her drawings with the critical eye afforded by time and distance. For all the Colonel's criticism, she could find few faults.

Her breath caught when she reached the place the sirens had been. The ragged edge of the torn page was all that was left. No, there was something. The faint impression of the graphite had left its mirror image on the opposing page. Faith traced its contours with a finger, remembering the sinister beauty of the creatures that had inspired her. She could hear their song faintly, like a remembered tune on a misty morning.

Shaking her head against the hypnotic sound, she flipped forward to the phoenix. The sight of it filled her with warmth, courage, and a sense of power. The next page would be Leviathan. Faith hesitated. Her stomach knotted at the memory of the storm and the demon come to life. It was far harder now that she knew of the Ink to assure herself she was not somehow to blame. With a bracing breath and a nod to the phoenix, Faith turned the page.

Leviathan was gone.

* * *

Faith took her seat at the writing desk stiff backed and scowling internally. The Colonel had acknowledged her arrival without looking up. He was busy with his own letters, the Guild writing box open on his desk.

Faith uncapped her inkwell and picked up her pen with abrupt movements. She pulled the first letter and a clean piece of paper in front of her. Her pen hovered but she did not write. She could not write for the storm raging in her head.

When the Colonel had ripped the sirens from her sketchbook, she had been embarrassed and afraid of his reprisal. Now, there was no threat of either. The deed was done, the sketchbook forgotten, at least by him. To discover that he had also torn out Leviathan only made her face hot with rage. He had said the sirens were indecent. But Leviathan? A symbol of God's own power taken straight from the Bible- what was indecent about that?

Why had he taken those drawings? Why had he taken her whole sketchbook for that matter? It was not because they were poor drawings. She was sure of that now. He had not been embarrassed by her efforts. He had been angry. Even fearful. What about the private sketches of a young woman threatened him so?

Faith set her quill down and turned to watch him. His eyes were red-rimmed and he held a handkerchief in one hand while he wrote. He squinted and frowned, stopping to dab at his watering eyes every few lines.

"Colonel, may I interrupt you a moment?" Faith asked, her voice even.

He looked up and dabbed again. "Yes. Can you not read my writing? My eyes are bad today."

"It's not about the letters. I have a question. Why did you enter my watercolors in the exhibit?"

The Colonel blinked, but whether from pain or surprise, Faith could not tell.

"You saw them? Good. It was a gift to you, to thank you for your help with the preparations."

"Why didn't you put my name on them?"

"It would not serve our purpose of finding you a fitting match if we made a spectacle of you. They are not as good as my usual work, but since I rarely do watercolor I decided to take the risk to my reputation."

"That was very thoughtful of you. I hope you do not regret it," Faith said. She could not put gratitude into her voice. It was enough that she kept the sarcasm out.

"They were received very well, actually." The Colonel did not seem to notice her frosty tone and went back to writing.

Faith turned back to the copying, seething with resentment. When had he intended to tell her of this gift? How dare he belittle her efforts and then attach his own name to them! After a time, the monotony of Faith's task dulled the edge of her anger but did not sheath it.

She was still frowning when the Colonel grunted in frustration and stood up. Pretending not to have noticed, Faith watched from the side of her eye as he packed up his writing box, closed the lid, and set it on its shelf.

"I'm going to put drops in my eyes and lie down for awhile. See what you can get done before dinner."

"Yes, Colonel. I hope you get some relief," Faith said as she uncharitably wished that he would not.

After he had left, Faith set down her quill and stretched. Her eyes flitted to the owl embossed box. She froze.

The key was still in the lock.

Faith peered around the door that he had left ajar. The hall was empty, the floor creaked faintly somewhere overhead. She heard a door shut.

Skin tingling, Faith went to the box. She listened again but could hear nothing but the sound of her heart pounding in her ears. *All I need are a few minutes. I will just try it out, a few lines just to prove I can do it, and put it right back. He would never know. Where's the harm in that?*

She carried the box to the desk. The key turned with a satisfying click and the lid lifted silently. Nestled in a velvet crevice was the miraculous pen.

What if he comes back? What if he finds out? Where is your integrity Faith Trumbull? She had never done anything so deceitful before. She had also never wanted anything so much. She knew it was wrong, but she would have no peace until she knew for sure.

Faith looked around the room once more as though to reassure herself that she was alone. Her eyes landed on the family crest. *Fortuna favet audaci.*

Faith picked up the pen.

There was no shock or sound of angels singing. It felt like any other pencil but with a grip too thick for her slender fingers. She adjusted until it felt reasonably steady in her hand and sat in the Colonel's chair. It was still warm.

She pulled a small stack of clean paper in front of her. Listening for movement in the hall and holding her breath, Faith drew the pen across the page.

Nothing. Her stomach clenched as disappointment and something like panic swept over her. Had she been wrong about the Talent? No. The Colonel had said it took concentration and self discipline. She was too distracted.

Faith took several deep breaths, marshaling her thoughts and emotions. She focused all of them on simply creating a line. A pencil line. Again, she touched the pen to paper.

This time, a strange sensation, both warm and cool at the same time, ran up her fingers and into her forearm. With elation and a sigh of relief, she saw the pen leave a smooth carbon line as she described a simple arabesque in the corner of the page. *Now what?* she thought. She needed an image. The sirens and leviathan flashed before her eyes. She banished them as too ambitious, too dangerous. The phoenix as well. Something simple. At a loss for anything better, she decided on an apple.

With the thrill of the Ink at her command, it was easier now to forget about the Colonel, to forget about being discovered. She built an image of an apple in her mind, not just what it looked like, but what it smelled, felt, and tasted like. What did an apple *mean*?

With this multidimensional thought firm in her mind, she began to draw. At first her effort was stuttering and unsure, the pen stopping with her doubts. She forced them away, telling herself it was no different from any other pen or pencil she had ever used. It began to respond to her thoughts as though it were an extension of them, revealing upon the page the image in her mind.

Faith sat back and looked at what she had done. It was perfect. It sat upon the page, ripe and tempting as the Colonel's. More so because it was hers. She picked it up and held it, sun warm and tree ripe as though freshly picked. As she had before, Faith pierced its skin. This time she giggled with delight to see the juice trickle out, shimmering enticingly. The smell made her stomach rumble and she longed to take a bite.

The Colonel had said not to eat it. But he had also said women could not use the Ink. She had proved him wrong once already. Faith opened her mouth to take a bite.

There was a sound on the stair.

Terror flooded out her triumph. Faith placed the pen back in its niche, closed the lid, and slid the box onto its shelf.

Footsteps in the foyer.

Faith grabbed the stack of papers, flipping them upside down with her drawing on the bottom. She raced around to the other side of the desk before slowing to a dawdling pace, as though she were casually crossing the room. Her nerves were drawn so tight, it was no act that she gasped when the Colonel pushed the door open.

"You startled me! I thought you were going to bed?" Faith pressed the papers to her chest, the apple over her heart. She was glad of the excuse for her breathlessness.

"I forgot something," he said. "What are those?"

"I dropped my pen and splattered ink all over my paper. I needed some clean sheets. These are from the stack on your desk. I hope that's all right?" Faith asked, making a move to put them back.

"No, that's fine," he said, dabbing at his eyes. The Colonel walked around his desk and stopped before the Guild writing box.

Faith retook her seat at her desk as casually as she could while her heart was in her throat. Trained to the Colonel's rigid requirements, it was second nature for Faith to notice how things were placed and put them back as she had found them. In her haste though, had she got it right? Was the box askew, too far to the left or to the right?

Either she had placed it correctly or his eyes were too troublesome for him to see. He turned the key, pocketed it, and left without another word. Faith waited to exhale until he was long gone.

He who replies to words of Doubt
Doth put the Light of Knowledge out
- William Blake, Auguries of Innocence

CHAPTER TWELVE

The Opening

Once Faith had tried the Ink, it consumed her every thought. Whatever restraint she had thought herself capable of withered in the heat of her obsession.

At first she floated on a rising draft of triumph. Not only had she proven she had the Talent, but it had felt so right. The tingling. The exhilaration. The Ink had not just brought the apple to life. It had brought her to life. But the thrill had soon faded without the Ink, leaving her feeling dull and empty in a drab and lifeless world.

If she were being completely honest, some part of that thrill had been the rush of her illicit behavior and the nearness of being caught. In turn, some of the dullness had to be from the near constant drudgery she manufactured in an effort to keep her mind from the Ink. That had been in vain. Though her fingers were stiff and sore, no amount of work was enough to distract her.

As she washed the floors she wondered anew what the Ink was made of. Was it divine? Did it exist in nature? Could it be made, or was it mined or harvested? As she scrubbed pots in the kitchen she considered how it worked. How did it answer to her imagination? More perplexing, how did her imagination answer to it? Did the pen tip really change? Did the apple really exist? How much was real and how much illusion, on the page or in the world around her?

When she was not working, she listened absently at meals and visits, sparing only the smallest part of her attention for the conversation. If she had been any less distracted, she might have been appalled at how well this was received. Both Eliza and the Colonel were content to talk without much interjection and William was content to sit in silence with his thoughts. At night she would pull the drawing from her dresser just to marvel at the apple that she had created.

Faith had told herself that she would be content just to know if she had the Talent. She had been very wrong. She wanted nothing more than to use the Ink again, to imagine, to create, and to see the images of her mind's eye appear before her earthly ones. She ached to test the limits of its power and her imagination. Her fingers tingled with her desire to hold the pen again.

Today though, all they would hold was a needle.

In early November, any hope of late summer heat was gone as winter once again occupied the city. An icy gale celebrated its victory outside the parlor window with furious abandon. The lamps were no match for the gloom, so Faith and her mother had taken up chairs by the window, angled not for conversation but to catch the cold, pale light. The dresses they were sewing spilled over their laps like silky throws.

They worked in companionable silence. Her mother's face was, for once, peaceful and content. What her upbringing had lacked in refinement, it had compensated for in practicality. There were few useful crafts, save maybe cobbling, that Faith's mother could not perform with competence. The realm of domestic industry was where she felt most at home; utilitarian accomplishment was the one thing that gave her satisfaction, and the admiration of the Colonel.

The Colonel had high aspirations for the coming social season and had set them to making new dresses for it. The exhibition had been a resounding success, resulting in the honorarium that the Colonel had predicted. It had been enough for fabric, ribbon, and beads but Faith's mother had insisted it was foolish to spend it on dressmakers when she was up to the task. When she had finished sewing the body, she gave each dress to Faith for embellishment.

Faith fished a precious bugle bead from the dish on the sill and glanced at the Colonel who was reading in a softly upholstered wingback. As she threaded the bead, she wondered about the Guild. More precisely, she wondered how she could get a pen of her own. As desperate as she was, she dared not sneak to use his pen again. Although she felt vindicated by the outcome, she was guilty that she had fallen prey to temptation in a fit of pique. Even if she could get comfortable with the deceit, it was too risky.

If she were a man, she reasoned, it would all be very simple. If this guild were anything like the old craft guilds, young men who showed promise would be brought on as apprentices. If they excelled they would become journeymen, free to ply the trade in lesser markets as they gained skill and experience. Upon the completion of a masterpiece and the approval of the guild, they would become masters themselves who could then take on apprentices of their own.

Once Faith had demonstrated she had the Talent, presumably there would have been some deliberation about personal character. Her recent deviousness notwithstanding, the Colonel could have no complaint on that front. If she were a man, she would not have needed to sneak and he would already have begun her training.

So, what did it mean that she was a woman? If he believed that women were incapable of using the Ink, there would be no reason to test her. But if she could prove that it were, in fact, possible, if she could find some way to show him that she had the Talent without betraying her deception, perhaps he could be persuaded to apprentice her. On the other hand, if the issue were one of permission rather than possibility, he might let her apprentice if she swore never to use it for anything other than what he deemed acceptable. Faith was not sure it was a promise she could keep, but it was one she was willing to make. First, though, she had to find out which it was.

She continued to thread and stitch beads along the hem of the dress as she considered how to broach the subject. Her mother had stopped sewing and was rummaging in the sewing basket at her feet.

"What are you looking for Mama?"

"That new skein we bought the other day. I thought I'd put it in the basket."

"Maybe it's still in the shopping basket. Do you want me to go look?"

"No. My arse is flat. I need a stretch. I'll go look for it."

Faith's mother stood and set the work in progress carefully over the arms of her chair. When she had gone, Faith seized her opportunity.

"Colonel, may I ask you something about the Guild?" Faith made her tone as innocently curious as she could.

He looked up from his book . "Yes, if it is appropriate."

"I hope it is. When we were at the Astor's, they have a floral painting above the mantle that is so *lifelike*, I think it must have been done with the Ink. I was just wondering if I am right?"

The Colonel looked at her from under his brows. "Yes, it probably is. They have a number of Old Masters' that were Inked."

Faith nodded and stitched another bead, as though her curiosity had been satisfied. Only after he had gone back to his book did she add, apparently as an afterthought, "That's odd though. I remember you said that women could not use the Ink, yet I'm sure that William said it was painted by a woman."

"You must have misunderstood." The Colonel did not look up from his page this time.

"No, I remember. Rachel Ruysch was the artist's name."

Something flashed across the Colonel's face. Faith would have missed it if she had not been watching him so closely. He still did not look up from his book, but he was not reading. His eyes were fixed on the center of a page.

"Rachel Ruysch was married to an artist. If her paintings incorporated Ink, it was by his contribution."

"Oh. I see." Faith felt a stab of disappointment, but whether Ruysch had used the Ink or not, Faith knew she herself could. Besides there was something hollow and evasive about his answer. She pushed him harder. "I had thought maybe it was possible for a woman to use the Ink, so long as she confined herself to fruits and flowers, like you had once suggested. I mean, in theory, if it were proved that a woman could use the Ink, would s-"

The force of his interruption sat Faith back in her chair. "Impossible! I will say it again so it will be clear and there will be no more discussion of it. Women may be susceptible to the Ink but are utterly incapable of controlling it. They inherently lack the emotional discipline and mental fortitude. There is no place for women in the Guild. It is best you resign yourself to this fact and not be distracted from your true duty."

He snapped the book shut with such violence that Faith jabbed the needle into her finger. She sucked away the welling drop of blood before it could stain the dress, a metallic tang filling her mouth as the Colonel stormed from the room. His words claimed an absolute truth Faith knew to be false. His anger told her there was more to the issue than he was saying. His burst of temper had made two things clear to Faith. She was determined to prove him wrong and she would have to find a way to do it that did not require his approval.

* * *

Faith became quietly observant of everything the Colonel said and did. She listened for clues about the Guild and its workings hidden in conversations. She noted who he met with, when and what they discussed, all the while maintaining an air of contented disinterest. It was not as hard as she might have thought. Having a purpose calmed the frenzy in her soul. Determination gave her patience.

In an ideal world, Faith could acquire pen and Ink without the Guild at all. If daVinci had discovered rather than created it, there had to be a source. The use of it had come so easily to her that she doubted the need for training. The Colonel had said it could be dangerous, and she was mindful that she did not know enough to know what to guard against, but she figured that if she proceeded cautiously she would spot the traps before becoming ensnared in them. The only thing she would give up by going it alone would be time.

However, Faith knew this was next to impossible. Not only was the Colonel unlikely to betray the source of the Ink in passing, it was even more unlikely that she would be able to access it. Faith was also certain that the Guild had taken thorough precautions against those who would circumvent their authority. It was, as the Colonel had said, the Guild's fundamental purpose.

Its other purpose, however, was to train those with Talent in how to use it. She toyed only briefly with the idea of disguising herself as a man. She also dismissed the notion of running away to England to train there. Not only would she have no money and no assurance they would accept a woman, but she would have to cross the Atlantic again. That she could not do.

What Faith needed was someone in New York with access to the Guild who would be willing to train her, even if it were against the Guild's regulations. She ruled out apprentices. They would be the easiest to sway but would not have the access or training she needed. A journeyman might do. A master would be better. She was not sure how she would find one with the right lack of integrity, if women truly were excluded from the Guild, and sympathy for her plight. She refused to let this deter her.

One peculiar complication she noted immediately was that she did not know many of the artists in New York. Of course she knew them all by name from the exhibition preparations, but none of them, save Mr. Smith, Mr. Waldo and, of course, Mr. Ingham, had ever been to the house. The Colonel had not introduced her to a single artist at the ball. Mr. Smith and Mr. Waldo were too close to the Colonel to go against him and Mr. Ingham seemed too honest to go against the Guild.

Days slipped past and turned into weeks without any useful developments and Faith began to lose hope. The Colonel had decided to take rooms at the Academy and move all of his canvases and supplies over there. To her dismay, she discovered while helping him pack that this included the Guild writing box. According to a letter Faith had copied in reply to a Mr. Wilkes, Baltimore was looking for historical pictures to adorn their public buildings. The Colonel was eager to pitch his services and would be leaving end of the following week. He wanted his things settled at the Academy before then, putting a hard stop to Faith's sleuthing about the Guild once the move was complete.

She tried to reassure herself that the Ink was her destiny. Fate would provide.

When everything was loaded on the carriage, Faith asked if she could accompany the Colonel to the Academy to help unpack.

"Doesn't your mother need you here?"

"She said she didn't. And I could use a break from the house. I haven't been out of it in days." Faith's primary goal in going to the Academy was to match paintings done with Ink to local names she might recognize, but as she said it, she realized she did want to leave the house. The Astors had returned to their country house before the flurry of the holidays in town. Faith was surprised to find she missed the distraction of those visits.

Ultimately, the Colonel agreed. They rattled the short distance to the Academy through snappingly clear air. The haze had begun to fade, Faith observed with relief. Maybe the interminable winter would end soon as well.

Porters carried the trunks and crates up to the Colonel's rooms with Faith trailing behind. It took them far less time to unpack than it had to pack and soon there was a pile of empty trunks and white sheets piled outside the door to the Colonel's new studio. As the Colonel busied himself with setting the disgorged contents in some semblance of order, Faith retreated to the hall to tidy the packing material. After, she planned to scout the galleries for possible Masters.

She had just picked up the first sheet when Mr. Waldo approached with two small canvases under one arm.

"Hello Miss Trumbull. I was told Colonel Trumbull is here."

"He is setting up his rooms. Please, go in."

Mr. Waldo moved past her with a nod and shut the door behind him.

Faith lifted the sheet high only to find the corner of it had been trapped by the door. She tugged to loosen it and the door opened slightly. This was enough to let her hear the two men talking. Faith did not think twice about the propriety of listening at doors.

"You brought the samplers?" she heard the Colonel ask. "Well, let's see them."

Mr. Waldo must have shown him the two canvases. There were a few minutes of silence before she heard the Colonel again.

"That one there needs to look into other trades. He'd be a better wainwright than a painter. The oil shows promise though. He'll have to be evaluated. Assuming he passes, who can we get to mentor him?"

"I already have my hands full," Waldo replied. "Jewett is pretty busy too. I don't know about Sully and Allston."

"What about Jarvis? Jarvis could start his training."

"Jarvis has two apprentices already."

"Two?!" the Colonel sputtered indignantly. "He's taken on another without my approval! Malbone should have thought twice about making him a Master. He's a rogue with a door. No respect for authority or procedure!"

"To that point, Colonel, shouldn't we get Guild Master West's permission first? Or wait until you are officially Guild Master? Just in case it doesn't come through."

"It's nothing more than a formality now. I'll be Guild Master by early in the new year. If we appeal to West, it will just be another body for the British Guild. No, I want American artists to be trained by the American Guild and I want to have them lined up. We need to prove the strength of our Talent. Munson can at least be evaluated before the Guild is approved. If he passes, I want a mentor ready to take him on."

Faith did not hear Mr. Waldo's response as footsteps echoed in the hall behind her. She quickly resumed folding the sheets. Mr. Murray came into view just as Mr. Waldo was leaving. Mr. Murray gave Mr. Waldo a hurried greeting as he passed him in the doorway and was already addressing the Colonel before Mr. Waldo could exit.

"Colonel! I'm glad I caught you! The directors are very nervous about you taking your history paintings back. If you were to make them an offer for a permanent display, I think you would find them most receptive but time-" Mr. Murray was cut off as Mr. Waldo shut the door securely on his words.

Faith did not have as much time to walk the galleries while Mr. Murray and the Colonel finished their business as she had hoped, but she had learned more about the Guild in one conversation than she had in all the previous weeks. *Jarvis.* She had heard of him- he was apparently very eccentric- but she had never met the man. She didn't know who Malbone was, or what the Colonel had meant about a rogue with a door, but it seemed the Guild was not as rigid as the Colonel made it seem. Maybe there were ways to circumvent its rules. Indeed, the Colonel himself seemed to be pushing the boundaries. It was clear his power was limited until he was Guild Master. If Faith had any chance of becoming a master, she would have to move quickly before that happened. *Maybe Jarvis is the Master I've been looking for. But, how do I meet him? And why would he help me?*

A Truth thats told with bad intent
Beats all the Lies you can invent
- William Blake, Auguries of Innocence

CHAPTER THIRTEEN
The Ruse

These questions continued to occupy Faith's thoughts leading up to the Colonel's departure for Baltimore. His absence was the best time to try Mr. Jarvis, but she could not conjure up a way to visit him without an introduction that would not create a scandal sure to get back to the Colonel. She thought of writing a letter from the Colonel hiring him to paint her portrait, but she had no way to pay, nor any assurance that he would be inclined to help. Adding to Faith's frustration, the Astors were back at their town house and Eliza had invited her to visit. Faith was not in the mood to listen to Eliza's endless prattle when time was so short and options were so few.

Faith walked the short distance to their house, thankful for little else other than the fur muff that Eliza had gifted her. Faith didn't think it had been given with any great affection- Eliza had more of them than any one lady could possibly need- but she was grateful for its insulation against the frigid wind. Her hair and face were less protected. By the time she arrived she was sure her nose and cheeks were bright red, her hair a wild mess. She sighed. Eliza secretly delighted in being superior and William would hardly notice, so why should Faith care what she looked like?

Faith decided she cared very much the moment she stepped into the parlor.

The furniture had been rearranged to place one of the velvet chairs between the fireplace and the window. Eliza, elegantly dressed and arranged, sat in the window's watery light. Mr. Ingham sat across from her, drawing board and pencil in hand.

"Faith!" Eliza greeted her with her usual enthusiasm. "I'm so happy you are here. I want you to keep me company while Mr. Ingham paints my portrait. I hear it's a long and tedious process," she said with a teasing look at Mr. Ingham.

"Any time it becomes unbearable, we will take a break," Mr. Ingham replied mildly.

Faith smoothed her hair as she took a seat. Her face was no longer red from cold but flush with embarrassment. She avoided eye contact with Mr. Ingham. How did he always catch her at the worst moments? Only the fact that he was focused on Eliza soothed her vanity, if not her envy.

Faith played her part, listening to Eliza talk about whatever gossip came to mind. Some of it Faith had heard before and knew it was being retold for Mr. Ingham's benefit. For his part, Faith was glad to see he took little note. He rarely spoke except when he asked Faith to reposition her chair so that Eliza's head might stay in a more flattering light while she talked. The best spot turned out to be close to Mr. Ingham, close enough that Faith could watch him work.

It did not feel like much time had passed before Eliza had grown uncomfortable in her pose and asked for a break. When Eliza left the room, Faith found herself alone with Mr. Ingham and the buzzing floral painting. It was the perfect opportunity to ask him about the Guild, but Faith was at a loss for how to start.

"Which do you find more off-putting?" Mr. Ingham asked, without looking up as he refined the details of his sketch.

"I beg your pardon?" Faith asked, wondering if he meant Eliza or something about his drawing.

"The painting. Do you find the buzzing or the smell more irritating?" This time he looked up and gave her a sly smile. Faith could not help but return it.

"The buzzing, certainly."

"Really? I find the smell more bothersome. Some think she did it on purpose, a reminder of our mortality. Personally I think she was playing a rich prank on her well-to-do patrons."

Faith could barely contain her astonishment that Mr. Ingham was openly discussing the Ink with her. Was he simply acknowledging the obvious from their encounter at the exhibition, that they were both subject to its effects? Or did he assume that the Colonel had brought her into his confidence and that she knew more than she did? Faith made a quick decision to play that it was the latter and see what she could get him to reveal.

"Either way, Mrs. Ruysch was very adept with the Ink." Faith said with false confidence. Saying the word Ink out loud sounded strange, as though he might think she were speaking in tongues.

He did not react other than to agree, "She was one of the best."

Faith felt a surge of vindication. Women *could* use the Ink!

"It's too bad that she was limited to flowers," Faith said experimentally.

"Limited? There were no limits to Ruysch's Talent other than her interests. She could have painted anything she wanted but her father was a botanist and flowers were her passion. They were popular with patrons as well. Her paintings sold for more than Vermeer's. Or Rembrandt's for that matter."

"She was a Master then?" Faith's body was thrumming with tension.

"Of course she was a Master. In fact, she was Guild Master of the Dutch for a time."

Guild Master. A woman. Faith was unable to disguise her shock.

"What?! I didn't think women could even be Masters!" The words were out of her mouth before she could stop them.

"There are few now, to be sure, but there are some. Did your Da tell you there aren't?" Mr. Ingham asked with a furrowed brow.

"He said they shouldn't... that it's more difficult for women," Faith said scrambling to cover her ignorance.

"Well, they are more imaginative than men, and that's a good thing with the Ink, but also makes managing it more of a challenge. It's a wee bit more dangerous and the Guild Masters can be a pretty cautious lot. They don't admit as many women as they should, in my opinion."

Faith should have been elated. Instead she felt she had been punched in the gut. The Colonel had to have known. It was recognition she had seen cross his face. He had lied to her. Outright lied to her. Any guilt that Faith had been harboring for her own actions evaporated instantly in the glare of his deception.

"I should very much like to emulate Mrs. Ruysch. I mean, not to become a Guild Master. To be a Master would be honor enough."

"Has your Da tested you?"

What kind of test? Did the apple count? "Yes, it was successful."

"Then what's stopping you?"

The Colonel. The Colonel was the only thing stopping her. But if she told Mr. Ingham that, he would be honor bound not to help her. If, on the other hand, he thought the Colonel approved... A plan was forming in Faith's mind. First, she needed his sympathy.

"Time is my enemy. The Colonel has been wanting to train me, but he is always so busy. Even now, he is getting ready to go out of town for who knows how long."

"What about another Master?"

"Just the other day he was talking to Mr. Waldo about finding a mentor and there was no one else with the time either," Faith said affecting an air of stoic martyrdom. "I have begun to feel I will never get to use the Ink."

"I remember how eager I was to start. You must be very anxious."

Faith waited a beat, hoping he would offer to train her himself. When he didn't she plunged ahead.

She brightened as though an idea had just come to her. "Oh! Do you think...? No, I hate to impose. You'll think me impertinent, but do you think *you* could be my mentor?"

Mr. Ingham sat back and rubbed his chin. Faith held her breath, afraid she had overstepped.

"I haven't trained anyone before. I'm young for a Master."

"That's to your credit! I'm sure you'd make an excellent teacher."

"There's other considerations, too. There's a lot of protocols and courtesies. I'd have to get permission, but I'm not sure from whom."

"I'm sure the Colonel would approve," Faith offered recklessly.

"Well, I should have his blessing, but he isn't a Guild Master yet. Ordinarily, the Americans have had to get West's approval, but I suppose if I were training you, I'd need my Guild's approval. But then, if you train with me, you'd get presented to the Irish Guild, but eventually there will be a Guild here. If you were to be admitted to the American Guild instead, it would have to be with everyone's approval." He ran a hand through his hair. "It's quite a muddle."

"And if they disagreed? I mean, about which Guild I would belong to."

"That could get... unpleasant. In the end, I would be obligated to go by my Guild Master's decision, not the Colonel's. But you'd be at the Colonel's mercy."

Faith swallowed at the prospect of the Colonel's mercy. "I had no idea it is so complicated! I couldn't put you to the trouble."

"I don't know how much trouble it'd be to me. I've never been one for politics. I suppose I could do it if my Guild Master agrees. And your Da, as a courtesy. The rest could be sorted later."

"Of course! There is nothing my father loves more than protocol and courtesies," Faith said. The bubble of excitement in her chest was growing by the moment. If she could fake the Colonel's approval, she would be under the authority of a different Guild altogether and completely out of his reach. The bubble pressed against her chest so she could hardly breath. "Would it take a long time to get your Guild Master's permission though? A packet to Dublin and back would be months!"

"The Guild has ways to communicate quickly. Wouldn't be more than a day or two."

"That's extraordinary!" Faith resolved to find out more about how those Inked letters traveled.

Just then, Eliza came back into the room. Mr. Ingham settled her back into position, leaving Faith to ponder how she would get the Colonel's permission without actually getting his permission. She could forge a letter. She signed his name better than he did. But how would she keep Mr. Ingham, or Mr. Ingham's Guild Master, from mentioning it to him? She didn't know if they ever corresponded, other than Mr. Ingham's letter of introduction, but she couldn't rule it out. And, what excuse would she use for their training? Doubts pricked at her bubble of joy.

Faith worked on a solution as she watched Mr. Ingham finish his study of Eliza. As he put away his drawing tools he explained that he would come back every other day for several sittings, depending on how long she could tolerate to pose for each. Eliza looked pained by the idea of so much sitting still. To Faith, it sounded ideal. There were few ways for a lady to spend so much time alone with a gentleman without creating a scandal...

When Eliza objected that too many sittings would unduly impact her social calendar, Mr. Ingham offered to quicken the process by only capturing her face and hair in person and finishing the details of her clothing and the background at his studio.

"I will need you to allow me to have your dress at my studio as reference."

"What a curious thought! What do you do with it? Drape it over a chair?" Eliza asked, her eyes round and her cheeks brightly colored. The idea of a young man in possession of her dress had her discomfited.

"It is best if I can find a model to wear it, but I have a mannequin available that will do well enough."

"Oh! Are you sure about the mannequin? I do want the best portrait but I don't know how I feel about someone else-"

"I will do it," Faith volunteered, seizing on an idea that was forming before her, like walking a bridge in dense fog. "I will model the dress. If you both think I'd be suitable, of course." Faith looked from Mr. Ingham to Eliza.

Eliza's face was mixed surprise and cautious relief. "Would you? I would feel better if you were wearing it rather than a stranger, but won't you be terribly bored? I couldn't ask it, really."

"It's no trouble. I've done it before for the Colonel's portraits. I'm very accustomed to sitting like a statue."

Eliza seemed doubtful about Faith's sanity in this regard but she looked to Mr. Ingham who voiced his agreement. Faith smiled genuinely as they began to firm up a schedule. Her sense of triumph dimmed when Eliza requested that she do the modeling at the house. That would not give Faith the degree of privacy she wanted for her nascent plan, but Eliza was still unnerved at the thought of her garments being so far out of her sight. Afraid that Eliza might decide to endure the sittings herself, Faith agreed.

Faith made her farewells along with Mr. Ingham, astonished by how late it had gotten. She asked Mr. Ingham to escort her home.

The eastern sky was already a dusky bruise; the light before them a bright wash of palest gold. Faith's hands sweated inside the fur muff in spite of the sharply cold air. She had secured both Mr. Ingham's willingness to train her and the time alone, or at least nearly alone, to do it in. Now, she needed a way to make sure the Colonel did not find out. She did not spend much time considering the flaws of the tactic that came to her. She was afraid a better idea would not materialize and she would lose her chance.

Faith stopped Mr. Ingham with a light hand on his arm. "An exciting idea has just occurred to me. The Colonel has so much on his mind, with the Guild and the Academy and these new commissions he is pitching. I hate to be a bother to him, or make him feel guilty that he isn't training me himself. Now, don't be afraid to say no, but I think it would be a wonderful surprise for him if we began my training in secret. We could start while I'm sitting in for Eliza and wait to reveal it until I've really got something to show, at your discretion of course."

Mr. Ingham considered her proposal warily. "I am not sure that is a good idea. If there were some objection, Colonel Trumbull would be angry with me and with my Guild Master. That is exactly the kind of political kerfuffle that I try to avoid."

Faith couldn't agree more. It would be a disaster. But she could think of no other way. "I promise I will take all the blame if anyone should object." Even if they would punish her by refusing to let her advance, they could not take away what she had already learned. "But honestly, what kind of objection could the Colonel possibly make? Against his own daughter?"

"I get the feeling your father does not enjoy surprises."

"He will love this one," Faith said with all the sincerity she could muster.

"I don't know," Mr. Ingham said doubtfully. "Training takes a long time."

"How long?"

"Most of us take a year or two before becoming Journeymen."

A year or two? Faith would just have to learn much faster. "Well, I obviously won't get very far while you are doing Eliza's portrait, but what if you did my portrait after that?"

Mr. Ingham stopped and folded his arms as he thought. He regarded Faith with a frank gaze that sent a delicious shiver through her even as she worried he could see right through her ruse. He reached up and coiled one loose tendril of her hair around his finger, tilting his head to change the angle of his view.

"I won't paint your portrait," he said finally, pulling his hand away. Faith's heart stopped in her chest. "But I can use you as a model."

"For other portraits?"

"Possibly. But an allegorical is what I had in mind. I'm thinking we've had too much of winter. It's time for spring. You would make a lovely Persephone. Or maybe,..." he trailed off. Faith's heart hammered under his gaze. "I'd still have to get my Guild Master's permission."

"Do you think he'd agree to keep it a secret?"

"Probably not, but I could botch the name somewhat. It wouldn't be the first time my handwriting had caused confusion."

"So you'll do it?"

"I'll do it."

"Thank you, Mr. Ingham! You've made me terribly happy!" On impulse Faith pushed up on her toes and kissed him on the cheek.

"You are very welcome," he said with a warm laugh. "But don't think I will go easy on you! I will expect discipline and dedication!" he said with false severity that made Faith giggle. She gave him a smart salute and they continued on down the street.

Faith seemed to walk on air. She was flushed with happiness and the feel of her lips on his cheek. In her heart, there was a spark of regret for all the lies she'd told that day, but the glow of her victory outshone it like the sun outshines the stars.

He who desires, but acts not, breeds pestilence.
-William Blake, The Marriage of Heaven and Hell

CHAPTER FOURTEEN

The Swoon

"Mr. Ingham will have to find another model," the Colonel said, as he picked up his teacup.

Faith's plan was already beginning to unravel.

"But Colonel, I will have plenty of time while you are in Baltimore. And Mama could chaperone." Faith pleaded, risking his ire at being challenged.

"While *I* am in Baltimore? We are *all* going to Baltimore." The Colonel set the cup back down with a sharp clink. It was a warning that Faith was too surprised to heed.

"All of us?"

"Yes, including Katherine. I will not be back here before Christmas so we will all go and pass the holiday in Baltimore. If Mr. Ingham needs a model before we are back, then he will have to find another young woman."

"How long will we be gone?"

"A month. Maybe less."

A month? The Colonel might be Guild Master by then and then all those protocols and courtesies would give him control of Faith's destiny. She could not get so close to her goal and fail now. It was all she could do to cap the welling spring of desperation that was threatening to overflow her heart and eyes. Yet, if she pushed too hard, he would push back. She had one last ploy.

"Might you reconsider and take the trip alone? You see, Mrs. Astor was wanting something bright and uplifting for the tea porch. She had suggested Eliza as a model for Mr. Ingham but she's already tired of posing and her portrait isn't even finished. If Mr. Ingham uses me as his model, then it will be my face that William sees every day. If Mr. Ingham uses some other model..."

The Colonel paused ever so slightly as he wiped his mouth with a napkin, but shook his head as he set it on the table.

"There's nothing to be done about it. I will not abandon you and your mother for Christmas and the trip cannot wait. I must make my proposal before Vanderlyn does. I'm the only artist qualified to commemorate our Revolutionary history- I was there after all- but that won't stop him from trying and I'd rather avoid the distraction. Before you help Katherine and your mother begin packing, I will need you to copy out these letters. One is the new bylaws for the Academy and the other is a proposal for the Academy to purchase some of my pictures for permanent display. The next meeting isn't until after we leave, but I want both proposals before the directors even if I am not."

"Yes, Colonel." Defeated, Faith took the pages. Hot tears of frustration burned in her nose.

Preparations for their trip progressed at such a breakneck pace that Faith did not have time to notify Mr. Ingham that she would be leaving. She began on several occasions to write him a letter but stopped each time. Not only was she reluctant to record any hint of their agreement, but the very act of fixing her defeat in writing somehow made it inevitable. A part of her was still searching for a way past this obstacle.

On the eve of their departure, with trunks and boxes stacked in the entry hall for the porters in the morning, Faith's mood was sullen and irritated, all the more so for her inability to indulge it. She kept a more neutral facade than her mother who kept glancing with bitter longing at the empty wine carafe on the sideboard. The Colonel had put alcohol strictly out of the question. He would not have her ill the next morning and delay their trip.

Faith sat up straighter as a spark of inspiration fell on the tinder in her mind and slowly flared to life. *That's it!* She would fake an illness. Something like her mother's fits. But without the drink.

As dinner ended and the evening wore on, Faith affected an increasingly lethargic air. She moved slowly and let a vague distraction creep into her voice. When she breathed out, she imagined her body deflating until it had collapsed on itself. Her shoulders slumped and her face was slack.

"Are you well?" her mother asked, frowning at her over the last bit of sewing.

"I am just tired," Faith said, closing the book she had been pretending to read. "I think I will go to bed early."

Faith stood and let herself sway ever so slightly. She put a hand to her head.

Her mother rushed to her side, placing her hands on Faith's cheeks and neck.

"You don't feel hot."

"I will be fine. It is just a headache. I have probably over exerted myself today and will be fine after some rest. Good night."

Faith felt the Colonel's eyes on her as she left the room. She took the stairs one slow, heavy step at a time, a small smile playing on her lips. When she got to her room, she dressed for bed but did not get in it. Instead, she sat in the straight backed chair and read until her back spasmed and her eyes burned. It was not until she saw the sunlight edge around her curtains, turning her room into a soft chiaroscuro of golden light, that she allowed herself to crawl under the covers. As she descended into half-sleep, Faith heard the rest of the house come to life and, after a time, the arrival of the porters. She did not rise.

Nor did she answer a knock on her door. Faith pretended to be sound asleep as someone opened it. From the sound of the steps and the weight on the bed, it was her mother who leaned over her and touched her forehead again.

"Faith. Wake up. The porters are loading the carriage."

Faith moaned but kept her eyes shut.

"Please, Faith. The Colonel will be put out if our departure is delayed."

Faith felt a small stab of guilt at the concern in her mother's voice. She let her eyelids flutter open and raised her head weakly, looking around as in a daze. Her mother opened the curtains. Faith gave a whimper and closed her eyes, her hands going to her head as she let it fall back to the bed. Her mother made a sound of distress and left the room. Faith heard a muffled conversation dominated by the Colonel's gruff tones and then his step on the stairs. He strode impatiently into the room and looked down at her with irritation.

"Can you rise?"

"Yes, I will try. It's just my head. And I feel so weak. I'm sorry Colonel. I don't mean to delay us."

"Sarah, help her to dress and she can sleep in the carriage."

Faith made a show of drawing back the covers and putting each foot slowly on the floor. She stood and swayed. And then she let herself fall.

Pain shot through her shoulder as it crashed awkwardly against the floor. She ignored it, glad it was her left. There was some excited conversation above her, a great shuffling of feet. She stayed limp as she was lifted back into bed. Time passed and Faith dozed, faintly aware of her mother sitting on the edge of the bed. A knot of dread formed in her stomach when Dr. Hosack arrived. She had not thought they would call the doctor.

He examined her gently and asked a number of questions, which Faith answered slowly and carefully. She did not want him to think she had anything infectious that would keep her away from Mr. Ingham if she were successful. When he asked about her menses, she blushed and demurred. When he asked if she had hit her head recently Faith saw an opportunity.

"Yes. On the drawer of my dresser. I bent to pick up something while it was open and hit it standing up." It was a real occurrence, though several days old and with no ill effect. Dr. Hosack felt under her hair.

"I cannot find a lump but that doesn't mean damage was not done." Mr. Hosack turned to the Colonel. "She will be fine but needs bed rest."

"Can't she rest on the trip?"

"Heavens no! She cannot be jostled like that."

"How long?"

"Until she is feeling better. It is hard to tell. A couple of days. Maybe a week."

The Colonel made an impatient sound and crossed his arms.

"Should I stay with her?" Faith's mother asked. The hopefulness Faith heard in her mother's voice was immediately dashed.

"No. Dr. Hosack, you are sure it is not catching? All she needs is rest for a few days?"

Dr. Hosack assured him that it was not contagious and agreed that she could be moved if it was done gently and not over any great distance. The Colonel left with Dr. Hosack. Faith lost track of time until the Colonel returned.

"Sarah, go down to the coach and get them to separate Faith's trunk from the rest of our things and take it to the Astor's. I have made arrangements for her to stay with them while we are in Baltimore."

Faith allowed herself to be roused and dressed by her mother and Katherine as she considered the effect of her deceit. Her plan had been for her mother to stay home, not to spend a month with Eliza and William Astor. Under her mother's care she could have met easily with Mr. Ingham. She was not sure how they would get the privacy they needed with the Astors all about. Still, she counted today a victory and would leave that problem for another.

Faith was led carefully out of the house with a veil to shield her from the light and bundled into the coach. At a funereal pace, it took an absurdly long time for the short distance. Once they arrived, Faith was settled in a luxurious bed of down and feathers in a large and well-appointed room. She kissed her mother goodbye and apologized to the Colonel and Mrs. Astor for her inconvenience. Mrs. Astor accepted the apology with far more warmth than the Colonel, even accounting for her natural reserve. The Colonel gave Faith a calculating look.

"Remember your duty," he said before leaving the room.

When everyone else had gone, Faith sat in bed and watched anxiously as a maid unpacked her things, until she too had closed the bedroom door behind her. Finally alone, Faith crawled from the bed to grab the small satchel of toiletries that had been set on the vanity table. Rummaging past her hair brush and comb, a tin of comfits and another of toothpowder, Faith's fingers closed on her sketchbook. Scrambling back into bed, she opened it to the page marked by the folded drawing of an apple and a short stub of pencil. With a contented sigh, Faith bent over the page and drew a dream of spring.

To see a World in a Grain of Sand
And a Heaven in a Wild Flower
Hold Infinity in the palm of your hand
And Eternity in an hour
                              -William Blake, Auguries of Innocence

CHAPTER FIFTEEN

The Tea

Faith tilted her face for the maid to apply her rouge. Jane's fingers were lighter and far more adept than Katherine's. She had curled and arranged Faith's hair without burning her once or stabbing a single pin into her scalp. Eliza's dress beneath her upswept curls left her neck and shoulders bare.

There was a knock on the door.

"Mr. Ingham is here. Are you sure you feel well enough?" Mrs. Astor asked, entering at Faith's invitation.

"Perfectly well, thank you, Mrs. Astor. You have been so kind to take me in."

"Not at all. Eliza and William enjoy your company. Although Eliza may be jealous. You look lovely in her dress."

Faith blushed beneath the rouge and thanked her hostess. She hoped that Mr. Ingham would think so, too. For once, he would not be catching her dusty, windblown, or startled. She was determined to be the picture of elegant grace. Jane had done her part. Now Faith had to do hers.

Faith grabbed the reticule in which she had hidden her sketchbook and Ink drawing and followed Mrs. Astor. It felt silly to carry a reticule within the house, but the dress had no pocket holes. Mrs. Astor led Faith to what they referred to as the summer parlor. It was a north-windowed room with even light that would be delightfully cool in the warmer months. In winter it was cold, even with a fire. Mr. Ingham was waiting within. Faith greeted him with such exuberance she feared her curtsy resembled a jumping marionette. So much for being poised and graceful.

"I hope it will be warm enough for you in here. There will be company in the main parlor later today and I didn't want you to be disturbed while you work. In here, I think you will be safe even from little John," she said, referring to her eldest daughter's seven year old son. Magdalena had left her husband and brought the boy to live with her parents while their marital issues were resolved. Faith was sure the boy had been a terror before, but the upheaval had done nothing to curb his tempestuous and entitled behavior.

"It will be just fine, Mrs. Astor. The lighting in here is ideal. Thank you," Mr. Ingham assured her.

"I would stay, but John, Jr. is particularly unwell today and Magdalena has received an upsetting letter from Mr. Bentzon. I will have one of the maids bring tea in a bit and Eliza will be in to keep you company. Please ring if you need anything else." With that, Mrs. Astor retreated, closing the door behind her.

Faith rocked onto the balls of her feet in anticipation. She had spent a few days in bed to do credit to her illness, at first reveling in the luxury of idleness that a house full of servants afforded. She had quickly become bored and restless. When Mrs. Astor had finally felt she was well enough to pen a letter to Mr. Ingham, Faith had been happy to make some progress but it had seemed an eternity for the day to arrive. Now that it was here, she was so giddy she thought she might float to the ceiling.

"Where do we start?" she asked Mr. Ingham.

"Well, you will sit there and pretend to be Eliza while I paint."

"I didn't mean the picture! I meant..." Faith dropped her voice to a conspiratorial whisper "the Ink."

"Oh! That." Mr. Ingham said with a teasing smile that made Faith's heart do a little jig. "The first lesson with the Ink is about discipline and self-control."

"You sound like the Colonel," Faith said sourly.

Mr. Ingham just laughed. He led her to a chair and arranged her just so, setting her arms here and pulling a curl forward there. The touch of his hand as it lightly brushed her cheek made Faith tingle. Then, without a word about the Ink, he began to paint. Faith's excitement faltered but she resolved to be patient. If he demanded a show of discipline and control, that is what she would give him. After all, she had spent her entire life hiding behind a facade for the Colonel.

She amused herself by watching him work. While he did not work quickly, he was looser than the Colonel. She liked the way he held the brush and how his whole arm moved fluidly but with control. His expression was serious with concentration, aging his youthful features in an appealing way. His eyes darted back and forth from the canvas to her. *What is he thinking? Am I all lines and shadows, like drawing a flower or a bird, or is he looking at me differently?* Suddenly self conscious about what part of her he might be focusing on, she clamped down on the urge to squirm. He did not seem to notice.

Just as Faith was finding her impatience to become unbearable, there was a knock on the door followed by Eliza striding into the room with a large striped hatbox in her hand. Her eyes widened and then narrowed at the sight of Faith all done up.

"Why Faith! You look beautiful! The neckline is a little looser on you, but I'm sure Mr. Ingham will adjust. I'm happy to see you do the dress justice." Faith accepted the back-handed compliment with grace as Eliza quickly made herself the center of attention. If they weren't going to get to the Ink any time soon, Faith welcomed the distraction.

"Hello Mr. Ingham! So nice to see you again. I hope I'm not interrupting. My new hat arrived and I couldn't wait to show it to Faith. You might like it too, Mr. Ingham. Perhaps you will want to use it for a painting."

Eliza untied the ribbons and lifted out a hat with immense ostrich feathers draping its ample brim and trailing languidly off to the side. Eliza put it on, the brim reaching to the edge of her shoulders.

"It's for spring of course, but isn't it exquisite!" Eliza said, tilting her head this way and that to make the feathers loll and ripple. "What do you think? " she asked, striking a pose.

Even with its astounding proportions, it was a beautiful hat and Faith said as much. Mr. Ingham concurred.

"Should we include it in my portrait?" Eliza asked, basking in the admiration.

"I've already painted your face and hair. It would be a shame- and would require you to sit again- to repaint it all. Besides, it would cover too much of your beautiful face," Mr. Ingham said without a shred of apparent irony.

"Oh, well then. Of course not." Satisfied with this diplomatic rejection, Eliza removed the hat and sat with it on her lap. She lingered, idly stroking the feathers and gossiping happily until a tray laden maid came to deliver the tea and inform Miss Astor that a guest had arrived. Eliza departed, leaving her hat in its box on the floor. The maid set the tea on a side table, asked if they needed anything else, and closed the door once again.

"Now that all of the anticipated interruptions are accounted for," Mr. Ingham said, "we may talk about the Ink."

Faith let out an audible sigh of relief.

"Were you able to bring a sample of your work, so I can get an idea where to start?"

With his permission to move, Faith fetched her reticule and pulled out the sketchbook. She put it into his hand and forced her own to withdraw. Her insides contorted and her skin prickled with heat as she scrutinized his expression for a reaction. His brow was drawn but she could not tell if it were concentration or disapproval. At times a faint smile tugged at his mouth. Was that pleasure or disdain? She bit the inside of her cheek but gave no outward sign of her internal struggle.

He paused at the spot where the sirens had been torn away, tilting the book in the light to catch the shine of their reflection on the opposing page, and again where Leviathan had been. The last pages were a riot of flowers, the drawings she had done while recuperating. He rubbed his brow with a free hand. Faith braced herself against his criticism.

"These are outstanding. Simply superb." He looked up at her with admiration such as she had never received before. It was so unexpected, Faith felt nothing for a moment. Then a warm light bloomed within and she found herself smiling broadly.

"You really think so?"

He nodded emphatically. "I do. Best I've ever seen starting out. Clearly I've nothing to teach you in terms of drawing. Can you paint as well?"

"I have some ability," Faith hedged. As wonderful as it was to hear, she did not completely trust Mr. Ingham's glowing praise. Although, he *had* been impressed by the watercolors at the exhibit. She wanted to claim them as hers, hungry for more compliments. Either Eliza was rubbing off on her or she was starting to understand why the young woman sought so much attention. Still, Faith held her tongue. Trying to explain why the Colonel would have put them up under his own name would only create complications.

"Well, we'll find out. Although I'd wager you can. But, wielding a pencil or a brush is one thing. The Ink is quite another. Do you have your sample?"

Faith handed him the folded page that she had held back. He spread it out upon his drawing board, holding the corners flat. At first the creases distorted the image, trapping it to its page. Mr. Ingham pulled it taut and the apple rose above the surface.

He picked it up in one hand, turning it about, and held it to his nose.

"Remarkable," he breathed. "This was your first time using the Ink? Your Da hadn't given you any instruction before this?"

"No," Faith said, wide-eyed with surprise. "Is it all right?"

"All right? It's astounding! I'm almost wondering what I have to teach you."

"Oh, I know so little. I have so many questions. Where does it come from? What is it made of? Why do the pens never run out? How does it change-"

Mr. Ingham held up his hands laughing. "I said almost. Drawing objects is just the start, but with a start like this... Your Da must be very proud."

Instinctively, Faith started to object but caught herself just in time. Instead she said, "It is hard to tell. He has high standards and is sparing in his praise."

"It is inconceivable that he wouldn't be proud. Now, let's get to this tea before it's cold and I will tell you about the Ink. What do you know about it already?"

"Very, very little. I would urge you to proceed as though I had never heard of it."

"That is hard to believe given your results, but I will humor you and start at the beginning," Mr. Ingham said as Faith poured out. "The Ink was discovered by daVinci-"

"I do know that bit. Sugar?"

"None, thank you. Do you want me to start from the beginning or not?"

"My apologies. Continue."

Mr. Ingham inclined his head and resumed, recounting the tale like a bard before a royal court. "As legend has it, *daVinci* came across a cave while hiking in the mountains as a young man. Standing outside the cave, he was seized by the notion of limitless possibilities concealed by its darkness. He wavered at its entrance, caught between fear and curiosity. Summoning his courage, he entered and found that it was not dark, but was lit from within by a floating pool of liquid light." Faith felt her skin prickle as she recalled the glowing pool from her dream. She handed Mr. Ingham his cup and poured her own.

"Thank you." Mr. Ingham took a sip before continuing. "Cautiously, daVinci examined the substance with a stylus from his drawing tools but could make no study of it in the cave so he emptied an inkwell and collected a sample. We can assume he investigated it as soon as he was back in the light of day, but whether he understood what he had discovered immediately or some time later is lost to history. In any event, it became apparent that the substance had many peculiar properties. One was that it responded to his thoughts. When he drew with it, it manifested everything that was in his mind- not just what he saw, but every other sense as well. What's more, he wasn't the only one who experienced its effects.

"He approached several of his contemporaries to see who was influenced by it, testing to see if they could use it in the same way he could. What he found was that most, but not all, could perceive its effects and some could use it, but curiously, the two did not always go hand in hand. All of the artists who had the Talent also had Vision, or else they wouldn't have been able to see their own creations, but not all of those who had Vision also had the Talent. These were some of the greatest artists of the Renaissance, mind you."

"Not all Old Masters are Masters, then?"

"You see, there are different definitions of skill in art. Success might be a better term. There are artists who can paint a pretty picture, perfect in composition, exacting in detail, and be quite successful with patrons. For these artists, painting is a set of formulae to be applied to the canvas. A few of the famous names fit into this category. For those with the Talent though, art is a way of putting your soul into the canvas. It has more to do with openness of mind and strength of conviction than with technical ability. It is possible, likely really, that there are those out there with immense Talent who are undiscovered because they cannot draw or paint to save their skins."

"And there are people who cannot see its effects at all?" Faith asked, thinking of William and, quite possibly, her mother.

"There are," he said, his accented r's rolling delightfully. "They were called *litterati* because they were so literal minded. Ironically this is now a term for those who appreciate art. More uncharitably, they are known as lit-wits within the Guild."

Faith laughed, sending hot tea up into her nose. When she had recovered, a frown replaced her smile as her thoughts returned to what he had said about undiscovered Talent. Having spent the last several months trying to get a chance to try the Ink herself, it felt unfair that some great Talent might go unrecognized for lack of exposure and opportunity.

"Why all the secrecy? In balance it seems quite harmless to let people use it freely in exchange for the pleasure they and their viewers would derive."

"Ah, an innocent spirit you are who can't conceive of the terrible possibilities of the Ink! Let me ask you, have you ever stood before a painting of some terrible deed and felt the fear and the dread, or the injustice overwhelm you?"

Vanderlyn's Marius and the General's murderous gaze immediately came to mind.

"Yes..." Faith answered slowly. "But if a painting can inspire those emotions in the viewer, is that not instructive? To feel the horror of war or another's suffering so that we might learn from it?" As the words came out, Faith realized how like the Colonel she sounded.

"It is, but only in the hands of the moral and well-intentioned. What if the scene of war inspired joy instead of horror because that was how its author perceived it? The Ink can be used to twist the politics, even the morality, of those with the Vision to perceive it. I don't know if daVinci experienced this first hand, or simply anticipated the problem, but this was one of the primary reasons he founded the Guild of Athena. After Caravaggio, the Guild took this lesson quite to heart. Only those with the proper character were even offered a trial and to everyone else the Ink remained entirely unknown."

Faith considered this as she nibbled a biscuit from the tray, wondering what happened if it were the character of the Guild itself that was the corrupting influence. She decided to leave that blasphemous thought to another session.

"Why Athena?" she asked between bites. "Is it because she was the patroness of craft?"

"It is, but also her manner of birth, bursting fully formed from her da's head."

The starburst above the owl. It made perfect sense now. What did not make sense was the Ink itself.

"What exactly is the Ink? How does it work? Precisely."

"The Ink is essentially liquid imagination," he said.

Faith cocked her head quizzically. He set down his cup and leaned forward with his elbows on his knees.

"Think of imagination as part of the ether that surrounds us, part of the air we breathe. It contains the elements of every thought, every idea, every color and emotion. Ordinarily, like the air, it is invisible. Now, imagine if you could concentrate it to the point that it becomes visible and tangible, like dew on a leaf. That is the Ink."

"If it contains everything, how do I make it draw what I want?"

Charles got up and pulled a cloth wrapped object from a satchel. He unwrapped it to display a simple glass pyramid.

"This is a prism. When you align it just so with a beam of light, it separates the light into colors." As he spoke, Charles sat the glass pyramid on the window sill, turning it until wan rays of colored light fanned out across the floor at her feet. "When you use the Ink, your mind is the prism, separating out the elements that reflect what is in your senses and depositing them on the page. The power of your imagination is akin to the quality of light that enters the prism. If it were bright and sunny out, the rainbow would be equally intense, but in this more diffuse light, the spectrum is muted. The Ink and your imagination together are the source, the pen is just a tool. The pen merely serves as a reservoir for the Ink and a conduit between your thoughts and the page."

"Then how is it that the pen changes?"

"The pen itself is nothing special. Well, theoretically, certain metals and minerals are supposed to have an internal structure that are ideal conduits for the energy of the mind. Pens made out of gold or diamond would have the optimal structure, but their other qualities make them impractical for obvious reasons. Instead, most are made of wood which, as a living thing- or a former living thing- strikes the perfect balance between effectiveness and practicality. Of course, there are some species of wood that are preferred, and some Masters push the boundaries of practicality by seeking out exotic specimens, but on the whole, the pen itself is nothing extraordinary. The Ink on the pen's tip responds to your expectations and beliefs just like it does on the page. If you believe you are drawing with pencil, it will be a pencil. If you imagine you are painting, it will resemble a brush, whatever kind of brush you believe to be fitting."

"Extraordinary! Why does it never need to be refilled?"

"There are many theories on that. Too many for now. I want to make more progress on the painting before we stop for today." Mr. Ingham made a move to stand.

"But wait! I have so many more questions!"

"One more."

"Where does the Ink come from? Does the Guild collect it from daVinci's cave?" Faith asked, already imagining hiking through the mountains to find it for herself even though it had to be on the other side of the ocean.

"That's two questions."

"It's one question, restated for clarification."

Mr. Ingham tilted his head, considering. "I'll allow it. When daVinci went back into the cave, the pool of light was gone. When he returned to the mountains several years later, he was unable to find the cave at all."

"Where did it go?" Faith asked, deflated.

"That's definitely a second question." Mr. Ingham stood and returned his cup to the tray.

"Please."

He turned back to face Faith and shrugged. "Nobody knows, really. Was it a gift from God, offered and then withdrawn? Had a boundary between this reality and the world of imagination thinned for a moment and he was there at just the right time? Was it the power of his own genius that created it?" Charles shrugged. "Whatever the answer, the Guild is still drawing on the original inkwell that he used to collect a sample."

"That's impossible!"

"You'd think," he agreed. "Just another strange property of the Ink. Each Master of the Guild receives a single pen dipped once in the Ink. The level of the Ink in the well has never lowered. So long as the artist never loses his imagination, the pen never dries and never runs out."

"So it is possible for it to dry up?"

"No more questions for today," Charles said, retaking his seat. He seemed amused by her pout of frustration.

"Do I get to try the Ink now?" Faith asked.

"You don't. Now you get to try the tea."

"Tea? We've just had tea." Now he was definitely amused by her confusion. His eyes crinkled at the corners.

Faith watched bewildered as he took her teacup from her hand and emptied it into his. Handing the empty cup back to her he said, "Tea. Describe it."

"You mean the actual tea? It's hot water and leaves, it turns brown after a bit..."

"Not that. Tell me about the experience of tea. What do you feel?"

"Feel? I'm not sure I have very strong feelings about tea one way or another. I mean, it is traditional..."

"That's not what I mean, but your answer illustrates the difference between drawing and using the Ink. Most people go through their daily lives, seeing only what they need to see to avoid tripping over things or telling the difference between a tree and a hatstand. Artists set themselves apart by being keen observers and then replicating what we observe. Even without the Ink, this can convey more than just what an image presents on its surface. For example, is the tea in the pot hot?"

"Well of course not. It's been cooling while we talk."

Charles nodded impatiently. "Yes, you know it has been sitting here. But if you had just walked into the room, how could you tell if the tea were hot, just by looking at it?"

"It would have steam coming out of the spout."

"Exactly," he said. "Since there is no steam now, it tells us that the tea is not very hot. There is some butter there. If it were getting soft and shiny, a viewer might know that the room is warm, but because the room is cool, it has stayed hard-edged and matte. Using the Ink though is not just about what you see, it's about what you perceive. You've had tea a thousand times, but have you ever really experienced it? Go ahead and pour out a cup- sugar and cream please- and describe it to me, not just how things look, but how they feel, sound, smell, and taste."

Starting to understand, Faith reached for the white porcelain teapot. The delicately curving handle, cool to the touch, felt inadequate to the weight of the tea that gently sloshed within. She steadied the bottom with her other hand, feeling the radiant heat concentrated there. The lid clinked as she tilted it to pour. Humid warmth and the smell of earth and spice spilled out with the amber liquid, the stream twisting in on itself with criss-crossing ripples, narrowing until it hit the bottom of the cup and swirled around its bowl. Flecks of leaves rode the current of the rising whirlpool only to spiral to the bottom when she stopped pouring.

Next, Faith plunged a small silver spoon into white dunes of sugar and scooped a mound. Tiny crystals fell away from the sides like sand in an hourglass, piling ever higher until a final grain triggered a sparkling avalanche that smoothed the miniature white landscape. Tilting the spoon into her cup released a diamond rain that hissed as it roiled the rich brown surface. The silver creamer was cold, a haze of condensation dulling its belly while it flashed brightly above the line of milk within. She poured slowly, watching the white column disappear beneath the surface only to rise back up in clouds like thunderheads on a summer afternoon. Stirring, the clouds swirled, white and tan and brown, until they diffused into one uniform shade. The spoon tinkled musically against the side of the cup until she laid it down with a soft clink on the saucer. Without taking a sip, Faith could taste its creamy sweetness in her mouth and feel its soothing warmth slide down her throat and spread through her center.

Faith looked up at Charles.

He nodded approvingly. "Very good. To use the Ink well, you must have that kind of understanding of your subject. If your understanding is mechanical and thoughtless, so your world will be. However," he held up a cautionary hand and his typically playful expression turned serious, "that very imaginative understanding can also be a danger. You described the sugar as both sand and diamonds. If you employ your impressions too literally while you use the Ink, they become part of what you create. In this case, all someone might get is a mouthful of grit and a broken tooth. Malevolent thoughts though, even unwitting ones, can have devastating effects. If, for example, you were thinking while you drew that cup of tea how much you despise me for not giving you a pen today, it might not be safe to drink."

Faith shook her head. "Are you saying it would be *poisonous*? How is that possible?"

"Dark thoughts manifest in dark expression. It can be unpredictable and deadly."

"Deadly? But it's imaginary!"

"Are you sure of that, now?" he asked with the teasing glint returning to his eyes. "Never forget this with the Ink. Whatever the artist envisions, whether good or evil, is what the viewer perceives. How strongly this is transmitted depends on the strength of conviction in the artist and the sensitivity of the viewer, but in the right combination, the Ink can have real physical harm. It is our perception that determines our reality. If the body believes it has been poisoned it will react as though it has been. Tissues might swell, organs shut down. What's more, unlike a real life injury, there is nothing for the doctor to detect, and therefore nothing he can do to treat it. The Ink can be deadly."

Mr. Ingham's ominous words made the hair stand up on Faith's neck. The room seemed darker and colder.

As though dispelling evil spirits that he had just conjured up, Mr. Ingham clapped his hands and sat back in his chair. His voice became incongruously bright. "All right! I think it is time to finish up my work for today. Are you ready to pose again?"

Faith agreed wordlessly and resumed her spot under the light of the window. She shivered, but not just from its draft. She was chilled, and quietly enthralled, by the Ink's power to create and to destroy.

He who Doubts from what he sees
Will neer Believe do what you Please
If the Sun & Moon should Doubt
Theyd immediately Go out
- William Blake, Auguries of Innocence

CHAPTER SIXTEEN

The Lesson

Mr. Ingham held the pen just out of Faith's reach. It was all she could do not to try to snatch it from his hands. She had spent the morning before Mr. Ingham arrived pacing her room in anticipation. And then, she had been forced to compose herself to sit while he painted for an interminably long time, enduring Eliza's chatting for much of it. The Colonel had trained her well to conceal her emotions but that didn't mean it wasn't torture. Now, the time had finally come and the Ink was almost within her grasp.

"Before I give this to you, you must swear to abide by the rules," Mr. Ingham said giving her a stern look that was so out of place on him that she stifled a giggle.

"First, the Ink is the property of the Guild. Using it is a privilege and not a right, no matter how Talented you are. If you break any of the rules or become unfit to use the Ink, including death, any and all instruments of the Ink that you may possess must be returned to the Guild. Do you understand?" Faith nodded that she did.

"Second, unless or until you become a Journeyman, you are only allowed to use this pen under my direct supervision and only to create what I instruct you to create." Faith nodded again.

"Finally, you must take frequent breaks. Using the Ink is very draining, especially for a novice. You must tell me if you feel at all unwell and we will stop to let you rest."

"Yes, Mr. Ingham, I swear," Faith agreed.

"And, you should call me Charles."

"Yes, Charles, I will," Faith said, her tongue curling appreciatively around his name. He handed her the pen.

Of course, calling it a pen was something of a misnomer born of an association with the Ink. It was not a quill or reed, but a wooden stick with a tapered end like the case of an ordinary pencil. Only, it did not seem to be of cedar. It was harder and a quick sniff revealed no resinous aroma. Nor did it have the shiny gloss or deep color of the Colonel's pen. It was dull and tan and not at all what Faith was expecting.

He must have seen the look of disappointment on her face. He chuckled.

"It may not look like much, and it's not as powerful as a Master's pen, but I assure you it will do the job. Don't underestimate it," Charles said as she inspected the tip. It looked like ordinary graphite except for a faint opalescent shimmer as she tilted it in the light.

"There are different strengths? How is that? Is it because of the wood? Or does it have something to do with the Ink itself? What can a Master's pen do that this one cannot?" The questions tumbled from Faith's mouth until he silenced them with a finger on her lips. Her mind went blank at his touch.

"Do you want me to answer questions, or do you want to try it?"

"Try it," Faith whispered when he lifted his finger. "Please."

Eyes twinkling with knowing amusement, Charles put his drawing board before her with several sheets of paper on it. Faith settled the pencil in her hand and looked up at him expectantly. She had already decided what she would draw first, she just needed his permission to begin.

"First, you will draw a pencil line."

Faith blinked. "That's it? Just a line?"

"That's it. An ordinary pencil line. Straight or curved, your choice."

"How magnanimous of you," Faith said dryly. She drew the same little swirling arabesque as when she had first held the Colonel's pen. It came easier this time.

"Show off. Now, a line of ink followed by a line of paint, medium and color of your choice."

As Faith thought about drawing with ink, the tip of her pencil turned into a perfectly trimmed quill with glittering Ink filling its groove. She squeaked in delight and drew the line. For the paint, she chose watercolor.

The tip became a slim rounded brush with soft bristles that narrowed to a neat point. She thought a moment about the color. With a mischievous smirk, she imagined a violent pink hue that she had never seen in the colorist's shop and swept it boldly across the page. She sat back and displayed it to Charles.

"You effectively just stuck your tongue out at me."

Faith's eyes went wide and she clapped a hand over her mouth. "I did, didn't I?" she confessed and started to laugh. He laughed with her but his tone was serious when he spoke.

"Remember, whatever the artist puts in, is what the viewer gets out. In this case, pure sass. Everything must be intentional."

"I will remember," Faith assured him. She took a breath and sobered herself.

"Now, you will draw a continuous line, a spiral. Every time you pass the starting point, you will change the color as I direct. Ready?"

When Charles instructed, Faith began her line, delighted at the warm-cool sensation that ran from her fingers to her wrist as she did. She was less delighted with the precision of her changes as he barked commands. If his instruction came too far ahead of the mark, her anticipation of the switch would cause her to change color too early. When his call came too close to the mark, she could not change fast enough. She got better as she went. By the time she had reached the edge of the page, she was tense and breathless but the changes in color lined up neatly across the outer bands of her spiral.

Charles seemed pleased and the thought made her glow.

"I think you are ready to draw your first object. Unless you'd rather rest?"

"No!" Faith objected too strongly. He raised an eyebrow. She reined in her enthusiasm. "I'm feeling very well and would like to continue, thank you."

"I suspected as much. Draw this," Charles said, taking a small ceramic pot off of the window sill and putting it before her. The remains of a withered plant lay on the dirt like a silvery web. "Take some breaths, close your eyes, and empty your mind first. Then get the sense of it and set your intentions before you start."

Faith gave him a skeptical glance for his choice of object before giving the pretty little pot and its sad resident her full attention. As she had with the apple, she filled her senses with every aspect of it, from the feel of the ceramic to the smell of the soil. Only instead of a dead plant in a shrunken ball of dry dirt, she drew it live and blooming from her memory of the fuchsia that used to dress the parlor window in Bath. The dirt was moist and dark, the leaves bright green and sharply pointed, the tubular flowers a deep purple beneath pink skirts. She could hear her mother's tuneless humming as they had sewed side by side before the window.

When she was done, she pushed the drawing toward Charles. His frown made her stomach knot.

"Have I not done it right?"

Charles crossed his arms and rested his chin in a hand. "Well, you have, and you haven't. Your command of the Ink is extraordinary. Granted I haven't trained anyone before but I've known a fair number of novices, myself included, and I've never seen anything like it. Not just the pot and flowers but the warm feeling of ... companionship? Contentment? The problem is that I asked you to draw what is in front of you, not something from your imagination."

"But, what's the point of bringing the imaginary world to life if it looks just like reality?" The pleasure of his praise mixed with the sting of his finding fault made her indignant.

Charles chuckled at her distress. "I know it makes little sense now, but soon you will understand. In the beginning, you must confine yourself to replicating what is in front of you without embellishment. You need to develop the discipline to control what you put into your creations. It seems counterintuitive to exert so much restraint over something that depends on imagination, but for everyone's safety everything you create must be done with intention and forethought. Once you have demonstrated that you have that control, and understand the dangers, you will be given your artistic license, so to speak, to indulge every flight of fancy. I promise."

Faith's brow knitted. Often since the Colonel had shown her the Ink, she had wondered how someone so rigid could be receptive to it. She would have pegged him for a lit-wit right off. However, if it were such control that was required, it was no wonder he was a Master.

In an effort to console her Charles said, "Don't fret. You are in good company if you find it hard to control your thoughts. As I said the other day, it is an especially common obstacle for women when learning to use the Ink."

Faith sat up straight, anger flashing in her eyes. She wanted to retort that he had also said it made them more powerful, but she held her tongue. The Colonel's lies had been meant to keep her from the Ink but had only made her determined to master it. The mere suggestion from Charles that she might not be suited annealed her resolve. If it were control that was wanted, then control is what she would give them. She would prove them all wrong.

Charles did not see her reaction. He had picked up the pot from her drawing, admiring it from every side.

There was a knock on the door followed by Mrs. Astor's stout form in the doorway. Faith gave Charles a panicked look, as though they had been caught doing something indecent. Charles seemed unconcerned. He continued to hold the pot of fuchsias.

"What pretty flowers!" Mrs. Astor remarked. "I had thought them all dead with the cold. How wonderful to see a spot of color. Faith, I have had a letter from your father and I have one for you as well. In the letter to me, he says that he has been asked to travel onto the capitol and asks if we would keep you here for another several weeks. I have no objection if you do not."

"That is very kind of you, Mrs. Astor. I would be delighted to stay if you are sure it is no trouble."

"Of course not. I will write to the Colonel to let him know you may stay as long as is necessary for his business. How is the picture going Mr. Ingham?"

"Very well, Mrs. Astor. With your blessing, I would like to come again tomorrow to finish the clothing and then I will finish the background from my studio after the Christmas holiday. After that, however, I wonder if I might have Faith come to the Academy to act as my model on another project. During public hours, of course. It would be far easier to work from there and far less dangerous for your beautiful rugs."

"My only concern would be Faith walking in this miserable weather. I will speak with Mr. Astor. Perhaps she can take the carriage with Mr. Astor and William on their way to the office."

Charles thanked Mrs. Astor who, after handing Faith her letter, withdrew from the room. It was not until after she left that Charles put down the fuchsia.

"She thought it was real!"

"You will find that when people are confronted with what they believe to be impossible, they will only see what they expect."

Faith fleetingly wondered what William would have seen had he been the one to enter. The idea of taking the carriage with him every day was hardly thrilling, but it was a small price to pay for the chance to work with Charles uninterrupted. The fact that she had weeks available to her instead of days made it all the more delightful. With a great weight lifted from her, she fairly floated through the rest of the day.

* * *

Faith bit the inside of her cheek near the corner of her lip and scanned her painting critically. Some things about the Ink were much easier than using regular paint. She didn't have to grind or mix anything or clean her brush. There were no smelly fumes or drips. She just thought about the color and consistency she wanted and it appeared. Keeping her imagination in check was another thing altogether.

Her painting was a faithful copy of the real tea service sitting before her. From the pattern of blue roses on the china and the texture of the biscuits to the glint of gilded rims and silver spoons, she could find no mistake of line, shape, or shadow. Of course, just making it look real wasn't enough. It had to feel real too.

It was far harder than Faith had anticipated to keep her imagination on the bit. She'd had to resist the urge to turn the flat roses into dimensional ones like a rambler winding around the teapot. To get the flavor right, she'd had to fill her mouth with the stout breakfast tea while she drew, drowning out a memory of the delicately colored, sweetly scented strawberry tea of childhood that she preferred to the deep brown, bitter grassiness of the one before her.

She was sure she had the taste right. Now it was the temperature that was giving her fits. In her effort to be reserved, her first pot had been cold. She had reworked it two more times- thankful for the ability to make corrections without turning everything into a muddy mess- with lukewarm results. This time she had channeled her frustration into making it piping hot. Before letting Charles see her fail again, she dipped a finger in the steaming cup.

"Ow!" Faith yanked her finger back, shaking a scalding hot drop from it that disappeared in mid air. Her finger burned. She stamped her foot in frustration.

"Well, it seems you got it hot this time," Charles observed flatly, turning away from Eliza's nearly complete portrait. "How does it smell though?" He leaned over the cup in her painting and breathed in. He coughed a little. "A bold brew of determination and showmanship. A little heavy on resentment for my taste but I hear it's a favorite with the Lords of Parliament."

Faith gave a short sarcastic laugh. "Very funny but I'd wager it tastes spot on. Try it!"

"After I planted the seed of poisoned tea in your fertile mind? No thank you. I'll draw my own."

"Would you?" Faith had yet to see Charles use the Ink himself.

"Not today." Charles went back to the painting. Faith knew their time was at an end for today and for several days after. Ordinarily she looked forward to Christmas with its color and lights and songs, but this year it felt like a holly encrusted prison. Without the Ink, everything was drab and lifeless. Melancholy descended on Faith like a thick fog. She covered a yawn and realized her finger still burned.

Examining it, she could see no evidence of a burn. It was neither pale nor red and yet it felt exactly like any other burn she had ever had. "If the Ink is just imagination, why does my finger still hurt?"

"Because your mind thinks it should."

"I understand that in the moment, but shouldn't it have dissipated by now? Particularly since I know in my mind it wasn't real."

"It will persist as long as any similar injury. Just be glad it is a burn and not a cut. Or a snake bite," was his less than sympathetic response.

Faith sat up straighter. "The asp in your painting? Could it have bit me? What would have happened?"

Charles smiled. "I suppose it could have bit you, but it's venom was solely meant for the Egyptian queen. You might have had a sore finger, but you would not have been poisoned."

"You have that much control that you can make it poison only one person?"

"I do. At least, I hope so. Didn't seem like we should test it out though. Just in case."

"Just in case," Faith repeated as a shiver ran through her. "But what about someone else who might see it in the Gallery?"

"That's why you aren't supposed to touch paintings."

Faith flushed. Charles finished up and rang the bell for a servant to show him out. As he gathered his things, he reached into his case and pulled out a wrapped package. "A gift for you, for Christmas."

"A gift?" Faith took it from him with a thrill of excitement. It's weight and contours told her it was a book, not a pen as she might have outrageously hoped, but she was touched that he had thought to give her anything. "Thank you."

A maid arrived while Charles was still gathering his things. She was telling him that she would send the footman to see him out when she noticed the tea things on their tray.

"If you're finished, I'll take this now," she said brightly as she crossed the room. Faith squeaked in protest as the maid's hands closed around the tray of her drawing, the real tea blocked from her view by Charles. Without the slightest perturbation, Charles turned and picked up the real tray.

"Here, let me help you with that," he said placing the real tea tray on top of Faith's drawing of it. The real and the imaginary trays merged into one as the drawing was obscured. The maid's face registered a moment of blank confusion before she shook her head as though to rid it of an intrusive thought.

"Are you all right?" Charles asked.

"Of course!" the maid protested with forced confidence as she lifted the real tray. Charles quickly slid Faith's drawing from beneath it and held it behind his back. "Thought I saw double for a moment is all. Just a trick of the light, I'm sure." She tilted her head toward the window as though that explained everything. As she backed out the door, Faith heard her mutter, "I haven't even touched the sherry today..."

When the door clicked shut behind her, Faith and Charles erupted into laughter.

"Poor woman! What must she have thought?!" Faith said through gasping breaths.

"I told you," Charles said, wiping the corners of his eye, "people see what they want to believe."

Everything possible to be believed is an image of truth.
- William Blake, The Marriage of Heaven and Hell

CHAPTER SEVENTEEN
The Portal

Faith sat slightly forward on the carriage seat to spare her back from the rattle of wheels over cobbles. Her hands, ensconced in the fur trimmed kid gloves that the Astors had given her for Christmas, were folded in her lap. Outwardly, Faith was calm. Only if Mr. Astor or William could feel the tightness with which one hand clenched the other would they know the level of her impatience. The short ride to the Academy, and her first sitting with Charles since before Christmas, felt interminable. Faith knew there was far more to the Ink than she had already learned. Otherwise she could not see how it would take over a year for most novices to become Journeymen. She was frantic to learn as much as she could before the Colonel's return.

Her step-father's letter had relieved some of the pressure. Although he had been unsuccessful securing a commission from Baltimore, his new friend Judge Nicholson had offered to go with the Colonel to Washington and introduce him to the Judge's connections there. Plans for the rebuilding of the Capitol after its sack by the British were underway. The Colonel intended to pitch his historical paintings of the Revolution to adorn a new rotunda. He expected to make the proposal a week or two after the new year and to be home by end of January. That gave Faith several more weeks than she had dared to hope to train with Charles. On the other hand, the Colonel also expected to be confirmed as Academy president at their meeting on the seventeenth of January. It would not be long after that when he would become the American Guild Master and Faith's quest would be over. She could ill afford the delays brought on by the holidays.

To be fair, spending Christmas with the Astors had been diverting. It had been sumptuous in the ways wealth afforded with elaborate meals and busy social engagements. Their church service, like their German customs, had been refreshingly different yet not so foreign from Faith's own traditions to be unsatisfying. Mr. Astor was particularly fond of music and every gathering had featured a gifted performance of some kind. Faith had found some of them as transporting as some of her favorite poetry, filling her imagination with sensation and images.

The Astors had made an effort to make her feel part of the family, but with the congregation of Eliza's older sisters and their children, including Dorothea Astor's infant son, Faith had found it all overwhelming. At times she had sympathized far too much with the overstimulated baby's crying, although not so much as to find it tolerable in the slightest, and had often retreated to her room. There she amused herself with the poems and new sketchbook that Charles had given to her, which she had opened the moment he left.

The poems she had already memorized. The sketchbook, already a quarter filled, poked at the sides of her reticule, which sat on the carriage bench between her and William. Mr. Astor sat in the middle of the bench opposite them.

Mr. Astor was an outdoorsman in gentleman's clothing. Left to his own devices, he would rather be rough shaven than clean, practically dressed rather than finely so, out rather than cooped up within. He put Faith in mind of a bear in a menagerie, allowing himself to be gently tamed to society's expectations by his wife and daughter, but restless and wild at heart. Even his fondness of music invoked the savage beast seeking solace. Even now, he seemed constrained by the frame of the carriage, an animal in a cage, a tempest in a teapot. In him, Faith saw a kindred spirit.

Over the holidays, Faith had also observed Mrs. Astor closely. After all, if she were to marry William, there was no better model of his expectations in a wife than his own mother. She had been surprised to find that in spite of the trappings of wealth evident throughout the house, from the art to the servants, the woman was frugal and business minded. Her expenditures were carefully considered against their social or pecuniary return. She was kind and gracious but with an economy of emotion for everyone but John Jr, the devoted care of whom probably left her with little else to spare.

Although she was a different animal entirely, more a brightly plumed, flittering bird than bear, Eliza had taken after her father. She was lively, vocal, and, although her attentions shifted with the breeze, passionate. William, in turn, had absorbed all of his mother's most sober qualities. He was solemn, still, and silent. He measured art only in terms of its investment value, ideas in terms of logic, and words in terms of their practicality. Faith could feel his dark eyes on her. His stare began to feel intrusive.

Faith met his gaze and gave him a tight smile, wishing the carriage would sprout wings.

"You look very efficient with your hair pulled back like that," he said in his monotone.

Efficient? "Thank you," Faith said after a moment's hesitation, realizing he meant it as a compliment. She had asked Jane to pin it up tightly so that for once Charles might see her as smooth and elegant. She had aimed for sophistication and landed on efficient? "How kind of you to notice," Faith said as she felt the carriage slow to a stop. Next time she would be sure to rival Eliza's curly upsweep for frivolousness.

William stepped out and handed her down, offering to walk her to the front door. Faith declined, nearly snatching her hand from his in her eagerness to escape.

"It is kind enough that you have detoured to bring me here. I could not let you be any later to the office than necessary on my account," Faith said.

William ducked his chin and stepped back inside the carriage. Faith rushed up the steps, slowing only when she slid alarmingly on an icy tread. Safely at the top, she hurried through the Academy doors.

Compared to the ball last fall, it was a dreary place. The whitewashed interior was gray in the shadowy winter light. Without the press of people, it had the hushed air of a church. The echo of Faith's footsteps on the stone floor made her flinch self consciously. Happily, though, they attracted Mr. Dunlap's attention and he showed her to Charles' studio room. He was ready and waiting with drawing board and pencils. For her, there was a seat angled before the room's single window. Off to the side there was a long work table and a pair of straight backed wooden chairs.

Mr. Dunlap lingered while Charles got her situated. Faith pretended that she did not mind his presence in the slightest as she silently willed him to leave. Against the wall near Faith's seat was a small pile of props and a coatrack draped with lengths of fabric. Charles traded her coat for a swath of spring green silk and a flower basket, arranging them first one way and then another. Unsatisfied, he tried a different drape, this time red, and then a deep black one, along with a succession of props. Tiring of this process, Mr. Dunlap muttered something about his duties and excused himself.

As soon as Mr. Dunlap had left, Charles' demeanor shifted from indecisive to assured. He went to the door that Mr. Dunlap had left wide open and closed it until it was slightly ajar. He hung a bell from a hook on the back of the door.

"What's the bell for?"

"Think of it as a loud knock on the door, in case we are about to be disturbed. I can't close the door without raising some eyebrows, but that will give us enough warning to change the subject. Now, let's get you posed for real."

"You're going to make me sit first? Even here?"

"Of course! I think I put on a good enough show for Mr. Dunlap that he won't expect me to have accomplished much before he comes back to check on us, but I will have to have something on the page. Here, put this on."

He handed Faith a dull tan smock. She rolled her eyes and pulled the robe up on her shoulders, crossed it in front of her and tied the sash at the waist. It was a shapeless, bulky thing that bunched in folds where it was cinched.

"This is ghastly!" Faith objected as she looked down at herself. "I thought you had a goddess of spring in mind, not some poor street urchin."

"Goddesses are overdone. What says spring more than a flower girl? Here." This time he handed her a saddle shaped flower basket. "Put your arm through the handle. Like this. Hmm... a little to the right, uh, I meant your left. Perfect."

Faith felt ridiculous, and very much in disagreement about the status of goddesses. She tried to keep her face smooth though as he stood back and looked at her. He shook his head, dissatisfied with something. Suddenly he snapped his fingers.

"Even a flower girl wouldn't go out without her head covered."

Holding up a length of black velvet, he laid it gently over her hair.

"A widow's bonnet?" she exclaimed. "Isn't that a little morose for spring?"

"Contrast," he replied as he arranged the folds of cloth. With his thumb, he gently lowered her chin. His touch was soft and she smiled in spite of her exasperation. He stepped away to take in his composition.

"Stay just like that. With that baleful look and half smile, you'll rival Mona Lisa for mystery!" Charles said as he picked up his drawing board and sat down. As he began his sketch, Faith tried to be the epitome of patience and restraint.

When Charles had finished a sketch and gave her permission to break her pose, Faith burst from the smock like Athena from Zeus. She grabbed the sketchbook from her reticule and thrust it into Charles' hands. The instructions in the note he had slipped between its pages had asked her to prepare a drawing of her favorite landscape with the requirement that it be free of any buildings, animals, or people. Faith had lived in London, with its manicured parks, and New York with its wild woods on the rolling hills that surrounded the city, but it was the countryside of Bath that had her heart. There were Roman ruins and a hill fort. High on one hill there had been a henge, its mysterious stones lit by beams of sunlight that broke through the scumbled sky as though touched by ancient forces. Above all though, Faith loved Prior Park.

The Colonel had been friendly with its owner, John Thomas, and she had been invited to walk its gardens any time she chose. In truth, Faith had longed to climb its spreading trees and roll down its steep hills like a carefree child, but walking its paths under a sky that threatened rain or watching the waterfowl from the Palladian bridge was the closest she had ever felt to completely free. That was the landscape she had drawn. She had picked a viewpoint she remembered well for its windswept panorama with a glimpse of Bath beyond the trees. In the gentle valley below the hill, the arched and colonnaded bridge spanned the spillway between the upper and middle lakes.

She held her breath while Charles looked over her drawing. His brow creased.

"What's wrong?" Faith asked, her heart in her throat.

"This looks like the watercolors that were in the exhibit."

Faith felt the blood drain from her face. "Yes, those were mine. There was a ... mix-up with the labels. Is that a problem?"

"That's not a problem. But I told you no buildings."

Faith let her breath out in a whoosh. "That's a bridge not a building."

He pursed his lips and shook his head. "I suppose it looks sturdy enough. Here is your pen. I want you to replicate this scene in Ink being very careful not to include any animals or people. It would also be nice if it looked less like it were about to rain."

"Have you been to Bath?"

Charles went back to his drawing while Faith set to work. She channeled every memory, every sense of place, into her drawing of the little valley and its hidden treasures. The feel of the grass and the smell of the trees. The breeze that tugged her hair and cooled her cheeks, the sun that warmed her back. It was all there when she placed the drawing in Charles' hands.

He stood looking it over for quite some time. In fact, he didn't move for so long that Faith thought his mind had wandered off. She cleared her throat with no effect, and then again more loudly. Nothing. Nervously awaiting his comments, she wondered if she shouldn't give him a nudge. She was about to call his name when he suddenly drew a deep breath and turned to her.

"This will do very nicely. Let me get my pen and we can be on our way," Charles said.

Faith's curiosity about Charles' pen prevented his words from sinking in for several heartbeats. "Wait, what? Where are we going?"

"To Bath, of course. Or, at least your version of it." Charles pulled a writing box like the Colonel's from a shelf beneath the work table. He opened it and pulled out his pen. It was different from the Colonel's, whose pen was smooth and glossy black like lacquered ebony. Charles' pen gleamed like polished rosewood with Celtic knot work carved along its length. It was beautiful, but Faith pulled her gaze from the pen and looked at Charles in confusion.

"I don't understand."

He smiled broadly and his eyes twinkled mischievously. "The Ink, as I'm sure you have guessed, can do more than make objects appear on this side of reality. It can also allow us to appear on the other side."

"Have you hit your head?"

"Not recently. That I remember."

"Maybe I'm not understanding what you mean by this and that side of reality. It sounds like you are suggesting that we are going to pop into this drawing and have a walk around."

"Precisely."

"Are you sober?"

"For an Irishman, I am."

"This drawing is barely longer than my forearm and I, if you haven't noticed, am quite a bit bigger and you bigger still! It would be easier to pass a camel through the eye of a needle!"

Charles just laughed and tapped his temple with a finger. "We will not be going in physically. Our minds will travel. In order for it to work though, you must believe it is possible. Do you believe?"

"I'm not entirely certain what I am endorsing, but I suppose..."

"The only limitation is what you believe to be impossible. Do you believe?" Charles asked, his tone serious.

Sobered, Faith answered "Yes," and realized that she did.

Charles had Faith sit at the drawing table with the landscape in front of her. He placed her pen in her hand.

"Hold onto this, no matter what."

Faith nodded, suddenly nervous. He took the seat next to her, his own pen in his hand.

"It's very simple. Just focus on your drawing and let everything else slip away." He was close enough that she could feel his breath on her ear. It was hard to focus on anything but his presence. "You were there when you drew it. Go there again."

Faith nodded. She looked at her drawing and immersed herself in it. It shifted and deepened. A tendril of hair blew into her eyes. She closed them, feeling dizzy. She pulled the hair away with a finger and opened her eyes.

Faith was no longer in the Academy studio. She sat on a verdant hill above a placid lake beneath a gently shifting sky. The breeze was strong and cool, the sun, when it broke from the scudding clouds, was warm on her skin. She put her hands down beside her and ran them through the grass with growing excitement. She also became aware of the cold wet earth beneath her and scrambled to her feet.

She twisted around trying to see how bad the wet spots on her backside looked. As she tried vainly to wipe them away, she was thankful Charles was not here to see that she had sat in a puddle. A flash of motion caught the corner of her eye and Charles appeared out of thin air before her.

"Oh!" she gasped. "How did you... I mean, I didn't think you could get here too."

He laughed, always amused when she got flustered. "Of course I can, and it's a good lesson too. The Ink doesn't just allow you to enter your own world. It allows anyone with enough Vision to enter the spaces you have Inked. The trick was landing in the same place. I went to the bridge first before I realized you were up here on the hill. Is there something wrong with your dress?" he asked.

She realized she was still fidgeting with her skirt. "Next time, I think I'll bring a blanket. It seems I've sat in a bit of a damp spot," she admitted.

"Let's see now," Charles instructed, motioning for her to spin around. "I don't see a thing wrong."

Faith ran her hands down the back of her skirt and was shocked to find it completely dry.

"Changes don't last long here. Unless of course you intend them too." Faith's face must have shown her puzzlement because he went on to explain. "Everything about your appearance is how your mind expects, or intends, it to be. Typically, your hair, your clothes, will be just as you ordinarily would wear them. So unless you very intentionally or firmly believed that your backside should be wet and stay wet, it would quickly return to its usual state. Remember, your body, your clothing, they aren't really here. They are even more imaginary than the rest of this place."

"And where are we exactly?" Faith asked.

"Welcome to Phantasia."

To create a little flower is the labour of ages.
  -William Blake, The Marriage of Heaven and Hell

CHAPTER EIGHTEEN
The Butterfly

"Phantasia?"

"Well, your little slice of it at least." Charles answered as though that explained everything. Faith raised an eyebrow. "*Phantasia* is a Greek concept that described the ability of an artist to create an experience in the mind of another. After his discovery, daVinci realized what the ancient philosophers were describing was the effect of the Ink, so he named this place Phantasia."

Did that mean they had the Ink in Ancient Greece, that there was more than one source? As tantalizing as that thought was, Faith let it fall away in favor of more pressing concerns. "But where are we exactly? Are you saying we are inside my picture?"

"We aren't inside the picture itself, we are inside the space you created by making the picture." Charles made a sweeping gesture that encompassed the entire landscape around them. "Everything you create with the Ink is made real here."

"Everything? Does that include the apple and the tea set and the fuchsia? And what about those lines and spirals you had me do?"

"Everything. Now do you understand why it is so important to control your thoughts as you create? Whatever you put down in Ink, you will encounter here."

Faith gave an uneasy glance at the lake, thankful that she had not had the Ink when making Leviathan. She looked around for her other creations but did not see them.

"Where are they, then?"

"They aren't visible here because they weren't part of your vision when you created this particular space. They are somewhere out there. Exactly where you encounter them depends on you."

"There is more than just this landscape?" Faith asked, her mind feeling stretched to its limits to take it all in.

"Phantasia is far more than what you see. In its biggest sense, it is all the world of imagination that has ever been imagined by anyone ever. Each person, however, occupies a portion of it. Like islands in a sea or clouds in the sky. It's where their minds go when they dream, or get lost in music or a story. Everything you've ever imagined is here somewhere."

Faith looked at the horizon of the hills as though she might catch a glimpse of all her hopes and dreams shimmering above it like celestial lights. She was both disappointed and a little relieved to see nothing but cloud and sky. There were things that she had imagined that she would be embarrassed for Charles to see, particularly some vivid dreams she had had since beginning her training. She felt herself flush at the memory and then tried to stuff it away like a pillow into its case, suddenly alarmed that her thoughts might manifest before them.

"So, all of the enchanted forests and fairies and unicorns of my childhood are beyond these hills? If we walked to the ridge, we would see them? " Faith asked, looking for reassurance that her more private imaginings would stay hidden.

"Only if they had been done with the Ink." Faith felt her shoulders relax. "Without the Ink, Phantasia is like a mist. Your imagination works upon that mist, much as it works upon the Ink, to manifest your thoughts but they are fleeting and changeable. Idle thoughts are here and gone in an instant. Cherished dreams and memories that you return to again and again have more substance. Only things done in the Ink become fixed and solid."

"You mean this can't be changed?" Faith asked with dismay. The landscape was just as she remembered, but without the deer and rabbits, birds and insects, it was not complete. And, if she were ever allowed to embellish, she had always thought the Park would benefit from more flowers.

"Of course it can be changed! The Ink can work upon itself just as you reworked that tea. Enduring would have been a better word than fixed."

"So when we go back to the studio," Faith hesitated at the strangeness of having to return to reality, "I could change my painting to add some flowers, and maybe some deer?"

"In time you can add anything you want. This is your world. Whatever you imagine will become your reality. For now, no animals of any kind. Flowers though, I don't see any reason to wait until we go back."

Faith had been looking down at the lake, picturing a field of violets along one tree shaded bank. His words made her turn and face him, wind whipping her hair across her face. She tucked the wayward strands behind her ear.

"I can draw from *inside* the picture?"

"Inside Phantasia, you can."

"But I haven't got a pen-" No sooner had the words left her lips, Faith felt the pen in her hand. She held it up in wonder as Charles smiled broadly at her.

"It only works if you are holding it in reality. That's why I told you to keep a tight grip on it."

"But I don't have the picture here, how can I change it?" Faith asked, half expecting the drawing itself to materialize just as the pen had.

"You simply draw on the world."

Faith gave him a disbelieving look. Nothing about drawing on the world sounded simple.

She listened carefully as Charles gave her instructions. Faith chose a spot on the hill and lifted her pen, positioning the tip in midair to line up with that spot. She attempted to draw a violet. Without the anchor of paper or canvas, she flailed awkwardly not knowing where to start and stop her lines. When she withdrew her hand, green and purple confetti fell to the ground. Charles urged her to try again.

"Close one eye this time. That will help you line it up."

Her second and third attempts didn't go much better. Both, one, or no eyes didn't seem to make much difference. She could feel her frustration rising.

"Faith, you are drawing as though you are still in reality. Try to remember that you are in Phantasia. Your intentions are what matter."

"What does that mean?" she asked with more salt than she intended.

"It means," he said patiently, "that your hands aren't really here. They are imaginary. If you imagine them being able to draw here, they will. They will do whatever you intend them to do."

Faith held up her hands to try again and then, as a disconcerting thought occurred to her, she let them fall.

"If my hands aren't here, if I'm not here, you're saying my body is still in the studio? What does that look like?" Faith felt a flare of nervous agitation at the thought of Mr. Dunlap checking on them, not at all sure what he would encounter.

"Relax," Charles advised in a soothing voice. "I'm certain you've been to Phantasia many times before, even in the company of others, without harm. It's exactly the same as being engrossed in a book, oblivious to events and conversation around you until someone or something intrudes and brings you rudely back to reality. If someone came into the studio without alerting us- unlikely with that bell on the door- he would see two people lost in thought as they look at a picture. What is strange to you now is that you are very aware of the separation. Trust me, that awareness is not shared by any observer."

"But if I change the picture, what do they see then?"

Charles pulled her hands together between his own. "These hands are not your real hands, but they are linked to them through your mind," he said, releasing one hand to touch her forehead gently, "which has the infinite capacity to be in both reality and Phantasia simultaneously. Any action you take to change the world here will be echoed by your actions there. To put it simply, it will look like you are drawing."

Faith was too distracted by the contrast between his words and the apparent *realness* of his touch to answer.

When she didn't respond, Charles said dryly, "That is only if you actually attempt to draw something."

Faith gave him a look and he dropped her hands.

"Trust your mind to guide your hands," he prodded. "Go on, now."

Faith closed her eyes as she tried to embrace the peculiarity of his suggestion. She tried to imagine herself drawing the perfect violet. When she thought she had convinced herself, she tried again. At last, she succeeded in drawing an actual flower and stem, getting the feel of tracing her own motions in the air. The dainty bloom hovered in midair for a moment and fell to the ground.

She stomped her foot. "Blast it! Why is this so difficult!"

"Careful," Charles admonished, picking up the flower and twirling its stem between his fingers. "Control your temper or those violets won't be as shy as they should be. You've got the flower down. Now you just need to center your intention on putting it in the hillside, not in the air in front of you. Plant it."

"Will you show me how you do it?" she asked, too agitated yet to try again.

"It's generally considered bad form to draw in someone else's world. Anything I draw here will exist in both of our worlds. I only brought my pen for emergencies."

While Faith's mind tripped over the concept of an emergency that would require his intervention, she liked the idea of their worlds being joined, whatever it meant. "I don't mind."

"All right then, if you insist." Charles brought his hand to his chin, thinking for a moment about what to draw. Having decided, he held his pen aloft. With a few short, curving strokes and a deft flourish, a small but brilliantly colored butterfly hung momentarily in the air before it fluttered its wings and bounced about in the breeze.

"Hold out your hand," Charles instructed. To Faith's delight, the butterfly flitted toward her and alighted on her open palm. For the briefest moment, Faith smelled wildflowers and heard the call of birds. Before she could wonder at the sensation, it was gone, leaving her with nothing but the tickle of butterfly feet on her skin. Its wings slowly opened and shut like a gentle heartbeat, revealing an intricate pattern of bright colors set off by swirling black bands.

"It's beautiful!" Faith exclaimed with a delighted laugh.

"Thank you! It is a rare species of butterfly that I just made up and its favorite nectar is from violets. Now, let's see some violets."

Faith took several breaths, matching them to the beat of the butterfly's wings. When she felt more focused, she released the butterfly with a wave of her hand and tried again. This time she had to spare less thought on the act of drawing the flower and was able to concentrate on it being firmly planted into the hillside. As she drew the upper portions, she thought of the hidden roots reaching deep into loamy soil. She was certain this time that it had worked. Faith felt a thrill as the butterfly flitted over to the flower and settled lightly on its curving stem.

"Well done!" Charles congratulated her.

Her triumph was quickly dampened when she realized how much work it had taken just to produce one simple plant. She was exhausted from the exertion. How was she going to fill a whole meadow with them?

"You don't have to do them one at a time," Charles told her. "What you need is some perspective. Just like a painting, if you draw them from a distance you can create a whole swath with just a few strokes."

"But won't that look like a sloppy mess up close?"

"Yes, if you intention is to create colorful blobs. Not if your *intention* is to create a field of individual violets. As you get better at focusing your thoughts, you will be able to do in one pass what it takes you fifty strokes to do now. Eventually, you'll be able to do multiple colors and textures all at the same time. You just have to be clear about what you intend to produce."

"If that's true, then you wouldn't even have to know how to draw or paint! The Old Masters could have just thought things onto the canvas!"

"Exactly," Charles agreed.

"But- but-" she sputtered, "why spend all this time making sure I know how to draw?! Isn't that kind of a waste of time?"

"Not at all! You can't achieve that kind of mastery without a deep understanding of what you are trying to create. That understanding can only come from the kind of careful observation and consideration that drawing requires. You must master the minutiae before you can ignore them."

Faith rubbed her forehead. It was all so strange, as though up were down and right were left. Her mind was sluggish and her body felt heavy. She became aware of Charles watching her, eyes narrowed.

"I think that's enough for today. Back to reality Miss Trumbull."

"No, I'm fine. I can..." Faith trailed off as the world blurred and spun. She came back into her body with a sharp breath. She was once again seated at the drawing table, pen in hand with her picture spread before her. It was just as she had drawn it except for a single violet on the hillside and a colorful butterfly dancing gently on the breeze.

If others had not been foolish we should have been so
-William Blake, The Marriage of Heaven and Hell

CHAPTER NINETEEN
The White Plume

The air was so shockingly cold when Faith stepped out of the carriage, she was glad for once of William's hand on hers. It was a tiny ember of warmth in a frozen world. Still, she released it quickly, eager to get inside to her lesson and the relative coziness of Charles' studio. Small dry snowflakes that did not seek the ground floated about her as she took the hatbox from William. His eyes flicked from the box to her hair, an artfully messy pile of loose curls today, with a furrow between his brows before he bid her well and stepped back into the carriage. She felt a flash of irritation at his disapproval, followed by a defiant smirk as she bounded up the Academy steps.

As Faith made her way to Charles' room carrying the hatbox before her, she realized her irritation had not dissipated. Now, though, it was directed at Charles. Her lessons had been daily, but entirely too short. Charles had kept up his show of creative indecision, sketching every possible permutation of drape, prop, and pose. Having exhausted the options in his studio, he had borrowed from others who had rooms at the Academy and had asked Faith to bring Eliza's hat. He claimed it was all intended to ensure the gossipy Mr. Dunlap's disinterest in supervising them, as well as to buy them time for more lessons. On the one hand, the slower Charles' progress on the picture she was modeling for, the longer they could work together. On the other hand, the number of days at Faith's disposal were limited. How much quicker could she be learning if they did not waste so much precious time on her sitting?

Charles had also said short lessons were necessary for her safety, lest she become too tired or weakened. Faith snorted at that and then, remembering where she was, looked around to see if anyone had heard. The building was unusually quiet. Even Mr. Dunlap was nowhere to be seen.

Faith's stamina with the Ink was growing rapidly. Her picture of Prior Park and the world it circumscribed had become less and less as she remembered it and more and more as she wished it to be. Its green hills abounded with flowers in perpetual bloom. A weeping willow's trailing branches now traced lazy circles on the water at the edge of the lower lake. The lake's surface was still devoid of birds and dragon flies, the woods around its rim similarly bereft of life, but Charles promised that with the progress she was making, she would be ready for animals soon. Not soon enough by Faith's estimation.

For now he had her working on buildings. The open ridges around the lakes were populated with a range of structures from a small shed to a rather grand country house. She had made a few mistakes on the interiors, resulting in peculiar sensations of growing bigger and smaller as she moved through the rooms. The black and white tiled floor in one had proven truly hazardous until she had sorted her vanishing point. While the correction had taken little time, the invisible bruises were a lingering reminder not to underestimate the power of the Ink. Although her progress was too slow for Faith's liking, she had mastered interiors and exteriors with a speed that had surprised and pleased Charles. That, in turn, had made her glow with pride.

Each visit to Phantasia was a magical revelation of possibility. Each new discovery inspired ever grander and fantastical ideas. Faith simultaneously chafed under the yoke of restraint, forced to plod along the path and pace that Charles prescribed, and longed for each metered revelation and the cascade of thrilling possibilities it inevitably created. Trying to soothe her irritation, Faith focused on the latter, wondering what Charles might teach her today. She had already started to ask as she pushed her way into the studio when the smell of smoke made her stop.

"What happened in here?" she asked instead, propping the hat box on one hip as she fanned her nose with the other.

"Blocked flues," Charles said apologetically as he turned to greet her. It was only when she saw that he was still wearing his coat that Faith realized how cold it was in the room. "There won't be any heat until the sweeps can clear it up, I'm afraid. Most of the Academy has left for the day, certainly everyone on this side of the building."

"Dunlap?"

They had been interrupted by Mr. Dunlap only once, the sharp clang of the bell sounding a tocsin through her imaginary world. It had brought her back to reality with breathtaking suddenness. Fortunately, the sound had surprised Mr. Dunlap almost as much, such that he did not question Faith's discomfiture when he turned his attention to her and Charles. The bell had worked once, but Faith worried that the busybody might think to be more stealthy next time he thought to check on them.

"He left. He's convinced there's a big snow coming and didn't want to be here when it started. He has a point. I would have canceled for today, but it was too late to get a message to you to tell you not to come."

"I would have ignored it. It's a perfect, and rare, opportunity to work without fear of interruption."

"Or chaperone," Charles said. Although his manner said he meant it as a problem, there was an opportunity in his words that made Faith's cheeks color and her heart flutter. As though he realized the implication himself, he added, "People might talk."

"Nothing to be done about that now. I'm here until the Astors come to get me. Might as well make use of the time," Faith said with forced airiness, trying to hide the strange excitement that stirred within her. "Can you be trusted?"

"Can you?"

Their eyes met. The air drew taut between them. Charles took a step toward Faith and her breath caught in her chest. He closed the distance between them, Faith's heart hammering harder the closer he came, until the hatbox was all that separated them. The usual teasing light in his eyes had turned to a smoldering ember and Faith could not look away. It ignited something within her and she burned in response. It was tantalizing and frightening all at once. She did not break his gaze but she did break the silence.

"Shall we begin?" Her voice was timid and thick with an emotion she could not place.

"Begin?" he asked, as though in a trance.

"My lesson?"

"Lesson. Oh, that!" Charles said, the spell lifting. He glanced down at the hatbox Faith still held before her. "Though, you did go to the trouble to bring the hat. Might as well make use of it, eh?" he said, throwing her earlier words back at her.

Charles took the hatbox in one arm and her hand in the other to lead her to a stool by the window. Faith began undoing the buttons of her coat as Charles took the hat from its box. He stood watching her with a strange look on his face that made her pause on the last button.

"Something wrong?"

"Are you sure you want to take off your coat? It's so cold in here."

Whatever fire Charles had started still burned in Faith. She felt feverish beneath the coat, the heat escaping around the collar and rising about her neck and face. Faith undid the last button and slid out of the hot wool, grateful for the chill air of the room.

"A winter coat with that hat? If we are going to do this, we are going to do it right." Faith sat on the stool and traded her coat for the hat, lifting it onto her head. She adjusted it this way and that but it would not settle over the mound of her hair. She handed the hat back to Charles and began probing her hair with her fingers.

"What are you doing?" Charles asked.

"I'll need to unpin my hair, or the hat won't sit right." Faith's voice was innocence but her thoughts were not so pure. With deft fingers, she found and pulled the pins that held her red-blond ringlets in place. The curls slid as each pin came free until, with one last pin removed, they fell in a seductive cascade down Faith's back.

Their eyes locked again, the spell recast, as Faith reached for the hat. Charles ignored her hand and settled it on her head like a crown upon a queen. His eyes flicked away as he adjusted the tilt of the brim and smoothed the tousled feathers. Then Charles reached for her hair, arranging the tumble of curls along her bare neck and shoulders. His touch, as light as the feathers themselves, sent shivers through Faith's body. She closed her eyes and trembled.

"You're cold," Charles said. Her eyes still closed, she felt him walk away and return with the rustle of fabric. He draped a length of deep blue velvet about her, the silk lining sharply cold on Faith's hot skin. Feeling the heavy fabric slide off a shoulder, Faith held it loosely in place with one hand.

"Stay just like that," she heard Charles say huskily. It was not until she heard the creak of his chair and the sound of charcoal on paper that she dared to open her eyes. The air still thrummed with tension that surged each time he looked up from his work and their eyes met. Practicing a restraint Faith could never have imagined the Ink would demand of her, she turned her focus upward, eyes on the brim of the hat and the quivering feathers that curled around its edge.

Can you lift up your voice to the clouds
So that a flood of waters may cover you?
Can you send forth lightnings, so that they may go
And say to you, 'Here we are'?

- Job 38:34

CHAPTER TWENTY

The Summerhouse

Faith stared bleakly out of the window as she held her pose. What she had once thought beautiful and serene now seemed wretched and infuriating. Big fat snowflakes fell in a heavy curtain outside the window, adding to the insurmountable drifts that had kept Faith from her lessons for more than two days.

Ordinarily she would have enjoyed the peaceful coziness of a snow day, or two, by the fire, but in the present instance she was too aware of time slipping by, and the inevitability of spending nearly all of her time cooped up with Eliza and William. Faith would have preferred to pass the entire storm in her room where she could draw and read without interruption or judgment. Such seclusion, however, would have been viewed as inexcusably rude, or would have roused suspicions of an illness that might have extended her confinement beyond the clearing of the weather and the roads. After years of hiding her drawings from the Colonel's disapproving gaze, she found herself unequal to the prospect of bringing her sketchbook into the relatively public light of the drawing room and exposing herself to the Astors' judgments. And so, Faith had found herself subject to the cruel irony of being asked to sit while Eliza herself attempted to sketch Faith's portrait.

Between cursing the weather and marveling at the improbability of Eliza running out of things to say even as she drew, Faith tried to escape, unaided by the Ink or Eliza's steady stream of words, into a sunny corner of her imagination. The lines of one of the Coleridge poems that Charles had given her for Christmas ran through her mind like a melody:

> *"In Xanadu did Kubla Khan*
> *A stately pleasure-dome decree:*
> *Where Alph, the sacred river, ran*
> *Through caverns measureless to man*
>   *Down to a sunless sea.*
> *So twice five miles of fertile ground*
> *With walls and towers were girdled round;*
> *And there were gardens bright with sinuous rills,*
> *Where blossomed many an incense-bearing tree;*
> *And here were forests ancient as the hills,*
> *Enfolding sunny spots of greenery."*

In her mind's eye, Faith traced the looping river as it twisted through rolling hills of wood and glade, the boundaries of its course defined by gleaming fortress walls and tapering towers. Within this border, she imagined the gardens along the river's burbling tributaries. Some were well-ordered, fragrant trees and flowering shrubs arranged in fountain-centered starbursts and labyrinthine spirals. Others were wild and tumultuous, plants spreading, leaning, climbing one atop the other in bright profusion. At its heart, Faith envisioned a palace with eight domed towers round a vast central one crowned with prismatic crystal.

> *The shadow of the dome of pleasure*
>   *Floated midway on the waves;*
>   *Where was heard the mingled measure*
>   *From the fountain and the caves.*
> *It was a miracle of rare device,*
> *A sunny pleasure-dome with caves of ice!*

The river carved an ever deeper valley on its run until it spilled from the edge of the land as from an island in the sky. As it fell, the river shredded on inverted rocky slopes, sculpting cavernous chasms on its way to an icy sea that roiled beneath the castle in the air.

Faith was forming the white capped waves of the frothing charcoal sea when she was pulled out of her reverie by Eliza calling her name.

Faith tore herself back to reality to focus on Eliza who was holding up her drawing board with an expectant look upon her face.

"It's quite lovely!" Faith perjured herself with as much enthusiasm as she could muster. Mrs. Astor got up from the table where she had been working alongside William on the shop's accounts. Mrs. Astor glanced skeptically from the drawing to Faith and back again.

"Perhaps you should stick to singing. You have such a beautiful voice," Mrs. Astor said to her daughter, but not unkindly.

Eliza turned the board around with a scowl. "I just need practice, Mama."

Mrs. Astor made to respond when Magdalena appeared in the doorway with an open letter in her hand. Her eyes were red and tears ran down her cheeks.

"He's so hateful, Mama," she got out before Mrs. Astor shushed her gently. Mrs. Astor apologized to William for abandoning him to the bookkeeping and promised to finish later if she had time, before she followed the distraught woman down the hall. Feeling restless and in need of distraction, Faith heard herself volunteer to take Mrs. Astor's place. The pleasant surprise on William's face, in contrast to Eliza's wrinkled nose, made Faith instantly regret the offer, but she picked up a pen and sat before the ledger. William began to instruct her on what to do, showing her the stack of receipts that needed to be entered. It was no different than the accounting she had done for the Colonel and she began writing before William finished speaking. He watched over her shoulder a moment before, apparently satisfied she had the task in hand, he re-took his seat.

"I don't see why you should bother practicing," William said to Eliza as he dipped his pen. His tone was placid but Eliza's response was not.

"Are you saying I'm hopeless? You haven't even seen it!"

"No, I meant that drawing is a worthless pursuit."

Eliza gasped with a wide-eyed glance at Faith. "William! How can you say such a thing. Colonel Trumbull is an artist and an esteemed one at that!"

William looked pained to have to explain what he thought was obvious. "Colonel Trumbull is a gentleman. You are a lady. Reading to expand your knowledge and the acquisition of language are all very useful. While embroidery is frivolous, sewing is likewise practical. Singing is a pleasant diversion that can accompany other tasks, but of all the so-called improvements that young ladies undertake, drawing is the least worthwhile.

Women have as much business being artists as Colonel Trumbull would being a lady's maid."

William's tone was cooly matter of fact, but it landed on Faith like an incendiary. Her numbers grew fat under the pressure on her nib.

Eliza expressed her disdain for this opinion with an exasperated groan and a click of her tongue. Then an impish smirk curled her lips. "For that, I will do your portrait next and I will hang it in the dining room for all to see."

William shook his head. "That's juvenile Eliza. Why can't you be practical and reserved like Faith?"

Faith looked up at William sharply, her pen hovering mid air. An uncomprehending moment passed before Faith realized he meant this as a compliment. She gave him what weak smile her smothered indignation would allow and swore under her breath that it would never snow in her world.

* * *

Faith was so excited and relieved to be back at lessons that she could have hurled herself at Charles as she crossed the threshold into his studio. Only the memory of their last encounter and the disconcerting tension that had alternately repelled and attracted them held Faith back. Doubt and fear tempered her manner. Had he felt what she felt or had she imagined it all? And if he had felt it too, what exquisite torture was she in for, and could she, as he had asked, be trusted with those feelings?

Instead of a triumphant entrance, Faith greeted Charles nervously and self-consciously. She studied him warily for any signs of reserve or awkwardness and found none. Nor did she sense any of the electricity that had crackled around them before, even when she doffed her coat and donned the hat to pose once more. He was as he had always been, casual, light-hearted, and charming. Feeling relieved and strangely disappointed, Faith began to relax. They fell into easy conversation as he worked.

"Do you think I should start another picture, Charles? Unless I start putting them in the air, I don't know where I'd fit another building."

"In the air?" he asked vaguely before giving her a knowing look from under his brows. "Ah, the Coleridge. Planning castles in the air, I see."

"Do you think it's possible?" Faith asked excitedly.

"Do you?"

"Yes."

"Then, it's possible. And how do you propose to get to and from this floating city? Winged buggy? Or winged horse?" There was just a hint of teasing in his voice, but no disdain.

"Phoenix," Faith said crisply. He nodded without pausing his work, as though this were the most reasonable answer. "Of course, the idea of winged horses isn't bad either," Faith added as she mused over it. There was a comfortable silence that stretched until Charles stopped and stepped away from his work.

"Are you ready for your lesson?" The question was entirely rhetorical.

"More buildings?" Faith asked with mild distaste. It was always a pleasure to use the Ink, but being confined to four corners was not the best use for it in her mind.

"I think you have demonstrated that you can draw a building without being in danger of it coming down around your ears if you sneeze," Charles said with a wink that made Faith's heart skip as usual. "We can move on."

"Animals?"

"Water."

"But, there's already a lake. Isn't that enough water?"

"That lake is entirely incidental. How much thought did you put into it? For all we know, it's an enormous puddle no more than inches deep at its center. How warm or cold is it? Not to mention, there are many other forms of water. Deep, shallow, running, still. Creeks and rivers, waterfalls, seas. And there's rain and what about dew?"

Faith rolled her eyes, knowing she had put just enough thought into the lake to keep it empty of birds and fish per her instructions, nothing more. "Fine then. Water it is! But where shall I put it? It's all so crowded already," Faith said with dismay as she looked at her picture.

"There's no need to stay within the frame of the picture. That's just the gateway. The world of that picture includes everything that was in your mind when you drew it. And if that doesn't go far enough, you can always add on from inside. I believe there ought to be a useful valley behind the hills here," he said, pointing to one of the hilltops.

"What if I did start another painting though?" Faith asked, thinking of her floating castle. "Would the two be connected?"

"If you want them to be." That seemed to be his answer to everything. Faith made a face and he laughed. "When you're Master you can create a sprawling empire of uninterrupted lands or an archipelago of discrete worlds at your pleasure. For now it's safest to keep it all in one place."

Faith did not think she would have the luxury of waiting until she was a Master, but since she could not share that with Charles, she agreed to stay within the bounds of the world before her. With a thought to time draining away, Faith urged that they should get started. One moment they were in the Academy studio, seated at the drawing table. A dizzying moment later, they were standing in the valley of the former Prior Park.

Faith began to walk up the hillside toward the ridge Charles had identified. Her imaginary legs soon grew tired.

"I do think it would be good to start another picture. It is irritating to have to walk across this whole tableau."

"You don't have to walk, you know."

"Let me guess. I just intend to be somewhere."

"You're catching on. Just be sure to take my ha-"

Whatever else Charles said was lost as Faith closed her eyes and imagined herself upon the hilltop beyond the wooded valley rim. She looked around, pleased with herself until she realized Charles was not there. She waited several moments. Then, with a sheepish aspect, she imagined herself back to where she had left him. He was waiting for her with an air of affected patience.

"As I was saying, you need to take my hand, so that I can reach the same location. A visitor to your world cannot transport themselves outside the confines of the picture frame. Two people imagining themselves in the exact same place that neither has ever seen before is about as likely as lightning striking the same location twice in a row."

"My apologies," Faith said contritely, offering her hand. He took it and she delivered them both to the hilltop.

From there, an empty vista of indistinct hills stretched to a far horizon. With Charles' guidance and a few false starts, Faith filled the nearest crease in the land with a small, pebbly stream. He then had her enlarge it, until it was a meandering river cutting into the flanks of the hills, complete with rills and falls and rushing cataracts. By then, Faith was hot and tired from exertion, but with no movement in the heavens to mark the pass of time Faith did not know how long they worked.

Charles watched her as she pushed hair away from her damp brow. "Have you had enough for today?"

"No," she said, knowing she should rest but dreading a return to drab reality. She did her best to hide her breathlessness. "I'm just warm, that's all."

"A north wind would cool you down. A gentle one, mind you."

"Draw the wind?"

"Well, not the wind precisely. You can draw the things that it affects."

"Like my hair," she said, holding the twisting tendrils back with one hand.

"Can't redraw that since you never drew it in the first place."

Faith looked skyward at the clouds scuttling visibly by overhead, beams of sunlight weaving in and out of them as they passed.

"The clouds?"

"That's one way to do it. Trees and grasses are another, but we've been here awhile and you look tired. We should leave that for another day."

"No, please let me give it a try?"

She hardly waited for his reluctant consent before raising her pen to the sky. Faith called to mind the cooling winds and darkening skies that relieved a humid summer afternoon. The clouds thickened, tumbling rapidly overhead. Her hair and skirts billowed around her. A roll of far off thunder reached her ears. The next moment, the clouds poured forth their bounty and she stood, arms thrown wide and grinning, in a drenching rain.

Lightning flashed, filling the air with electricity. Faith's skin tingled with its charge. She felt Charles grab her hand and looked to see his brow creased with worry.

"End the storm or go-" his words were drowned by a clap of thunder. He spoke again as the rumble faded. "If we get struck by lightning, we could be killed. We have to go back!"

Faith shook her head and began to lead him by the hand. "I know a shelter! Come with me!" There was a place hidden in the woods where she had sheltered from many storms. Somehow she knew it would be here.

Faith hitched her skirts in both hands and ran for the woods that clothed the sides of the valley. Mud splashed with each footfall and her heart pumped wildly. Faith felt a freedom unlike any she had ever known. Drawing deep gulps of air and tasting the rain on her lips, she lengthened her stride, feeling the power in her own body. Joy burst inside her and escaped as a peal of laughter as she sprinted the final distance to the relative shelter of the tree line.

From there, she led them down the meandering paths of memory to a small clearing where she found the Summerhouse, just as she remembered it. It was not much more than a freestanding covered porch, a place to sit out of sun or rain, and take in the view of the valley below.

They ducked through the cascade of water pouring off the eaves and stood in the dry, dim shelter, panting and laughing at their sodden clothes and hair. Looking for a place to sit and watch the rain, Faith found the old cane chairs pushed against the back wall. They each pulled one forward and collapsed into them with a wet squelching sound.

"You are wild," Charles said, running his fingers through his thick , wet hair. Faith smiled broadly as she grabbed her own hair and wrung it like a towel.

"You know what would be perfect on a rainy afternoon like this?" Charles said. "Tea."

"I just made a mess of the weather, and now you want me to set tea?"

"You already have a tea service in your world."

"Let me guess. I just need to intend it to be here?" Faith asked.

"You've got it."

Faith closed her eyes and visualized the tea service. She heard the jangle of porcelain knocking together and opened her eyes.

"It worked!"

"Yes, but a table would be nice to go with it."

"So demanding," Faith muttered as she raised her pen. "No, wait! I have a better idea." Moments later the tea service sat upon a thick blanket between two enormous, overstuffed floor cushions.

"How very Bedouin," Charles said with a crooked smile as he lowered his long frame to the ground.

Faith plopped onto her cushion.

"Shall I pour out?" she asked in a mockingly haughty tone.

"Not that bitter stuff you drew before."

Faith winced, remembering the resentment laden tea she had conjured. "I have something better." Faith refilled the pot and cups, this time with the summer tea she had imagined all along. A fresh burst of steam carried the scent of strawberries. Charles sniffed appreciatively and picked up his cup.

He glanced at her over the rim, hesitating for a heartbeat, before taking a sip. Faith watched him nervously for any ill effects.

"Much happier," Charles said. Faith exhaled. "I don't know about those biscuits though. With your permission, I have something better."

Faith nodded, eager to see what he would create. Charles drew up a plate with dark brown bread and a mound of softened butter.

"Just like my Mam makes," he said, breaking off a hunk and slathering it with butter. "Only better. But don't tell her I said that."

He handed the bread to Faith. The smell made her ravenously hungry. She took a bite without a second thought. The butter was salty, the bread thick and slightly sweet. It was delicious. She followed it with a sip of tea, astonished at the sensation of warm liquid sliding down an imaginary throat.

They ate and drank in silence for a while, listening to the storm rumble overhead and the rain splash through the trees. Little bursts of wind eddied under the shelter overhang, ruffling Faith's hair. She was disappointed to realize that she was already dry, the magic of Phantasia having restored her to her typical appearance.

"This reminds me of the first time I used the Ink," Charles said "only it wasn't quite this dramatic."

"Tell me about it. Were you very young when you found out you had the Talent?"

"When I was a wee lad, I didn't have much opportunity to see that kind of art. But I do remember once, my Da took me to a museum and all these paintings were moving and jabbering. It was fascinating, and a bit terrifying I don't mind admitting." Faith looked away as she smiled, remembering her own reactions, several of them in front of Charles. "Of course, I thought everyone saw them that way. That had to be why the museum was so popular, right? That was when I decided to become an artist, but it wasn't until one day I'm in my drawing class slaving over a windy landscape when Master Cuming puts this odd pencil in my hand and tells me to redraw it, only make sure I'm thinking about the wind and the trees and the sounds and the sensations. Apparently I did a pretty good job because I had to hold the corners of the paper down to finish it and when I did, it fair blew my hair back."

Faith laughed at the image in her mind and Charles chuckled self-deprecatingly with her.

"That time I thought I was crazy. Then Master Cuming tells me about the Ink. Then I thought *he* was crazy."

When their laughter faded, Charles looked at Faith as he tore off another piece of bread. "I'd wager your father saw your Talent early on. No mistaking it."

Faith gave him a weak smile and shifted in her seat. In her mind's eye she saw the torn edges in her old sketchbook. She didn't want to ruin this moment with thoughts of the Colonel, or let it drift into dangerous territory. She cast about for a different subject, looking over their surroundings.

"Charles, how is the Summerhouse here? I never drew it."

"You must have created it when you first drew the Park. Kind of like the tea inside the pot," Charles said with a nod towards the tea, "your world includes more than what is visible on the surface."

"What do you do if you make a mistake?"

"Like this storm?" he teased.

She made a face. "I know I can repaint the sky, or change the contours of the hills, but what if you create something and later regret it, or there's something hidden that you didn't even know about? Will it disappear if you destroy the drawing?"

"The drawing is just a portal, a doorway. What's done in Ink stays in Phantasia forever. The only thing that changes is how you get here."

"Surely there must be some way to erase a mistake. Can you just wish it out of existence?"

He gave her a considering look as though wondering if she had something to confess, but did not press. Instead he said, "Whatever is done with the Ink has a permanence about it. You can change it into something different, turn it to thin air if you can, but you can't get rid of it entirely. The best you can do is treat a mistake like any regret: try to make the best of it. And if you can't do that, try to forget about it. The parts of Phantasia that you never visit, even the Inked ones, tend to fade over time. Still, it's best to tend your garden carefully and try to keep the weeds out in the first place. In the end, we all have to live in the world we create."

Faith's lips twisted and her brow creased as she turned the puzzle of Phantasia and the Ink this way and that. In some ways it felt so familiar, and she had learned so much. In other ways, it was still mysterious and unfathomable. She knew there was so much more to know but wondered if she could ever comprehend it all.

"And where is this world exactly? Are we in my mind? In yours? Does Phantasia have a location?"

"You might as well ask where Heaven and Hell are located. We think of them as upstairs and down, but you don't see the pearly gates when you look up at the sky and no one ever found the devil digging a hole. For me, personally, I think of it a bit like Heaven, invisible but somewhere above."

Faith nodded, agreeing that it was like Heaven. Better, in fact. Faith smiled and reclined luxuriously. She let a comfortable silence fall between them as she basked in the contentment of the moment, visions of heavenly cities drifting in her mind.

"We need to be getting back," Charles said, setting his cup and saucer on the tray. Faith's face fell.

"I thought we were going to wait for the rain to stop!"

"Did you mean for it to stop when you started it? If not it will continue indefinitely." If that was the case it would rain like the Flood. Faith did not ever want this moment to end.

Reluctantly, Faith raised her pen and painted her sky a brilliant, cloudless blue. The rain and wind ceased. Every leaf and blade sparkled in the sunlight as though bedecked with diamonds.

With a sigh, Faith closed her eyes and called to mind the studio room, the chair, the table, and her own body sitting with the image of this sunny world in front of her. Everything tilted and she tingled from head to toe.

A fine woman shows her charms to most advantage, when she
seems most to conceal them.
- Dr. John Gregory, A Father's Legacy to his Daughters

CHAPTER TWENTY-ONE
The Masquerade

The ginger tabby cat dozed on a pile of fabrics in the studio. It wasn't a very pretty cat. Its fur was rough and dirty. The tip of one ear was missing while the better part of the other was gone. It was an alley cat after all. But, its perpetually hungry condition had made it curious enough to investigate the small bits of meat Faith had offered to it. Thus distracted, the instantly irate beast had been netted in Charles' coat, and the whole hissing mess of claws and teeth carried upstairs to the studio room. Once there, it had dined cautiously on the bait that had got it into trouble in the first place. Ultimately preferring the studio's warmth to the snowy street, the cat had forgiven the indignity of its capture and found a soft place in a tangle of cream linen and blue satin to fall asleep.

Faith sat on the floor, several feet away from her reluctant subject, with a drawing board across her lap. She had initially enjoyed the novelty of sitting on a floor. The thought of her scandalized father, if he should have seen such a thing, amused her to no end. Eventually, though, the hard stone had flattened and numbed her backside and an ache extended both up her back and down her legs. She shifted every few minutes, trying to find a more comfortable position.

Faith leaned to the side to get a view of Charles at his easel. He had settled on the sketch of her wrapped in velvet beneath Eliza's ostrich plumed hat as his subject, and had finally begun work on the canvas. He had blocked in her form and started on her face. He had an unusual, and tedious, technique of layering thin glazes to give the skin a lifelike glow. It was strange for Faith to watch her own face emerge shade by contour, as though looking in a fogged but clearing mirror. She was glad of the slow progress on the canvas, but she had had a letter from the Colonel. His proposal for historical paintings to hang in the new capitol rotunda had been well received in the debate before congress. He expected it to be passed and would return home immediately after. Even if the painting were not complete by then, she knew her lessons would quickly end. She wished she knew better how long it would be before the Colonel returned.

She had pushed herself to master water, from dew-spangled webs to crashing waves, as quickly as Charles would allow. She ignored both fatigue and the foreboding she felt when creating deeper, wilder bodies of water. She pushed all fear out of her mind, assuring herself that she was fully in control of her thoughts. Still, she had watched carefully for signs of inadvertent consequences: an unexpected ripple, unintended shadows. When none materialized, Faith congratulated herself on her progress. Charles had been impressed enough, in spite of the quickness, to grudgingly allow her to begin work on animals.

It was no particular task to draw the resting form of an animal that stayed still long enough to let Faith capture a clear mental image. But, animals moved. Not only was it hard to draw them if they were in the act of moving, but it was also hard to understand how they moved when they were not. The ginger cat, once sated, had been particularly problematic. Faith had a vague impression of a cat's movements as smooth and haughty, but her true awareness of the way they moved had fallen far short of what she needed. They had been forced to prod their model into action. Consequently, the cat in Faith's Phantasia had a distinctly perturbed and disdainful manner.

The other problem was that animals thought. They had instincts and reactions. They had purposes of their own that they didn't care to share. Between the movement and the intellect, it was too much for Faith to incorporate all at once. So far her attempts had created graceful idiots or intelligent marionettes and very little in between.

Another surprising feature of drawing living things was that their well-being was tied to her own. Apparently, the impact was directly related to how much she invested in the drawing. To snap a twig or pick a flower was inconsequential because Faith had not imbued the flora of her world with any truly living properties. They were primarily decorative. However, when the small beetle that was her first attempt at an animate being had accidentally been crushed a few days later, she had felt it like a pinch in her mind. As she had worked on the cat, she had felt each awkward step, each misshapen body part, as though she had given birth to a monster. Or that she herself was the monster. At times she had to hold back tears that took her wholly by surprise. She could only imagine how it might feel if the cat were to get hurt. An injury to it would be an injury to her soul. And it was only an alley cat.

By afternoon, she was emotionally and physically drained, but determined to get it right. There was still so much she wanted to know, and she needed to learn how to Ink people before the Colonel returned. She knew Charles would never let her work on people until she had completely mastered animals.

"I think he's ready," Faith said.

Charles placed a few strokes before setting down his brush and turning to her. "Let's give it a try then, shall we?"

They both moved to the table where Faith's landscape lay spread out on the table. Faith limped over stiffly, one foot asleep.

"Where did you place him?" Charles asked.

"The Summerhouse."

Pens in hand, they both gazed at the drawing with a soft focus until Faith felt the now familiar spin. The studio around her blurred and resolved into the cool dim interior of the Summerhouse. She had created a table for the tea tray as it was less likely to be stepped on there. Charles had been amused, pointing out that even if they took a hammer to it, it would reassemble itself the moment she stopped thinking about it. The cat, cleaner and more smoothly coated than its model, was curled in one of the large, overstuffed cushions.

"Let's stir him a bit," Charles suggested, going over to the cat and gently stroking its head and back. The cat opened one bright yellow eye, then another. "Well, it has eyes. That's a start."

Faith winced at his jest. The first cat she had drawn hadn't had eyes behind its sleeping lids. The blank sockets when it had first opened them would haunt Faith's nightmares for quite awhile.

The cat, irritated by the disturbance, rose, stretching its back in a high arch, and moved off haughtily towards the tea table. It jumped gracefully onto the edge and sat, perfectly balanced, as it raised a paw for cleaning. Having washed up, the hungry cat started licking the butter from the plate.

"Shoo! Shoo!" Faith called, waving her arms at the opportunistic animal. He hissed his objection before jumping down and sauntering away.

Charles just laughed. "Given your source material, I think that you have done an excellent job capturing the essence of that cat."

Faith was pleased and relieved. It had taken all she had to give to create that cat. She wondered if she had it in her to create a person, but pushed the thought aside.

"Does the cat have a name?" Charles asked just as motion caught the corner of Faith's eye. Charles' brilliant butterfly was bobbing drunkenly from flower to tree to flower. The butterfly had also caught the cat's attention. Faith knew that cats liked to chase all manner of things and apparently she had been successful in giving it this trait. It immediately gave chase.

"Oh no! Your butterfly!" Faith cried, following behind.

"Wait! It's all right-" Charles called after her, but she took off down the path, trying to capture the predatory feline. Charles ran after her.

The butterfly led them all a merry chase down to the lake where it fluttered out over the water, leaving them at the edge. The sky was clear and blue. The water was smooth as glass and bright as polished silver. The cat stopped at the waterline, eyes darting between the butterfly in the air and its perfect twin reflected in the water. Giving up on its quarry, the cat touched its nose to its own image in the water and drank, rending its reflection with a flurry of ripples.

Faith came to a stop behind the cat. Something about the lake troubled Faith but she could not put her finger on what it was. Her eyes followed the diminishing ripples as they collided with the reflection of the bridge, twisting its balustrade and columns as the tiny waves lapped gently against the pilings. She suddenly realized why the lake bothered her so.

"Charles, why don't I have a reflection?"

"Because you aren't actually here."

"But none of this is here. It's all imaginary."

"Not the parts done with the Ink. In this world, that's as good as real. You, on the other hand, have not been done in Ink so there is nothing for the water to reflect."

"That's right. I'm just- what did you call it- a construct for the benefit of my mind?"

"You are. You appear however you expect yourself to look." As Charles spoke, a neatly buttoned coat appeared out of nowhere to cover the rolled shirtsleeves that Charles had been working in. Faith clapped a hand over her mouth. A moment later, the coat was gone again without him having lifted his pen.

"I can change my clothes to anything I can think of?" she asked Charles breathlessly.

"If you can believe in it, you can wear it," he answered with a broad grin. "Though that's the easy bit since we change clothes all the time. You can also conjure up just about any prop. Those are temporary, o' course. They go away when you drop them." Suddenly an open umbrella appeared above Charles' head. He let it fall and it disappeared only to be replaced with a bow and nocked arrow. He drew and loosed the arrow with practiced motions. The arrow buried itself in a distant hillside and vanished. "I used to amuse myself by seeing how far I could shoot them before they disappeared."

Faith looked down at the heavy skirts and winter boots she had worn to the studio. No sooner had she formed the thought that they were out of place on such a warm sunny day, they became a summer frock and light slippers. Working against the ingrained notion of impropriety, Faith willed herself to be barefoot and the slippers disappeared. She felt the cool wet grass of the shoreline beneath her feet. She lifted her hem and stepped into the water, mud squelching between her fictional toes, cold water swirling about her non-existent ankles. Faith laughed in delight and kicked the water playfully. Glinting beads of water arced through the air, landing with a chill on sun warmed skin. Realizing she could be dry in a moment if she chose, Faith let her hem fall. It floated on the surface before sinking to cling about her legs.

Charles laughed at her antics. "That's not all, you know. You can also change your physical appearance. Your hair, your eye color, your height. Of course, all of that is much harder since it goes against who we are used to being but I've often wondered if I might look better as a blond." His dark hair turned a sandy blond that made his eyes look blue. Or perhaps he had changed his eyes as well.

"I like you just as you are" Faith said as she waded out of the water and his appearance returned to normal. Faith, in turn, imagined her hair a deep brunette like Eliza's. She lifted the ends to inspect the dark brown waves but was unimpressed. Tossing the tresses back over her shoulder, they became ginger spirals once again. Faith gasped as a startling possibility came to her. "Could I make myself invisible?"

"Theoretically, you could, for a moment or two. I'd think the second you try to move, your mind will envision a body to do it."

Faith frowned at that. She would have to try it, but not while Charles was watching. "I could be a princess, then."

"Why stop there? You could be a queen!"

"Or a..." Faith trailed off, trying to think of what else a woman might become. Queen. Princess. Lady. Governess. Seamstress. Washerwoman. Beggar. Whore. Spinster. Wife. Mother. Save the first few, she could find nothing in the rest to desire. A queen then, but not like any other. She conjured an image of a shimmering silken dress, fitted from bodice to the waist from which it fell in serrated tiers. From palest gold at her shoulders, adorned with scarlet feathers, it darkened to deepest crimson at the hem, its layers like inverted flames. A string of rubies circled her throat as more dripped from her ears and wrist. Her hair, half restrained with jewel encrusted combs, fell in a tumble down her back.

Charles' eyes went wide with surprise. Faith had a moment of doubt and the illusion blurred threateningly.

"Is it too much?" Faith asked.

"I've never seen anything like it...," he said in something of daze. "It's stunning. Your majesty." Charles made an elaborate bow and when he stood he too was wearing evening dress. His tailed coat of shining silk was colored to match her dress. Faith smiled playfully and returned his bow with a deep curtsy.

"My Lord. Is that a waltz I hear?" she asked. The dance's rhythmic strains drifted in her mind and on the wind. Charles took one of her hands in his and led her to the bridge. The curious cat followed, leaping onto the balustrade. It found a vantage point to sit and watch, tail swaying in time to the music.

When they had reached the center of the bridge, Charles turned to Faith and put his other hand upon her waist. She lifted her skirt with her free hand and they began to move. As the dance carried them along, the sunlight glinting off the lake glared in Faith's eyes. That wouldn't do.

"One moment," she said, pushing gently away and calling her pen to hand. She painted the sky velvet black. The sun she turned into a bowl of pure silver light that poured itself upon the lake and surrounded it with a scatter of stars. Pleased, she returned to Charles.

"Better, don't you think?"

"Much better," he agreed, pulling Faith to him again. They resumed the dance, floating along the length of the bridge, carried by the music in the air. The only other sound was the rustle of silk and the whisper of their feet skimming lightly over the stones. In the light of Faith's moon, Charles' eyes were a soft green that belied the intensity of his gaze. Faith met it with a burning one of her own.

Their feet slowed though the music continued on. They came to a stop, perfectly framed within the bridge's arching gallery. Charles' hand tightened on her waist, pulling her closer. Faith closed her eyes and raised her chin. His lips on hers were soft and warm, his arms around her strong. A delicious tingle ran through her body with a jolt each place they touched. Faith's heart hammered and her lips asked for more. Charles' hold on her tightened and then released.

Charles pulled away, the arms that had pressed her to him now holding them apart. He shook his head as if to clear it of some unwanted thought.

"This isn't right," he said gently, letting his arms fall and stepping back.

"What do you mean? It's just as I imagined it would be," Faith said. His kiss had told her he returned her feelings and it had made her bold.

He gave her a small smile. "That's partly what I'm afraid of." He silenced her indignant objection with a finger on her lips. "All I meant was that you've put me in a trance. Not just the music, the moonlight, your dress," he said gesturing at each in turn, "but all your other wild ways. You've tempted me to do something I would never do anywhere else and risk your reputation."

"No one has to know," Faith protested.

"That doesn't make it right."

"What would make it right?" Faith asked with mounting frustration at the restrictions she encountered with every movement of her heart. "We could court openly on the other side. Then, you could train me without the charade of modeling and portraits."

Charles shook his head. Faith felt the first flush of embarrassment as her certainty faltered. The music had stopped. The air was silent except for the gentle spill of water under the bridge.

"You and I both know your Da has other plans for you."

Rage flared in Faith at the mention of the Colonel. It was maddening enough to fear discovery, knowing he might soon have the power to bar her from the Ink forever. To be reminded that he already had the power to control her ordinary life, to tell her how to act and whom to marry, was too much to bear. Even here, in her own world, his specter floated between her and Charles, coming between her and joy in every place she might seek it out.

She opened her mouth to protest that he was not her father, that it was his power over her that was not right, but the words were drowned by the roar of rushing water. The lake seethed, sending waves against the bridge to break across its span. Water surged over Faith's feet.

A great hill of water rose at the center of the lake until it was broken by a horned and scaly head with smoking nostrils and eyes of burning fire. The head hovered above its arching neck for a sickening moment, rows of wetly glistening teeth lining its open maw. Then, it struck.

The ginger cat leapt from the shadows of the bridge, hissing with claws spread wide, and landed on the face of the monster. In frantic fury it scrambled to find purchase on the scaly cheek, swiping one burning eye. With a terrible screech, the monster thrashed its head, sending the cat into the side of the bridge with a gut wrenching crunch. In her mind, Faith felt the blinding pain of the cat's broken bones in her own body. Her legs crumpled beneath her. She fell, striking her head on the stone balustrade. Lights exploded behind her eyes. Through them, she could just barely see Leviathan. The moon surrounded its head like a halo, the back of its open mouth glowed like a great forge. Faith braced herself against the coming flames.

Something fluttered in her vision.

Charles's butterfly, its wings a translucent kaleidoscope before the beast's incandescence, danced before its remaining eye. In that moment, Charles was beside her, lifting her with one arm about her. The other held an enormous shield that blotted out her vision of the monster, the moon, and the butterfly. All she could see and hear was Charles. His voice was calm and soothing, but his eyes were filled with fear. Faith did not know which to believe.

"Go back Faith. Back to the studio. Back to yourself. Back to reality."

Faith fought for a moment to remember the studio, herself, reality, certain that they were not one and the same. Her thoughts turned to mist as she seized them. Her head hurt too much to protest. Faith closed her eyes and followed Charles' voice. The world spun and then went black.

No bird soars too high if he soars with his own wings.
-William Blake, The Marriage of Heaven and Hell

CHAPTER TWENTY-TWO

The Plea

Charles paced the parlor, hands clasped behind his back. His footsteps made angry thumps as he crossed the carpet. Faith had never seen him in any but an easy mood. She was chagrined to be the cause of his agitation, but not enough to keep from pressing her case. It would be even more upsetting if he did not agree.

"Please, Charles. I'm only asking *because* I have so much to learn," she said.

He stopped and rounded on her, a finger raised, hot words on his lips. He stopped himself before they issued. He folded his arms across his chest. Deciding it would be better not to provoke him further, Faith stayed silent and waited for him to speak.

Faith was perched on the edge of the settee in the Astor's parlor after several days in bed. She was woozy and her head hurt, but she poured her limited energy into looking well. Her memory after the confrontation with Leviathan was spotty. Alternating periods of light and dark were stitched together with a constant thread of pain. She had fuzzy visions of Charles and Mr. Dunlap hovering over her and the lurching of a carriage. She could remember Charles carrying her through the house, the smell of his coat and the feel of his arms beneath her before laying her gently on the bed. From then, all of her moments of clarity were populated with the Astors, her maid Jane, and the kindly concern of Dr. Hosack.

She had been tormented by cold sweats that left her shivering under blankets piled so high she could barely move beneath the weight of them, only to become feverishly hot as though Leviathan's flames washed over her. Bright light spawned a crippling headache that concentrated behind her left eye. But, every time she closed them she saw glowing eyes amid a tapestry of scales and a needle lined jaw lunging toward her. Of course, she shared none of these thoughts. Apparently Charles had only told them that she fainted, which, in due course, they took as the precursor of a mysterious infection. There had been cold compresses and warming pans, vile tinctures and infusions, weak broth and plain bread. Fortunately, she had not been bled.

Faith had steadily improved, but even when she could tolerate un-curtained windows, the world was still colorless and heavy. When she was well enough for visitors, the only one she wanted to see was not among them. She had missed Charles and, even with the serpent lurking in the depths of her imagination, she missed Phantasia.

When Mrs. Astor had told Faith that Charles had finally come to see her, she had insisted on getting out of bed and dressing. She knew she would have much to answer for about Leviathan, but she also could not delay her training much longer. For all she knew the Colonel was already on his way home. The more recovered she seemed, the easier things would be on all fronts.

She had come up with an idea to continue her training even after the Colonel had returned. Charles had not taken kindly to the idea.

He stopped pacing, looking to the ceiling as though to ask for divine guidance.

"You could have killed yourself. And me. Why on earth would I let you practice with the Ink unsupervised?"

"I know it would be safer practicing with you, and I completely understand why you have your doubts, but when the portrait is done we have no excuse to meet anymore. At least, not one you find agreeable." Faith pouted and it was not an act. Although the Colonel had been his excuse, Charles' rejection had stung.

"Faith, that's not fair." Charles ran his hand through his hair.

"Then why haven't you visited before now?"

Charles answered in a harsh whisper, darting glances at the closed door. "I'm dancing a fine line between propriety and ruining your reputation as it is. I was here once before, but returning Eliza's hat and friendly concern over your well-being only carries so far. It does not get me a private audience in your bedchamber when you are ill. Mrs. Astor was none too pleased that I asked to speak with you alone in the parlor."

"Hang my reputation! What good is it to live a life of virtue on the outside when it makes me feel like I'm dying on the inside?"

"Faith, you're ill and emotional. You don't know what you're saying," Charles said gently. "A lady's reputation is not something to be treated lightly and I'll not be the one to ruin yours. Besides, it's clear to anyone with an eye and a brain that your Da is setting up a match for you, and not with me. If I interfere with those plans, he could ruin my career here."

"His plans? What about my plan? No one cares if he ruins everything I've worked for." Faith said, bitterness making her reckless.

Charles stopped and looked at her. "What are you talking about?"

Faith blanched. She had almost said too much. "I-I just meant... my plan to surprise him. With the Ink. It's just that he will be home soon. With the lost time, there's no way I can be ready to reveal my progress."

"Ready? You've already learned more than any apprentice has in so short a time. He could not fail to be impressed!"

"I'm afraid you do not know his standards like I do. What is extraordinary to anyone else is a shortcoming to the Colonel. I would be too embarrassed to reveal myself and fall short. I can not go to him until I have done all I need to earn a Journeyman's pen, including people. I need to be able to practice more than your time can allow and to continue when he comes home. If you have another solution, I am open to it, but the only thing I can think of is to keep the pen with me. I promise I will only work on what you allow me to work on."

"Is that so? How do I trust you? How do I even know what is safe for you to work on? Somehow, in my very presence, you created a monster of Biblical proportion. Literally!" he nearly shouted before looking hastily at the door. He paced the carpet with clipped steps before stopping again. This time his voice was lower. "Why didn't you tell me?"

"I'm sorry," Faith apologized, truly agonized. "I've been on ships that nearly wrecked twice in my life. How many people does that happen to? I can't help it. Deep water inspires such dread in me that I cannot subdue the feeling that something dark and sinister is there hunting me. I didn't tell you because I thought I had learned to control it like you have taught me to control all my other thoughts and emotions. I thought I could control that too. I know better, now. I know my limits. I won't do anything that I'm not completely sure about unless you're with me."

Charles raised his arms and snorted. "You have no limits." There was a brief silence as he visibly gathered his temper. "My apologies. That was unchivalrous. However, you have put me in a very difficult position. On the one hand, that was frightening enough that I daresay you might finally have discovered a respect for the Ink. And, you are right that continued practice is the only way to improve. On the other hand, it would be foolhardy of me, after an incident like that, to blithely put a pen in your hand and send you on your merry way. And then you want me to teach you people? What are your feelings about people? You might release the four horsemen!" His voice had grown loud and animated by the end of this rant.

He took a breath and added quietly. "The right thing to do is to continue at a moderate pace, practicing under supervision. If that continues past when your father gets back, so be it. You have made extraordinary progress already. In spite of your assertion to the contrary, that should be more than enough to pleasantly surprise him and he, or I if he wishes, can take up the remainder of your training."

The finality of Charles' tone made Faith's heart fall. From his perspective, it was a perfectly reasonable decision. From Faith's it was devastating. There was no way to explain to him how critical it was that she master as much as possible before the Colonel found out without revealing the lie she had told to get Charles to help her in the first place. Once her father got home, she knew her training would be done if she did not have a pen of her own before then. Even so, she ran the risk of discovery which, once he was Guild Master, would mean the end of it all for Faith. The idea of touching Phantasia only through dream and daydream for the rest of her life made Faith's soul quake with hopelessness. Grief tightened her chest and burned in her nose. She tried to hold back the tears that welled up but she could not. They started as silent drops trailing down her cheeks, and quickly grew to whimpering sobs.

With a pained look Charles offered her his handkerchief. She pressed it gratefully to her face, stemming the flow of tears that now dripped from her chin onto her lap. She was embarrassed to cry like this in front of him, but she was so overwhelmed that she could not hold it back.

Charles looked nervously at the door, either thinking he should get help or worried that someone would think that he was responsible for her hysterics. Apparently giving up on either thought, he sat next to her on the settee and patted her shoulder reassuringly. When that had no effect, he put his arm around her shoulders and drew her in. Faith turned into his chest and wept freely. She felt the hot tears press into the smooth fabric of his lapel, the strength of his arms around her, and the steady rise and fall of his breath as he murmured to her that it would be all right. She wanted to believe him, but how could it be all right? Even if she somehow became a Master of the Guild, would she ever be free of the Colonel's dominion?

After a time, her sobs ran their course. She stayed in Charles' steadying embrace drawing ragged breaths, not wanting to pull away. Eventually though, he held her gently away from him where he could look at her face. She swiped at her nose and eyes with the sodden handkerchief, aware of how frightful she must look.

"I'm sorry I upset you. I did not mean to be so angry but you gave me quite a scare. That creature really could have hurt you and when you fainted, I thought it had. I was worried about you."

"You were?" Faith asked weakly.

"Of course! I do care about you. I do not want to see you hurt."

In the ashes of her disappointment, Faith felt a warm ember flare within her heart. Charles's feelings for her were not yet strong enough to make him go against the Colonel, but if she could stoke his affection to sufficient passion, Faith was sure she could convince him to stand up for her. If she could marry him rather than William Astor, everything would be different. They could create a beautiful world together both in and out of Phantasia.

Enlivened by this new hope, Faith pressed one more time. "I really am sorry, Charles. It was a terrible accident and I know the blame lies entirely with me. I would never hide something like that again. I just... It's...I just can't express how important Phantasia is to me. You've already taught me so much, but can you teach me everything? Isn't there a point where I need to learn on my own, even if it means making some mistakes?"

Charles' hands fell from her shoulders as he considered her words. Surprisingly, he nodded reluctantly. "I understand. I felt the same drive to learn the Ink. And, you are right. I cannot teach you everything. There is much for even Masters to learn after they have earned their pen. I daresay you have already taught me a thing or two, I just don't want you to get hurt again."

"With your guidance, which I swear to God I will obey, I cannot possibly get hurt again," Faith assured him.

He gave her a skeptical look. "If, and I haven't agreed to do it, if I give you the pen to use here, you must limit yourself to no more than an hour at a time until you are fully recovered-"

Faith opened her mouth to protest that she was already fully recovered but he held up a hand to silence her. "I will determine when you are recovered. No more than an hour." Faith agreed meekly.

"I think it is also quite obvious," he went on, "that you may not go anywhere near water again without my presence. If water or anything else gives you even the slightest misgiving, if you feel anything other than joy and contentment while you are creating something, then you must wait to work on it with me."

"Absolutely," Faith promised. "How will I work with you though?"

"We will meet in Phantasia. The butterfly connects our worlds. I will also keep your painting of the tea set as a direct portal in case you turn the butterfly into something monstrous that I am forced to erase." A hint of his usual teasing had returned and Faith was relieved to see it. "We will work out a schedule to meet but I reserve the right to inspect unannounced to ensure that you are adhering to these promises."

"Yes, Charles. In the meantime, what should I-we- do about the monster in the lake?"

He rubbed his chin in thought. "I don't know that we can change your feelings about the water itself, but maybe we can come up with something that makes you feel safe. If you feel safer, maybe you can create water without putting big beasties in it or at least keep the beasties from raising their ugly heads."

Faith thought of the ginger cat and her bones ached at the memory. Perhaps if she turned it into something larger and stronger it could protect her.

"What if I turned the cat into a lion, or a tiger? It came to my defense once already. I think it would make me feel safer."

Charles raised a skeptical eyebrow. "Another man-eater? I'm not sure that makes *me* feel safer."

"Does it have to be something real?" Faith asked. Without telling Charles that she thought she had seen Leviathan in the ocean, she described to him how her vision of the phoenix had carried her through the awful gale. In

Faith's mind, it was not inherently aggressive but could defend her absolutely from the beast.

"That could work," he said thoughtfully. "You can pencil it on your own. We'll start with ordinary birds, but I don't want you Inking anything bigger than a finch or fiercer than a rabbit without me. No stormy weather, no fire, and absolutely no people."

Faith couldn't hide a small pout about the fire. "We were supposed to do fire this week."

"Well, quite a bit has changed since then."

"I can't very well make a proper phoenix without fire."

Charles sighed. "I suppose that's true, but you won't be doing it on your own, will you?"

"No," Faith answered contritely. "What can I practice on my own?"

"Well, I can show you how to make mechanical objects. I can also teach you how to make time."

"Time for what?"

"Time itself. When you draw plants and animals now, you've been thinking of them as existing that way forever. The violets you drew will bloom exactly the same, never growing, never dying. With the right intention though, you can draw a seed that will, over time, grow, bloom and die, just like a real plant. You can make night and day progress on their own and the stars move across the sky."

"That sounds wonderful," Faith breathed. "Does that mean that you will let me keep the pen?"

Charles consulted the ceiling one more time. Looking back down at her with a sigh he said, "I am certain I will regret it, but I'll let you keep it."

"Can we begin tonight?" Faith asked as she blinked against the blinding pain behind her eyes.

Can you bind the chains of the Pleiades, or loose the cords of Orion?

Can you lead forth the Constellations in their season, or can you guide the Bear with its children?

Do you know the ordinances of the heavens? Can you establish their rule on earth?"

- Job 38:31

CHAPTER TWENTY-THREE

The Demand

The first evening constellation of Faith's world was already rising while the last pink light of day was fading on the horizon. Charles was late.

Faith reclined in the crotch of the enormous fruit tree at the heart of her palace courtyard. The palace itself had not yet been built, nor had the island it rested on been made to float above the sea. In fact, it was not really an island at all so much as a large swath of land enclosed on all sides by rivers. Charles would not hear of her creating anything resembling a lake or sea that might hold a true island, and he would have taken her pen immediately if she had been so bold as to attempt a floating city.

She did not begrudge the injunction against large bodies of water. The creation of her phoenix, which had evolved incrementally over the course of a number of birds, had been successful so near as they could determine. They had been to the lake many times under Charles' supervision and had not seen so much as a ripple on its surface. Still, the experience with Leviathan had shaken Faith. She would not have admitted it to Charles, but in spite of the trust she had put in Helios to keep her safe, she was just as afraid of deep water in her world as she was in reality.

That the palace had not yet been created could not be blamed on Charles, however. While Faith had a reasonably clear picture in her mind of the exterior, an image that seemed to have come to her from dream or memory, she had met with insurmountable indecision about what she wanted *inside* of the palace. She had been surprised and curious to realize that she did not have any clear vision of what a pleasure dome should contain. Except, of course, for gardens.

That is where she had begun, with the walls and fountains and beds of a magnificent central, to something, courtyard. Centered in one half of the formal garden was a grand fountain while the tree in which she now sat was centered in the other half. All of the beds around and in between were a riot of season-less blooms and draping vines, a mix of her earthly favorites and those of her own design. The tree itself was an amalgamation unknown to the natural world, birthed from another fit of indecision. At first, she had thought to create an apple tree upon which she could hang the apple that represented the start of her journey with the Ink. Then, she had realized that true apple trees were upright, irregular, and covered with stiff leaves that did not convey a sense of lushness that she felt appropriate for the center of her private Eden. No, she was quite certain that Milton had it wrong when he had immortalized the apple as the forbidden fruit.

Faith could think of no tree known to her that exhibited all the characteristics she desired, so she had created her own. It had the spreading form and substance of an oak, and the large, heart shaped leaves of a redbud. The new growth was delicate with a weeping habit that swayed elegantly, and aubergine in contrast to the deep green of the older leaves. It bore both flowers in fragrant wisteria-like racemes and fruit simultaneously. These she had excepted from the progression of time so that they hung in perpetual perfection. The fruit itself was not limited to one variety, but was a medley that, in real life, would have required a fleet of merchant traders sent to the corners of the world to acquire. Among the oranges and plums, cherries and pomegranates, there was one, single apple.

During the day, the air buzzed with the busyness of bees and the whirr of hummingbird wings as sunlight dappled the pure white stone of the walls and pavement. Now that night spread its shadow over the garden, the damask scent of blue flowered roses and the sensuous fragrance of jasmine were fading, allowing the delicate sweetness of moonflowers to rise from their pure white throats to greet their lunar mistress. Until the sky darkened completely and the moon filled the garden with her silver light, the courtyard was lit only with bowls of fire set on pedestals around the perimeter. An even brighter light came from the fountain. By day it burbled soothingly as water flowed from the mouths of marble nymphs and dolphins who cavorted within a scalloped basin. At night, fire burned on the surface of the water, falling in a cascade of multihued flames. There was also Helios. The phoenix preened itself upon its perch, casting its own warm glow upon the ground beneath it.

Faith plucked a pear from the tree as she watched the tea set for Charles' arrival. She had moved it from the Summerhouse to a stone bench along one garden wall. It resembled a curiously modern offering on the altar of an ancient god. She took a bite of the pear. Its flesh was cold and buttery soft, the skin and juice a perfect mix of bitter and sweet as it filled her mouth. It would help her stave off the fatigue she felt stealing over her physical body where she had left it in her bedroom.

Since Charles had let her keep her pen, Faith had only been able to work at night. At first she had been limited by the nausea, headaches, and exhaustion that she refused to admit to. As she had recovered her strength, she had found herself tempted to spend all night in Phantasia, showing a contempt for the coming day that no book, no matter how riveting, had ever inspired. With no way to measure the passage of time, it had been too easy a temptation to indulge. It had been Mrs. Astor's concern at Faith's tired appearance and constant yawning that had prompted Faith to create the constellations so that she could measure the passage of night. When the Great Bell rose above the horizon, it was time to return for sleep. Faith noted with frustration that waiting for Charles had wasted one of her precious hours.

Faith was nearly done with the pear when Charles finally appeared. Holding it between her teeth, she clambered down the tree trunk, bare feet gripping the knotted bark. She swung from the lowest branch and landed lightly in front of Charles.

He raised an eyebrow at her entrance or appearance, or both. She had taken to wearing fitted britches and loose shirts with rolled sleeves while in her world. They were more conducive to climbing and running - and flying she secretly thought, once she was truly the master of her world. They were infinitely more comfortable than the tight bodices and sleeves of her conventional attire, and more practical than trailing skirts. Her hair she wore in a long braid. Charles had seemed amused by her sartorial choices but had not commented on them. Since they had begun to meet within Phantasia he had been reserved.

Tonight he was more than reserved. "I hope you aren't ruining your appetite with food from here. It feels satisfying but it doesn't feed your body." Charles frowned with uncharacteristic irritation.

Faith made sure her cheeks looked flush and plump. She tossed the pear core to the side. It vanished before it hit the ground and reappeared whole where Faith had plucked it. "The Astors keep me well-fed. This was just a snack while I was waiting for you. I'm fine. Where have you been?" His testiness was making her grouchy in turn.

"I do have clients and familial obligations, Faith. Teaching you is not my only occupation."

"Of course, but isn't there some way you could let me know that you'll be late? Or if you can't come at all? I know you Masters have some way of sending letters that is much quicker than the post."

"Mirrors," he answered cryptically. A pained expression compressed his lips and he ran a hand through his hair. "Since you mention it, I've had a letter from your Da." He held up a folded packet of parchment with the Colonel's handwriting and a blob of dark purple wax.

The blood drained from Faith's face.

Faith had had her own letter from her step-father, receiving the news with mixed emotions. With the endorsement of former presidents Jefferson and Adams, Congress had approved a commission for four large historical paintings, with an advance of eight thousand dollars on the first one. It was a great success and an even greater sum. The Colonel would be in a magnanimous frame of mind when he returned, which could only help Faith in her scheme. He had also said that he had to wait until after the inauguration to receive the payment and would return after that, around the Ides of March. It gave her several more weeks to complete her training, but only that. Faith knew she would not have much time or opportunity after he returned before the American Guild would be founded and he became its Guild Master.

But what had he written to Charles about? He would not have written to him about the commissions, and not with that seal. It had to be Guild business. Whatever it was had Charles in a mood. With a conscious thought to her complexion and keeping her voice light, Faith asked, "Really? What did he have to say?"

"The Guild Council has approved the formation of the American Guild."

"And he is to be Master?" Faith asked with a sharp intake of breath.

"He is."

The breath left Faith as though she had been kicked in the gut. She had known it was coming, set all her plans against the eventuality. Now that it was imminent, she felt wholly unprepared. She became aware of Charles watching her closely.

"How do you feel about that?"

Faith imagined a happy smile onto her face. "I'm thrilled for him, of course! Is there anyone else more deserving?"

Charles did not answer, searching her face as he turned the letter in his hands. Faith swallowed hard against rising fear. What else had the Colonel told Charles? "Does it say when his appointment will be official?"

"April thirteenth. There will be a ceremony at the Guild Hall."

Two months. Faith had two months before the Colonel would be the Master of her destiny on both sides of reality.

"That's wonderful!" Faith said with unfelt warmth. "Do you think I have time to master people before then? I would so like to become a Journeyman before he is Guild Master. It would be like a gift to commemorate his triumph." The lie was like oil on Faith's tongue.

Charles ran his hand through his hair again and frowned. Faith's neck prickled. Something wasn't right.

"Why are you so eager to learn people?" was all he asked.

"Why are you so reluctant to teach me?" Faith countered, her voice smooth and level.

"People are unlike anything you've created yet. They aren't like cats and birds. Their impacts are different, more profound."

"I don't understand. What about all the portraits that have been Inked? What about your own Cleopatra? Or Vanderlyn's Marius?" Faith shuddered at the memory of the fearsome general, realizing he made a poor example. "I don't believe that any of those subjects meant more to their creators than Helios does to me. I've poured my heart and soul into that bird, instilled it with every noble, loyal, and protective ideal I can imagine. Nothing could impact me more." Faith had placed absolute trust in the phoenix to safeguard her. So intense was Faith's attachment to the firebird that even outside Phantasia, she thought she could perceive its presence like a mote of light in the dark.

"You're right, people can be Inked in a superficial way. Most portraits are, if they are even Inked at all. They're meant to capture a sentiment or a concept more than a person. When I painted Cleopatra, I wasn't trying to resurrect her from the dead. She represents self-determination and courage in the face of calamity. She's an idea in human form."

"That doesn't sound so dangerous. Why can't I start with that?"

"Because it never ends there. It always starts with simple figures. Automatons to liven a lonely world. Servants are popular. They bring a sense of power and luxury that most of us lack in life. Farmers are another. Some find beauty in the untamed world while others find peace in seeing it subdued and put to productive use. In your case probably gardeners," Charles said with a wave of his arm that encompassed more than the garden courtyard. "A host of them to tend to all the things you've set to growing now that you've played with time. At some point though, everyone is tempted to create someone real. Whether it's the love they've lost, or the one they've never had. Or maybe its some well intentioned effort to manufacture the ideal. It almost always leads to tragedy."

Faith had thought one day to create her real father, but Charles' tone told her to keep that to herself. "I don't see how. I've already created animals that I've invested with life. I don't see the difference between them and people except the contours of their shapes."

"Have you though? Really created living beings, I mean. You said yourself, Helios is an embodiment of every noble thought. The cat is your idea of a cat. The deer that I see wandering by the lake are your ideal of deer. They don't fear people-"

"Why should they? No one here will harm them!"

"Faith, they don't fear people because you don't want them to. You want them to eat from your hand and follow you about like some fairy tale. And that's fine!" Charles said, grabbing and squeezing her hands. "It's your world to create as you choose. But don't fool yourself into thinking you have bestowed upon any of these creatures something like a soul."

Faith shook her head stubbornly. "Whether they have a soul, as you call it, or not, you have not objected to their creation. I still don't see how people are different."

"They just are. I don't know that I can explain to your satisfaction. People have an intrinsically stronger claim upon us. No matter how strong our feelings for an animal, even one of our own device, they pale in comparison to the feelings that are possible between two people. Remember your first efforts to draw the cat and how its deformities affected you? It is infinitely worse when we try to create another person. You feel every flaw as your own."

"But you can correct them, can't you?"

"You can, but before it drives you mad? And even if you did *correct* it, what have you achieved? Is it more beautiful? More devoted? More compliant? Is it more like what you want for another, or more like what you want for yourself? What is the measurement of perfection- when it makes you happy or when it makes itself happy? What happens when the two conflict?"

Faith pulled her hands away, "At the risk of sounding vain and self-serving, why should I be concerned about the happiness of a figment of my imagination? Obviously I would not create something just to make it live in torment. I understand how that would undermine my own spirit in turn, but if something is happy making me happy...?"

"Nothing is wrong with it if you have no higher expectations of something you create. Take Helios for example. The phoenix serves a purpose in your world, a purpose that would be undermined if it were capable of deciding it did not want to come to your aid. The problem with people is that the distinction is more easily blurred. We expect people to live and breath, to have ideas and motivations of their own. When we create them ourselves though, it is too easy to forget that there cannot be perfection without flaws. Without free will you have no life, you have nothing but an immaculate dupe. What good is it to have someone's undying devotion if you have done nothing to earn it?"

"Are you saying that no one should be creating people at all? An entire world, devoid of humans? That sounds lonely even to me."

"That's not what I'm saying. As always, it is a matter of intentions. The problem here is two fold. First is the danger of self-deception when setting those intentions. The second goes deeper than that. People have been known to lose themselves to Phantasia. The appeal is undeniable: a world you can design to your ideals of beauty and pleasure. When it comes to people, you can fill it with sycophants and lovers who never challenge, never question, never doubt. It's an easier existence than reality, one that is tempting never to leave. But, all the time you spend in Phantasia, a little of your soul gets left here. Spend too much time and you have nothing but an empty shell to return to. You end up trading real life and real relationships for a false existence."

"Is that what you are afraid of? That I will abandon myself to Phantasia and become some sort of ghost? Or do you still not believe that I have control over my thoughts and intentions?"

Charles gave her that searching look again. "Both."

"What?!"

Charles sighed. "You are too determined, too much in a rush to know everything all at once. If it weren't for the limits I set-"

"Which I have adhered to diligently!" Faith interrupted. Even when the Astors had decamped from the city to Hellgate, putting an end to their sittings at the Academy if her accident hadn't already, Faith had resisted the temptation to sneak off to her bedroom during the day and make up for the lost time. Instead, Faith had once again resorted to labor as a distraction, with the unintended consequence that her industry had endeared her to William more than any more feminine art could have.

"If it weren't for my limits," he repeated sternly, "you would not take such precautions on your own. You would only stop when you were too exhausted to continue and I don't think that you have an appreciation for how dangerous that is. You have learned too much, too quickly. It is the counterstroke to your immense Talent. You are technically proficient but you don't have the depth of experience to truly understand the consequences of your actions."

"I've made one mistake! Granted it was a big one, but everything I have done since then has been the epitome of purpose and self control." It was the cruelest irony that Charles could have no idea how much discipline it took to hide her deceptions, or her feelings for him. "What else would you ask of me before you believe I am ready to move on?"

"Patience."

"I don't have time for patience! The Colonel will be home in two months and I must be ready by then!" Faith's desperation made her reckless.

It made Charles angry. "I'll not compromise my judgement because you have imposed some arbitrary deadline to your studies. We've already discussed this. When your Da is Guild Master, it will be up to him what exceptions to make for your Talent." Charles punctuated his tirade with the

Colonel's letter. The letter slipped from his waving hand and slanted to the ground at Faith's feet.

Faith bit back a protest as she bent to pick it up. The moment she touched the letter, an impression of a fire-lit study and the layered smell of books, scotch, and cigars flitted across her senses. She did not spare a moment to dwell on the sensation. How could she tell Charles that once the Colonel took over, her chance to learn would be over? And that if Charles didn't agree to keep her secret, she would be cut off from the Ink altogether?

Faith looked at the folded parchment in her hands as she tried to think of a different angle of approach. It was addressed to All Masters, Guild of Athena, Citizens and Residents of the United States of America. The Colonel had not sent it to Charles alone, which meant it was unlikely to have included anything particular to her or their arrangement. She relaxed ever so slightly, though Charles' manner kept her wary. Faith held the letter out to him and softened her voice.

"All right. If it's not to be people, what will you teach me before he returns? What else do I have to learn that I need your guidance for?"

Charles rubbed his forehead and looked around. Fire and time had come easily to her. Mechanics like carriages and latches were a different matter. Faith had found them to be an all or nothing proposition. If she knew nothing except for the desired result, it was quite easy. If she knew a little about how something worked, Faith found she needed to understand the mechanism completely before it worked at all. Improvement there was a matter of practice; there was nothing more Charles could teach on the subject.

He made a frustrated noise and snatched the letter back. "You know there is little more I can teach you." He looked up at the sky, the moon arcing toward midheaven, as he considered in silence. At last there was a sigh and Faith knew she had won at least a partial victory. She kept her demeanor deferential nonetheless.

"I won't agree to you doing any people in Ink, not even almost humans like faerie folk or nymphs, but I will let you start the pencil studies. Before we worry about what's on the inside, I have to see you can get the outside right. I know you can do faces, but I doubt you have a good enough grasp on the rest. You'll need models to study."

Faith's internal exaltation was quickly followed by an illicit thrill at what sounded like a scandalous suggestion. "Live models?"

"Are you daft? Of course not. I think it would raise some eyebrows if you even tried to use the casts at the Academy. But, I do know a man with some very useful books. Lord knows I shouldn't introduce the two of you." He shook his head, clearly doubting the wisdom of his plan. "Come to the Academy tomorrow and I'll take you to see him."

"We are still at Hellgate. We won't be back to the city until Sunday."

"Monday then. Bring a market basket."

"For what?"

"We are going down to the shops for painting supplies. Tell the Astors the Colonel has asked in his letter that you pick up some things before his return."

"Pearl Street? By the docks?" Faith asked. It was an unsavory place. Who was he taking her to? "What do I do in the meantime?"

"Practice patience. And remember that I can take that pen away if I see fit, so you'd better resist the temptation to figure it out on your own."

Faith took an involuntary step back. "Charles, you can't!"

"I can and I will if you give me cause. It takes more than a castle and a crown to be a queen. It takes even more to be a god."

Man has no Body distinct from his Soul. For that called Body is a portion of Soul discerned by the five senses, the chief inlets of Soul in this age.

-William Blake, The Marriage of Heaven and Hell

CHAPTER TWENTY-FOUR
The Cold Cellar

Faith stood in the foyer of the Academy waiting for Charles. Once again, he was late. Her gaze wandered unseeing over the few visitors who had come to the exhibit. Apparently its initial popularity had waned. The Colonel would not be pleased with that.

Beyond this fleeting observation, all of Faith's attention was directed inwards at the tumult of emotions that had been worrying at her since she had last seen Charles in the garden courtyard. She was excited to meet the mysterious expert on the human form, but her enthusiasm was tempered by the agitation that Charles' words had sown in her thoughts.

While in church the day before, not listening to the sermon, Faith had contemplated what it meant to be a god in her world. The idea that Helios had no choice in its creation or purpose unsettled her. It was too much like the oppressive expectations and restrictions that weighed upon her in reality. She increasingly objected to the idea that she had been born to fill a purpose or perform a duty that was dictated by someone else, whether that someone was the faceless despot of societal mores or her step-father. In turn, Faith did not want to create things that were subservient to her whims, whether animal or human. But how, she wondered, did one bestow free will upon one's creations? How much control, how much stifling of one's own desires, did that require? Was she capable? And did she dare? God had given his creations free will. From what she understood of the matter, it had not gone well.

Her last meeting with Charles had upset Faith in more prosaic ways as well. His reserve following the incident with Leviathan, and the rejection that had preceded it, had already stung her sharply, but his demeanor in the courtyard had made her anxious. There was something in that letter that had upset Charles, and Faith could not shake the suspicion that it had something to do with her.

Most troubling was Charles' threat to take her pen. Faith's hand went instinctively to her knot of gathered hair, touching the pen that pierced it like a hairpin. It poked too awkwardly at the sides of the small reticule that hung at her wrist to carry it there, and she wanted to have it on hand. The wood was already changing with her use. The wood was still flat and buff colored, but faint vines of gold and silver had started to twine their way up the shaft. The subtle metallic glints made it resemble a decorative hairpin all the more. Reassured that the pen was still secure in her updo, she let her hand fall again. A small smile touched her lips at her cleverness in hiding it.

As she waited, Faith tried to reassure herself that Charles' mood might have had nothing to do with her or the Colonel's letter. As he had pointed out, he had concerns other than Faith and her training. Whatever the cause of Charles' short temper, Faith hoped it was resolved today. She missed their easy interaction and his open frankness.

When Faith heard Charles' voice at the top of the stairs, she turned up to him with a smile. It immediately soured when she saw the beautiful young woman he was escorting down. She had raven hair, skin like cream, and bright blue eyes. Charles was laughing, his own gray-green eyes crinkled at the corners. A lightning bolt of jealousy struck Faith. Perhaps she had been right that his withdrawal had nothing to with herself, and everything to do with him being in love with a different woman.

Faith spun quickly away, avoiding eye contact as she ducked into the shadows beneath the staircase. The last thing she wanted was an introduction. She heard them pass by, letting her eyes follow their backs out the door. When Charles had seen the woman off, he found Faith in the foyer.

"Who was that?" Faith asked, unable to take the distaste our of her voice.

"Miss Ann Low. She is a client, Faith. I do need to make a living, particularly after having spent so much time on your sitting."

"I'm sorry I put you in such a difficult position. She is very beautiful. I'm sure you enjoyed the sitting."

"She is. And it does make the task more pleasant," he answered mildly, refusing to take her bait. "Are you ready?"

Faith sat primly in the carriage, hands folded in her lap. She had been determined not to show one whit of emotion the entire day to prove her discipline. That plan was ruined by the scowl she could feel upon her face. The only small consolation, if it could be called consoling, was that Charles seemed more amused than irritated. Was it the Ink or Charles that had undone a lifetime of practice disguising her true feelings? Whichever, she was going to be in trouble when the Colonel returned if she did not get the skill back.

Faith watched the brightly sunlit world slide by outside. There was the barest hint of spring in the air. The remaining snow was shiny and pockmarked, and puddles filled the dips in the streets. The buildings got older and closer as they neared the docks. Shortly after they turned past the Battery, the carriage came to a stop in front of the colorman's shop.

"We are actually shopping? Or is your man inside?" Faith inquired.

"Shopping. I need some supplies and you'd best purchase something as well to cover for our outing."

As Charles considered his selections, Faith ordered a pound of flake white and a pint of walnut oil. When their purchases had been settled, they left the colorman to wrap them and walked up the street.

Faith looked about curiously. It was not often she saw this part of town. She marveled at the diversity of character and class that surrounded her, from the sun darkened longshoremen at the docks to the brightly liveried servants on errand, from the greasy peddlers to the smart shopkeepers just visible behind their glass.

Ahead of them on the street was a strange character who stood out even among this motley crew. He wore an elaborate coat, trimmed in shiny black fur, a top hat, and was accompanied by two of the largest dogs Faith had ever seen. The cane he carried in one hand was clearly for show as he walked with a jaunty step, a market basket swinging from his elbow. Faith pointed out the man to Charles as a curiosity. Charles' expression was pained.

"That," he said, "is who we have come to see."

They hurried their pace and caught up to him as he paused at the corner of the next block.

"Jarvis!" Charles called. The man stopped short, his basket swinging wildly, and the two dogs stopped with him. He turned on his heel, the tail of the coat billowing out. "Charlie!" he shouted, holding out his arms. Every eye on the street turned to see the commotion and just as quickly turned away again. *Charlie? This is Jarvis?* Faith's curiosity was more than piqued.

The two men shook hands before Jarvis turned his attention to Faith with mischief in his eye. The dogs sat patiently next to the market basket, their heads even with her chest. Charles made the introduction.

"Miss Faith Trumbull, this is Mr. John Jarvis."

"Ah, Miss Trumbull!" Jarvis exclaimed. "The esteemed Colonel's daughter. Or," he dropped his voice to a conspiratorial whisper, "should I say the soon-to-be Guild Master's daughter? I am delighted to make your acquaintance," Jarvis said as he gave an elaborate bow, knocking his hat off his head such that it rolled down his arm and into his waiting hand. Faith had no idea how to respond to such a greeting, but a deep curtsy seemed the only response equal to such a performance. Jarvis smiled, seeming to enjoy what she assumed was a startled look on her face.

"And this is Rex and Ulysses," he said pointing first to the all black dog and then to the black and white harlequin. Faith curtsied to the dogs as well. "Pleased to meet you gentlemen," she said. The dogs panted uninterestedly but Jarvis grinned.

"She'll do," he said nudging Charles in the ribs.

After Jarvis had replaced the hat on his head, he leaned toward Faith, his voice low once again. "Charlie here tells me you are interested in knowing more about the human body."

Flustered by the vaguely inappropriate nature of this statement, Faith replied, "Yes, just for drawing though."

"That's what they all say!" Jarvis whispered before he stood back up laughing. "Of course! Just for drawing. Follow me!"

Jarvis led them back to the Battery and up the steps of the Customs House. His canine companions loped up beside him and followed him through the front doors. Feeling as though she had stepped into a pocket of Phantasia, Faith smiled at the absurdity of two giant dogs trotting through the Customs House. Apparently, Jarvis lived in a wing on the second floor.

They topped the stairs and Jarvis fitted his key to the lock on the door. He turned it with a click and tried the handle. It was still locked. He studied the door for a moment before brightening.

"Oh, I forgot, I never locked it in the first place." He turned the key again, unlocking the door. The dogs trotted inside while Jarvis held the door for Faith. She paused in the doorway as the scene within greeted her. She had never seen such total chaos in a living space. There were two easels set up, both with portraits in various stages of completion. There were several palettes and mortars near the easels. Brushes abounded, some wet and some dried with paint, surely ruined, sitting upright in cups, others balanced on the edge of the palette, and one lying flat on a table, its bristles hanging off into the air. Compared to the strict regimen and precisely ordered equipment the Colonel used, Faith wondered how Jarvis got anything done.

Jarvis invited her to have a seat while he got some refreshments. Faith looked around her. There were a few chairs and some small side tables but every surface and much of the floor was covered with books, papers, and dishes.

"Where?" she asked.

"Indeed, where?" he said stroking his chin and looking around at the mess as though seeing it for the first time. "I wonder who left this place in such a state."

"Do you share it with someone?" Faith asked.

"Oh no, it's just me and my manservant. I really do get tired of cleaning up after him though," he said with apparent seriousness.

"Where *is* Tom?" Charles asked as Jarvis' eye swept the room.

"Gave him the day off. Least I could do after keeping him up all night. You left early."

"It was two in the -" Charles broke off as he caught Faith's pointedly questioning look. He gave her a guilty smile.

Jarvis saw what passed between them and chuckled.

"This looks like a good spot," he said and strode to a chair, lifting the pile of books and paper and dropping them unceremoniously onto the floor. Faith walked over, trying to avoid stepping on anything and sat with as much dignity as being presented at court.

"Judging by your accent, Miss Trumbull, I bet that you like tea. Shall I get some?"

"Only if it's no trouble," she replied.

"Hmmm," he said thinking. "I'm not sure what has become of the kettle. It may still have shaving soap in it as the cup I usually use had beer in it this morning. How about some champagne instead?"

"Champagne?" Faith repeated. She was only allowed to drink champagne on very special occasions, which were particularly rare mid-afternoon.

"Yes, that does sound good. Let me just pop into the cold cellar," Jarvis said, heading back towards the kitchen.

"Cold cellar?" she asked in confusion. "How can you have a cellar on the second floor?"

Charles called out, "Wait, Jarvis, don't..."

Faith could clearly see into the kitchen from her vantage point. Jarvis walked to a tall narrow canvas leaning against the back wall. It was probably about six feet tall and two or three feet wide. On it was painted a simple wooden door. Exactly the kind that would lead to a cellar.

Given her training with the Ink, Faith was not especially surprised when he reached out and pulled the door open. What did astonish her was when he stepped right into the painting and disappeared down a set of steps. Her mouth agape, she listened to him rummage around below. She heard a bump, muffled curses and a crash, and after a little more scuffling, Faith heard him come back up the stairs. Bit by bit, he appeared above the lower edge of the canvas until he stepped back out into the kitchen carrying a dusty, green glass bottle. He rummaged around for some glasses, blowing in them to scatter any dust or other debris and wiping their rims on his jacket.

The cork popped like a bottle of champagne and the gold liquid bubbled and sparkled like champagne, but Faith wondered if it really was. Surely, it was just Ink. He couldn't possibly store real bottles inside a painting. Or could he? Up until a moment ago, she would have said no one could walk into a painting either.

"Is it real?" she asked.

"You injure me, Miss Trumbull. Of course it's real. Vanderlyn brought me a case last time he came back from France."

Faith looked at Charles for confirmation. He nodded.

They toasted the Guild and Phantasia and Faith gingerly sipped the champagne. It was deliciously cool and crisp. The bubbles tickled her lips and tongue.

"It calls for strawberries, does it not?," Jarvis added after taking a sip of his own, "It's too bad they are out of season. I could draw some up, but I think real Champagne requires real fruit. As it happens, I had just picked up oranges fresh in from Spain. Where is that basket?"

"You left it in the hall. I set it inside the door," Charles told him, standing to get it.

"Thank you Charlie! Let's see how oranges get on with Champagne."

The three of them sat for a few moments sipping champagne and peeling oranges amidst the vortex of debris while Rex and Ulysses napped, lying upside down in a patch of sunlight by the window. Jarvis dropped his peels on the floor while Faith set hers on an empty plate near her feet. She was thankful for the moments of silence. She could not have conversed while her mind spun with the possibilities of being able to walk physically into Phantasia. Could her pen do that, or was that one of the mysterious differences between Journeyman and Master pens that Charles had alluded to? If so, she was no longer content just to be a Journeyman.

After awhile, conversation did begin. Jarvis told hilarious stories that had Faith equal parts entertained and scandalized until Charles reminded Jarvis of the reason for their visit.

"Ah, yes!" Jarvis exclaimed and went scrounging through piles of books next to one of the easels. When he couldn't find what he was looking for, he stopped and thought for a moment. Snapping his fingers he said, "This looks about the right size," and picked up a book in front of him. He walked over to a small table. Lifting the edge of the table, he pulled out the book that had been supporting one leg and replaced it with the one in his hand.

"When I first came to this city," he said, "I didn't know a thing about painting portraits, but I thought the other painters were so bad -this was when your father was in England of course-, that I figured I must be able to do better than they. I did all right for a time, but when a doctor friend gave me this book, the sun really came out."

Faith took the proffered book and read its cover. *Human anatomy and movement: With a special emphasis on musculoskeletal and cranial features.* Not exactly a snappy title. She opened the book to reveal scientific drawings of skulls and facial muscles with skin stripped away. Flipping further, the whole body was represented with drawings of skeletons, with and without muscles, positioned in various ways. It was disturbing but fascinating at the same time.

"Where did they get this information?" Faith asked.

"Dead people."

Faith decided it was more disturbing than fascinating.

"And this will help?"

"You see my dear, a little knowledge is a dangerous thing. You are better off knowing nothing. Ignorance truly is bliss in Phantasia. But once you know a little, you have to know everything to make it work. Take faces for example. If you were as ignorant as a babe, you could draw up your mother's face just by the sights and smells and sounds you associate with her without knowing a thing else. But by now, you have been tainted with knowledge. You know that we all have eyes and ears and a nose, and yet we all look different. And so we struggle to get the likeness just right. When you understand what's truly under the skin, that's when you can really capture a person."

Faith saw Charles give Jarvis a stern look, as though warning him he was going too far. Faith was sure there was some meaning in Jarvis' words beyond what she was hearing, but she didn't know what.

Faith nodded and thanked him for the book. In any event, it was source material that she could use without exposing herself to ridicule and shame.

Jarvis looked at her then with a serious expression. "Be sure you have this down in regular media before you attempt to Ink. Only when you can draw the form without a thought can you devote your attention to what is in the heart and mind."

"Yes, I will. Thank you, Mr. Jarvis," she said, chilled by the sober tone from an otherwise flippant character. "When should I get it back to you?"

"Just call me Jarvis," he said, the twinkle back in his eye. "Keep it as long as you need. I have it all up here," he said, pointing to his own head. Faith smiled. With a mind as chaotic as his living space, she wasn't sure how much help that was.

"We should be getting back," Charles suggested, "or the colorman will have closed up and Mrs. Astor will be wondering what has happened to us."

Faith stood to go, clutching the book to her chest.

"Thank you very much Jarvis. I have enjoyed meeting you and I hope to see you again soon. In the meantime though, and if we should meet again, I would ask that you not mention our visit or the reason for it to anyone. I'm sure Charles has told you that I'm hoping to surprise the Colonel. I would hate for him to find out from someone else and ruin the surprise."

"Talk to who?" Jarvis answered. "About what? Who are you and what have you done to my house? Out! Out, you vandals!" he said, shooing them towards the door with a hearty laugh. As Faith passed him going out he took her by the elbow. He opened the cover of the anatomy book and slipped a slim paperbound volume within it. "One is for the bodies, the other for the soul. Where one fails, the other endures," Jarvis said with an enigmatic smile.

When a girl ceases to blush, she has lost the most powerful charm of beauty.

- Dr. John Gregory, A Father's Legacy to his Daughters

CHAPTER TWENTY-FIVE

The Rogue

As the carriage rumbled back up Broadway towards the Astor's, Faith resisted the urge to see what Jarvis had tucked into the anatomy book. Something told her Charles would not approve. A part of her regretted that Jarvis had not been her mentor all along. Certainly not the part that had fallen in love with Charles, but the part that was guilty she had tricked him into training her. Jarvis did not seem the kind to be particularly troubled by rules and courtesies. What had the Colonel called him?

"Charles, do you think the Colonel knows about Jarvis' cold cellar?" Faith asked.

Charles shifted in his seat. "Why do you ask?"

"He once called Jarvis 'a rogue with a door'. I'm wondering if that was what he meant."

Charles snorted with laughter. "It's an apt description to be sure, but no, he did not have that door in mind. Nor was he referring to his eccentric behavior."

"What did he mean then?"

Charles considered what to say before shaking his head with a sharp exhalation. "I suppose Jarvis has let the cat out of the bag so there's no use trying to put it back. When an artist becomes a Master in the Guild, he is given more than just his pen and Ink. There are a few trifles, like the seal and things for official correspondence." Those were something Faith wanted to know more about as well, but she did not interrupt. "The most important is that each Master is given a doorway in the Guild Hall that opens directly from his world. It's how we get to the Hall for meetings, and a way for the Guild to keep a check on those who might be misusing the Ink. When your Da said Jarvis had a door, he wasn't referring to Jarvis' cellar- though for all I know that might be how he gets to the Guild Hall. All your Da meant was that he was a Master."

"The Guild Hall is in Phantasia?" When Charles had mentioned the Guild Hall, Faith had envisioned a physical edifice much like the Academy, only in Paris or Rome perhaps, without considering that Masters from all over the world would have to journey to it. It seemed obvious now that it would be in Phantasia. "That only makes sense, but where? Whose world is it in?"

"DaVinci's. He created it."

Faith felt her eyes go wide. The great man himself! "Extraordinary! Can you leave the Guild Hall and have a look about? What must his world be like!"

"I've had an amble or two. It is... intriguing. He was an eccentric fellow himself."

Faith sighed. "I can only imagine."

"Indeed," Charles answered dryly.

A tantalizing thought popped into Faith's mind. "Is that where they store the Ink?" They must have it on hand, at least for whatever ceremony attended newly made Masters.

"It is," Charles said, shifting in his seat again. His face and tone were suddenly guarded. "Under more than lock and key."

Noting Charles' wariness, Faith looked out the window so he could not see her keen interest in where the Ink was kept. If she could find a way to access it herself, she could circumvent the Guild entirely. She had no doubt they guarded it well, but she was sure she could find a way. First, she would need to get into the Hall itself. She let a few moments of silence pass.

Still looking out the window, Faith asked, "These doorways into the Hall, are they like Jarvis' cellar door?"

"If you mean just a painting of a door, no. They are usually well hidden, deep in some other 'scape."

Now Faith turned to face him. "No, I was just wondering if you stepped bodily into Phantasia? It must be such a peculiar sensation!"

"That it is. But, it's rare enough that anyone does it. Anyone but Jarvis that is. Most of us only enter Phantasia in our minds, like you and I have been doing. Going physically presents its own complications. It's only for the most particular occasions."

Like the foundation of a new chapter and the elevation of its Guild Master, Faith thought to herself. Faith wanted to know more, more about the complications and where Charles had hidden his own portal to the Guild, but she did not want to rouse Charles' suspicions any more than absolutely necessary. She shifted to what she hoped was a less closely guarded secret.

"Then how is it that you can send and receive mail so quickly amongst the Masters? I thought, when you mentioned it just now, that being in Phantasia was the answer to that mystery, but if you seldom go in bodily, there must be another way."

"Mirrors."

"Yes, you said that the other evening, but I don't understand."

Faith noted with relief that the tension around Charles' eyes eased ever so slightly..

"Honestly, I'm not sure I do myself. Mirrors have peculiar properties when it comes to Phantasia. Some aspects of the imaginary world are, quite literally, reflections of reality. For those things, mirrors are some kind of threshold between the two."

"You aren't suggesting we can pass into Phantasia through a mirror?" Faith asked. As unlikely as it sounded, what she had already learned and witnessed about Phantasia had taught her nearly anything was possible.

He shook his head emphatically though. "Not at all! Nothing real can pass through a mirror. It would shatter just as you'd expect. But the reflection in the mirror, particularly when Ink is involved, now that's a different matter."

Faith frowned in confusion. Charles took a breath and leaned forward in an effort to explain.

"If you took that book, written in ordinary ink" he said, pointing at the anatomy book on her lap, "into Phantasia, carried it physically in through Jarvis' cellar door, the writing in it would stay exactly as you expect. But then, if you were to write in that book while you were there, in *our* Ink, when you came back out, you'd find the words reversed. A mirror image. The same would be true of anything written in Ink on this side of reality. If you took it into Phantasia, it would be reversed."

Faith's first thought was the Colonel's letter that Charles had dropped in the courtyard of her world. The writing had been direct, not retrograde. But then the memory of the night she had learned about the Ink burst upon her thoughts. She had thought the Colonel had been writing in some secret cipher. Now, at least that small part made sense! She might still call it a cipher, but he had been writing backwards, Inked letters intended to be read in Phantasia. And, she remembered, the folding mirror.

"What part does the mirror play?" she asked.

"That's even harder to explain. I suppose the first answer is that it's not so easy to learn to write in reverse- at least in the mirror you can check that you're doing it right. The more complicated explanation is that if the creation of something in Ink, like a letter, is captured in a mirror's reflection, that image is, well, captured." Charles ran his hand through his hair, a rumpled lock falling over his forehead as he searched for the right words. "The image, the reflection I mean, then exists somewhere between reality and Phantasia, whatever realm or plane is the domain of mirrors. It can then be sent, more or less instantaneously, to any other mirror and retrieved at the other end."

Faith rubbed her forehead as a vision flashed in her mind of hundreds of letters, confined to passages the thickness of a pane of glass, sliding along an invisible network connected by each earthly mirror. It seemed a wonder she had never seen one fly across her own reflection. Or perhaps she had and simply failed to register the improbable. And what of her reflection? Could it shoot between mirrored worlds and take a piece of her consciousness with it? She asked Charles as much and he shook his head.

"Not unless you were made of Ink," he said.

"How do the letters get to their destination?"

"Do you have to ask?"

"Intention," Faith said, knowing the answer. "But when I travel in my world, I have to know where I am going. If I don't know where the recipient is, how can I send something to them?"

"That's the exceptionally bizarre part. The mirrors seem to know."

"That's the part you find bizarre? The whole thing is like a torture rack for the mind. I know mine feels stretched to its limits." Faith's fingers moved to her temples. The Colonel's letter had been addressed to all Masters in the United States. Now that she thought about it, a simple mirror knowing which were Masters and where they currently resided was a particularly strange phenomenon. They could not be simple mirrors.

"Does it work with any mirror?"

Charles' eyebrows shot up. "Honestly, I've never tried. The mirrors are part of the kit the Guild gives to Masters, with instruction on how to use them, but not on how they're made. Perhaps they have been marked in some way. Only the High Council would know. All I know of it is that I pen the letter in Ink before the mirror, address and stamp it, and off it goes."

Faith let her fingers fall and leaned back in her seat. She was suddenly exhausted from the day's revelations, the gears of her mind grinding under the strain. New paths and possibilities had been illuminated, a way to secure the power of the Ink for her own without threat of the Colonel, the Guild, or even Charles taking it from her, but for now the glare was too bright to see the way clearly. She promised herself that there would be time enough later, if only she did not forget anything. She let her mind wander back over their conversation, absorbing it without trying to understand it. When she got back to the beginning, she remembered that Charles had agreed Jarvis was a rogue, but not for his manners.

Without sitting up, Faith asked, "What's a rogue?"

Charles' reaction was something between a smile and a grimace. "You mean Jarvis? As you might imagine, Jarvis came by his Ink in, let's say, unconventional ways. He trained here in the States, rather than under the British Guild. To many with proper Guild training like your Da, that makes him a rogue."

"I don't understand. I thought the Guild held tighter control of the Ink than that. How is it possible that he was able to train without Guild permission and then become a Master anyway?" Faith wished she'd have known the answer to that months ago.

"Some Master's are more cavalier about the rules than their oaths to the Guild might imply. Jarvis' mentor was one. You could say I have joined those ranks." All hints of a smile disappeared from Charles' face, leaving only a scowl. Faith's heart hammered with slow dread. She wanted to know what oath he thought he had broken, but was too afraid to ask.

"What happens to those who break the rules?" she asked instead, her stomach like lead.

Charles looked out the window. "It's a matter of discretion. At best, censure or a fine. At worst, termination."

"Execution?!"

Charles' eyes met hers for a moment. "Not typically," he said with an unsettling shrug before his eyes slid away again. "I meant being cut off from the Ink, excommunicated from the Guild, if you will. I can imagine it's a fate worse than death, but it's rare that they go so far"

"Why is that?" Faith sat forward in her seat. If termination was unusual, maybe she had reason to hope.

"Each Master might differ, but what the Guild as a whole values most, above and beyond the Ink itself, is authority. You might assume then, that they would brook no contempt and come down hard on the smallest indiscretion. Really though, they can't always afford to be so heavy handed. They don't want to risk driving a rogue to ground. The Guild won't admit it officially, but there are rumors of rebel groups formed by those who have been cast out. An angry rebel with a vendetta against the Guild is almost its worst nightmare."

"Almost? What could be worse?"

"True rogues. These days, anyone with Talent who operates outside the Guild is called a rogue, but the term was originally used for those rare individuals with such profound Talent that they are, essentially, a source unto themselves. They are the ultimate threat to the Guild's authority because they cannot be cut off. It's ironic really. If daVinci were alive today, he'd be considered a rogue, criminalized instead of venerated," Charles said with a derisive snort.

"Is Jarvis a true rogue?"

Charles chuckled, still turned away. "He's exceptional but not like that."

"Are there any alive today?" Faith asked keeping her voice casual. If the Colonel did threaten to cut her off, she wanted to know where to find other sources. Somehow Charles read her mind. He finally looked at her, eyes narrowed.

"I only know of one for sure. He's the author of that other book Jarvis slipped to you as we left." Faith's eyes went wide. Charles gestured, inviting her to look at it. Faith pulled open the anatomy book's cover to reveal a slim, paperbound volume with a hand colored cover. At the top, a couple walked beneath bare trees whose branches pulled and twisted as in a great wind. At the bottom, another couple embraced across an abyss, one supported by clouds, the other bathed in fire. *The Marriage of Heaven and Hell*. There was no author on the cover. Faith looked up curiously.

"William Blake." The name seemed vaguely familiar. An Englishman. Someone the Colonel had spoken of, and not kindly. "He's what you might call a mad genius. If he's not being accused of blasphemy. That's one surprise your Da won't like, so you'd best keep it well hidden. Neither heaven nor hell will help you out if he sees that, I'd wager."

Faith swallowed. When she worked up enough spit to speak, she said, "If the Guild is afraid to punish these rogues, what do they do?"

"If they aren't a threat, the Guild's preference is always control. They bring them into the fold if they can. Jarvis was wild but not dangerous so they made him an official Master. Not to control him- God knows that would be a thankless task- so much as to know what shenanigans he's up to. Blake is more controversial. The Council was split on him. His views are too subversive for many, but Guild Master West is a generous and tolerant man and stood for him. They came to an agreement. Blake's not a Master, but he has agreed to certain limitations and the Guild agreed to let him be if he adhered to them."

"It's good to know they can be reasonable." The knot in Faith's stomach would have loosened if Charles' manner were less grim. "If they can't or won't be brought into the fold, though, what then?"

Charles turned away again. "They'll stop at nothing to have control," he said to the window glass.

Faith's breath snagged in her throat. "Execution?"

Charles' silence was all the confirmation she needed.

The silence stretched as the carriage traversed the next few blocks. Faith wanted to find hope in what Charles had said. The Colonel might not want women in the Guild, but she could hardly be seen as much of a threat to its authority over the Ink. She was no true rogue, and her training could not have been more unorthodox than Jarvis'. If they had made their peace with him, there was hope that she could as well. After all, she was a British citizen by birth and heritage. Perhaps Guild Master West would stand for her too. And yet, Charles' morose demeanor had her insides in a tumble. They would be at the Astor's in moment.

"Charles, please. What is bothering you?"

He did not respond immediately, only clasping his hands together and looking down at them. When he finally raised his gaze to hers, there was a smile on his lips but it did not reach his eyes.

"I have a lot on my mind, that is all. I do not wish to trouble you with it."

"I don't want you to hide from me. I want to go back to the way things were... before." Faith hesitated to name that momentous evening that had been equal parts bliss and terror. "If you're in love with someone else, just tell me. I just want us to be friends again." Faith's eyes stung with burgeoning tears but she blinked them back.

"I am not," he said with a small but genuine smile, "I promise I will tell you when the time is right. But, now, you must go away."

"Away? But, when will I see—" The carriage lurched to a stop. This time Charles' eyes crinkled at the corners.

"I meant this is your stop. I will be gone for a few days, but I will leave a note on the tea tray to let you know when I am back. That doesn't mean I won't pop in unexpectedly, so be on your best behavior and don't let Jarvis' books carry you away." The footman opened the door and Charles stepped out first to hand Faith down. He spoke quietly in her ear, his breath warm on her neck. "Practice people and patience. *No Ink.*"

Charles waited by the carriage until the house door had been opened. By the time Faith turned to wave goodbye, her answer was the crunch of wheels on gravel as Charles was carried away.

* * *

Faith spent the next few weeks in a near constant blush. With the exception of Classical sculpture, Faith realized that she had never seen a real man in less than his shirtsleeves. When she had drawn men in the past, they were nothing but arrangements of clothing with a head nestled on top. As ready as she had thought herself to be, she had to admit at least to herself, that if she had tried to Ink men without the benefit of Jarvis' book, she would have created nothing but animated, empty suits of armor. That there were muscles, sinews, and *appendages* under that clothing came as something of a shocking revelation.

As though that weren't enough in itself to put her modesty in a tizzy, the Blake work was a spiritual cartwheel that turned every notion of the sundry and divine on its head. In truth, Faith understood few of the passages and grasped at the rest, but even that was enough to know it was every bit as scandalous as Charles had said. The principle idea was that Good and Evil were united in all men, not by the mechanisms of creation and original sin, but inherently, such that there was no path to righteousness that did not include the Evil body and its desires. When Blake described the Body as a construct of the five senses, themselves the embodiment of the Soul, she knew he was talking about the experience of the Ink. Or was he referring to reality? In his mind, the two seemed switched, Phantasia the true expression of Body and Soul while "reality" was its weak reflection.

Above all, the most enthralling part was when Blake bargained with an Angel to compare the pleasantness of their respective fates. With the Angel in attendance, Blake was shown a hell-scape of smoke and fire as his eternal reward. When Leviathan rose from the flaming sea of Blake's vision, Faith closed the book in sympathetic alarm. When she later summoned the courage to keep reading, the Angel fled in fear of the demon, leaving Blake to his doom. And yet, once the Angel left, taking its self-righteous condemnation with it, Blake found himself in a paradise of his own construction. Was he suggesting that the contours of the Eternal Reward were not determined by piety and deeds but, like Phantasia, a matter of belief and expectation? Or, more shocking still, were Heaven and Hell Phantasia itself?

Faith read and re-read, searching for understanding. One thing she knew for certain was that the Colonel would pop like a stoppered kettle if he were to read it. That only served to recommend it in Faith's estimation. Even so, it set her mind awhirl and kept her cheeks a rosy pink.

All of her studies were, of course, by night. As promised, Charles had returned several days later and, as promised, he seemed much more his usual self, though the restless melancholy was not entirely gone. The bright energy of burgeoning spring offering an easy excuse for a long walk, they arranged to meet in person during the day, midway between the house and the Academy, for Charles to check her un-Inked work. She observed with sinister delight Charles' own deep flush and discomfiture at her female nudes and took it as confirmation of her success. Men took her longer to finesse, but after a couple weeks of work and more blushing on both their parts, he finally gave her permission to Ink a human-like figure.

After a lengthy interview, he had agreed to let her start with a care-taker for her gardens. She had wanted fairies, arguing that they were not truly human would present few of the risks he had warned about. Although she had promised they would be the impish but generally harmless and fully clothed kind, rather than the ones that stole people into hidden worlds, Charles had objected. It was as though he could read Faith's mind toying dangerously with the idea of hidden worlds within her world. In the end, she had no bargaining power. She agreed to whatever he would permit.

So employed, the nights had passed quickly, up to the time of the Colonel's anticipated return. Faith was determined that she would find ways to continue her studies, and one way or another would acquire a Master pen of her own, but she resigned herself that the freedom she had so far enjoyed was at its end. As the mid-point of March approached, she hid away the books and drawings, except one, in her trunk so they would not be discovered by accident in the confusion of a hasty packing.

When the Colonel's return became overdue, Faith found herself as restless and nervous as after a month at sea. Looking for a numbing distraction, she had offered to relieve Mrs. Astor of her bookkeeping and had been accepted gratefully. In the background, Eliza was practicing a love song she planned to perform at the Easter Ball the Astor's would be hosting at Hellgate to celebrate the end of Lent. In keeping with the Astor's love of music, there would be a number of professional performances and Eliza was determined to be give a good showing among them. She had been singing nearly non stop for a week and there were two weeks to go. She had a pleasant voice and decent pitch, so it could have been worse, but the syrupy lyrics and repetition were wearing thin.

A sour note followed by silence brought Faith's full awareness back to the room. Faith looked up to see Eliza taking a drink and clearing her throat. When she turned back, she felt William's eyes on her from the desk where he worked. He had stopped writing and was watching her with unusual intensity. Faith found herself biting at the inside of her cheek.

"Is something wrong?" she asked with veiled irritation.

"No. Quite the contrary. Your walks agree with you." He frowned and looked down. Faith thought she saw his cheeks coloring. She realized with a start that he was flustered. She had not thought him capable of the emotion. "Perhaps you will permit me to walk with you today?" he finally asked with a bashful glance.

Faith nearly choked on her response. She was supposed to meet Charles, but could not think of any excuse to go alone that would not give offense. "That would be lovely. Thank you," she forced out.

When they had finished their work and had a light lunch, Faith returned to her room to dress for her walk. The sun had recuperated from its long illness, caressing the land with unveiled warmth, but the wind still pried with cold fingers. Faith shrugged into a warm pelisse and grabbed her gloves. She frowned as she hefted her reticule, feeling the weight of her sketchbook within. With a muttered curse she pulled it out. She would not be able to show her newest drawings to Charles with William around, so best not to have it with her. She lifted up the folded shifts and nightdresses in her trunk, followed by the lining she had loosened and slipped the book on top of her other contraband.

William joined her in the foyer and they set out. At the street, there was a moment's indecision on which way to go. Faith turned instinctively towards the Academy and Charles, but William rightly suggested that going through the park to the river would be more pleasant. With a silent prayer that Charles would understand why she stood him up, Faith gave in and walked with William towards the river.

The air was clear and soft, the sky bright cerulean, the clouds a blinding white. The front gardens of the houses that they passed were showing signs of life. Green blades and pink flushed leaves were emerging in the beds. Only Faith's house, shuttered and empty these many months, still hibernated. She spared it an uneasy glance as they passed by, but was soon distracted by the sense of nascent life that filled the park between the house and the river.

Snowdrops and bright hyacinths had broken winter's spell and scented spring's cool breeze. Fat, swelling buds set like jewels in prongs of chartreuse sprigs lined every branch and twig. Birds flitted from tree to earth, snatching newly wakened life from the warming soil. They chirped and chitted excitedly. Faith imagined she could feel the pulse of the earth and the flow of sap within the trees. The air seemed to vibrate with pent up energy, ready to erupt in vernal exuberance. It was as though Demeter rejoiced two-fold at Persephone's imminent return after the previous year's missed reunion.

Even William was not immune to the feeling of vitality that permeated all about them. He spoke with uncharacteristic animation, in part about the weather. If not its beauty, then its prospects for the family business. Faith listened as they reached the river, paused and headed back toward the house. She commented when necessary, eyes fixed on the road ahead. As they neared Faith's house again, a carriage swung into view.

The carriage angled to the curb and came to a stop. Dread clutched Faith by the heart as the footman swung down and opened the door. The Colonel stepped out.

For the first time in weeks, Faith's cheeks were white as snow.

CHAPTER TWENTY-SIX
The Proposal

The Colonel was a man of military and Puritanical precision. He rose, ate, and retired at precisely regular times each day and expected his household to do the same. After three months of late nights, late mornings, and idle days with the Astors, returning home was a shock to Faith's system. Not only were there the usual household chores, with no bevy of servants to tend to them, but there were the added tasks of restoring a home which had been unused for so long. Dust and cobwebs had to be cleared, while the pile of laundry miraculously redoubled every night. The temporary position their cook had taken in their absence had turned permanent. Faith and her mother spent half their days in the kitchen until the Colonel found a suitable replacement. Drained and desperately in need of sleep to prepare for the next day's work, Faith had not had a single moment in Phantasia since their return, not even in dream.

Even if she had been better rested, the warmth of the church packed with Easter faithful and the drone of the sermon wove a soporific spell that had Faith dozing upright in the pew. A sharp squeeze of her hand brought Faith awake again. She gave a grateful sidelong glance at her mother. Sarah's eyes remained on the pulpit, but a gentler squeeze of Faith's hand acknowledged her reassuringly.

The comfort Faith took from her mother's presence, now that she had returned, had caught Faith by surprise. Although the trip had been their first extended separation, Faith had not thought she missed her. So often indisposed by drink or bitterness, or both, Sarah had been little more than a disembodied presence in an upstairs room, more apparition than mother. Now that she had returned, they had worked side by side, recalling the quiet contentment that Faith had captured in a drawing of a fuchsia what seemed like years before. Whether baking bread or crafting the flowers that adorned their Easter bonnets, they often worked in companionable silence. When they did speak, particularly out of earshot of the Colonel, Faith found a smile chasing her lips at her mother's pragmatic and unfiltered observations about everything from the way Mrs. Wadsworth ran her D.C. household to the absurdity of holding the inauguration outside on a platform in the open air because Congress could not agree on how to conduct an indoor ceremony. As her mother described the burned out hulks of buildings that were still left from the British depredations, Faith detected more than a little perverse pride and satisfaction.

The Colonel, for his part, had been in high spirits. Looking past her mother, Faith could see his self-satisfied profile. It was no wonder why. The rotunda commission had provided the long-sought public validation he so desired, while the deposit for it had eased his financial concerns. He was finally, officially, the president of the American Academy of Fine Art, which, as he predicted, had indeed purchased a number of his paintings for permanent exhibit. And, in a matter of days, he was about to become the first Guild Master of a new American Guild of Athena. Riding a cresting wave of success had made him more gracious and equanimous than she had ever seen him. It almost gave her hope that she might win him over with a display of her Talent and earn his blessing on her bid for Mastery. Almost.

In spite of the Colonel's uncharacteristically liberal mood, Faith herself felt no such laxity. She felt like she was being watched even when he was not present; any time his gaze fell on her, Faith feared he would somehow see her secrets laid bare. She felt so different inside, no longer the meek and love-starved child who had only wanted to please him, it was hard to imagine that it did not show on the outside. Faith worried that her ability to hide her true feelings behind a demure mask had slipped. She half-hoped it had, pathetic as her old self seemed now.

And yet, she feared discovery. Not out of guilt for deceiving him; the only measure of that emotion was for Charles alone. The Colonel had lied to her about women having the Talent. It was only fitting that she should return the favor. As emboldened as Faith felt, if she were honest with herself, it was confrontation with the Colonel that she dreaded. That, and the consequences. In the light of day, she cleaved to the prospect that the Guild would see reason even if the Colonel did not. In the fearful dark of night, she agonized over what would happen to her, and what would happen to Charles, if her scheme were discovered.

When the Easter service ended, Faith stood with relief and shuffled out of church with the rest of the throng. Once outside, bright sunlight began to melt her grogginess. What remained was quickly dissipated by the energy of the crowd about her as they promenaded up Broadway with what seemed the entire population of the city. Ladies in their finest dresses and bonnets had turned out to see and be seen. People laughed and waved, walked and gawked, calling out to friends and strangers alike.

Too poor for real flowers when she was younger, Faith's mother had learned to make false blooms that were the envy of the real. With sheets of brightly colored paper, she and Faith had adorned their naked hats and prayed that it wouldn't rain. A gust of wind lifted the brim, but there was not a cloud in sight. Faith raised a hand to resettle her hat, careful not to crush the red and yellow roses that clustered around the crown. Standing on tiptoe, Faith scanned the bobbing sea of heads, hoping to catch sight of Eliza, proudly wearing the white plumed hat that Charles had immortalized, or, more hopefully, of Charles himself. She saw neither but was unconcerned. She would see them both at the Astor's ball that evening.

Faith's renewed vigor began to flag before they had walked all the way back home. Her legs felt heavy when she sat at the kitchen table to eat a cold lunch while the waiting carriage was loaded. When they were ready to leave, she nestled into the corner of the carriage seat with great relief. She unpinned her hat and laid it on her lap, letting her head rest against the window frame. Wrapped in a traveling cloak and rocked by the cradle of their movement, Faith was asleep before they'd reached the edge of the city. The last thing she saw as her eyes slid shut was the Colonel watching her with a beatific smile that made a shiver run down her spine.

* * *

Faith awoke to a knock on the bedroom door.

Roused from a deep and dreamless sleep, she struggled to remember who and where she was and why. Hazy memories of the afternoon came to her slowly. The carriage lurching to a stop before Hellgate's soaring front porch. Being ushered into a guest room on the second floor, a bed for her mother and the Colonel, a cushioned pallet on the floor for her. The relief of loosened stays and and sinking onto the makeshift bed. Curling up like a cat in a golden square of light.

Now, the sunbeam had shifted, leaving her in shadow. She shivered. Her mouth was dry, her head thick and groggy. There was another knock at the door. She hadn't dreamt it.

Her mother's head lifted from the bed, looking no more alert than Faith felt.

"I'll get it, Mama," she said, pushing to her feet. Reality coming back to her, Faith looked about for her Easter hat. With relief, she saw it hanging on an obliging hook next to the armoire.

Faith opened the door and peered around it. Katherine and Jane waited in the hallway holding trays, one laden with tea, the other with brushes, combs, and an assortment of cosmetic pots. Jane bobbed a polite curtsy. Katherine nodded belatedly.

"Sorry to disturb you Miss, but we've been sent to help you get ready for this evening."

"Already? What time is it? Have we missed the bell?"

"No, Miss. You're to be down early, so we've been told."

Faith was suddenly wary but she opened the door wider to let them in.

Cold water on her face washed away some of Faith's sleepiness. Jane applied her cosmetic arts to this clean canvas, darkening Faith's brows, reddening her cheeks and lips. When Jane began to brush her hair, Faith asked if she would leave some of the curls long in back. Faith thought maybe Charles would be reminded of that day in the studio when she had unpinned her hair.

"Begging your pardon, Miss, but wouldn't it be better up? That is Master William's preference." Jane paused, and then, as though she sensed the retort about William's preferences that was forming in Faith's thoughts, she hurriedly added, "and it would look most pleasing with your dress."

Faith's eyes narrowed. "How do you know what dress I'm wearing?"

"It's just here," Jane replied, stepping to the armoire. She lifted out a dress the color of palest butter. "It's a gift from Mrs. Astor."

"Is it now?" Faith stood to examine the dress, holding it against her. It was beautiful, exquisite in every detail from the beaded lace overskirt to the embroidery on the sleeves and hem. "I'm already too much in her debt for keeping me all these months. Why should she make me such a gift?"

Jane did not respond but her wide eyes and pressed lips told Faith she wished she could. Faith shot her mother a questioning glance. Sarah shrugged and shook her head, eliciting a protest from Katherine who was fighting to secure a tress, just so. Her mother had no explanation, but her expression said she shared Faith's misgivings. Something was going on.

Not wanting to appear ungrateful in front of Jane, Faith said, "I suppose I'll find out when I thank her for it." Jane nodded, her eyes bright. Faith retook her seat cautiously, allowing Jane to finish her work. When it came time to dress, Faith was not at all surprised to find there were also matching slippers, and that the dress and slippers both fit her perfectly. Jane was adjusting the sash at the waist when a bell jangled out in the hall. The rest of the guests who had retreated to rest were being called to dress.

There was a knock at their bedroom door and Jane scurried to answer it. "Just a moment. She's about ready," Jane said to whoever was on the other side. Jane left the door ajar to give Faith one more appraisal. Jane signaled her approval by clasping her hands together beneath her chin before returning to the door. She opened it wide, revealing a footman in the hall.

With a wary look at her mother as they filed out, Faith allowed herself to be escorted down the stairs. The footman led them to the formal parlor off the entry. The double doors were closed but Faith could hear muffled conversation within.

"A moment, Missus, Miss," the footman said, holding up a hand for them to wait. He opened one door and stepped inside to announce them. Conversation abruptly ceased. In the silence, a profound dread gripped Faith's heart in an icy fist and fixed her feet to the floor. She would rather walk into a sinister wood in blackest night than pass through the parlor door. The footman stepped aside and jerked his head, imploring her to enter. Faith's fingers tangled in her skirts. Just as she tensed to hike them and run, the Colonel appeared in the doorway.

"Come, my dear," he said, his voice soft and entreating, his eyes like steel. The hand that found her elbow was just as hard, pulling her firmly across the threshold. The Astors were there. All of them, even Dorothea and her husband. They stood about the room, some at the window, some behind the settee. Eliza stood with one hand on the back of a chair, her face eager with some unshared secret.

They closed in as the Colonel steered Faith across the room. She felt their eyes on her. They were smiling. Or were their teeth bared, like beasts about to feast? The Colonel stopped her in front of the fireplace, in front of William who stood alone at the center. The silence screamed in Faith's ears, or was that a voice inside her head crying at her to run away? The doors to the parlor clicked shut.

"Miss Trumbull, it has been suggested by our mutual parents that we would make a good match." William paused, glancing at the each of them in turn. When he turned back to Faith, her eyes met his. They were somber and humorless. The only sign of emotion on his face was the depth of the perpetual crease between his brows and a particular slowness of speech, as though inspecting each word before offering it. "While their wise counsel alone would be sufficient to guide me, I have had the pleasure of getting to know you these past several months. I have observed with admiration your industriousness, your usefulness, your reserve and practicality that are so rare in a woman. It would be an asset to have a wife with your qualities. I would be pleased if you would consent to marry me."

No! Never! Faith screamed the words in her mind, but she could not find the breath to utter them. Her hand went to her throat to pull away the invisible coil that was tightening around it. She turned to run but was held firmly in place by the Colonel's vice like grip. Faith caught her mother's eye. It was full of sadness as she gave a tragic sigh, like her portrait in the entry hall.

A pain lanced through Faith's elbow and down her arm. Her eyes, wide-eyed with panic, met the Colonel's. They burned a warning, like a viper about to strike. The pain in her elbow sharpened. There was no way out.

As waves of despair broke over her, drowning out the wailing of her heart, Faith found one last breath. As though it came from another body, another world, she heard herself utter, "I accept."

CHAPTER TWENTY-SEVEN

The Unraveling

The Colonel transferred her hand to William's and stepped away with a smug smile.

Faith seemed to watch from a distance, as though she looked out from Phantasia upon her own body. She saw, as though in slow motion, William take a small box from his father. He placed the ring within it on her finger. The witnesses applauded, converging on them. Their happy exclamations were muted and distorted to Faith's ears as though their voices passed through water.

As Faith took her place at William's side to receive the Astor's guests, soon to be her guests, she was thankful for the strange space between her mind and body. She saw no faces, and heard no names. Their mute congratulations washed over her, failing to confirm what she did not want to be true. A welling font of tears built within her but, estranged from her body, Faith could not cry. The empty girl in the buttercream dress could not either.

She faltered only once. A tall Irishman with eyes like storm and sea received the news with a lightning flash of shock and, was that dismay? There and gone again, only the afterimage as evidence it had been there at all. He shook William's hand and said, "You're a lucky man," and stepped down the line.

His eyes met Faith's and pulled her back into her body. Charles said nothing, but she *felt* his hand take hers. He bent his head and brushed his lips against her hand. In that butterfly's kiss lived all that Faith had loved and lost. Her foundations shook and her lip trembled as her facade began to crack. And then, his hand left hers. He turned away and Faith again retreated somewhere high and far.

Faith floated through the evening in a surreal haze. She danced the first dance with her betrothed, weighed down by his heavy steps and the ring upon the finger that did not seem to belong to her. William breathed a sigh of relief when the dance was over, or perhaps it was Faith's own sigh of despair. She tried to remember when she had danced her last dance as a single woman. If she had known, would she have enjoyed it more? Or less? As she stood dutifully next to William on the side, she wondered if she would ever dance again.

Faith watched the others glide and turn, join hands and part again. She looked for women she knew to be married, to see if they danced with men other than their husbands, if they danced at all. She did not know about such things. All the rules and courtesies she had ever been taught had been in pursuit of this very moment, to secure a husband. After that, what then? Did it cease to matter what she did? Did she cease to matter? From behind her veil of detachment, Faith could not make out the dancers. They were a blur of colored motion until Charles stepped into view.

Everything about him stood in crisp detail, like Ruysch's more than life-like flowers. He was dancing with a vivacious, dark haired girl. Jealousy pierced the veil and caught Faith's heart. The girl turned and she saw it was Eliza. Charles smiled at her, but Faith, who knew him so well, could see it was a mask like the one her own face wore. The dance ended and he bowed. As he straightened, his gaze met Faith's. He gave her a half bow from across the room and headed for the doors.

Faith tried to call after him but the sound could not make it from her soul to her mortal tongue. Her throat was stopped by a lump; to dislodge it would burst the dam of tears. She made a move to follow him, but her way was blocked by people babbling incoherencies. She nodded and smiled and mumbled in return as her spirit tried to flee the hot and suffocating room and find Charles, wherever he had gone.

The couple in front of her finally moved on and Faith saw a path to the door. She put a hand on William's arm.

"I need some air."

"I will come with you."

"No!" Faith softened the desperation in her voice. "No, it wouldn't do for both of us to abandon the party. I'll only be gone a moment." Faith did not give him a chance to respond and walked swiftly for the door.

The tears were already pooling on her lower lids when Faith burst from the front doors onto the broad veranda. Without a wrap, the spring night air washed over her in a cold wave. Her skin prickled but she welcomed it on her hot cheeks. She looked for Charles but she couldn't see through the stars the porch lights made of her tears. Faith hurried down the front steps and out into the cloak of night.

No longer caring what people would say or see, she balled her skirts in her fists and ran down the sloping lawn towards the shore. Pebbles ground sharply beneath her thin slippers and branches caught at the lace of her gown, but she ran until exertion and heaving sobs left her no more breath to run. Faith stood on a small promontory above the East River and cried.

She stayed there, arms clutched about her middle, until her sobs slowed and the tears ran dry, leaving nothing but icy tracks on her cheeks. Her vision cleared, Faith looked up at the moon. It was just past full, drowning out all but the brightest stars. Like everything around her, they seemed strange and diaphanous. It was not her moon, or her constellations. They gave no comfort. She wanted to retreat to her palace garden and Helios, to Phantasia where she felt alive and powerful.

Later, she promised herself. She could not reach Phantasia now, but it had not yet been taken from her. She had not brought her pen to Hellgate, but she had brought a gateway. For now, she had to navigate this reality and its devastating turn. With deep draughts of cool air and concerted effort, Faith steeled herself to return to the ball.

Faith removed a glove, turning it inside out to wipe her cheeks dry. She could see dark stains of rouge against the pale fabric. Would they be able to tell she had been crying? If anyone commented on her pallor, she would plead tiredness and hopefully be allowed to retire.

As she began to replace the glove, Faith was confronted by the sapphire ring William had given her. It was a symbol of her attachment, the purchase price of her freedom. Under the moon, little sparks of brilliant blue light flashed in its depths, a chunk of starlit night or a shard of ocean's deep set on a golden band. She thought of hurling it back where it had come from, into the night, into the sea. And then, impulsively, she thought of hurling herself. Moonlight sparkled on a swath of disturbed water and the old, ever-present fear returned. Faith pulled the glove over the ring and walked slowly back up the hill.

Light and music spilled from every window of the house, forming an incandescent halo that pulled Faith back like moth to a flame. She stopped on the veranda to neaten herself under the porch lights before going in. Just another refugee from the frivolity within, no one paid her any mind as she plucked leaves from her overskirt and tried to smooth away the scuffs on her slippers. She ran her hands over her hair, feeling for loose strands and snags.

She was wondering if the window glass at her shoulder would serve as a mirror when she became aware of two gentleman sitting in wingback chairs just on the other side. Faith ducked away instinctively, pressing herself against the shutter. Their voices carried past the open sash.

Although their faces were hidden by the chairs, she recognized one man's voice. Mr. Dunlap.

"I only encouraged you to come because I thought you might secure a good commission or two out of it. I had no idea about the engagement. If I had known this was nothing more than a triumphal for the Colonel, I would never have urged you to make the trip."

"I believe you, but it makes me wonder that either of us were included on the guest list to begin with. Given the news of the evening, the Colonel had to have some say in who was invited. Could there be any other purpose for including me other than to gloat?" another voice with an accent somewhere between French and drunk.

"About the engagement?"

"No. I don't care one whit for the insipid girl. Never met her until tonight and wish I hadn't. Not a single spark of wit." Faith flinched and shrank further back. The man continued on. "But, it's about the only thing that conniving bastard hasn't taken from me. The Academy was - "

"Quieter!" Mr. Dunlap waved a hand above the arm of his chair. The other man lowered his voice to a hoarse whisper.

"The Academy was mine! I was the one commissioned to build the collection while he was playing diplomat. Then ever so mysteriously I was abandoned, stranded in Europe with no way to pay for the acquisitions or my way home. He turned the Livingstons against me. Probably Mr. West as well."

"You know I have little love for the man, but I'm not sure that was Trumbull's doing. The Livingstons did not manage the Academy well. There was no money to be sent."

The other man grunted. "I know he's had a hand in it all. He works from the shadows, pulling the strings like a puppeteer. When I finally got back to New York, I knew the Academy was lost to me, so I determined to start my own. I'd have had my own school and my own exhibit and be out from under his rule. And then one by one, all my plans died on the vine. My rotunda project was on the verge of approval and then Clinton buried it. It was Trumbull's man Murray that waylaid my Marius and Ariadne, telling me they'd gone to Peale in Philadelphia instead of New York. And then it was Murray again who told me I'd been evicted from my own exhibit!"

The disgruntled man's voice had risen again. Dunlap countered it with a soothing tone.

"Do you have proof that he had a hand in all this?"

"From his conspirator himself!"

"Murray?" Mr. Dunlap asked with surprise.

"No. Smith. Trumbull arranged with Smith and Waldo to move the directors to evict me, only Smith took it too far and Trumbull left him swinging. Smith was furious after that. Came and told me himself."

"If that's true, then Smith got what was coming to him."

"Agreed. Despicable fellow." There was a pause as the man ruminated on his distaste for Mr. Smith. If the story had not been familiar, the mention of Marius and Ariadne was enough to reveal his identity. *Vanderlyn*. Faith could not remember meeting him tonight, but that was hardly surprising. Vanderlyn, his face still hidden, raised his glass to take a drink. Mid- sip he re-collected his original train of thought and spluttered with renewed animation. "But now! Now! Not only has Trumbull secured the Academy and all that goes with it for himself-" the man pointed at Dunlap for emphasis, sloshing the contents of his glass, "but now he's Congress' new pet! If it had been known that Congress was soliciting work for the new capitol, I could have put in a proposal. Instead he snuck in the back door under Judge Nicholson's robes. The coward. He's afraid of me. He know's I'm the superior painter!"

"Now John, I agree that he has slipped a little, but he is best suited to the project. Before you had even picked up a pencil, he was traveling all about the country capturing the likenesses of all the luminaries of the Revolution.

Unless you have a similar collection, he has the fairer claim to paint our nation's history. While you were at your mother's breast, he fought in the War. He was at Bunker Hill, an aid du camp for General Washington... The Colonel is one of the few first-hand witnesses left alive."

Vanderlyn gave a caustic laugh that drew other eyes in the room. "The Colonel! How he banks on that title! The man's a fraud."

"I'll agree he's a pompous ass, but he's hardly a fr-"

"A fraud, I tell you!"

"Keep your voice down, John. The man is well respected as a war hero and a patriot, even by those who don't like him." Dunlap said with volume before he leaned in conspiratorially. "In what way is he a fraud?"

"Did you know that he wasn't actually at Bunker Hill? He was in Roxbury when the shots were fired. He couldn't have smelled the smoke for half a day even with a strong wind, let alone witness the action 'first-hand' as you say! You mention Washington. He was aid du camp for Washington for fewer than 20 days and he was a Colonel for all of seven months, a commission he ultimately rejected in some fit of pique because General Gates and Congress did not adequately bow and scrape to entice him to remain! According to those I have consulted, he never saw a bit of action in the entire war. That sword he carries? Looted from a fallen Hessian after the battle was complete. I tell you, *Mr.* Trumbull is no patriot. He is a fraud and a scoundrel!"

There was a pause in which Faith silently urged Mr. Dunlap to come to the Colonel's defense. If what Vanderlyn was saying were true, the Colonel was hardly the man he held himself out to be. The man she had believed him to be. His entire identity was founded on the esteem of his military service. His title, his personal connections, the Hessian sword that he carried on his hip even tonight. His career as an artist was predicated on his unique position as eye witness to America's birth. Surely he had to have been in service for more than seven months when the war had gone on for seven years? It didn't make sense.

Dunlap did not come to his defense. His voice grew even lower, forcing Faith to edge closer to the window. "I must confess, I am not entirely surprised to hear this. There has been other talk consistent with the picture you paint, as it were. I have heard through Verplanck, who has it from Gore, who was himself at the Trumbull's wedding, that it was a most unusual affair. The lady arrived unescorted in a coach that deposited her alone and drove off. Having no one to stand for her but a woman- friend or convenient stranger I do not know- Mr. King offered to give Mrs. Trumbull away. When he inquired for whom he had done such a service, Trumbull's only response was 'Mrs. Trumbull!' Can you believe it?"

"He would not identify her to one of his closest friends? He was hiding something."

"It is tantalizingly mysterious! I have done a little investigating on the matter myself, out of curiosity. Archibald Robinson told me that her maiden name is Hope, the daughter of a William Hope of Perthshire, Scotland. That is all well and good, but where does the name Harvey come from, which I have also heard used in reference to Mrs. Trumbull? If she had been previously married to a Mr. Harvey, a young widow perhaps, such would not be terribly unusual and there would be no reason to be so secretive. Verplanck offers one theory. He says that there is reason to believe she is one of the illegitimate daughters of Lord Thurlow- you know, the former Lord Chancellor?- by his mistress who went by the name of Mrs. Harvey. Of course, it was later revealed that the mysterious Mrs. Harvey was the Duchess of Kingston. It was all very scandalous."

"I don't know, Dunlap. If Mrs. Trumbull were the get of a Baron and a Duchess, even an illegitimate one, don't you think she'd have better... *manners?*"

"One would hope," Dunlap said with such sarcasm that it made Faith's cheeks burn for her mother. "But it is said that Lord Thurlow provided nothing for the girls, particularly the third who, get this, married against his consent." There was a dramatic pause. Whether it had its intended impact, Faith couldn't tell from where she leaned against the window casing Dunlap continued. "At least that is what Verplanck has said, and Clinton, in confidence, told me that he believes the story as well. Of course, there is another, more salacious option. Mrs. Trumbull may have been married to a Mr. Harvey before the Colonel came along, but he may not have expired before the Colonel took over his affairs, as you might say."

"You're saying the self-righteous Colonel, with a pious ram-rod up his arse, had an affair with a married woman? Oh, that's rich." Vanderlyn chuckled maliciously. Faith clutched a hand to her middle. Her gut had turned to stone.

His seed having hit fertile ground, Dunlap tended it with vigor. "It would not have been his first indiscretion! Robertson has told me that

Colonel Trumbull, many years ago, had an affair with a serving girl in his brother's household and got her with child. It would seem she was the profligate type- he claimed it could have been any number of men- but she pinned it on Trumbull and the Select Men made it stick. Robertson did the boy's portrait. Well, he's a man now. Serves in the British Army."

Vanderlyn snorted. "Further evidence of Trumbull's patriotism."

"Indeed. As I was saying though, Robertson did the portrait and said he is the very image of Trumbull. Of course, Trumbull calls him his nephew, but I know Trumbull's family and there's no place for John Ray among their ranks."

Cousin Ray. Faith's head spun. Dunlap continued his gossipy speculation.

"Having once ventured that way, it is not hard to believe that Trumbull did it again. If this time his affair were with a married Mrs. Harvey, his reticence on the subject becomes quite understandable. It leaves one to wonder what the inducement to marriage really was."

Dunlap's voice had trailed off suggestively. The other man answered "Do you mean a settlement? Did Trumbull pay the other man for the insult, or, I wonder, did the husband pay Trumbull to take her off his hands?"

Dunlap laughed heartily. "He'd have been well rid of her at any price! Which begs the question, why would the emphatically well-born Colonel Trumbull marry such a woman, especially if he could have paid to settle the whole affair? The only reason I can see is if the lady were already pregnant."

"*Incroiable*! But surely, Gore or King would have noticed she were with child, unless she were not showing yet."

"It is my belief that the girl was born before the wedding."

"You mean the girl whose engagement was announced tonight? The girl everyone is fawning over isn't Trumbull's daughter, or even his step-daughter, but his illegitimate by-blow?" Vanderlyn chortled in peevish delight."I wonder if Astor knows!"

"I suspect not!" Dunlap answered, "But, after his second daughter's elopement a few years ago, and his eldest estranged from her husband, perhaps the man is resigned to scandal. New money can withstand far more than old, in any event."

"I'm of half a mind to take Astor aside. It would serve the proud Colonel right."

"You wouldn't want to make an enemy of the Astors or the Colonel directly. If you really wanted to make trouble for the Colonel, there is an easier way. The Astors might even thank you for averting disaster. It seems his intemperance runs in the blood."

Vanderlyn sat forward, revealing the edges of his profile. "The girl?"

"The very same. While Trumbull was away in the Capitol, Miss Trumbull spent an inordinate amount of time at the Academy in the company of a painter. Ostensibly he was painting her portrait, but I had occasion to observe them and although I may have only one working eye, I can see it was more than just a sitting."

"With whom?"

"Ingham."

There was a long pause while Vanderlyn swirled his glass. Faith felt as though she were spinning like the liquor within it. "He's a good man. As much as I would relish muddying the Colonel's reputation, I wouldn't want to drag Ingham's with it. Although, he should be warned to steer clear."

"I think he already has. And, I agree that I wouldn't want to do him harm, but like father, like daughter. She won't stay faithful to young Astor for long."

A commotion somewhere deeper in the room, caused Dunlap to snicker softly. "Ah, the merry widow as we speak. Mrs. Trumbull is in her cups again."

"All these bloody rooms look the same! If I can't find a bloody privy, I'm going to have to crawl out that window and piss outside!" Sarah said loudly into a stunned silence. Faith peered around the edge of the window to see her mother walking with a precarious sway towards her. To Faith's growing horror, she tripped, stumbling forward several steps before landing across Vanderlyn's lap.

"Madame!" he said, trying to extricate himself. Mr. Dunlap was on his feet, lifting Sarah to hers.

"Ah, bugger me," Sarah said, wiping at a spreading stain on her dress.

"Is that an apology, Madame?" Vanderlyn asked brushing off his coat with a look of disgust.

"No, you bloody frog. Either you've spilled your drink on me or I've gone and pissed myself."

Her cheeks burning with fury and shame, Faith ran into the house and to her mother's side.

"It seems Mr. Vanderlyn has spilled his drink on you, Mama. Come upstairs with me and see if your dress can be saved." Shooting Dunlap and Vanderlyn each a look that would have shamed Leviathan for murderous intent, Faith escorted her mother out with one arm around her waist and one hand beneath her elbow.

About half way up the stairs, her mother tripped and slid several steps face down. When she rolled over, Faith reached out to help her up but was pushed away. Sarah fumbled through the folds of her dress. When she found her shoes, she pulled them off and tossed them away before lurching back to her feet. Gathering her skirts nearly to her waist, Sarah went scrambling up the rest of the stairs. Faith retrieved the shoes, ignoring the eyes that followed her until she was out of sight and safely in their bedroom. Faith leaned her back against the closed door and sank slowly to the floor.

Instead of meeting with sense, delicacy, tenderness, a lover, a friend, an equal companion, in a husband, you may be tired with insipidity and dulness; shocked with indelicacy or mortified by indifference. You will find none to ... understand your sufferings; for your husbands may not use you cruelly, and may give you as much money for your clothes, personal expense, and domestic necessaries as is suitable to their fortunes. The world would therefore look on you as unreasonable women, and that did not deserve to be happy, if you were not so.

- Dr. John Gregory, A Father's Legacy to his Daughters

CHAPTER TWENTY-EIGHT

The Truth

Faith held her head in her hands, trying to steady it against a world that spun violently around her. In a mere matter of hours, she had been engaged against her will to a man she did not hate but could not love and had learned that the fundamental viewpoint from which she had understood her world might be nothing but a false perspective.

The knowledge that the Colonel was not Faith's real father had defined the context of her life. Faith had rationalized the Colonel's reserve not only as the product of his rank and status, but as the natural result of a connection by law instead of blood. Surely, it was a rare man who could come to love another man's child as his own? He had given her his name but Faith had understood that she would have to earn, if not his love, his respect and affection. When she had so often failed at that, she had consoled herself with the fantasy of a real father who, moved by innate nature, would have swaddled her in unconditional love. From that angle, the panorama of Faith's life had been lonely, a vast expanse of empty space relieved by occasional beauty and joy, but it had made sense.

Now she had been violently knocked aside. To see her life from this angle, the sight lines were all askew, the landscape ugly and distorted. If the

Colonel were her real father, all of her rationalizations evaporated like mist under summer sun. What could she have possibly done to deserve his cold detachment and constant disapproval? Whatever her faults, only an unnatural beast treated his only child with such cruel disdain. No, not his only child. Children. If the rumor were to be believed, she was not the only one. Faith pictured Ray's face. The resemblance was too obvious for him to be unrelated, the product of another man's indiscretion. If the resemblance was not familial, it had to be paternal. Did Ray know? He must. How did it feel to be a nephew to all and a son to none, a Trumbull in name but never in fact? The Colonel's superficial acknowledgment made Faith the favored of the two. The idea that she should be grateful for the Colonel's name suddenly made her nauseated.

The Colonel. Faith's mind tripped over the title. He carried the rank as he did the Hessian sword, proud testament to his duty, bravery, and honor. But had he truly earned them? The way he spoke of witnessing the birth of the nation as it was brought forth in gun smoke and blood, she'd assumed he'd fought hand to hand, winning his reputation and the Hessian sword in valiant combat. Now she could not be sure. Which lies were his and which were malicious gossip?

Faith knew some things to be true. However short his service to General Washington, Faith knew by her own hand the Colonel had the General's ear, as well as those of other men of history. It was also fact that the Colonel had been held in England as a political prisoner in retribution for the hanging of a British officer by the States. By his own account though, it was not the hardship one might suspect. He was treated more as guest than inmate and had his art to distract him when visitors were few. If he had already acquired the Ink, she realized now, he would have passed the time blissfully unaware of the walls around him. Compared to her fate, Faith thought, it was a sentence to be envied.

For all his posturing, had the Colonel ever felt the sting of sacrifice for his country? Although he may have attained the rank fairly, it seemed to Faith dishonorable that he would insist upon the title after so many years and so little service when there were those who had fought long and paid far dearer for it. Even if he had earned the honor in some small measure, there was no act that justified her being raised by a Colonel rather than loved by a Father.

But was it true? Could she believe the idle talk of two men who clearly bore no love for him? Nothing offended the Colonel so much as a challenge to his honor and he found nothing so despicable as a lack of integrity in another. Did that make him a paragon of virtue, or were these the defensive postures of a tender conscience, loud protestations meant to distract attention from his own misdeeds? He had lied about the Ink, about women in the Guild. Faith was certain he had master-minded Vanderlyn's misfortunes. Was it too much of a stretch to believe he was a philanderer as well, who treated his own children like insect carcasses stuck in his web of lies?

If it were all true, he could not have concealed these things alone. There were accomplices to his hypocrisy. Her mother knew the truth and had kept it from her. The anger that had been bubbling up like magma from the cracks in Faith's foundation surged at this fresh betrayal. She tried to temper it with cool reason. She needed to know the truth.

Looking up from her hands, Faith's awareness came back to the room. The first thing it encountered was the sound of falling water and her mother sighing gratefully from behind the privy screen. A moment later Sarah emerged, shaking down her gathered skirt without a hint of unsteadiness.

"Now that's better. I really did need to piss, or whatever ladies call it. If they even have a word for something they don't admit to doing," Sarah said, her words clear and sure. "Come, untie me. I'd hate to have to ring for Katherine."

Her rage momentarily displaced by astonishment, Faith rose obediently. She unlaced the back of her mother's bodice and helped her out of her dress. Sarah only wobbled once, steadying herself with a sure hand on Faith's back as she stepped out of the puddle of fabric on the floor. She gave another sigh of relief and threw a dressing gown around her shoulders.

"You aren't drunk at all!" Faith said when she had found her voice.

"A little tipsy maybe, but who could get drunk on that watered down punch? As it is, I had to drink so much, it's no wonder I had to piss so bad."

"Mama! What was that scene then? I nearly died of embarrassment!"

Her mother eyed her up and down. "You seem well enough. I'm sorry for it though. You know, you weren't the intended victim."

"The Colonel?"

"Him. The Astors. The whole wretched lot of them. That was a deuce's trick they pulled on you. On us."

"You really didn't know about it?" Faith asked, suspicion rekindling her anger.

"Of course not! He knew I'd do what I could to prevent it. I'd have put on a production that made tonight look like a street skit. Not that it would have been more than a nuisance. I might have scared the Astors off but he was bound to get his way eventually. The best I could do now was get a little revenge. Who knows, maybe the Astors will call it off still." Sarah pulled back the covers of the bed and flopped down on it. Her lips curled in a smug smirk. "I can just see the look on the Colonel's face now as he makes his excuses."

Faith found herself almost smiling at the thought, until she remembered that she would have to make her own apologies. "That's well and good for you. You'll stay abed. I'm the one that will have to face them in the morning."

"I really am sorry, my love. I only have so many tools at my disposal though. Some men you can just twist their whirligigs, but that man, the only way to get to him is to threaten his honor."

Faith's outrage flared back to life. Hands on her hips, she asked "Is that so? I've heard some things tonight that make me wonder if he has any. Or you, for that matter."

"What has you in such a tizzy? I've already apologized twice." Sarah sat up and began to adjust the pillows behind her.

"Is the Colonel my real father?"

Sarah's hand faltered for a moment. She continued to fuss with the pillows and did not answer.

"Mama. Is the Colonel my real father?"

Sarah fell back against the pillows, her face pale and pinched. "Why do you ask?"

"I overheard some men talking. They said some horrible things. If they're true, then I- I just need to know the truth."

"Banbury stories. Bugger the lot of them."

"Mama."

"Fine! What did they say?"

In spite of her anger, Faith found it hard to repeat what she had heard, to accuse her own mother of lies and adultery. She began with the least culpable of the allegations. "For one, they said that you are the illegitimate daughter of Lord Thurlow and the Duchess of Kingston."

Her mother laughed caustically. "That rumor is still going 'round? Does anything about me say daughter of a duchess to you? I need to get some sleep Faith. If you are going back down, turn down the wick before you go." Sarah turned over on her side.

"I wasn't finished." Irritation gave Faith the push she needed. "They said that you and the Colonel had an affair, while you were still married."

Her mother turned slowly back to face her. All humor had fled. "What else did they say?"

"They said that cousin Ray was his bastard by a servant girl and that- and that-" Faith's voice wavered and broke. She took a breath. "And that I'm his bastard too. I need to know! Is he my real father?"

Her mother smoothed the coverlet. When she spoke, her voice was just above a whisper. "Yes, he's your father."

Faith's outrage burst forth. "How could you lie to me like that? To tell me I was an orphan, when really I am base-born?"

"It was for your own good!" her mother responded with a fire of her own.

"How could it be?"

"Faith, don't act the fool. You're a smart girl. Do you know what happens to poor women with bastard children? Nothing good. It was the only way I could be sure you'd be taken care of. It was necessary."

"Maybe for the outside world, but why lie to me? How could you let me think I was one thing when I'm something else?"

"And what are you exactly? Does what you're called mean so much? Because if it does, let me remind you that to all the world you are Faith Trumbull. You have his family's name, which is no small thing in this blasted country. And you have the benefit of his reputation which, by the way, would be worth next to nothing if the truth were widely known. So tell me, child, how would your life have been better knowing the truth? Would it have served you well to know your real father is a cold, hypocritical prig? Are you relieved to hear it confirmed?"

"No! I feel betrayed. And angry. And, and, *dirty*. To know that I'm the result of an adulterous affair!"

"That part isn't true." Sarah's voice had lost its edge and her face was pained. The sudden change in her demeanor caught Faith off guard and her own anger contracted. Still, she was not ready to let go of it entirely.

"How do I trust you? How do I trust either of you?"

"You said you wanted to know the truth. Then hear the truth." Her mother's voice was calm and resigned as she patted the bed next to her.

Faith cautiously took the proffered spot on the bed. She both wanted to hear what her mother had to say and was afraid of what she might reveal. Faith leaned against the headboard, her feet curled beneath her. "Go on."

Sarah took a breath and began with a wry smile. "First, in case there are any lingering doubts, my father was a Scotsman, not a lord, though my mother was an Englishwoman. She died just after I was born, but I am certain she was no duchess. We lived in a small town outside of London. I had an older sister; she died same time as my mother. I had a brother too. He used to carry me about on his back, pretending to be my horse, so all I can remember of him is the nape of his neck. He and my father both died, leaving me an orphan before the age of 10."

"How awful! Of course I knew you had no family left but I didn't know you had been so young!" Faith's own complaints felt trivial all of a sudden. "What did you do?"

"I was taken in by a well-off widow- at least by country standards- and she saw to my education, though it was no fancy thing with governesses and singing lessons. I learned to read and keep accounts and how to run a country house. I might have stayed there forever if it hadn't been for the pastor's wedding. People came from all over- biggest to-do the town had seen in ages- including a woman, Elizabeth Halbrook, who had been a friend of my mother's. She saw me on the street and stopped like she'd seen a ghost. She said I looked exactly like my mother had last time she'd seen her, before she married a wealthy merchant and moved to London. When she learned I hadn't any family left, she insisted I move in with them, so I found myself in London at sixteen years old.

"They put me to work in their millinery shop, in exchange for room and board and some small credit. That was where I met Leland Harvey. He was a footman in some grand house or another who'd been assigned to follow their high-in-the-in-step daughter on her shopping excursions. He was handsome and brash with a smile as bright as noon day sun. Ah, did he look good in his uniform!" Sarah said wistfully, as the memory played behind closed eyes.

When they opened again, they were bright and wet. She cleared her throat. "Well, I'll spare you the details of our courtship. Suffice it to say we fell in love. Between us, we didn't have much money and we had even less family or connections, so we eloped and rented a tiny run-down flat in the worst part of the city. To us though, it was paradise. It was as if some fairy lord had cast a spell on us. When all we had was bread, we tasted cake. When everything was black with soot, all we saw was gold and silver. He got a promotion and I got pregnant. When Michael was born, our only fear was that we might die of happiness because we were already in heaven."

Sarah paused and took a deep breath. "And then smallpox swept the city. It took them both and left me all alone again." Tears spilled over Sarah's cheeks.

"Oh, Mama!" Faith's own eyes brimmed with tears that doused her anger. She threw her arms around her mother.

"I can still see the sores on the back of his dimpled hands..." Sarah's words were lost to quiet sobs. Faith held her shaking shoulders and cried with her. They stayed that way until Sarah sniffed and dashed her eyes with the back of her hand. She sat up straighter.

"I don't know why it spared me again. I spent the next years wishing that it hadn't. I thought about going back to the widow, but found out she had died as well. Agnes offered to take me in again, but I couldn't go back to the shop; the memories were too painful. They found another position for me, and that's how I was there the night John Trumbull came for dinner.

"He was in London on some business between England and the States about merchant vessels that had been taken at sea. Part of his job was to determine the value of the cargo seized and so he had been meeting with various merchants. To this day I am surprised that he noticed me. I had become quiet and sad. I saw death all around me and had come to believe that I was cursed. Hardly compelling company. Like Elizabeth though, I reminded him of someone else, a woman he had been in love with who had died tragically young. At first, our connection was nothing more than shared misery, but it quickly grew from there.

"He was handsome and confidant, with all the manners of a gentleman. And he was passionate, about everything from politics to art. He became infatuated with me and after so much loss, it went to my head like liquor. He said I was his muse and convinced me to model for him. He made me feel alive again. And not just me, everything. Even the pictures he made seemed to come to life."

Faith blinked as her mother's words sank in. Had her mother been able to see the Ink then? Could she still see it now? She started to ask, but her mother's eyes were far away and she did not want to pull her out of the past.

"I trusted him. He was always going on about honor and duty. Maybe it was because I had no reputation to protect, but it never occurred to me to question how a man of honor would do the things we did. It wasn't until I got pregnant with you that I realized what a dangerous game I had been playing. I was terrified. He could have denied it and walked away. When I told him, I saw the thought cross his mind. Without money or a husband, there was no way I could keep you safe. I couldn't bear to lose another child." Her voice hitched again, but she pressed on doggedly. "We argued. He said he couldn't marry so far below his station. I cried and pleaded, threw myself on his mercy and honor. I threatened him too. Threatened to parade my belly around town and tell everyone it was his. I don't know which worked, or maybe it was too much to drink, but one night he came to me in a fit of guilt and confessed about Ray."

"So what those men said was true?" Faith asked, "He got a woman with child and abandoned them?"

"He paid a settlement, but yes, in every other way he had abandoned Ray."

Faith's teeth ground together at such callous disregard but she only nodded at her mother to continue.

"I saw an opportunity that night. I told him this was God's way of forcing him to atone for his sins. That if he wanted to hold himself out as an honorable man, he would have to do the honorable thing. He was so desperate for redemption, I thought he would agree to anything. I made him promise that not only would he marry me and give you his name, he would also seek out Ray and do everything he could to ensure the boy's future. He agreed, with one request: that we do everything we could to hide the true nature of your conception. It seemed in my best interest, in *your* best interest," Faith's mother said with a pointed look that made Faith duck her eyes, "to preserve his standing as best I could and so I agreed to the lie.

"I was too far along by then to marry without it being noticed, so he got me a room in a part of town where no one knew me. I was worried the whole time that he would back out, but if he's true to one thing, it's his word. After you were born and my figure recovered, we married. Since no one in his circles knew me from Eve, we agreed not to say anything at all and let people fill in as they would. Early on, everyone assumed you were a child of my previous marriage because, of course, they thought him incapable of anything indecent. When you were older and the order of things got muddled, everyone assumed you were his natural daughter."

At that point Sarah's voice took on a note of caustic sarcasm. "Everyone except a *particular* member of his family who could rival him for self-righteousness and outdid him for connections. She knew about Ray and figured out our secret. She denounced me to the rest of the family, called me a harlot and a fortune seeker. I could see the pain it caused him to be called out by his family that way, not the least for the loss of financial connections. I thought for sure he'd abandon me, but he took his vows seriously and cut off ties with them."

"I'm surprised he supported you!" Faith said, not hiding the disdain in her voice.

Her mother tilted her head thoughtfully. "In a way I think his sensitive pride worked in my favor. Questioning his judgment in marrying offended him so deeply that he became all the more attached to me just to spite them."

Faith looked at her mother and saw her clearly for maybe the first time ever. She had always seemed so small and fragile, but to hear how much pain and loss she had endured and still had the courage to carry on, Faith knew there was steel hidden in her core. If there were any justice in the world, the woman had deserved another chance at happiness. Instead she had the Colonel. Hoping for some small measure of redemption, she asked, "Were you ever happy with the Colonel?"

"Perhaps at first, but whatever there was didn't take long to fade. Although he sided with me, the row with his family took its toll, as did the wars. I was relieved to go back to England, but even there it was not the same. Neither of us was welcome anywhere and we blamed each other for the trouble. When money got tight, blame turned to resentment and all the life and color faded from our lives. I can see it in his eyes. I am the cause of all his troubles."

No, thought Faith. *I am*. In that moment, everything was clear. She knew why he had treated her so coldly, why she could never earn his approval. Why he was so determined to marry her off and why he would deny her the Ink. She was the physical embodiment of his failures. What was also achingly clear was how much her mother had endured: a loveless marriage founded on guilt and desperation, a bargain struck out of duty rather than love. A wave of shame washed over Faith for having judged her mother so harshly. Tears ran down her cheeks again.

"I'm so sorry, Mama. I never should have doubted you. You've put up with so much for me. I feel- I feel it's all my fault."

Sarah pulled Faith to her, cradling her against her chest. She stroked Faith's hair like she had when she was a child. "Hush now, dear. I'm no Goody Two-Shoes. I'm the one who should say I'm sorry. I haven't been there like I should these past few years. Even so, you should know that even though the Colonel may not have brought me happiness, you always have."

A sob broke loose from Faith's chest and she buried her head against her mother's chest and cried. Her mother's hand on her head stayed gentle but her voice grew sharper.

"And now that bastard has given you to a dullard. I knew you'd have to marry someday, but I had dared to hope it would be to someone you love, to experience even just a sliver of the joy I had once." Sarah sighed, again resigned. "I suppose it could be worse. I don't think William is the kind to beat you, or treat you cruelly. Thanks to your family name, he will look on you as equal to his station and if you manage him and his business well, you will never be short the diversions that money brings."

"Is that the best we can hope? To consider ourselves fortunate if we are not beaten?" Faith asked, sitting up a little.

"I'm afraid so, child," Sarah said with resignation. She tilted her head as she wiped tears from Faith's cheek. "Do you still like to draw?"

Faith gave her a wry smile, tasting the salt on her lips. "I do."

"Well, if he becomes too tiresome, develop an affliction and use it to get some time for yourself to draw. It will give you some peace."

Faith and her mother exchanged a knowing laugh, but the mirth was superficial. The tenderness Faith felt for her mother at this moment was only outdone by a building hatred for the Colonel.

Faith stayed in her mother's arms until she felt Sarah's breath become soft and even. A gentle snore jolted Faith from her thoughts. She got up and settled her sleeping mother more comfortably in bed. She debated whether to return to the party downstairs, as duty demanded, or give up for the night. Her mother's advice to develop an affliction brought a smile back to her lips. Perhaps she was right. If her mother could tolerate her marriage, surely Faith could tolerate hers. If she had Phantasia to retreat to, she could tolerate anything.

Faith went to the door and locked it. The Colonel could find somewhere else to sleep tonight. She struggled to get out of her dress on her own, wincing as she heard a seam tear somewhere. Faith hung the dress in the armoire and took down her Easter bonnet from the hook beside it. She pulled a red paper rose from its crown and crawled into bed beside her mother. She carefully unfolded the paper and smoothed it on her lap.

Looking down at the perfect apple which now shimmered above the page, Faith let her focus grow soft and her mind drift. She felt the familiar spin and opened her eyes to find herself sitting on a tree branch high above her palace garden. She began to climb down but another thought took hold. She reached out for Helios and the next moment the bird was there. She grasped the scarlet feathers and swung fearlessly from the tree to sit astride his broad shoulders. The firebird took off with powerful downward strokes that threatened to dislodge her. A bolt of doubt crossed Faith's mind at the wisdom of trying to fly. Should anything go wrong, she did not have her pen. Reminding herself she could always retreat to reality, Faith flattened herself to Helios' back and turned her face to the wind.

Faith knew Charles would not approve. Tonight though, she did not care. They soared across the vistas of Faith's imagination as the constellations of her world turned slowly overhead. They flew over mountains, through valleys, and beneath misty waterfalls where moonbows danced. The only place they did not cross was the deep and wild sea.

Somewhere on that maiden flight, Faith's physical body, drained by the day's whipsaw of emotions, fell asleep, her head pressed against her mother's shoulder and an apple clutched tightly in her hand.

* * *

The knock on the door felt like a hammer inside Faith's head. She opened an eye to see bright morning light streaming in through the window. The door knocked again.

"It's the Colonel. Come unlock the door," Faith heard the Colonel say. Though muffled, she could hear the impatience in his voice.

"Bugger," her mother muttered and turned away.

"Coming" Faith called out, as she pulled a dressing gown around her and stumbled to the door. She turned the key. Faith stepped back a pace as he burst in before she had even touched the handle. The Colonel deposited his jacket from the night before and began to unbutton his waistcoat. He looked at Faith.

"Why did you lock the door?"

"I asked her to," Sarah said from somewhere under the coverlet. "I didn't want one of those blasted servants bursting in and waking me up."

"Well, Katherine will be here in a moment. You'll need to dress quickly. I expect you downstairs for breakfast looking pleasant and contrite." The Colonel pulled a fresh shirt and waistcoat from his luggage and disappeared behind the privy screen.

"I'll stay up here. Someone will need to pack," Faith's mother objected.

"Katherine will do it," the Colonel's disembodied voice countered.

"She'll muck it up like she always does."

The Colonel made a frustrated sound and stepped back into view, adjusting his collar as he moved. "Very well. Faith, I expect you down in ten minutes."

"Ten min-"

The Colonel shot her a warning look. "Yes, Colonel," Faith said bobbing her head. The words tasted like bile on her tongue.

On his way out the door, the Colonel blew past a startled Katherine on her way in. "Ten minutes," he repeated.

Faith and Katherine scrambled frantically. Faith arrived at breakfast, breathless and without a second to spare. It was an awkward meal. Faith found it hard to meet any of the Astor's eyes for embarrassment and refused to meet the Colonel's lest he see the hatred in hers. When the meal was over and their things loaded up to leave, Faith leapt into the carriage with relief.

It wasn't until they were halfway back home that Faith remembered the apple. Her eyes darted to the hat resting next to her on the seat. It was missing one red rose. Panic gripped her heart and squeezed. Had he found it? Did he know? Faith looked up at the Colonel in fear. He was watching her with a smile like a cat that had eaten a canary.

Prudence is a rich ugly old maid courted by Incapacity.
-William Blake, The Marriage of Heaven and Hell

CHAPTER TWENTY-NINE

The Time

The only thing harder for Faith to conceal than her anxiety was her loathing for the Colonel. For the first two days after returning from the Astor's, the missing apple occupied her every thought. She looked for it everywhere, trying not to look as if she were looking. She slowly realized the Colonel must not have it. If he had, he would have been outraged and confronted her. He had been far too chipper for that.

Even so, her worries only dimmed slightly. So long as she did not have it, someone else might, and that someone might bring it to his attention. The last she remembered having it was in bed alongside her mother. She prayed some lit-wit maid, or even William himself, would find it. They would have no inkling of its significance and throw it out. If someone with more imagination found it though, in the bedroom they had occupied, it would not take long for word to get back to the Colonel.

And then he would take her pen and cut her off from Phantasia. Faith cursed herself for being so careless. While she had feared discovery all along, there was a part of her that trusted Charles to keep her secret indefinitely. It had been comforting that night, curled at her mother's side, to know that whatever was ahead of her in reality, at least she had a Journeyman's pen and Phantasia to escape to. Now even that was in jeopardy.

If Faith were truly honest with herself, she had decided not to settle for anything less than a Master's pen moments after she saw Jarvis disappear through a painted door. Now though, with the threat of discovery stalking her, she had to get it quickly. She had already discarded her delusions that the Guild might officially award her with one. She knew that the Colonel would never let that happen, no matter which Chapter she appealed to. She had also realized, as she contemplated being terminated by the Guild, that she did not want to be given what could subsequently be taken away.

They couldn't take away what they didn't know she had.

The morality of this had not concerned her for an instant. Her hatred for the Colonel and her knowledge of his own betrayals and deception were liberating. She no longer cared what he thought about her. Relieved of the burden of trying to earn his favor, she felt lighter and stronger and more certain than ever about the path she wished to carve for herself. If he would stand in her way, she would simply find a way around him.

Nor did Faith consider it theft. Surely her power to use the Ink gave her a claim upon it. By what right did the Guild control it? The fact that they would admit the Colonel to their highest ranks told Faith all she needed to know about the Guild and its motives. It could only be an elitist and capricious body governed by self-righteous, power-hungry men and she refused to be beholden to it.

She would take what was hers by right, and this was the day. Today was the ceremony that would create the American Guild and raise the Colonel as its Master. Faith did not know when it would be held or what it would entail. What she did know was that it would be in the Guild Hall and she was certain that if Leonardo's Inkwell were ever on display, it would be on such an occasion. All she had to do was follow the Colonel to the Hall, observe the proceedings to figure out where they kept the Ink, find a way to return in person, and claim a drop of the Ink for herself.

As Faith sat in church that morning, she tried not to dwell on the myriad variables and unknowns in her plan. She reassured herself that the solutions would present themselves as she went. Her only focus was the first step. Her concentration was such that she did not even hear when the first of the Banns were read for her impending marriage.

When they returned home, the Colonel glanced at the long case clock on the landing and informed Faith and her mother that he would be going to the Academy that afternoon and might be late for dinner. Faith smiled inwardly. She had expected such an announcement. Her mother was not as sanguine.

"On a Sunday?" Faith's mother asked.

"Some urgent business that the directors overlooked."

"What could possibly be so urgent to draw the directors out on a Sunday? Did they miss the rent?"

"None of your concern!" the Colonel answered impatiently. He compressed his lips as he grasped at composure. "That is, don't trouble yourself to think on it. If I am not back before dinner, please have Cook set me aside a tray. I will eat when I return."

Faith's mother shrugged, not looking the least put out that he would be gone all afternoon. Faith noted the Colonel's temper with amusement. He hadn't been this snappish in weeks. She wondered if he were nervous. In any event, this was the moment she had been waiting for.

"I've had word the Astors are back from Hellgate. I thought I might visit them this afternoon." Faith said innocently, ignoring the suspicious look her mother gave her. It would be the perfect excuse to leave the house for hours unaccompanied. Faith had reasoned that the Colonel's doorway into the Guild had to be the romantic landscape she had uncovered in the carriage house last summer. It was the only one big enough to step into that wasn't a portrait or a bloody battle scene. The fact that it was no longer in the carriage house- she had checked- confirmed her suspicion. She was certain it was waiting for him at the Academy.

"You may go, but take your mother with you." He looked at Sarah who did nothing to hide her displeasure at this suggestion. "They will be family soon. It would go easier on us all if they were to get to know you under more *sober* conditions. Be ready before I leave and I will escort you."

Faith had not anticipated he would send her mother. A wrinkle in her plan, but with the new understanding she and her mother had reached, it was one Faith was sure she could iron out.

As it was, her mother's reluctance to go dovetailed perfectly with Faith's scheme. Neither Faith or her mother had finished getting ready when the Colonel began pacing in the foyer. He shouted up to them.

"I'll need more time!" Faith shouted back.

"I must leave now or I'll be late!"

"You want me to look my best don't you? Go ahead to your meeting. Mama and I can find our way."

With an exasperated noise he agreed. The slamming of the door and the rattle of the transom confirmed his departure. For good measure, Faith pressed her forehead against the upstairs window and watched until he was well up the street.

"What on earth made you want to go to the Astor's and how in hell did I get dragged into it?" her mother asked.

"I'm sorry, Mama, but you know you weren't the intended victim," Faith said.

Sarah gave her a suspicious look. "What are you onto?"

"Don't trouble yourself to think on it," Faith said with a teasing smile. "Just tend to your affliction and if he asks later, tell him you sent me on and went to bed and you don't know a thing. Because you don't."

Sarah's eyes narrowed further. "Is it a man?"

Faith thought a moment then shook her head. "No, Mama. This is for me," she said and kissed her mother gently on the forehead.

Faith slipped on her softest shoes, tied on a bonnet, and checked the window one more time. The Colonel was no where in sight. She squeezed her bewildered mother's hand and stepped lightly down the stairs, glancing at the clock as she passed. A moment later she closed the front door quietly behind her.

Excitement and apprehension drove Faith's feet faster than she wanted. It took a conscious effort to walk at a decorous, unremarkable, pace. She did not want to attract attention, nor did she want to catch the Colonel up. As she stepped carefully over a puddle in the street left by yesterday's rain, she caught her reflection in the mirror-like water. Her face was hidden by the perspective and the shadow of her bonnet, the blue behind it both sky above and below. She had a moment of dizzying disorientation, losing a sense for what was up and down, which was real and which was image. Some grit fell from her passing shoe, sending ripples through the image.

Faith looked ahead, trying to regain her bearings. She was exquisitely aware of all the mundane details around her. The smell of horse manure from the droppings in the lane. The buzzing of insects and the chirps of birds. The sudden warmth on her shoulders when she stepped out of the sheltering shade of a building. The crunch of other people's steps, the mumble of their conversations. And yet, she felt disconnected from it all. She knew things that few around her could comprehend. She was apart, separated from this world by her knowledge of another.

As Faith closed the distance to the Academy, she shook off these strange musings and brought her focus to the task at hand. Up to now, she had merely been for a walk on a beautiful day. Once she entered the Academy, she was committed to her plan. With a sharp exhale and set jaw, Faith stepped into the foyer.

She scanned the space with eyes and ears. The light was dim and she saw no one about. The only thing she could hear was the thudding of her heart. She had not expected to see anyone. Certain that the director's meeting was a ruse, the only people who should be here were those artists who kept rooms, and only if they kept their portal painting here. She doubted Charles was here, though the temptation to check was hard to resist. Those who were here would have entered Phantasia in mind or body, leaving no consciousness to notice her. Relieved to have her reasoning confirmed, Faith headed to the stairs.

A throat cleared behind her. Faith startled, a hand to her heart.

A hesitant voice asked "Pardon Miss, can I help you?"

Faith spun, a little too quickly. The young man stepped back in surprise. She tried to emulate Eliza's coquettish laugh. She might have sounded deranged instead. "Oh! Hello! You startled me! I didn't think anyone else would be here. I'm here to see Colonel Trumbull. I'm his daughter."

The boy- in this moment far more boy than man- looked terrified at the mention of the Colonel. "I-I'm not supposed to let anyone in. Special meeting."

"Of course not! And you're doing a fine job. But I'm not just anyone. He'll understand. In fact, I think he would be put out if he thought I'd come all this way to see him and was turned away."

The boy pondered his impossible decision. Faith saved him the trouble. "I know where his rooms are. I'll see myself up and we'll pretend you never saw me."

"Oh- all right."

Faith waggled her fingers at him in a girlish wave and pranced over to the stairs. When he had disappeared back into the cast room, she settled into a more stealthy gait and tried to rein her galloping heart. She listened so intently that every faint creak or shuffle sounded like cannon fire in her ears. She stopped outside the Colonel's door. Looking both ways down the hall, Faith leaned her ear against the door. Nothing. She checked the light under the bottom for shadows. Still nothing.

With her hand on the latch, she took a breath and uttered a prayer. If he were still in the room, if she had misjudged in any way, her quest would be over for good. There was no quick talking that would explain to him why she was there. She winced at the squeal the latch made and pushed the door open. Gratefully, she found an empty room. Faith dashed in and closed the door behind her. As she caught her breath, she took in the room. His desk, table, scales, and supplies were all in pristine order just as she would have expected. The small Signing of the Declaration that was to be the model of his first capitol commission sat on an easel in one corner. The landscape leaned the opposite wall, its covering a white pile on the floor.

Faith untied her bonnet and pulled her pen from her hair as she debated whether to go in physically or mentally. It had occurred to her that it might only be possible to get there by following bodily. On the other hand, if she got lost, she could get trapped and not know how to get out. It would also be harder to hide without the ability to shift her imaginary appearance. If she went in mentally, she could return to reality in a blink if she were in any danger. She would just have to make sure she was back before the Colonel was, or he would encounter her catatonic body in front of his painting.

Faith sat on the floor before the picture as she had in a faraway memory. She gripped her pen tightly and focused on the small clearing at the fore. The space deepened and stretched. A warm breeze carried the sound of sheep grazing on the hillside. She felt the pull and spin. When it stopped, she was standing in the small clearing, hemmed in on two sides by a rocky outcrop. Where the studio had been moments before, was a grassy hill broken by more rocky projections. There was no clear path that way. Taking the only way open to her, she stepped beyond the boulders and found herself at the head of a trail. It wound its way down the hillside and along the river in the valley. From there it cut back uphill and disappeared into a stand of trees. The roof of the manor house was just visible among them.

Faith changed her clothes to shirt and britches, both the color of soft moss. At this distance, she would not stand out clearly. She hurried down the hill, eager to make the tree line before the Colonel might look back and see movement on the trail. Faith slowed when she entered the shelter of the trees. She stepped off the trail and moved stealthily from trunk to trunk. She wished she knew how far ahead the Colonel might be. Had he stopped along the path somewhere? Or was he already at the Guild Hall?

The path let out onto a broad clearing that sloped far down to the river on one side and up to the house on the other. The sky had deepened to twilight and the front windows were warmly lit. Smoke lifted from one of the chimneys.

Faith wondered how long she had already been here. It seemed like only minutes but the sky suggested otherwise. It was impossible to tell how time might flow in the Colonel's world. Afraid she would lose the trail if she dallied any longer, she threw caution to the wind and sprinted through the clearing toward the house. She headed for the foundation below the front windows, where the plantings would hide her while she peeked inside. Faith quickly realized that she had misjudged the height of the sills; she couldn't see over them at all. The most she could see was the upper half of a doorway on the far side of the room if she stood on tip-toe.

Faith was craning this way when a familiar head came into view. Faith ducked out of sight from the Colonel. Fear surged through her to think he would somehow know she was here. Pressed against the foundation wall of the house, she reassured herself he had not seen her. She stood up again to risk another look through the window. There was a woman with him now. She was young and pretty with rosy cheeks and masses of golden blonde curls. The smell of lavender perfume filled Faith's nose. Just as Faith was wondering who this woman could be, the Colonel pulled her close and kissed her passionately. When they separated, he touched the woman's cheek with a gentle hand. Faith saw his lips form the words "I love you" before he turned to leave the room.

Faith crouched down with a hand over her mouth. Her skin crawled with disgust. *Who is this woman?* Was she a member of the Guild or was she a figment of his imagination? Charles's words of warning about the dangers of creating people rang in Faith's ears.

A clock chimed inside the house and Faith jumped. She still didn't know how he would get to the Guild Hall. Was the door inside the house or somewhere else? She waited outside to see if he would emerge. When he did not Faith skirted the base of the house until she found a back stair to a servant's entrance. The door at its top was unlocked. Apparently the Colonel did not worry about intruders in his world.

Working her way down unfamiliar hallways, Faith stopped and listened every few feet. She heard nothing. Either the Colonel had left without her seeing or he was in a closed room outside of her hearing. Faith rounded a corner and found herself in the main entrance hall where a grand staircase led to the upper stories. She decided to try upstairs.

She had taken two steps up when a sweet voice behind her asked, "May I help you?"

CHAPTER THIRTY

The Guild

Faith turned slowly to face the young blond woman. She looked barely older than Faith. Although her complexion was flushed and glowing there was a strange emptiness about the eyes. Faith wondered if she were well.

The woman didn't look alarmed that Faith was standing there.

"I was hoping to see Colonel Trumbull," Faith said as though it were the most ordinary social call.

"Oh, John has gone to a meeting. He will be gone awhile, but you are welcome to wait for him."

John? "Oh! Uh, that is what I wanted to see him about. Can you tell me where it is?"

"In the drawing room, of course."

Faith stepped back down the stairs, coming closer to the other woman. The smell of lavender infused the air around her. And there was definitely something off about her eyes. They were lifeless as a doll's.

"Who are you?" Faith asked impertinently.

"I'm Harriet Wadsworth Trumbull," the woman replied with a sweet smile.

A shiver went down Faith's spine as though a ghost passed through her. The Wadsworths were close family friends of the Trumbulls. One of Faith's uncles had married a Wadsworth girl. She wracked her brain for the name Harriet. It came to her suddenly and her stomach clenched with revulsion. Harriet Wadsworth had died when she was eighteen. Nearly twenty years ago. For some unholy reason the Colonel had recreated the dead Wadsworth girl as his wife and kept her in this house.

And then Faith remembered what her mother had said about the Colonel when they first met. He was mourning the loss of a love who had died young. Faith had a sudden urge to return to reality and wash away the foul taint that seemed to coat her skin. She forced herself to focus on the Ink. She needed to see the Guild meeting first.

"Can you tell me where the drawing room is?" Faith asked.

"I'll show you." Harriet led her to a doorway across the hall and ushered her into a small parlor. There was a fireplace, two chairs, and a long case clock on one wall. "Are you sure this is where Colonel Trumbull went?"

"Yes, he goes to the drawing room when it is time."

Confused, Faith asked, "And is it time?"

"Time draws near," the woman said cryptically with the same pleasant smile.

The woman was like a child's toy, a doll made to speak. Her look was fawning and empty, her mannerisms flat and repetitive, her words hollow. She was little use. Faith was about to give up in frustration when her eye landed on the clock. When it is time. Faith remembered hearing the clock chime when the Colonel had left. She stepped to the clock, looking it over carefully. It was completely ordinary except... it had no hands on the face. *Time draws near. Time draws. Draws.* Faith brought her pen to hand, ready to draw the hands. *But what time?* The clock had chimed the hour but she hadn't counted it.

"Harriet, what time did Colonel Trumbull leave?"

"When the time was right, of course."

"Yes, but when is the right time?"

"There is a time for everything," Harriet said.

Her syrupy voice and nonsensical replies made Faith want to smack the smile off of Harriet's face. Still, as cryptic as her answers were, they seemed to offer clues. *A time for everything. Ecclesiastes.* It was one of her father's favorite passages.

Wishing she had taken the Colonel's advice about reading the Bible more to heart, Faith closed her eyes to block out Harriet's irritating presence. *To everything there is a season, and a time to every purpose under heaven.* She could almost see the page in her mind. Chapter three.

Faith reached up to draw the hands at three o'clock but stopped short. If she drew in the Colonel's world, it would link their worlds. The idea that she might leave something behind that could lead him to her made her go cold all over. She had little choice though. She drew the hands. The pendulum swung but nothing else happened.

Faith cursed under her breath. Perhaps it was a specific verse. She recited the chapter to herself, counting off the verses on her fingers.

> *A time to be born, and a time to die; a time to plant, and a time to uproot;*
> *A time to kill, and a time to heal; a time to break down, and a time to build up;*
> *A time to weep, and a time to laugh; a time to mourn, and a time to dance;*
> *A time to cast away stones...*

Faith stumbled over the next few lines. Though she couldn't remember the words, she could see the indentation on the page and ticked off two more fingers. She remembered the final two verses.

> *A time to rend, and a time to sew; a time to keep silence, and a time to speak;*
> *A time to love, and a time to hate; a time of war, and a time of peace.*

A time to keep silence and a time to speak. It had to be verse seven. Faith redrew the hands at seven o'clock. The mechanism began to whir followed by sonorous chimes. There was a click, barely audible, and both the wall behind the clock and the clock itself swung inwards. Faith dashed into the open doorway, erasing the clock face as she passed. Faith's last vision of the Colonel's world was of Harriet standing alone in the drawing room, hands folded in front of her, staring with an empty smile at the closing door.

Faith shuddered as it clicked shut. Charles was right. Real people should never be imitated.

Suddenly remembering herself, Faith looked quickly about her. She had been so eager to be away from the disturbing imitation of Harriet Wadsworth that she hadn't even thought to look where she was leaping. She found herself in a wide, curving hallway lined with doors. Fortunately, there was no one there to see her.

The door she had just come through was a plain affair on this side: A raised panel door, painted dark blue, with an ordinary iron latch. She was relieved to see that there was a latch on this side before she remembered that she was only in Phantasia in spirit.

The hallway curved out of sight in either direction. Faith picked one and started walking, giving a thought to making her steps silent on the gleaming marble floor. Her eyes slid over the doors as she passed. Each was different than the last, some radically so. These must be the Master's doors; behind each was a different world including, somewhere, Charles'. The idea was exhilarating and overwhelming.

Along the left hand wall she came to a window where a door should have been. She looked out of it onto a rolling countryside with patchwork fields in green and gold divided by stands of narrow cypress trees. At the edge of the fields, there was a lake that gave back the reflection of a great domed building surrounded by smaller towers. Her breath caught at the image. It was the same as what she had seen in her mind when thinking about her own pleasure dome. It took her a moment to realize she was looking at the Guild Hall and that she was in one of those towers.

Faith hurried along the hall of doors, knowing it would have to let out somewhere and hoping there would not be anyone around when it did. Wishing she could be invisible, Faith recalled what Charles had said when the idea had first struck her. It was possible with enough conviction, but probably hard to maintain. She decided to give it a try. At first Faith told herself to imagine that she wasn't there. It seemed to be working until she felt the tug of reality. Scared she would end up back in the Colonel's studio and have to start all over, she abruptly made herself fully present. Changing her mindset to one of transparency, Faith imagined herself more as a ghost. Holding up a hand to her face, she watched the form dissolve until it was a hazy veil but it did not disappear entirely. She could not be sure whether this was the limit of her imagination or the effect of new-found caution but it would have to do.

Until the floor leveled out onto a straight run of hallway, Faith had not realized she had been walking on a subtle incline. The straight hallway was short, ending on an archway that framed an intersection with another hall. Faith stepped into the cross vaulted intersection and found herself in a grand arcade of pillared arches that circled the interior of the Guild Hall's central dome. Spanning the bottom of each arch was a carved marble balustrade over which Faith could hear the echo of voices.

Not entirely confident in her transparency, Faith stayed concealed behind a pillar as she chanced a look over the railing. Above her there was another arcade and above that was the massive domed ceiling. It was painted like a soft blue sky. Inked clouds shifted and moved across it along with winged cherubs and a host of angels. Evenly spaced corbels supported the dome where it met the upper arcade. Figures dressed in bright colors perched atop each corbel. There were both male and female figures, though the women were oddly masculine. Some were reading, some were writing on scrolls, while others sat chin on fist watching what transpired below. Faith thought that they were sculptures until she noticed the moving quills and saw one turn a page.

Following the gaze of the thoughtful watchers, Faith looked down. There were two more levels above a large circular space at the bottom, the center of which was occupied by a round raised dais. Seats were arranged around the dais in a spiraling pattern. From Faith's high vantage, they resembled a pinecone or the center of a sunflower. The dais was occupied by a podium and several robed and wigged men arrayed about a long table. At one end was an open book on a stand. On the other was a plinth draped in purple silk, a small, glass inkwell at its center. Even from a distance, Faith could see the inkwell glow, casting kaleidoscopic shards of color and light all about it.

The Ink. She had found it. Now all she needed was to figure out how to get a drop of it.

Faith pulled back from the railing and moved along the arcade, watching for openings in the exterior wall. At the next cross-vault, she found what she was looking for: a staircase. As Faith ducked into the stairwell, a resonant voice rose up from below.

"Commensurate with the establishment and foundation of the American Guild of Athena, to which you have just borne witness, the High Council of the Guild has approved and will now appoint its first Guild Master. Will Master Colonel John Trumbull please ascend to the dais."

Faith tripped on the first step and if she had been there in body might have tumbled all the way to the bottom of the stair. As it was, she arrested her descent with force of will born of fear of making any noise. She paused at the next landing to catch her breath and then carried on. What transpired next in the ceremony was lost to Faith, muffled by the stone walls around her, but had all the characteristic intonation and pacing of an oath being taken. She told herself it did not matter. All she needed was the Ink.

When she reached the bottom of the stairs, she peered around the doorway. She could see someone leaning on the railing across the room but the arcade outside her stairwell was empty. Faith glanced down to confirm that she was still transparent, or nearly so, and edged cautiously to the railing. The floor of the assembly was sunk beneath the arcade, the heads of those seated just below her feet. It put her on the level of the dais. She could clearly see the Colonel as he lowered one hand and pulled the other from the top of a Bible. Instinctively, Faith shrank back farther behind a pillar.

The man holding the Bible gestured to the end of the table with the Inkwell on its plinth. The Colonel bowed solemnly and approached the Ink.

"Your pen, sir." A white wigged old man with a nasal voice took the Colonel's proffered pen and, with dramatic slowness, dipped it once into the Ink. He held it above the well, giving the shaft three light taps and then returned the pen to the Colonel in a high arcing gesture. For all his theatrics, it was quite anticlimactic.

"Please mark your name in the ledger of the American Guild, the first among its members."

The Colonel took his pen and walked to the book.

When the Colonel turned his back to sign his name, Faith was able to tear herself away from the spectacle and concentrate on the next steps in her plan. She glanced at her own pen with a moment's hope that she could approach the dais unseen and sneak a drop of Ink as the ceremony broke up. Surely there would be a bit of shuffling chaos to serve as a distraction. She immediately discarded the idea. Not only did she not trust her invisibility, but she suspected she would need to be here in person for it to work. Even if she could use the imaginary pen in her hand, it would be the one the Colonel would confiscate if and when he ever discovered her.

No, she would need a different pen. It didn't matter what it was made of- a stick would do- but it would have to be here physically. For that, she would have to wait until after the ceremony to find out where they stored the Ink so that she could come back another time. Yet, if she stayed too long, the Colonel might return while her body still sat on the floor of his studio. The only other option was to look around now and see if she could figure out where they kept the Ink and how to get back later.

A round of applause erupted behind her and made Faith jump. The Colonel had finished signing. It was official. He approached the podium with a triumphant look upon his face and addressed the assembly. He began with what Faith knew to be falsely humble thanks that suggested gratitude for an unsought honor. Faith's lip curled in disgust. She tuned him out as he launched into a monologue about his vision for the American Guild. Instead, Faith moved slowly around the arcade, observing everything as she went.

She was nearly half way around when his words caught her up short.

"...in keeping with this vision, and in emulation of the wise example of the Paris Academy and its esteemed Guild, the American Guild will be entirely closed to women."

A murmur rippled through the crowd. The motion of disgruntled heads bobbing and turning caught Faith's eye. All around the room, the movement drew her gaze to the women in the room. They were overwhelmingly outnumbered by the men, but they were there.

Liar! Faith shouted at him in her heart. She was so angry that she passed the next section of arcade blindly, forcing herself to retrace her steps to see what she might have missed.

"And now I have the pleasure of announcing the first Masters who have been invited and who, with the agreement of their current Guilds, have accepted admission into the American Guild..."

Faith only half listened as he announced the names, waves of applause washing through the assembly after each. She had seen a doorway whose position was out of place in the pattern of staircase and tower entries. As she made her way there, the Colonel's voice cut through her thoughts like a whetted knife.

"Master Charles Cromwell Ingham..."

Faith spun instinctively towards the dais. The Colonel's back was to her, the approach to the dais, and Charles as he gained it, directly in her line of sight. Their eyes met and Faith felt herself seen. A look of surprise and recognition crossed Charles' face. The Colonel's shoulder began to turn just before Faith vanished completely.

Where is the way to the dwelling of light
and where is the place of darkness
that you may take it to its territory
and that you may discern the paths to its home?

- Job 38:19

CHAPTER THIRTY-ONE

The Confession

Faith surged back into her body with a sharp inhalation. She lurched to her feet and ran from the Colonel's studio like the hounds of hell were after her. She gave not a thought to the sound of her steps on the stairs or the boy who stood on watch. She burst out of the Academy doors and into brilliant, disorienting sunlight.

She threw up her hands against the glare and skidded to a stop. After the twilight in the Colonel's world she had not expected it still to be day. What time was it now? How long had she been in there? How long before the Colonel returned? Whatever the answers, Faith had to get home before he did.

Gathering her wits, she began the walk back, briskly but not unreasonably so. She found it easier to control her feet than the wild panic that flailed about within her. Had the Colonel seen her? She didn't think so. But Charles certainly had. He had seen her and recognized her. It would take no great leap for him to reason why she was there sneaking around. What would he think? He was bound to be angry. What would he do?

Faith needed to talk to him.

There was no way to reach Charles until after the ceremony, after the Colonel had returned and retired. Then, in the safety of solitary night, Faith would try to reach him in Phantasia. And beg him not to take her pen.

When Faith arrived home, she went first to the kitchen. The smells, surely inviting any other night, made the pit of vipers in Faith's stomach writhe violently. She told Cook she would be skipping dinner.

"Oh, you do look poorly," the woman agreed. "Pale as a ghost. You go on. I'll take your Mama a tray."

Faith thanked Cook and went upstairs. Her thighs quivered with each step. She paused outside her mother's door, trying to steady herself. If Cook had noticed, her mother would too and she did not want to worry her. When she thought she had herself together, she poked her head around the door. Her mother was in bed with a book on her lap.

"How was your visit?" her mother asked.

Faith realized she was wringing her shaking hands. She pressed them together. "Fine. It went well."

"I'm not convinced."

"Well, please convince the Colonel that it did. I've got a headache now and am going to go to bed early."

Her mother's skeptical look only deepened but after a heartbeat she nodded. "I will tell him. If you need some sleep there's a tincture there in my vanity drawer. The dark glass bottle. Just a few drops, mind you."

"Thank you, but I'll be fine. Oh, uh, Cook said she will bring a tray up in a bit, so you don't have to go down if you don't want to."

"Take it."

Faith did as she was told and retrieved the bottle from her mother's vanity. The glass stopper rattled as she carried it to the door. "Good night, Mama. I love you."

"I love you, too, child. Whatever is troubling you, I hope you find peace with it."

Not trusting her voice anymore, Faith nodded and backed out. Once in her own room, she set the bottle down on the dresser and locked the door. Exhaustion pulled at the threads of her frayed wits. She undressed and lay down on the bed, thinking she would try to sleep while she waited for nightfall but sleep would not come. She turned and tossed and eyed the bottle of tincture. She could not risk sleeping through the night and missing Charles.

Faith got up and walked through the things she wanted to say in her mind as her feet paced the floor. She was tired of the stress and strain of all the lies, tired of masking what she felt and thought. She had long wanted to unburden herself of the guilt she carried for lying to Charles, but had not known how or when to do it. Now that she had been discovered, she had no choice but to confess. She found a relief there that offered some solace for her soul. She would repent and ask for Charles' absolution. He would be angry, but she knew he loved her as she loved him. He would forgive her and they could move forward with open hearts.

With this resolve, Faith's steps changed from frantic to eager as the sky purpled outside her room. The door below opened and shut, announcing the Colonel's return. Faith froze like prey that scented danger. She listened as his heels clicked across the foyer floor and faded down the hall. She did not move when silence returned, waiting for him to finish his meal and retire for the night. She was still standing, now in the dark of a moonless night, when she finally heard the creak on the stairs and the click of his bedroom door.

She waited still, another hour maybe, before pushing her discarded dress against the base of the door and feeling in the dark for her tinderbox. Her hands still trembling, she scraped her knuckles as she struck the flint. The tinder caught and she lit a spill, carrying it to the candle on her dresser. Under this low, guttering light, Faith pulled the bottom drawer all the way out, revealing her drawing of Prior Park laid flat along the bottom of the cabinet.

Setting both the drawing and the candle on the floor, Faith curled her legs beneath her. As she had earlier that afternoon before the Colonel's painting, she let her focus go soft and felt herself pulled into Phantasia. She arrived at the top of the hill, looking down upon the bridge with the city in the distance. If Charles came to her, he would be in the palace garden. Now that she was in her world, she could just imagine herself there but the events to the day had left her shaken and the lake below brought back disquieting thoughts. She reached out for Helios. An exhale later she heard and felt the beat of his wings and found herself enfolded in his reassuring glow. Pen in hand, she flew with him to her palace garden.

Charles was not there. Faith walked the circuit of the courtyard thrice, glancing between the tea set and the stars and back again every few paces. A flash of color and movement caught her attention in the moonlit garden. Charles' butterfly pulsed slowly on the lip of a moonflower. If he would not come to her, she would have to go to him.

Faith called the butterfly to her with an outstretched hand, the touch of its delicate feet carrying with it the same image of a wildflower meadow as the first time she had held it. She seized onto the image, cupping it against the movement of her thoughts like a precious flame. And then she was there, on a grassy, flower strewn plain that stretched towards a distant shore. A rustic cabin sat on its edge, a candle burning in the window. Faith made her way toward it.

Faith approached the cabin door, full of apprehension. She knocked. There was no answer. Trying the latch, she found it unlocked. She opened the door only a little way, slipping in quickly as though it were somehow a less intrusive way to enter uninvited.

The room was pleasantly warm. The faint scent of cigars and scotch perfumed the air. There was a desk with Charles' Guild writing box, or at least its facsimile, sitting open on it. Bookshelves lined one side opposite windows that looked out to sea. In front of them, the picture of Faith in the white plumed hat rested on an easel, its background a perfect match to the scene behind it. Charles, his back to her, sat looking at the picture, or at the rolling waves, she couldn't tell which. He held a glass of amber liquid balanced on his knee.

He did not turn to see her. She stepped around to face him.

"I can explain..." she offered quietly.

His only response was a slight tilt of his head and a raised eyebrow that said he very much doubted it. Faith had no choice but to fill the silence.

"I know you saw me at the Guild Hall today. I-I followed the Colonel in. But, only to observe! You've taught me so much about the Ink, but the Guild itself has remained such a mystery. I desperately wanted to know more. I needed to know more." Faith's voice had grown more pleading with each syllable. She took a breath, reminding herself she was here to apologize. When she began again she was contrite. "I know that doesn't make it right, that what I did is against the rules. I'm sure even being here right now," she said with a glance around the room, "is at least a breach of etiquette, but it was important for me to see you right away, to tell you how very sorry I am."

Faith paused to see if her words were having any impact. Charles still did not look at her, his gaze somewhere between the room and the horizon. Faith began to wonder if he could hear her. Was it some trick of Phantasia that she was invisible in his world? She moved between him and whatever held his gaze.

"Charles, can you hear me?" she asked, waving a hand. "I'm here to apologize. Can you forgive me? Please, Charles, answer me."

With this last, his eyes finally flicked toward her. He took a drink from his glass.

"I'm curious. If you were so desperate to see the Guild, why didn't you ask?"

Taken aback, Faith sputtered. "Ask you? I didn't think it was poss- I mean-"

Charles cut her off with a gesture. "Why didn't you ask your Da?"

"Well, you heard him during the ceremony. Women won't be allowed in the Guild," Faith answered, her thoughts milling like startled sheep in a pen.

"True, but you could hardly have known that before you decided to sneak in. So, I ask again. If all you wanted was to observe, why didn't you ask the Colonel?"

Faith wrung her hands as she flailed about for an answer. Charles didn't wait for it. "How long have you known women would be excluded from the Guild?"

Faith turned away. His voice was terrifyingly calm and his eyes seemed to cut right through her. She looked to the floor for strength. She had come here to confess. She knew he would be angry but she had not realized it would be so hard.

"Since the beginning," Faith answered meekly.

Silence.

She turned around to find him scowling at the bottom of his glass. "I see," he finally said.

Pent up anger and frustration violently shoved aside Faith's guilt and apprehension. "Do you? Do you have any idea what it's been like for me, what would drive me to such lengths? What do you know of the Colonel, truly? To all outward appearances he is a gentleman, a man of perfect integrity and courtesy. But can you imagine what it is like to have him as a *father* who will not even permit such an intimate term? Let me tell you what he's like, so that you can *see* the whole picture."

Faith's voice rose as the headwaters of indignation spilled forth, "All my life I have had to contort and constrain myself to meet that man's expectations. When I was a child I wanted to climb trees, splash in puddles, laugh and shout like children do. Instead, I had to speak quietly and stay on the path. I watched the other children play from the window, my mother my only playmate, while he preached honor, dignity, and duty. I came to accept that it was my role to be obedient and agreeable, subservient and silent. That my entire future was to marry well, manage a household, bear children and die respectfully. I thought that if I didn't neglect my duties, gave no cause for complaint, I might one day win his affection and approval. I have given up waiting for that day!"

Faith was pacing now, punctuating her words with flying hands. "The only thing that has kept me from despair has been my art. From the moment I learned to draw, it opened a gateway into a world where I could see and do all of the things this world would not allow. Never once did he encourage me. He offered no lessons. But, I thought if I could keep my art, even hidden, I could accept any fate. He wouldn't even allow me that one vice.

"I did not go looking for the Ink. He revealed it to me. He showed me a world of freedom and power that no woman can ever experience in this reality- an Eden of my own design!- and then closed and barred the gates! Why? Only because I am a woman! He told me that women can not even *use* the Ink but I knew in my heart that he was wrong. So, I took his pen when he wasn't looking and I tasted the forbidden fruit. After that, I could not stop any more than I could stop my heart or breath. After that, I knew everything he said was lies. Women can use the Ink. Women can enter the Guild. Only I cannot by virtue of my parentage.

"Oh, Charles, can you fathom the cruel irony?" Faith let her hands fall to her sides as tears ran down her cheeks. "Had I been born a man, he would have rejoiced at my Talent. I might have been the first to sign the ledger beneath his name. If I had been born a man, I would not have wanted for acceptance or agency, the very things that make the Ink more precious to me than life. What is life worth without self-determination?"

"Do you really think the Ink is less precious to me because I am a man?"

Faith blanched, unsure of her reply.

"You have no answer? Surely, you considered how I would be affected by your schemes?" Faith looked down at her hands, unable to meet the cold anger in his eyes. "I thought not. You say the Colonel drilled honor and integrity into you? I say he missed the board. You lied to me and tricked me without once considering the honest path. Have you ever thought to ask permission or is it only your intention to demand forgiveness?"

"What do you mean? Are you suggesting you would have defied the Guild if I had simply asked?" Faith asked incredulously.

"You've just said you knew the Guild admitted some women. You blame the Colonel for your plight, but he is not the entire Guild."

"You wouldn't have. Protocol and courtesies, remember?" Faith's voice undermined the certainty of her words.

"You didn't even try! And if you remember, I did bend the rules for you. Repeatedly! Faith, your situation is truly lamentable. If you had come to me in honesty, it wouldn't have been easy but we could have found a way."

Faith shook her head against the guilt and horror that began to press tight against her heart.

"You don't believe me?" he asked. With a groan he stomped to the desk and slammed his glass down. He pulled a letter from the writing box and waved it at her. "Let me tell you what I've been through for you. When the Colonel announced his appointment and invited us to join, he laid out the bylaws of the new Guild. I've known since early March that he intended to exclude women. Can you fathom the irony? I thought you were innocent, that the news would be a shock. I couldn't bring myself to tell you, to see the disappointment in your eyes. I should have ended your lessons and taken back that pen the moment I got the letter. Instead I took you to Jarvis and let you press on. I figured what did it matter if you learned one more thing before it all came to an end. I even thought about letting you keep the pen and pretending like it never happened."

Faith was crying freely now. Relief and gratitude overwhelmed her. "Charles! Would you really? Can we just put this behind us and move on? I swear I'll never tell a soul."

Charles was motionless, an inscrutable look on his face. "After I've learned how you betrayed my trust and put my own future with the Guild in jeopardy? You ask too much."

Faith sniffed in surprise. "But, Charles-"

He cut her off sharply. "I spoke for you with my Guild Master. Your conduct is my responsibility. Like you, I've thought about what it would be like to be cut off from the Ink, and now your actions have made that a possibility. Not just the Ink, my whole livelihood. Do you think the Guild will allow me to continue as a painter if they eject me from the Guild? At least as a woman you get to marry and have someone take care of you. I am the one that has to provide."

"Get to marry? Have you heard nothing that I said? You've met the man the Colonel has matched me with. He has condemned me to a dull and visionless existence!"

"You may well have done the same to me."

"It doesn't have to be that way. I can't bear to lose you and the Ink when I know I have a claim to both!"

Faith threw her arms around his neck and kissed him. He tensed when her lips touched his, but his arms went around her waist and pulled her close. He returned her kiss with urgency. Faith's lips parted and she tasted the salt of her tears. She pressed herself to him.

Charles pulled away. He wiped a tear from her cheek with his thumb and brushed her hair back with his other hand. There was deep sadness in his eyes. He dropped his arms and stepped back.

"You have no claim on me and I have no claim on you. You are already spoken for. Even if you were free, you've broken my trust and that is not easily mended."

Her eyes wide, Faith pleaded. "Please, Charles. Please give me a chance to prove myself to you. Let me keep the pen, and I'll prove that you can trust me."

"What about the next time your curiosity knows no bounds or you feel slighted by some injustice? I cannot let you endanger both our futures."

"No, Charles, you can't. Please. I made such a mistake. Such a selfish mistake. I'm so sorry. I'm so very sorry."

His shoulder's slumped and his eyes slid from her to the floor. "You might be, but only about being caught."

"What are you going to do?"

"What's right."

"And what am I to do?"

"Go home, Faith," he said, not unkindly.

I went to the Garden of Love,
And saw what I never had seen:
A Chapel was built in the midst,
Where I used to play on the green.

And the gates of this Chapel were shut,
And Thou shalt not writ over the door;
So I turn'd to the Garden of Love,
That so many sweet flowers bore.

And I saw it was filled with graves,
And tomb-stones where flowers should be:
And Priests in black gowns, were walking their rounds,
And binding with briars, my joys & desires.
- William Blake, The Garden of Love

CHAPTER THIRTY-TWO
The Bonfire

For the second time that day, Faith came back to her body with a sharp inhalation. This time though, she did not rise. She collapsed to the floor, shattered. Faith cried, her back heaving with great shuddering sobs, hands pressed to her mouth to muffle her despair.

All was lost. Charles. The Ink. Any hope of freedom. Everything she held dear in this world would soon be taken from her.

There were brief lulls in her grief when the torrent of tears slowed to a steady stream and the barest hint of hope tried to shine through. It was during one of these respites when Faith moved herself to put her picture back in the base of her dresser cabinet and return the drawer that concealed it. During another she dared to think that Charles might have a change of heart. She knew he loved her. She had felt it in his kiss. He was justifiably angry. Who better knew the pain of betrayal than Faith? But, she tried to assure herself, he might come to forgive her.

That would have to be a worry for the day. For now she was spent and the night nearly with it. She lurched to her feet and splashed cold water from the basin on her face. As she felt for the towel, her hand brushed the tincture bottle. A few drops, her mother had said, and she would sleep. Hoping for a dreamless one in which she could forget the day, Faith held the dropper above her tongue. The tincture was vilely bitter and her stomach recoiled violently. She drank straight from the water pitcher in a vain attempt to wash the taste away.

She put out the candle and crawled into bed. Closing her eyes against the dark, Faith slept.

*　*　*

When she awoke, the sun was already high in the sky, streaming past her open curtain. The light stabbed at her skull. Her eyes felt sticky and strange. In the mirror the whites were red and the skin puffy and pale. Faith splashed more water on her face and waited for the swelling to go down before she could show her face downstairs.

She had just finished dressing when she heard a familiar voice in the hall below.

"I'll show myself out. Good day, sir, and thank you for your understanding."

"Good afternoon, Mr. Ingham. I appreciate your honesty."

Faith tore open the door of her room and ran to the top of the stairs. Charles was retrieving his hat from the stand.

"Charles," Faith called, desperation cracking her voice.

Charles looked up only briefly. His face was somber, his eyes expressionless.

"Good-bye, Miss Trumbull," he said with a nod and walked out the door.

Faith grasped the railing for support. White knuckled, she drew in deep draughts of air trying to stifle the renewed threat of tears. She would have to face the Colonel and she would need all of her strength and composure to do it. She turned her focus from what she had lost to the cause of her strife. A simmering resentment for the Colonel annealed her nerve and fortified her with fierce determination. The fight was not yet over. She still had her pen, her pictures, and her sketchbooks. No matter what he did, he could not take her Talent.

When her knees and spine felt equal to the task, Faith descended the stairs.

The Colonel was sitting at the dining table before a cup of tea. His face had a far off contemplative quality. Other than his ever-erect posture, there was nothing to suggest that he was in anything other than a peaceful mood.

Not knowing what Charles had actually said to him, Faith modeled her behavior on his. She poured herself a cup of tea and took a biscuit from the sideboard. She sat down at her usual spot and took a sip. The flow of saliva thus aided, she asked with casual curiosity, "Was that Mr. Ingham I saw leaving?"

The Colonel's eyes returned from wherever they had been and focused on Faith. He looked her up and down coolly, as though seeing her for the first time and taking the measure of her. "Yes, it was."

"Of course, it's not my affair, but I'm curious why he was here. Was it a social visit?"

"It was not. We will get to the reason for his visit in a moment. Did you follow me to the Guild Hall yesterday?"

A little stunned that he had driven straight for the mark, Faith felt a small flash of hope nonetheless. If he was asking, perhaps Charles had not shared everything.

"What are you talking about? What Guild?" Faith dissembled.

"Don't play coy with me. The Guild of Athena."

"The one with the magical Ink? I'd nearly forgotten all about it. You made it quite clear that the Guild was not open to me."

"Yes, I thought I had, which is why it made little sense that several of its members reported seeing a young woman, of about your description, make a vanishingly short appearance. I might have discounted that, as it is an imaginative place. It would not be the first time someone saw the flash of an image or the ghost of a memory. On further investigation, however, I learned that a similar young woman, claiming to be my daughter, had entered the Academy and that one of my paintings had been tampered with. This was all very extraordinary until Mr. Ingham's visit."

The Colonel's voice was conversational, but his eyes bore into Faith's. Her palms began to sweat. She placed them flat on her lap where he couldn't see them tremble.

"I will ask one more time. Did you follow me to the Guild Hall yesterday?" the Colonel asked with a challenge in his tone.

"Why ask, if you are so certain?" Faith answered with a challenge of her own.

"To hear it from your serpent's tongue," he said, voice dripping with acid.

"Are you calling *me* a liar?"

"You incited Mr. Ingham to train you under false pretenses, did you not? And then you lied to me yesterday about going to the Astors, a claim which we can verify this afternoon, so that you could sneak into the Guild like a thief in the night. Or are you saying that it was Mr. Ingham who forced you to take up the Ink and trained you in violation of his oath and set you as a spy amongst the Guild? If that is the case, we will have to deal harshly with him."

"Charles is innocent! He has done nothing wrong," Faith leapt to his defense knowing it weakened her own.

"Then you admit you are a deceiver and a conniver!" The corners of the Colonel's lips curled in a sadistic smile. "As it happens, I am inclined to agree with you about Mr. Ingham. He comes from a far more liberal Guild than mine and was only recently made aware of my feelings on the matter. That he allowed you to continue after my intentions were made clear was foolish and demands discipline, but I will recommend leniency on the matter. How was he to apprehend that all of the worst attributes of your sex were to be found in someone claiming to be of my blood? The fact that he came to me and confessed says a good deal about his integrity. A quality you, however, are utterly lacking."

A white hot flame burst in Faith's head. "*My* integrity is lacking? What about yours? I'd sooner question your integrity than the existence of unicorns! They are far more likely to be real! If I have no integrity then it is because you had none to give, *Father*," Faith spat with venom.

The Colonel's smile disappeared and his face darkened. "How dare you impugn my honor you impertinent snipe!"

Faith made a derogatory noise in her throat. "Honor. Yes, it was very honorable of you to sire not one, but *two* illegitimate children. I know about your indiscretions, if that is what I'm to be called."

The Colonel's shock was gratifying but he did not back down. "Then you also know that I have atoned for my sins. My penitence has cost me a great deal more than I could have imagined. You were nearly my ruin. Not only did I diminish my standing by marrying a poor orphan, but was forced to cut ties with my family over the affair. I have put up with your mother's scandalous behavior without complaint and tried to raise you into a respectable woman. I spared you the ridicule and degradations of society, and this is the thanks I have? A drunk and a manipulative chit!"

"Oh, poor, *honorable* Colonel Trumbull. What a trial I have been to you. I've only spent my entire life trying to be the meek and biddable simpleton you deem so appealing. And, I ask you, for what? Not a single shred of approval or affection, not even the acknowledgment that I am of your blood. And then tell me, why do you cling to a title you barely earned forty years after the fact? Is it because your honor is so tattered that you must dress it up with an emblem of false pride?"

The Colonel pounded the table with his fist that made the dishes rattle. "I have served this country dutifully and my honor is perfectly intact. I have provided for you, tried to raise you to your station, and match you in a way that will spare you what I have endured. Based upon the present circumstance though, it would seem I was quite right to withhold my approval. You have not earned it. A marriage to the Astors is more than you deserve."

"Don't pretend you've arranged that for my benefit. You want it for you and your precious legacy. It can't be for me because I don't want it."

"Then you are a foolish, ignorant child. How can you object to a favorable marriage- to enjoy wealth, comfort, a fine house to care for, and to be a prominent member of society? I hardly think it is too much to ask that you do your duty as a woman and put the needs of your family above your whims."

"Like Mama? To be unloved, disdained, to be beholden to a man who resents her for an outcome of his own making? To live with a man who prefers the company of an unholy perversion, who professes his love and commits profane acts with a woman you have raised from the dead to simper and fawn over you? It's no wonder she drinks!"

The Colonel visibly paled. For a moment, he looked like he might be sick. His voice was quiet, momentarily drained of self-righteous rage. "You *were* there."

Faith abandoned all pretense. "Of course I was there! What did you think would happen when you showed me the Ink? Did you think I could forget about it? Would you have given up after you first discovered what the Ink could do? I had to know and I knew I couldn't turn to you, my own father, to help me. So, I tricked Charles, but only because of your lies about women and the Ink. You said yourself, he had done nothing wrong. But, then, he did stop training me and I had to know more. So, yes, I followed you. Other than discovering what a lecherous, deceitful hypocrite you are, what harm did it do? If you were an honorable man, you would have encouraged me to be there. If you hadn't held me back..." Faith trailed off, the truth striking her like lightning. "That's why you did it. You're threatened by me. Otherwise, you would have held me up, if only to augment your position."

"Your conceit knows no bounds. You were nearly my ruin when you were born and I will not have you get in my way again. I will put a stop to it all right now. You will never touch the Ink again. In fact, you will never draw again. If you so much as draw in the dirt with a stick, I will take the stick from you and beat you with it. You will marry William Astor, repent your sins, and put your mind to being the upstanding young woman that God demands."

"God gave me this Gift. He didn't give it for you to take it away. If he did, then he is no God of mine."

Faith's blasphemous words sent the Colonel into an apoplectic rage.

"Jezebel!" he shouted at her as he stood, knocking over his chair. The Colonel stormed from the room, leaving Faith sitting in stunned silence.

She heard his footsteps on the stairs. Too late, she realized where he was headed. She took the stairs two at a time but could not make it to her room before he had locked the door. Faith pounded on the unyielding wood and cried to him to open up.

"What is going on?" her mother cried, coming into the hall. Faith slid to the floor. Her mother knelt and cradled her in her arms.

"Don't let him do it!" she pleaded with her mother, knowing she was as powerless as Faith to stop him. She could hear the thuds and bangs inside her room as he ransacked her drawers and turned the contents out onto the floor. When he finally opened the door, Faith's room was in complete disarray. Her dresser and her vanity drawers had all been disgorged of their contents. Even her mattress had been pushed aside, its covering torn. Feathers drifted in the air.

The Colonel stepped over her carrying the bundled sheet from her bed, the sharp edges of her sketchbooks visible in its folds. He paused for a moment in the hall, his hand raised above her head. Faith cowered, afraid that he would strike her. He reached down and pulled the pen from her hair.

The Colonel carried the entirety of Faith's world down the stairs and through the kitchen. Grabbing a lamp from its hook, he strode determinedly outside. Faith followed, trying to claw him back. He pushed her away and she fell against her mother. In the courtyard behind the house, the Colonel threw down the bundle and broke the lamp over it. Flaming grease ignited the sheet. The flames greedily gnawed the edges of Faith's books until they burst fully into flame and were swallowed whole. The terrible bonfire burned with brilliantly colored flames and the ashes of Faith's world floated to heaven like butterflies.

It indeed appeared to Reason as if desire was cast out, but the Devil's account is, that the Messiah fell, and formed a heaven of what he stole from the abyss.

-William Blake, The Marriage of Heaven and Hell

CHAPTER THIRTY-THREE
The Reprisal

Faith's heart seemed to lift up out of her body with the ashes and embers as they rose into the air. She felt the multi-hued flames sear away her hope, her joy, her love as though they burned inside her. When the funeral pyre of her inner world had burned itself out, so too had every emotion except hatred, anger, and determination. Her heart felt like the smoldering, black lumps of charcoal that remained; her body was an empty husk.

All that was left to her was revenge. Unlike her mother's reprisals, Faith's would not be petty.

Faith returned to her room and locked the door. She tearlessly put order to the chaos the Colonel had made of her room. Her hands worked of their own volition while her mind plotted. When she found the bottle of tincture in the pile of bed linens that he had tossed aside, Faith's plan was complete. She would have to move quickly.

Faith laid out two clean shifts and dresses, a bonnet and her coat next to an empty pillowcase on her remade bed. She packed a small bag of toiletries, shoving her tinder box and a handful of candle stubs on top. And then she sat and waited. Her mind and heart were almost peaceful in their resolve.

Her patience was rewarded when a soft thud and the rattle of the front door transom signaled that the Colonel had stepped out. She confirmed with a glance out the window before creeping down the stairs with the dark glass bottle in her hand. The house was silent and still. Even the usual clangs and bangs from the kitchen were absent. Everyone had retreated from the drama of the day like frightened rabbits.

Faith made her way to the Colonel's study and the decanter of liquor he kept there. Fatih held the tincture bottle up to the light. Most of it had spilled but there was a good swallow or more left in the bottom. She eyeballed the decanter, not sure of the necessary ratios. She shrugged and upended what was left of the tincture into the decanter. As a man of strict routine and probably more in need of a drink this night than most, Faith was sure he would poor a glass. How much, or whether, he would drink it if the tincture's bitterness was not adequately masked, she could not guess. Some things would be left to chance.

With a silent prayer for justice, Faith left the study for the kitchen. She collected some bread, cheese and cured meat into a pile next to the crate of soda water and covered it with a flour cloth. She pocketed the key that hung by the door and returned quietly to her room. She set the empty tincture bottle in plain sight upon her dresser. She would take all the blame for her actions.

Again, she sat and waited.

The Colonel returned, dusk descended, and then gave way to night. A tray was brought and left outside Faith's unanswered door. When she was certain all had retired and the house was long silent, Faith rose and dressed. She put one clean shift over the other, and then pulled on both dresses. The layers of fabric were tight and restricting, but it would be easier to wear rather than carry them. She left her room, depositing her coat and bonnet, pillowcase and shoes at the top of the stairs. She then made her way to the Colonel's bedroom door by candlelight.

Unsurprisingly, it was locked. She set the candle on the floor and smiled faintly as she pulled the skeleton key from her pocket. The lock clicked loudly in the silence. Faith waited, listening before opening the door. The Colonel was asleep in bed, his breathing undisturbed by either the creak of hinges or the light of the candle. Faith's smile grew less faint.

Holding the candle high, she scanned the surfaces of his room. Her eye fell on a familiar set of keys. As she stretched our her hand to grab them, the long case clock whirred and chimed the hour. The Colonel's breath caught and he shifted in his sleep. Faith froze, her skin tingling. His breathing steadied again. Her hands closed on the keys, suppressing their clink within her palm, and turned to leave the room. On her way out, she spotted his waistcoat draped over a valet stand. She squeezed the fabric, feeling a hard shape within its folds. Faith pulled another key, this one small and ornate, from the waistcoat pocket and slipped out the door.

Back in the kitchen, she returned the skeleton key to its hook. Faith filled the pillowcase with the food she had set aside, layering in bottles of the soda water. They would be heavy and they would not last long, but she hoped it would be long enough for what she had to do. When she had put on her shoes, donned her coat and bonnet, Faith slung the heavy bundle over her back. She staggered slightly under the weight, but moments later she was descending the front steps of the house, her life on Hudson Square behind her.

She did not look back until she stopped to adjust the weight on her back. By then it was just another door front on an ordinary street. She was not sure exactly when it had ceased to be her home, but now it was merely a house.

Faith was sweating and panting heavily under her burden by the time she reached the Academy. Her arms and back ached. She paused a little way from the Academy steps, letting the bundle fall at her feet and working blood back into her fingers. She looked up and down the street and around the entrance. She had been worried that the Colonel would have posted a guard at the door. If that were his intention, he had not made the arrangement yet. All was deserted.

She shouldered her provisions once again and lurched up the front steps. Using one of the keys she had taken from the Colonel's room, she unlocked the Academy's front door and slid inside. Faith stood still and listened for several moments, remembering the sentry who had surprised her just yesterday. It was strange to think so little real time had passed when she felt she had died twice in that span.

It was cold and dark in the lobby. The only light was a lantern at the foot of the stairs left burning for the benefit of those few artists who sometimes slept in their rooms. She wouldn't need her tinder box after all. Using the hooked pole left lying on the floor beneath it, she lifted down the lantern. Holding it awkwardly before her with the bundle in her other hand, Faith made her way slowly up the stairs and to the Colonel's room.

Faith was just putting a key to the lock when something pressed against her ankle. She jumped in alarm and dropped the key. It clattered like the banging of pots on new year's eve. Faith gasped and the ginger tabby arched and hissed. Faith exhaled sharply when she realized it was the cat she and Charles had rescued that had curled about her leg. "Shoo! You don't want to be around tonight!" she whispered to the cat as she bent to get the key. She gave one last look around the hall to see if the noise had drawn anyone. Satisfied, Faith entered the Colonel's studio and dropped the heavy bag gratefully.

Her eyes darted around the room in search of the Guild writing box and found it tucked beside the Colonel's neatly ordered desk. She lifted it to the desk and fished out the small key she had taken from the Colonel's waistcoat pocket. A lucky thing she had thought to look for it. She could have smashed the box- it wasn't going to survive the night- but she would have regretted the noise it would have made. She opened the lid and a smile spread across her face to see the Colonel's glossy black pen nestled in its slot.

The last piece of her plan secured, Faith worked quickly. She uncovered the Colonel's landscape, letting its sheet fall in a pile at its base, and turned the canvas to face the wall. Next, she gathered up every canvas in the room, including the Signing, and piled them about the base of the Colonel's landscape. Using paper from the Colonel's desk and spare lengths of raw canvas, Faith packed the gaps between the pictures. Lighting one candle stub after another, she dripped and splashed liquid wax over the lot.

Then, she took up the pen. Adjusting the Colonel's pen to fit her grip, Faith drew on the landscape's reverse. She Inked a wide grassy field that stretched for miles toward a sharp horizon with nothing but blue sky beyond. She did not bother to fill the whole back of the canvas. She only needed enough to pass through.

When her picture was complete, she dragged the heavy bundle to its threshold and, with a silent thanks to Jarvis, heaved it onto the grass within her picture. The bundle hit the canvas and bounced back.

It hadn't worked. The first hint of dread crept up her spine. If she could not make the portal work, her efforts had been for naught. Maybe it had worked, she thought, trying to calm her racing thoughts. Maybe she had to pass through with the bundle herself. Finding focus, Faith let her eyes rest on the picture. Sure enough, it deepened and stretched, beckoning her with a spring time breeze. She stretched out her hand, pressing it past the plane of the picture. She felt a strange sensation, like a band of cool water, pass over her hand and arm but she encountered no resistance. With a small sound of triumph, Faith stepped halfway in and lifted her pack over the threshold and into Phantasia.

As her head passed the picture plane, Faith's view of the studio suddenly changed to a great dome of sky above a green plain. She looked around frantically, unable to see the boundary between the worlds from this side. If she could not see it, how could she find her way back? She flailed about with her hands, feeling for the portal. A cool band slid down one arm. She froze, holding her attention to that spot. There was a faint haze, a kind of shimmering veil that hung in the air. Picturing the studio in her mind, Faith stepped into the veil. Relief flooded through her when she felt her foot make contact with the hard floor on the other side. A heartbeat later, she was back in the studio.

A noise in the hallway made Faith freeze. There was a faint shuffle, and then nothing. Probably the cat.

Faith picked up the lamp and tilted it, drizzling its oil over the sheet at the base of the canvas. Taking a twisted bit of paper from between two canvases, she lit it in the lamp. A greedy flame ate at the paper, peeling back blackened edges to reveal a burning red core. She sprinkled the tiny embers on the canvas kindling at her feet and watched them bloom and grow.

As the flames extended curious fingers toward the Inked canvas at their center, there was a knock at the door. Faith whipped around in surprise, her skirts swishing aside some of the burning paper. The door pushed open and a pale, drowsy face peered around it.

"Colonel? I saw a light under the door..." The face froze, eyes wide. Not wasting a moment, Faith threw down the lamp. She leaped over the growing flames and landed on soft grass. She smothered the smoldering hem of her dress, waving away the smell of smoke. Looking back the way she had come, all she could see was a faint glimmer of prismatic flame against the backdrop of her world.

You never know what is enough unless you know what is more than enough.

-William Blake, The Marriage of Heaven and Hell

CHAPTER THIRTY-FOUR
The Sacrifice

Charles stared at the ceiling above his bed. He had been staring at it since the coffers had been black wells of shadow. Before that, he had tossed and turned. He must have slept a little, or there was no other way to explain the dream. There had been a bright pool of water with blue and violet flames burning at its edges. A siren song had drawn him irresistibly to it. No sooner had he reached its edge, but Leviathan's terrifying head had burst from its surface as through a pane of glass. Charles had awoken feeling the sting of flying shards and smelling the beast's smoking breath. Now, the recesses in the ceiling above reflected the pale light of morning and still untroubled sleep eluded him. He knew he had done the right thing, so why was he tormented by it?

Visions of Faith floated in the empty space before his eyes. He saw her at the top of the stairs, her beautiful face ravaged by crying, the desolation in her voice when she had called to him. He also remembered how she had looked the night she came to him in his world. She had been fierce and vulnerable, desperate and yet determined. And tantalizing. He had never met anyone so uninhibited by the demands of reality. Her capacity for joy and beauty was limitless. She was like a rainbow made of lightning. Delicately, breathtakingly beautiful. Wildly, startlingly dangerous.

Even in his world, she bewitched him. He remembered her kiss. He had not thought anything could be more difficult than the first time he had pushed her away, before that demon had risen from the lake. This time had been even harder. She had lied to him, betrayed his trust, put his livelihood and connection to the Ink in jeopardy. She had shown herself to be self-centered and devious. And yet, it had taken every ounce of strength he had to turn her away.

Charles groaned as the memory of her touch and smell threatened to begin his torture anew. He rolled to the side of the bed and sat up. He ran a hand along his jaw feeling the stubble rasp beneath his fingers. If he wasn't going to sleep he might as well shave. As he lathered up, he wondered that he had ended up the responsible one. His Mam would have a hearty laugh if she knew.

His eyes following the track of his razor in the mirror, Charles was just finishing the last stroke on his neck when a flutter of movement caught his attention. He turned but there was nothing behind him. Out of the corner of his eye, there was another flash of color in the mirror. Before he could look closer, he heard a hard knock on his front door.

Charles threw on a shirt and headed for the door, wiping the last bits of lather from his face. A heavy hand knocked again. Charles opened the door with mounting irritation. He jerked back in surprise to see the Colonel standing there, the hilt of his sword raised to knock yet again. What shocked Charles more than the Colonel's presence was his appearance. He was bleary eyed and disheveled. There was a dark smudge on one cheek and when he moved, the smell of smoke came to Charles' nose.

"Get dressed. Immediately. I'll be waiting in the carriage," the Colonel barked without greeting or pre-amble.

Charles stopped him as he turned to go. "Wait. Is she all right?" There was only one reason he would be here..

The Colonel turned back slowly, his eyes hard. "She might be, if she can be made to see reason. Bring your pen. Hurry."

Charles dressed as quickly as he could with dread growing all the while. What had Faith done now? As he pulled his pen from the Guild chest, he glanced at her tea set on a table across the room. He debated whether to use it now, to find out what was going on. The Colonel was waiting though, and not patiently. Charles ran out, locking the door behind him.

As Charles took a seat in the carriage, the Colonel rapped the side with his sword and yelled up to the driver.

"Back to the Academy. Make haste!"

The driver took his charge to heart. Charles braced himself as they clattered at breakneck speed up the streets of New York. The Colonel swayed on the seat opposite him. His face was set as if for battle. When the

Colonel did not offer up an explanation, Charles was forced to ask. The Colonel spoke matter of factly.

"I was awakened rather urgently this morning by Mr. Dunlap with the news that there had been a fire at the Academy over night."

"A fire! Has it been put out?"

"Yes. It seems that one of the apprentices has been sleeping at the Academy. He will be reprimanded for that, but it gave him opportunity to discover the arsonist in action and raise an alarm."

"Was Faith there? Was she hurt?" Charles asked, trying to understand how he had become involved.

"She was the arsonist."

"What? The boy must be mistaken. Why would she do such a thing?"

The Colonel fixed Charles with a hard eye. "Retribution. After you came to me, I considered the appropriate punishment for her deceptions. When I examined her, she expressed no shame, and further condemned herself with a display of foul temper that would make Satan blush. She gave me no other alternative. I burned everything."

"Everything?" Charles asked, his heart clenching.

"Drawings, sketches, paintings. Ordinary, Inked. The pen you gave her. Everything. From now on, the only thing she will ever create is babies."

Charles swallowed at the cold finality in the Colonel's voice. He could only begin to imagine how Faith had felt to see her art, the visible expression of her soul, destroyed before her eyes. There were some things beyond the bounds of his imagination, but Charles did not think it could have been worse if the Colonel had burned her body at the stake. Charles was repulsed that the Colonel could speak so remorselessly about it.

"Where is she now?" Charles asked, a knot of fear forming in his chest.

The Colonel gave a dry chuckle. "The boy thought she jumped out of the window. Having inspected the damage myself, I know she stole my pen and ran off into Phantasia."

"Yours world or hers?"

"Hers."

Charles sat back, only a little relieved. If she was in her own world, she was safe from the Colonel and the Guild, at least for now. That she had gone in bodily was the greater threat. She was impetuous enough when she knew the risks; he doubted she had any idea what mortal danger she had put herself in. One thing though was clear. Charles understood now why the Colonel had come to him.

"And you want me to bring her back?"

"I want you to bring back my pen. Her actions have forfeited any concern for her."

Charles blinked at his callous disregard. "And if I refuse?"

"Then she will be at the mercy of the Guild. If her own father does not ask for leniency for her, I doubt they will offer any of their own accord. However, I would prefer not to involve the Guild in such a personal matter."

"I see." Charles did see. Not only was it too dangerous for the Colonel go after her himself without a pen, he would not want to face the Guild so soon after his appointment to tell them that his own daughter had gotten out of his control, stolen his pen, and was running amok in Phantasia. A part of Charles wanted to force that reckoning on him, but not at Faith's peril.

"I remind you, I hold you responsible for this predicament. None of this would have happened if you had not trained her," the Colonel said, his eyes carrying a warning that Charles was at risk of sharing her fate.

Charles was unconcerned for his position - he would gladly defend it before the Guild if it came to that. For Faith's sake though, it was better if he were the one to try to bring her back.

"I'll do it."

Smoke still clung to the ceiling of the Colonel's studio when they walked in. The smell of wet ash was heavy in the air. Puddles of sooty water stood between abandoned buckets. A pile of portrait canvases, burned along their lower thirds, resembled a host of men and women peering out from the charnel of hell. In the middle of it all was a single large canvas leaning against the wall. The stretchers had burned up both sides but the center had stayed intact.

Charles sighed inwardly. It had been a stroke of luck on the Colonel's part that all had not been destroyed. Faith had meant to injure him in every way possible on her way out. It was a stroke of luck on her part, that the fire had not destroyed the rest of the Academy and killed those who had been here.

The Colonel ordered everyone out of the room. The fire captain protested that there were still embers that could reignite. The Colonel brought the full weight of his military bearing on him. The fire captain left in disgust, motioning to the two other members of the fire brigade to follow him. The Colonel locked the door behind them.

"Fortunately, the boy had the presence of mind to save the *Signing*. It has some smoke damage but should be fine once it's cleaned. That there," he said motioning to the large canvas, "was my portal. She drew her own on the backside."

With splashing steps, Charles approached what was left of the canvas. All he could see was a grassy field. He would have had to duck to enter when it was whole; he would almost have to crawl through what was left between the charred edges. If it had burned completely, she would have had no way back. He needed to find her quickly.

Pen in hand, Charles crouched down and ducked his way through the portal. He felt the cool line of the boundary wash over him and stood to look around. Ahead the open plain spread to an empty horizon. Behind him, the land dropped off abruptly in rocky cliffs. Stepping closer he could see an icy sea far below and hear its rhythmic roar.

In the space between Charles and the edge, the Colonel struggled through the opening on hands and knees.

With a frustrated noise, Charles helped him up before pausing to mark the location of the boundary in the grass.

"Where are we? The edge of a plateau?" The Colonel asked, turning to see the cliff's edge behind them.

"An island. A floating island in the sky."

The Colonel looked at Charles as though he were stupid. "Impossible."

Charles shrugged. "Not to her."

"Where is she, do you think? How far to the other side of this plain?"

"About twice five miles, I'd wager. Look, Colonel, we are on an island in the sky. There is no way to look for her unless you have some idea how to master flight. We're going to have to wait for her to come to us."

"If we can't get off this island, then how will she get on it? She's here in body, not in spirit. She can't just will herself from one place to another."

Charles sighed. "She flies. On a giant phoenix."

The Colonel's eyes seemed to bulge out of his skull at the mention of the phoenix. Charles was sure this would not go well if the Colonel were here when Faith showed up. He told him as much.

"How do I know that you'll get the pen back? She has manipulated you before."

"I will get it back. Just let me talk to her alone."

The Colonel gave Charles a distrusting look but returned to the mark on the grass. He dropped to the ground and disappeared from sight.

Unnerved by his proximity to the cliff edge, Charles began walking toward the center of the island. It wasn't long before a second sun appeared high in the sky. It grew as it approached, resolving into an enormous bird in shifting shades of crimson, vermillion and gold, trailing a tail of fire.

Helios landed in a swirl of beating wings. Charles raised his arms against the hot drafts of air that washed over him. Holding tight to the bird's harness, Faith slid to the ground. She paused to shake down her skirt before walking towards Charles. Her steps seemed shaky and her face was gaunt, but she was smiling.

"You got my message," she said.

"Message?"

"The butterfly. In the mirror. I think I've figured out how it works."

Charles shook his head. "I didn't."

"Then why are you here?" The smile faded. Her eyes and voice were guarded.

Charles glanced back towards the invisible portal. "The Colonel. The portal wasn't completely destroyed."

Faith's face turned to living stone. "Then you're here doing his bidding? To get this?" She held up the pen.

"That's why he sent me here, but that's not why I agreed to come. I'm here for you."

"You've reconsidered?" There was a hopeful note in her question that rang painfully in Charles' heart.

"Marrying you? Faith, I can't make you any promises that way. You've lied to me and broken my trust." She crossed her arms over her chest and backed a step away. He hated to hurt her, but giving her false hope would be more cruel. "Even if we mended that, it's not in my power to make that promise. I doubt the Colonel would give us his blessing, and without it... You'd be ruined. My family... We'd be outcasts. This isn't some fairy tale.

Our actions affect more than just ourselves and I can't tell you I'm prepared to make those sacrifices."

"Do you love me?"

"That's besides the poi-"

"Do you love me?"

"God help me, but I do."

Faith threw her arms out to her sides. "Then join me here! We'll build a palace on this island-"

"I can't join you here. And you can't stay. I've come to bring you back."

"Then you've wasted your time," Faith said turning away. She called over her shoulder, "When you go back, do me *one* favor and destroy the canvas."

"Wait! Faith! You'll die here!" She stopped and turned slowly. "Being here in your body isn't the same as being here in your mind. You can't move or change things just by thinking. How easy is it to ride in that dress? How exhausting is it to get from one place to another?"

"I have all the time I need to figure those things out."

"I can see the burns on your hands from Helios' flame." Faith pressed her hands to her stomach. "What happens if you fall, or Leviathan comes back again? How much food and water do you have?"

"I'll find a way out."

"How? It's devilishly hard to find the boundaries between Phantasia and reality even when you know where they should be. If you do, you might find that the picture is in storage, tight against a wall, or in the hold of a ship at sea. It might be twenty feet up in the entry of some grand house. And if you do get out, how will you buy food?" Faith scowled and looked away.

"She probably plans to steal it," the Colonel's voice appeared at the same time as his sword blade at her side.

Charles whirled to face him. "Are you mad! You'd threaten your own daughter with a sword?"

"Don't worry Charles, he's a coward. He won't use it." In spite of her words, Faith raised the pen, her knuckles white as she gripped it.

The Colonel snarled and lunged at Faith, trying to knock the pen from her hand. The flat of the blade hit her wrist and sent it flying.

"Helios!" she screamed. The bird moved in a burst of searing flame. It snatched up the pen just as the Colonel reached the spot. He swung his sword wildly, the tip dragging down Helios' side. The bird screamed in pain as scarlet feathers flew. Faith cried out and fell to her knees, clutching at her own side. The Colonel drew back, ready to strike again. Charles lunged at him, knocking him to the ground. Charles found the sword in their rolling struggle and wrested it from the Colonel's hand.

"Enough!" Charles yelled, holding the sword high as from a grasping child. Helios leaned down over the Colonel where he still lay in the grass. "Stay there," Charles admonished the Colonel, "or that bird will peck your eyes out and I'll do naught to stop it."

Charles went to Faith. Dropping the sword to the ground, he knelt beside her and took her in his arms. She was trembling. Tears ran freely down her cheeks.

"I know you don't have much to return to, but you can't stay here," Charles said gently, brushing her hair back from her face.

Faith shook her head. "I can't go back either. I'll only die a different kind of death."

"Is William so very awful? You'll have money and a household to run. And children someday. Maybe, you'll come to love him?"

"Perhaps, in time. But perhaps not, and then what? Why should I be forced to make that gamble? And what about William? Doesn't he deserve someone who will love him for who he is and not resent him for what he isn't?" Faith dashed away tears with the heel of her hand. "Charles, I lived my entire life before I found the Ink as someone else. I was what the Colonel wanted me to be, what society wanted. If I go back, I'll have to be what my husband wants and then my children. And what do I care for money or houses when I can build palaces and dress like a queen? Why do I need children when I can populate a whole world? For once, I want to live as myself, for myself. If I had never known the Ink, it might have been different. I have been given an extraordinary gift. Am I so wicked that I want an extraordinary life?"

"It won't last long if you stay here like this."

Faith nodded, acknowledging that fate. "I'd rather have a short life of bliss than a long life under a man's thumb."

"And what about love? You may love your creations, but they cannot love you back."

"Love?" she snorted bitterly. "What love is waiting for me back in reality? My father bears no love for me, and you won't make good on yours. If what you say is true, love isn't available to me in either world."

"What about your mother?" Charles did not know much about the woman, but he had heard her tragic sigh captured in her portrait. If there were anyone that Faith needed, who needed Faith, it had to be her.

Faith went pale and her arms tightened around her middle. She closed her eyes, fresh tears sliding down her face. She was silent for a long time.

When she opened her eyes, Faith said, "You're right. My mother has lost enough. I will go back for her."

Faith rose slowly and called to Helios. The bird dropped the pen. The Colonel scrambled to snatch it from the grass, making a triumphant noise as his fist closed about it. Herding them with his sword, the Colonel ushered Faith and Charles back to the faintly shimmering veil between Phantasia and reality. As Faith crossed the threshold, Helios raised his mighty head and issued a mournful cry that rent the fabric of the world and echoed across all Phantasia.

If the doors of perception were cleansed everything would appear to man as it is, infinite.

For man has closed himself up, till he sees all things through narrow chinks of his cavern.

William Blake, The Marriage of Heaven and Hell

CHAPTER THIRTY-FIVE

The Marriage

Faith watched in the long mirror of her mother's dressing room as Sarah adjusted the ties and folds of Faith's wedding dress. It was an elegant thing made of beaded ivory lace and pale silk with a short train behind. Faith's hair was twisted up smoothly, the way William preferred. A single sapphire nestled at the base of her throat while its smaller kin hung from her ears. All were gifts from the Astors and all were stunning. None were what Faith would have chosen for herself. She looked like an old sepia drawing, faded, yellowing, drab and lifeless.

Faith's mother appeared at her shoulder. "I wish you could be as happy as you are beautiful."

"I'm just nervous, Mama."

That was a lie. In reality, Faith felt nothing. She wasn't nervous about getting married today. Nor was she frightened or even sad. She no longer cared about anything except the secret promise she had made to her mother. Her mother did not know that Faith had come back for her, but it would be a worthless gesture nonetheless if she made her mother unhappy on her account. Faith smiled, willing some of its brightness to reach her eyes. She found she did not resent the charade so much, now that she had chosen it of her own volition. "I will be happy enough if you come to visit regularly."

Sarah made a skeptical face. "I doubt your mother-in-law will feel the same. I don't think she has forgiven me yet for your engagement."

"Once we have moved to our own place, I can hardly see how her opinion matters."

"Hmm. You have much to learn about marriage," Sarah said with a wry twist to her mouth. Her face suddenly brightened. "Oh! I have something for you."

"Another wedding gift?" Faith asked as her mother opened her armoire.

She pulled out her Easter bonnet. "No. I'd be a poor woman indeed to make a gift of something that was already yours." Sarah pulled a red paper rose from its brim and handed it to Faith.

Faith's eyes went wide as recognition dawned. "Oh, Mama! You've had it all this time? I'm so relieved!"

"I meant to give it back to you before, but with all the fuss and then the wedding preparations..." She trailed off with a sly look. "Something told me it wasn't something you'd want the Colonel to see."

Faith cradled the paper flower in her hands as though it were made of crystal. Her eyes stung with threatening tears. "Thank you, Mama! Oh, thank you! You can't possibly know what this means to me."

"You're welcome?" Sarah said, eyeing Faith quizzically. "You're right, though. I have no idea what it means."

"Let me show you," Faith said, her fingers carefully but eagerly prying apart the folds. When the drawing was unfolded, Faith crouched to the ground and smoothed it against the floor. She looked up at her mother.

"Do you see it?"

"It's an apple." There was a waver in Sarah's voice as though it were a trick question.

"Yes, but so much more than that. Look." Faith picked the apple up from its page and held it on her palm. Her mother's eyes flicked from page to apple and back again, growing wider in amazement with each glance.

"That can't be..."

"It can. And it is. With the Ink anything is possible."

"The Ink?"

Faith laughed and shook her head. It would be too complicated to explain. Better just to show her. "Here," she said, cupping one of her mother's hands in her own and setting the apple gently within it. Before she let it go, Faith looked her mother in the eye and said, "You have to believe or it will disappear." Her mother gave a small nod and Faith let go.

At first, Sarah held the apple at arms length as though it might grow fangs and bite. When nothing dangerous happened, her arm relaxed and drew it close. Sarah turned it between her hands. Curiously, she sniffed around its stem.

"Smells like an apple, doesn't it?" Faith asked, a true smile lighting up her face to see her mother's wonder.

"But how?"

"I have a special Talent. Sometimes when I draw, I can make people feel more than they can see. With the right tools I can make whatever I imagine come to life. That's what the Colonel tried to take from me, but you've saved one little piece of Phantasia. It's enough. I may not be able to create anything new, but at least now I can go back."

Sarah tilted her head. "Go back where? What is this place?"

"It's hard to explain, but it's a world away from here where all my creations live. When the Colonel burned my drawings, I thought I would never be able to go back. Maybe in dream but not, well, not in the same way as before. But, with that," Faith pointed to the apple, "I'll be able to go back any time."

Faith's mother looked down at the apple, turning it in her hands again. This time though, it was not in wonder but in contemplation. Abruptly, she thrust the apple back at Faith.

"You should go back."

"What do you mean?" asked Faith, taking the apple reflexively.

"Go back. To where your imagination lives. You were there before?"

"Yes. And now that I have this, I *will* go back again."

"But only to visit? Why not forever?"

Faith shook her head wistfully. "I wish that were possible, but a body can't stay there long. I'd have to be made of Ink itself to stay forever. Besides, I couldn't leave you alone again. You've already lost so much. I won't abandon you."

"Once you get settled and busy, I'll hardly see you except for holidays."

Confusion knitted Faith's brow. "Mama, is that a reproach or are you trying to get rid of me?"

"Lord no! A mother loves her children and wants them close always, but a decent mother would never choose her happiness over her child's."

"I don't understand."

"Look." Faith's mother gestured at the mirror. "Do you see how radiant you are, and all because of an apple. If that is what an apple can do..."

Faith looked at herself in the mirror and gasped. She still stood in ivory lace and satin, but where she had looked pale and dull before, now she was aglow. Her skin and eyes were bright, her cheeks and lips flushed. Strands of fire seemed to glint in her red-gold hair, shamed only by the shining crimson apple she held to her chest.

Faith held the apple up before her face, remembering the day she had created it. She had been so determined to prove herself; she had put her heart and soul into its creation. It had not been enough to look or smell or taste like an apple should. What did an apple *mean*?

An epiphany struck Faith so hard and swift that starbursts formed before her eyes.

Was it possible? Charles had said there were those whose Talent was so strong they were a source unto themselves. Was Faith a rogue? *Forbidden fruit*. She had called it so herself. Had a part of her known all along?

Faith dug a nail into the apple's skin. The juice swelled and trickled down. An opalescent juice, not clear. Faith lifted a drop with her finger and smeared it across her forearm. With a thought as light as whimsy, Faith changed the smudge from blue to violet to red, and then to a pink that had never been seen in nature. Her smile was resplendent.

Ink. She was the source; she could be the creation. She *could* disappear into Phantasia and stay forever.

Disappear and leave her mother alone with the Colonel. Faith retreated from her revelation. She took a physical step back and shook her head.

"No, Mama, I will stay. Everything I need is here. I may still have to marry William but what I have can't be taken away by the Colonel, or the Guild, or anyone. It was mine all along! I promised myself I would stay with you and try to make up for all the love we've lost and that's what I intend to do. The apple will be enough."

"Bloody hell, child. Don't be a fool! You think I'd rather spend my days looking at your mopey face and pasted on smile- don't think I can't tell- than to know you are blissfully happy even if it's invisible to me? If you can live as no woman on this earth has lived, then you must do it. If you have a chance at the joy I had, you'd make a mockery of it not to seize it. "

Faith threw her arms around her mother and squeezed her tight. Tears of gratitude and regret, elation and loss seeped from between her closed lids. Her mother's arms closed around her. They were warm and strong.

"I love you, Mama," Faith whispered into her mother's neck.

"I love you too, dear child, but you are like a caged bird. It's time you were set free. Go on," Sarah said, disentangling herself from Faith wet embrace. Her own tears glistened in her eyes. "I'll be fine. I derive great joy from tormenting the Colonel and now I will be able to do it without harming you as well."

Faith smiled through her tears, a laugh caught in her thickening throat. She turned to face the mirror once again, holding the apple to her lips. Faith paused for half a heart-beat, not in doubt but in anticipation, and sunk her teeth into the scarlet skin.

Crisp flesh tore away with a satisfying crunch as the juice flooded her mouth. It was tart and sweet and exactly what an apple should taste like, but it was also so much more. A cacophony of flavors, every taste she could imagine, erupted upon her tongue, all mingled together yet each note distinct. A sensation simultaneously warm and cool traced the juice's track down her throat and to her center. It gathered there like an expanding star until it could grow no more and still be within her body. It spread like fire through her limbs and radiated from her eyes, her fingers, and her feet. In her reflection, Faith glowed with an incandescent light as though she had been clothed in rays of the sun. The light burned away her mortal flesh, leaving her sentience and consciousness, thought and perception, the intangible elements of her soul, to take whatever form they willed.

Faith reached out to herself, to her reflection. Her fingers touched as on the surface of a pool of water. She plunged forward, hand and arm merging, icy lace melting into a gown of burning flame, sapphires becoming rubies, until she and herself were one.

When Faith had entirely gone from reality, the glass shattered.

Shards littered the floor like jagged pools of water. The sweep of a crimson wing and Faith's retreating image were repeated across the mosaic of broken mirrors until they went empty and staring once again, giving back only a reflection of the ceiling overhead. A blank and creased sheet of paper lay beneath the broken glass. Near it was a single scarlet feather, the fluffy barbs at its base trembling in an unseen breeze.

Sarah nudged a shard with her toe. "Perhaps I'll take up drawing," she said to no one in particular. Then she heard the Colonel's steps upon the stair and began to scream.

CHAPTER THIRTY-SIX

The Commission

A hushed chatter filled the church hall. The wedding guests were gathered in twos and threes among the aisles and in the entry, passing the time with amiable nothings while they awaited the arrival of the bride. Charles was trapped in one such conversation with a friend of Mr. Astor's and his wife. Charles had already forgotten their names.

A twitter of excitement rose near the doors and surged through the room like a wave.

"It seems she has arrived!" said the associate of Mr. Astor.

"How exciting! We should take our seats." exclaimed his wife.

Charles gestured gallantly that they should proceed ahead of him. "I am not so closely related. I will take a seat toward the back." Charles watched the couple go with something like relief, but it was hard to distinguish against the melancholy that had plagued him since bringing Faith out of Phantasia. He was not sure why he had decided to come today. Was it to see the deed accomplished, their fates sealed with vows? He was quickly reconsidering his desire to witness the event. Like a salmon running upstream, Charles fought his way up the aisle and back to the entrance.

A moment's indecision as he neared the doors saved him from a collision with the Colonel. The man was in full stride, his face flushed and stern. Charles dodged to the side. The motion drew the Colonel's glance and broke his step. His eyebrows shot up in recognition and he pointed at Charles.

"You! Stay right here!"

Charles thought to give the man a mocking salute before turning to leave, as return for addressing him so rudely, but morbid curiosity stayed his hand and heel. The Colonel did not look like a man about to celebrate a marriage he had gone to great lengths to arrange. There was something wrong and if he needed Charles, it had to be about Faith.

Charles' eyes followed the Colonel as he walked forcefully to the front where the Astors milled to take their seats. He saw the expectant smiles turn to questioning frowns, a flash of irritation and then concern. The clergyman was called over to conference and there were dismayed nods all around. The Colonel ascended to the pulpit and addressed the murmuring assembly.

"Thank you all for coming to celebrate what should be a most joyous occasion. However, it is with great sadness and concern that I must announce my daughter has fallen ill this morning. We will have to put off the wedding until she has recovered. With your prayers, that will not be long. I beg your understanding at this difficult moment. Dr. Hosack, if you would meet me at the entrance."

The room buzzed like a shaken hive the moment the Colonel turned from the podium. A spike of activity against the general motion of turning and shaking heads revealed the doctor as he slid along his pew. He had only made it to the aisle when the Colonel was beside Charles once more.

"I assume Faith is not ill," Charles said darkly, "or you would not have need of me in addition to the doctor."

"She has stolen another pen and run off into Phantasia again."

"What? She couldn't have! Whose pen could she have taken? How?"

"Do you have yours?" the Colonel asked with a challenge in his voice.

"I don't typically carry it to weddings," Charles answered, his sarcasm unmetered.

"Well, you'll have a chance to prove it later. You'll need it to help me get her back."

Charles opened his mouth to refuse but Dr. Hosack's arrival stopped him.

"Dr. Hosack! Thank you," the Colonel said, as he shook the man's hand.

"What symptoms does she have?" the doctor asked, his face wrinkling with concern.

"You'll have to see for yourself when we get there. Mr. Ingham, are you coming?" the Colonel asked, a note of steel in his voice. Fearing for Faith's safety if he didn't, Charles followed them to the waiting carriage.

* * *

"What happened here?" the doctor asked, his voice spiking with alarm as they surveyed Mrs. Trumbull's dressing room. The shattered remnants of a mirror covered the floor. A single scarlet feather lay among them.

"Mrs. Trumbull says a bird flew in the open window and struck the mirror."

"Was Faith cut? Have you stopped the bleeding? Really John, I should see her at once."

"I'm afraid Faith is beyond your aid now. It's my wife I need you to attend. She was hysterical."

The doctor's face paled. "Oh John, I'm so sorry."

The Colonel patted his shoulder. "Not everything is as it seems, but I can't explain now. Please, see to my wife. You'll find her in my room down the hall. We will talk later. Please speak to no one about this until we do."

Dr. Hosack nodded, though clearly mystified, and left the room.

Charles rounded on the Colonel the moment the doctor was gone. "Is she all right? Have you harmed her?"

"You know as much as I do," the Colonel said, waving his hands at the glittering mess at their feet. "She was here with her mother, I heard the glass break and came rushing in to find my wife in a fit. Faith was gone."

Charles bent and picked up the feather. It shimmered like fire as he turned it in the light. "Helios."

"Exactly. She must have stolen another pen and created a portal on the mirror."

"I still don't understand where you think she got a pen."

"It's the only explanation."

"Not if she's a rogue. A true rogue."

The Colonel's face drained of all color, but instead of shock, his eyes narrowed in anger. "Impossible. I refuse to believe it."

Charles held up the feather, a piece of Phantasia persisting on this side of reality. Could he not see the significance? "Colonel, what you believe is irrelevant. It's what Faith believes that - "

The Colonel threw up a hand. "Stop. Never suggest such a thing again."

Charles ran a hand through his hair and took a steadying breath. He had never wanted to punch a man so much in his life, but that would do nothing to help Faith. Not yet at least. "What now?"

"We go get her. You must have a way into her world. Some link formed while you were training her."

"And then what? Will you imprison her? No cell or chains could hold her now. Just leave her be!"

"Do you have a link or not?"

"I refuse to be party to this." Charles stepped over the glass on his way out the door.

"I order you as your Guild Master."

Charles turned back. "Then I resign my association with the American Guild."

"Then you will also forfeit your right to practice here. You'll have to go back to Dublin."

"We'll see what the High Council says about that."

"You want to put this before the High Council?" the Colonel gave a short, derisive laugh. "Then I will tell them how you trained her in secret against my wishes, and see where they allow you to practice, if at all!"

"And I will tell them how you failed to report a stolen pen. A pen stolen from you, by your own daughter, a day after you got the job. And then I will tell them how you struck your own daughter with a sword to get it back."

"Don't you threaten me! How I discipline my child is no affair of the High Council. Nor of yours!" the Colonel's voice had risen steadily. He was shouting now.

Charles had an only slightly tighter rein on his temper. "You have no way into her world without me, and I will not help you."

The Colonel threw up his hands and grunted. He began to pace, glass crunching under his feet. When he stopped, he looked Charles straight in the eye. "You'll follow the High Council's decision?"

"I will," Charles said warily. He did not trust the Colonel's scheme, whatever it was.

"Then we will go to the Council this afternoon and get their determination. I will not bring up your indiscretions and you will not insinuate that I have acted improperly. Agreed?"

Charles didn't like it, but he could see no way around it. "Agreed."

* * *

Charles should have been overawed at his surroundings. He was standing in daVinci's own study, a wood paneled and frescoed masterpiece behind the Guild Hall's central chamber. The room was lined with bookshelves holding gleaming leather tomes and miniature models of his inventions. A bronze horse stood on a marble pedestal in the corner, a smaller twin to the colossus that guarded the approach to the Guild Hall. A brass armillary glinted by the window with what must have been a kind of telescope at its side. On another wall, a vitrine protected a display of neatly ordered pens. Each one distinct, like the doors, they were the pens of long past Masters. Rubens, Rembrandt and Vermeer. Michelangelo and Raphael. And at their head, daVinci's own pen.

Any other time, Charles could not have contained his curiosity. Under the circumstances, the three High Council members who had been available at such short notice had his undivided attention.

"My daughter, who has some Talent, has done something impetuous," the Colonel was explaining. "It appears that she has stolen a Master's pen and run away into Phantasia."

All three of the Council members began to speak at once.

"Volé un stylo? Mais Comment?"

"From where?"

"In body?" asked Guild Master West with evident concern.

Guild Master Goya glanced at his fellow Council. When they were silent, he addressed the Colonel in his heavily accented English. "Are you certain? We have had no reports of a stolen pen. If one had been taken and not reported, that would be a serious problem on its own."

"I agree," the Colonel responded without the slightest hesitation. Charles had to admire the man for his nerve. He was here as supplicant and yet his bearing and demeanor was that of a respectful equal. "If it is discovered that someone has failed to make such a report, I will deal with him appropriately. However, it is possible that the theft has yet gone undetected by the Master in question. We have only just discovered it ourselves and is why we summoned you so urgently in spite of the disturbance to your rest." Guild Masters David and West had put a thought to appearing wigged and robed. Although, when Guild Master West covered a yawn, his wig briefly became a night cap. Guild Master Goya had not bothered and was at ease in what appeared to be his nightclothes.

Guild Master David leaned forward. "Pourquoi ferait-elle une chose pareille?" he asked, his r's strangely slurred.

Guild Master West gave him a sideways glance. "In English, if you please."

"I do not please," Guild Master David sniffed. "I prefer not to insult my tongue with your horrible sounds."

"Mes excuses, Guild Master David. It's all right, Guild Master West." the Colonel said with a nod to each. "We all understood. In answer, I do not know why she would do such a thing except that she was to marry today. Perhaps the nervous excitement overwhelmed her and she lost hold of reason."

"I'm confused, Colonel Trumbull- forgive me *Guild Master* Trumbull," Guild Master West said, correcting himself, "was your daughter an apprentice? I know your feelings on women and the Ink and I am surprised to learn that she was being trained."

"Yes, it surprised me as well," the Colonel said with the slightest sidelong look at Charles, "but the tender heart of a loving father can be swayed against reason. If I were to test my conviction, who better to indulge than my own daughter? Unfortunately, she became increasingly frail of mind and excitable, confirming what I had known all along about women's lack of suitability for the Ink. This is what ultimately led me to prohibit women from the American Guild. I had discontinued her training and tried to put her off of art altogether, but it seems she retained enough to be dangerous. I am most embarrassed that this trouble has stemmed from my own household and would humbly appreciate your understanding in the matter."

Guild Master David was nodding sympathetically. Charles ground his teeth to keep himself from calling out the Colonel's lies and half-truths. In spite of his agreement, he was tempted to tell the Council all he knew.

"What do you propose to do?" Guild Master Goya asked.

"The solution is simple, our meeting here merely a courteous formality. I will go into her world and bring back the pen she has stolen."

"And your daughter," Guild Master West prompted.

"I beg your pardon?" the Colonel asked, "What about her?"

"You said you would bring back the pen. I presume your primary intention is to bring her back. If she is in bodily, she is in great danger."

"Of course, Guild Master West. Her safety is my highest concern. I thought that was assumed." The Colonel sniffed and turned to acknowledge Charles for the first time since they had first announced themselves. "To assist me, I ask permission for Mr. Ingham to come as well. He worked with my daughter while I was out of town and is familiar with her weaknesses."

"She is only a young girl, n'est-ce pas? Why would it take both of you?"

Charles stifled a cough as he watched the Colonel try to come up with an answer. "Indeed, Colonel. I am unclear on that point as well. Why do you need me?"

"You don't want to help him bring her back?" Guild Master West peered at him sharply over the edge of his glasses.

"I do not." Charles wished he could stop there. The only reason he could give for not wanting to help the Colonel might only make them more determined to go after Faith, but West's raised eyebrows already asked the question that was forming on his lips. Charles sighed inwardly and answered. "I do not believe she has stolen a pen, or that she is in danger. I believe that she is a rogue, a true rogue, and that we should leave her be."

The Council shifted in their seats as they exchanged shocked glances. The Colonel glared at Charles.

"If this is true, she could completely undermine the Guild's authority," Guild Master Goya said

"She is no rogue!" the Colonel shouted, his urbane facade cracking at last.

"Then you underestimate her. Her Talent is extraordinary. I've never seen anything like it." Charles turned to address the Council. "Do you know how she got into Phantasia? She walked through a mirror."

"She drew a portal on a mirror," the Colonel corrected.

"With whose pen? If she's a rogue, it would explain why none is missing," Charles said.

Guild Master West broke in. "Do you think she's dangerous, Mr. Ingham?"

"She is not," Charles answered.

"Respectfully, Mr. Ingham cannot make that determination. Who can possibly know the mind of a woman and a hysterical one at that?"

Charles rolled his eyes and began to protest but Guild Master Goya held up a hand. "If she has stolen a pen, it must be retrieved. If she is a rogue, if such a thing is possible, it is imperative that she be brought back and interrogated before the whole High Council. We will need to test her and confirm and to see if she can be brought under the Guild's control. If so, she would be a great asset."

"And if not?" Charles asked, a lump in his throat.

"Then she will pose a threat to the Guild that must be removed. I doubt it will come to that though. A young woman should not be so difficult to control, no matter her Talent."

Charles shook his head doubtfully. "So, we are to go then. That is your decision?"

Guild Master Goya looked to the other members. They each nodded.

"Yes," Guild Master Goya said, "the Council commissions Guild Master Trumbull and Master Ingham to enter Phantasia and apprehend the Guild Master's daughter."

"Unharmed," added Guild Master West.

He who mocks the Infants Faith
Shall be mockd in Age & Death
He who shall teach the Child to Doubt
The rotting Grave shall neer get out
He who respects the Infants faith
Triumphs over Hell & Death
The Childs Toys & the Old Mans Reasons
Are the Fruits of the Two seasons

- William Blake, Auguries of Innocence

CHAPTER THIRTY-SEVEN

The Siege

Charles' and the Colonel's footsteps echoed in the hallway as they made their way up the northwestern Tower of Doors.

"How dare you tell them she is a rogue!" the Colonel said between breaths.

"I did not break our agreement. Besides, wouldn't it be a feather in your cap to have brought another source of Ink to the Guild's disposal?"

"Being the father of an aberration will never be a source of pride."

Charles stopped before an age-polished oaken door with a Celtic shield carved in raised relief on its face. The Great Beast at the center of the spiraling knots was faintly traced in gold and silver but the rest was adorned only with careful craftsmanship. Charles set his jaw and ducked his chin as he opened the door to his world.

It opened to a set of spiraling stairs that seemed a continuation of the tower's curving hall, only instead of gleaming marble it was rough, gray stone. The interior wall about which they turned was cut ashlar, the exterior wall a tumbling ruin that was all but gone. The canopies of tall trees filled the gaps instead of stone. Breaks in both revealed a rolling countryside that spilled toward a windswept sea.

The base of the stairs let out before the keep of a castle ruin. Charles led them out the massive gates into a raised clearing where the head of a bridge would have met the land. The wide ditch below them, a one-time moat, was filled with wildflowers. A multihued butterfly fluttered through the poppies and daisies in search of the violets that clustered among them.

"Hang onto me," he told the Colonel over his shoulder. The Colonel grasped his forearm with strength surprising for a man of his years. Charles tightened the grip on his pen and held his free hand out towards the butterfly. It bobbed and drifted closer until it hovered just above his palm. The moment its delicate feet touched his skin, Charles' mind was filled with Faith. His world blurred and spun.

His vision cleared again as the butterfly floated from his hand. The Colonel's hold on his arm was quickly withdrawn. They were on a wide, empty plain that ended on an abrupt horizon.

"Are we in the same place as before?" the Colonel asked.

Charles did not think so. The field before had been verdant and warm. Here, the ground was gravelly and barren. What little green there was huddled in spindly clumps. The air was biting cold. Charles turned toward the sound of pounding surf to see an ice strewn ocean, its slate-dark waters in the shadow of a floating island.

"That's where we were before. It looks like she's been busy."

The Colonel spun to see where Charles pointed. The top of the island was no longer bare or flat. Its perimeter was ringed with gleaming white walls and towers that rose and fell with the contours of the land. Where forested slopes converged and dipped, bright rivers spilled over the island's edge. Wind and rock shredded the cascading tails into veils of rainbowed mist. The rocky underside of the island tapered to a sharp point that seemed poised to strike the heart of the sea. The inverted slopes were pockmarked with the black mouths of caves, rimmed with icicles like glittering teeth. A large swell washed the island's narrow tip, pushing water through the caves to be ejected as thunderous plumes of seawater and ice.

In contrast to its frozen base, the island's summit was awash in warming sunlight. Faith's palace, fully constructed now, sat on a high promontory at one end of the island. Imitating a familiar form, it was a high central dome surrounded by towers, only Faith's towers gleamed with silver and gold like the spikes of a crown. The dome was formed of crystal panes and scintillated like a jewel.

"The impertinence!" The Colonel shouted. "She's made a mockery of the Guild Hall!"

For all their similarities in form, the two buildings could not have been more different in execution or intent. Faith's version was too painfully beautiful to be called a mockery of anything except that which ordinarily went by the name. He would not take up the argument with the Colonel though.

"There's no way we can get to her. She knew we would come and she's put us on an island of our own."

The Colonel spun around again, verifying their predicament. The rocky plain on which they stood was just above the surface of the ocean, which surrounded them on all sides. They were on a large, but lonely, pedestal in the sea.

"We could fashion a ship and get to the mainland over there."

Charles shook his head. "You do not want to go out on that water. There's a beast that lurks in her world you do not want to awaken."

The Colonel paled and his eyes went wide. "Leviathan," he breathed, the word nearly lost against the ocean's roar.

"How did you know?" Charles asked, but the Colonel shook his head as though ridding it of some terrible thought. Charles continued. "Even if we got to the mainland, that doesn't get us any closer to that island. She can wait up there a lot longer than we can wait down here."

"Then we will have to draw her out," the Colonel said, looking from the island to their plateau and back again. He held up his pen, gauging the distance.

"What do you have in mind?"

The Colonel did not answer but began to draw. It began as a dark line on the plateau's edge that thickened and drew closer as the Colonel worked. The creak of wheels and the shouts of men carried on the wind. They reached Charles before his eyes understood what he was seeing. Squads of men in sharp uniform were wheeling enormous cannons towards them. Behind them, raised and bayoneted rifles turned the horizon to a spiny ridge.

"Artillery?" Charles shouted as a heavy cart passed behind him on its way to the rise above the beach.

"It will either draw her out to face us or I'll knock that island back into the ocean!"

"You could kill her! West said she wasn't supposed to be harmed!"

"I won't let her upend the Guild just when I've almost reached the top of it! If she's a rogue, she's already dead to me."

"This is about power?"

"This is about legacy. Immortality!"

"I won't help you with this," Charles said, backing up.

"That's fine. Just stay out of my way."

An officer stepped up next to Charles and saluted the Colonel.

"General Trumbull. The first line is in place."

"Very good. Fire when ready. I want the proper bearings established by the time the second line is in place."

"*General* Trumbull?" Charles threw his hands up in disgust.

"Fire!" he heard a soldier yell over the wind. Even with warning, the explosion made Charles jump. The air convulsed and his ears rang. He followed the ball's trajectory until it hit just below the middle of the island in an explosion of rock and ice.

"Higher!" the Colonel's shout echoed over the field.

"You can't do this!" Charles yelled as he lunged to grab the pen from the Colonel's hand. He caught the older man's wrist but he wrenched away with surprising force. Charles balled his other fist and swung, striking a blow across the Colonel's face. Pain exploded through Charles' hand but it was overwhelmed by satisfaction. The Colonel stumbled back and fell. Charles started after him but rough hands suddenly had his arms and shoulder. He was pinned between two soldiers.

The Colonel rose, wiping blood from his nose. His left eye was already starting to darken and swell.

"You've done me a favor lad," the Colonel said as he touched the skin around the eye. "That eye never was worth a damn. Now, I don't have to try to close it myself. Get him away from here."

The two soldiers escorted Charles a good way from the emplacement before turning him loose with a shove. Charles found himself on an empty ridge above a stretch of sandy shore. Another cannon firing made him stop and watch. With each concussive boom, they were getting closer to their mark. It would not be long before they hit the walls. And after that, they might manage to hit the palace itself. He had to do something to stop this madness but what? He could not fight the Colonel's entire army. Any attempt to draw them off would be answered in a moment. He needed to talk to Faith, reason with her, but how?

The only way to the island was to fly. He had teased Faith about winged carriages and horses, neither of which he had the conviction to try. He wished he'd had more time to inspect daVinci's models. He knew some of them were capable of flight. There was only one method of flight Charles had ever witnessed. It was slow and hard to direct, and his understanding of its mechanics were very rudimentary, but it would have to do. If he could get to the island maybe he could get her to meet with him. If that didn't work, he could at least get the Colonel to stop firing by getting between the cannons and the island.

Ignoring the recklessness of this plan, Charles brandished his pen and set to work. Ahead of him on open ground, Charles drew something that looked like a small wooden boat with a hot furnace and smokestack in its center. Above it, he drew an enormous sphere of tightly woven fabric that narrowed to a funnel. It was netted and lashed with an imposing web of thick ropes to the boat, which in turn was secured to the ground by more rope. As hot air filled the balloon, it lifted the little ship and strained against its moorings. Charles checked the direction of the wind. The balloon was leaning to the beach and the spume of the surf was blowing back out to sea. It seemed the Colonel had already ensured the wind was aimed towards Faith's floating island.

With a prayer, Charles climbed in and made to cut the mooring lines. His empty hand passed by the first one harmlessly, reminding him with an embarrassed flush that he could not just make a knife appear at will. Taking a moment to draw one, Charles again slashed at the mooring lines and rose into the sky. He watched the ground disappear beneath him as the ship swept quickly over the beach and past the breaking waves. It wasn't until he was well past the line of surf and over open water that he saw the approaching storm.

Have you entered into the springs of the sea,
Or walked in the recesses of the deep?
Have the gates of death been revealed to you,
Or have you seen the gates of deep darkness?...
Declare if you know all this.

- Job 38:16

CHAPTER THIRTY-EIGHT

The Monster

From the tallest tower of her castle, Faith watched with growing fury. She had known the Colonel would come, and that he would use Charles to do it. Anticipation, though, had not lessened the sting of betrayal to see that Charles had come so quickly to the Colonel's aid. She could just make them out, conferring among the positioning cannons how best to lay siege to her world.

A flash followed by a loud report announced the Colonel's first shot. She felt it hit the island like a tremor in her mind. Her knuckles grew white on the balcony railing as she considered what to do. She could erase his army from here, but he would only redraw another. She would have to confront the Colonel directly and find a way to take his pen. She needed a closer look.

Another shot fired. This one sent a shiver through the halls.

Faith called to Helios. The great bird called back and flew toward the tower. As he neared, Faith took a running start and leapt the balcony railing. Her stomach rose into her chest, her body weightless as she fell. The tower wall raced past until Helios swept beneath her. Faith settled herself behind his arching neck and took the slim leather harness in her hands.

Helios banked to circle around the palace, revealing Faith's courtyard garden with its great tree and flaming fountain far below her knee. She would not let the Colonel harm what she had so lovingly created. Before they had passed the farthest tower, Faith was gathering the wind and clouds to her. When they had finished the turn and straightened for the Colonel's army, Faith and her phoenix rode on a rolling wave of storm. The tumbling thunderheads glowed with Helios' fire and the flash of lightning.

Faith descended upon the island. The wind rushed past her ears, stung her eyes, and stole the air before she could breath it in. Though the billowing darkness of her anger obscured the island and their approach, the Colonel did not stop firing. Cannonballs whistled through the air. With a wave of her hand, Faith turned them to seed heads that broke and scattered in the wind. She passed directly over and behind the artillery emplacement, rendering the cannon useless, but was met with a volley of rifle fire. She turned the hail of bullets into rain that fell back from whence it came. Another volley, another shower, and the soldiers reloaded in a muddy slick.

Helios circled wide and out of range as Faith began to form her plan. Her thoughts were interrupted by a flash of white against the storm-dark sky. A giant balloon with a small ship slung below its belly was being tossed about in the wind as by a child. Faith turned Helios, speeding toward the hapless craft. As they neared, Faith saw a man silhouetted against a furnace fire, clinging to the ropes. She knew it was Charles.

The balloon jolted in another gust and embers flew from the furnace's stack. They settled on the skin of the balloon and the ropes that bound it. Some died out but others caught and spread. Red rings of flame with growing black centers ate at the balloon like a pox. Faith released the storm but it was too late. The balloon burst fully into flame. The ship that had been suspended from it fell to the ocean below.

"*Charles!*" Faith screamed out as she saw him fall. Her only desire was to save him and her world bent to her need. In the space between two heartbeats, Helios was there beneath him. Charles landed with a heavy thud that Faith felt across her own shoulders but Helios did not lose a beat. Faith reached for Charles as he slid unbalanced and drew him in with a harness of his own. Helios leveled out, gliding gracefully just above the reach of the windblown waves.

Relief and fear mingled with Faith's still simmering anger. When she yelled over her shoulder, her tone was harsh.

"What were you thinking? You could have gotten yourself killed!"

"I was trying to stop him!" Charles yelled back.

"So you're not on his side?"

"Of course not! The High Council ordered me to bring him here. They think you might be a rogue."

"They want to put me in a cage and mine my imagination, don't they? I have to put a stop to this." Would the Colonel never let her be? Seething hatred tightened Faith's grip on the harness. She would end this, once and for all. She spurred Helios on with her knees and her thoughts.

She heard Charles' voice behind her, though the wind tried to snatch away his words.

"...the Colonel, they won't stop. They'll send more..." Faith turned her head, trying to hear. "Come before the Council. Negotiate."

"Surrender?"

"No- Faith look out!"

Faith's head whipped around. A white ring of bubbles had formed on the surface, a glassy swell rising and spreading at its center like a liquid volcano. Sharp horns pierced the growing mountain of water.

"Helios! Pull up!" Faith pressed herself flat to the bird's neck as Leviathan's shining hulk rose in front of them. Helios banked hard to one side. She heard Charles call out and turned to see him hanging from the harness. She reached out a hand. The serpent lunged and Helios reared up, wings back-beating violently. Charles was thrown forward out of Faith's grasp. The harness broke and Charles fell to the water below.

Faith's relief to see Charles' head bob above the surface was short lived. Leviathan was too close. Even if the beast did not attack, Charles would be swamped by the swells that rolled off of its contorting body. She needed to draw Leviathan off.

Helios closed the distance with the serpent, spiraling up its rearing neck. When they reached the level of its fearsome head, its dawn-lit eyes met Faith's. Cold terror washed over her. She leaned close to the firebird, drawing on its warmth and courage as they soared past. The sea monster's head pulled back as it tensed to strike. Faith urged Helios higher, faster.

The serpent hurtled toward them in the air. The mouth opened wide, revealing hundreds of teeth like daggers. Its pitch black gullet glowed like a forge. The fire in its throat swelled and burst forth. Faith shut her eyes and cowered. Searing heat washed over her. She smelled burnt hair, but it was her own. The firebird flew on, un-singed by the demon's breath.

The serpent reached the top of its arc; the teeth snapped shut. Helios shuddered. Faith braced herself, waiting to be pulled into the icy depths.

Drops of water hit her warm skin like cold evil. The bird called out in fury and she heard a tremendous splash, but the rush of dark water didn't come. The phoenix's wings were still beating swift and strong. Daring to open her eyes, Faith looked behind and saw the narrowness of their escape. The long tail feathers were broken and shredded.

Insulted and defiant, the phoenix wheeled high in the sky, tracing a shadowy circuit above the serpent whose body whipped the sea into a matching circle of foam. As the two legendary beasts studied each other, Faith had an idea.

Helios peeled off, flying straight up into the sun. Losing them in the light, Leviathan turned to look for other quarry. It ducked its head beneath the waves and swam, slick sections of undulating body breaking the surface in rhythmic succession until it dove deeper and disappeared from view. Faith traced a white wake of bubbles, but then, those too disappeared. Faith knew it had not given up; she did not have long to act.

She scanned the heaving surface, churned frothy by Leviathan's coils, for any sign of Charles. A ways off, she saw the wreckage of his airship, and then an arm wave as he reached to grab onto it. A trailing rope wrapped around his hand, Charles heaved himself onto the bits of hull and plank that still floated.

With a few deft gestures, Faith turned the wreckage of the airship into a thick-hulled sailing craft. She had just set the mast and sail when the ship was carried high on a mound of water pushed by Leviathan's return.

Keeping the sun behind, Helios plummeted toward the creature's rising form. Too late, the serpent saw them. Talons found purchase just behind its head. Enraged, the serpent snapped and writhed as the phoenix climbed into the sky. Helios' wings beat hard and fast, the load becoming heavier as each massive coil left the water. The phoenix strained. Out of the water, the serpent struggled for air and against its own mass. The writhing slowed. Still, the bird climbed higher.

Faith looked in amazement at the serpent's length, stretching from the bird's claws to the water below, linking heaven and sea like a scaled umbilical cord.

And then, Faith saw the cannon ball as it buried itself in Helios' side.

She and the phoenix gave a united scream of pain. Her mount torn from beneath her, the harness ripped from her hands, Faith tumbled from the sky with the firebird and the serpent. The freezing water met her like a wall.

Her skin lanced with a thousand icy needles, the dark water closing overhead, Faith fought for consciousness. One thought gave her purpose. *Charles*. She needed to save Charles. Save him from the beast as he had saved her.

Faith struggled towards the light overhead, one arm lifeless at her side. She pulled with the other one, kicking frantically. Her head broke the surface only to be sunk by a rising swell. When she emerged again she spat and choked on salty water. Spinning about, she spotted the mast and sail of Charles' ship. A long shadow darkened the water between them. As it rose, the shadow paled to iridescent scales tinted blue-green by the water. Faith heard its keening moan and knew Leviathan was not after Charles. It was coming for her. Helios was down; she was powerless to fight it. This would be her end.

Tethering her sanity against a maelstrom of fear, Faith allowed herself one thought: getting Charles to safety. With a last breath before she turned to face the beast, she filled his sails and sent his ship skimming toward the shore. Knowing she would not survive to see him safely there, Faith called out to her world for aid and felt it answer back.

Leviathan's shadow fell on her as she turned to face it. Its horned head blocked the sun, turning the rays into a hellish halo. And then, it seemed the sun was in its mouth. A blinding ball of flame filled the black cavern behind its teeth. The icy water was driven away by a plume of fire, engulfing Faith in a searing bath of flame.

And then the sea came rushing back. The teeth snapped shut around her.

She was suspended in a watery void, formless in its blackness. The sound and fury of the beast and ocean were gone. All was silent. It was no longer cold, or warm. It was nothing. It was peaceful. It was death and Faith was unafraid.

Accepting her fate, she opened her lungs and drew the water in. There was no choking, no pain, no layering of black upon blackness. She hung there, still conscious, wondering at her fate. She took another breath. And another.

And then she laughed. She laughed in joy and wonder, in gratitude and shame for having taken so long to understand. This was her creation. There was no body separate from the soul. This world was her and she was it.

Helios had been her hope. Leviathan had been her fear. She was both and from both she drew her strength.

Faith took another breath and opened her dawn-lit eyes. Diving deep beneath the ocean waves, she stretched her sinuous lengths and glided toward the shore.

What is now proved was once only imagined.
-William Blake, The Marriage of Heaven and Hell

CHAPTER THIRTY-NINE
The Revelation

Charles raced to lower the sail. Between wind and surging swells, the beach was approaching far too quickly. He had tried to turn the ship but that only put him broadside to the waves. Having lost his pen in the fall, he couldn't stop from running aground, but he could try to lessen the impact.

An eerie sound, as though the sea itself were moaning, froze him at his task. He turned with dread, searching for the source, to find Leviathan rising again. He was relieved to see it moving away from his ship until he saw Faith, a pale dot in the looming shadow of the beast. Charles ran to the rail, grabbing for a pen he no longer had. Powerless, he saw the great jaws open to reveal the fire that burned within.

The burst of flame lit up the day as though it had been night. Charles' arm flew up to shield his eyes from what they did not want to see. His heart cried out for Faith. He watched the surface, praying to see that she had somehow escaped. Moments stretched, the monster dove, and still Faith did not appear. Hope turned to an ache that filled his soul.

Even if Charles had not been distracted by grief, he would not have seen the submerged rock that caught his ship. Charles was pitched by the impact as it tore through the hull with a splintering roar. Thrown overboard, he tumbled in the water not sure which way was up. Something grabbed him by one arm, and then the other. He pulled away frantically, air escaping as he tried to see what had attacked him in the murky water. His eyes found two delicate faces surrounded by wave tossed hair. They were somehow familiar, like a forgotten dream. He stopped struggling, willing to be led to the depths of the ocean by such exquisite beauty. They gave him cryptic smiles and pulled him to the surface.

Charles gratefully filled his lungs with air and let Faith's sirens carry him to shore. He remembered where he'd seen them now, the faint reflection of a torn out page, and wondered that he had not realized then the power that Faith had.

They were in the shore break now. The water bowed to a gathering wave and Charles' knee dragged a gravelly bottom. He tried to stand but the wave swept his feet away. The sirens had released him when the water fell again. He found himself on hands and knees and scrambled to his feet. He stumbled up the sandy beach and up the rocky slope to the top of the plateau. Finally safe from the sea's grasp, he collapsed on his back and stared blindly at the sky.

He heard the crunch of gravel near his head. "Do you think it killed her?" the Colonel asked.

"That was your intent, was it not?" Charles said darkly, refusing to look at him. "You're the one that shot her from the sky."

"I was firing at Leviathan. I was trying to save you. I didn't mean to hit her."

There was something in the Colonel's voice that made Charles sit up, weary as he was. The Colonel's face was white and drawn, except for the black eye Charles had given him. His proud bearing was diminished.

"Either way, you've won," Charles said.

"Have I?" The Colonel looked like a lost child, uncertain and a little afraid.

"Can we return now? We'll inform the Guild that she was killed and that will be the end of it."

The Colonel nodded. With relief, Charles reached out his hand to summon the butterfly.

It was Leviathan that answered.

The great serpent surged out of the surf, sending a wave up the cliff and onto the plateau. The sea spray hit Charles as he fell into the monster's looming shadow. The Colonel stepped between him and the serpent.

"Attack!" the Colonel yelled and his army answered.

Charles covered his ears against the cannon's roar and rattle of rifle fire. The shot bounced off Leviathan's scales with metallic clangs like discordant music, but the beast remained unmarked. The Colonel swung his pen with wide strokes, painting a net over the serpent that fell taut under the strain of leaded weights.

Leviathan tossed its head beneath the constricting net and gave a broken roar that sounded like the devil's laughter. The bright forge of its chest was stoked and with a fiery breath the net burned away. It then turned its flame against the Colonel's army. Drawn to be fearless and resolute, they did not turn and run but were consumed. Charles watched, transfixed with horror, expecting them to scream and blacken, but they did not. The soldiers merely froze in place as multihued flames turned them to dust and blew away.

When the plateau was clear, the fiery eyes turned back to the two living men. Charles held up his hand again.

"Hang on to me Colonel," he said, willing the drifting butterfly swiftly to his waiting palm. Instead it floated up on a draft of air and danced around Leviathan's smoking snout. Before his eyes, the monster began to dissolve, becoming a jumble of light and shadow like a rough underpainting of its former shape. It shrank and blurred and then began to take form again. When it was fully resolved, a woman with red-gold hair stood before them on the beach. She wore a rippling gown that seemed to be made from waves and cloud. The butterfly alighted on the woman's outstretched hand.

"Faith?" Charles breathed in doubt. It seemed impossible that she could be alive or that she had been that creature. But of course, anything was possible in Faith's world.

She gave him a radiant smile. "Charles. I'm so glad you are safe."

He wanted to go to her and hold her in his arms, but she looked too magnificent and his knees felt too weak. He knelt instead, as to a queen. As to a goddess.

Faith's eyes turned to the Colonel and her smile faded. "And you Colonel, though you do look worse for wear. Since I am done hiding my thoughts and feelings from you, I will admit, your black eye gives me satisfaction. It is the least you deserve."

"I have done nothing wrong. I have acted in the best interest of the Guild at every moment," the Colonel said, though with less conviction than Charles had heard from him before. His bearing was still proud but there was something of fear and wonder in his face as he looked at Faith. Even the Colonel was not immune to the impact of her splendor.

"Defiant to the end?" Faith arched an eyebrow. "You have acted in *your* best interest, without regard for anything or anyone else. You may declare that you have not been wrong, but you have not been right either. Nor have

I. I have made many mistakes. Still, that is something you and I will have to reckon with on our own. You are defeated here. Now, my concern is with the Guild."

"They have ordered that you be brought before the High Council," the Colonel said.

"Ordered? Me?" Faith laughed. "They have no power over me."

"They control the Ink. They control you."

Faith's brows drew down and an impish smile curled her lips. "We will see about that."

Afraid of what she might be scheming, Charles tried to change tack. "If we go back empty handed, they will send others."

"You're right," Faith said drumming her fingers on her chin. Then she nodded to herself and said, "Until their curiosity is satisfied I will have no peace. I will agree to meet the High Council at the Guild Hall. Tell me the date and time and I will appear before them."

"How do we know you will show?" the Colonel asked.

"I am as eager as they to settle this once and for all. Now, you two must leave. I have some... cleaning up to do," Faith said with a sweeping glance around the beach. Something caught her eye out in the water. "Oh- I almost forgot. You'll need your pen back, won't you Charles?"

"I'm afraid it's lost."

"Not at all." Faith strode out into the water, the hem of her dress riding on the breaking waves, becoming one with the foam until she seemed to wear the surf itself. One of the sirens rose from the water, holding Charles' pen aloft.

"Sirens!" the Colonel shouted throwing up his hands, "cover your ears!"

Faith laughed as she walked gracefully back to shore, unhindered by the water's rise and fall. "They were never true sirens! Lucky for you, I had no desire that men be lured to their doom when I drew them. I just liked the idea of mermaids who could sing so beautifully."

The Colonel lowered his hands warily and Charles looked at him in dawning shock. "You knew all along she was a rogue! It was you who tore the page out of her book."

The Colonel did not answer but his shifting eyes gave Charles his answer. Charles took his pen from Faith. Their fingers touched for a moment. It was if he had touched the sun.

"What shall I tell the Astors?" the Colonel asked.

Faith looked down at the sand for a moment then raised a somber face. "Tell them that I am dead. They should not feel rejected or slighted, particularly William. None of this is their fault. Besides, it's close enough to the truth. In fact, my death should relieve you of a great many burdens, Colonel."

Again the Colonel did not answer. Exhaustion was crashing down on Charles. He swayed on his feet.

"Go now. Get rest. And I will see you before the Council," Faith said. The butterfly appeared before them as out of the air. The Colonel grabbed Charles' arm, his grip notably weaker than before. The butterfly landed on Charles' palm and spirited them away.

Without contraries is no progression. Attraction and repulsion, reason and energy, love and hate, are necessary to human existence.

- William Blake, The Marriage of Heaven and Hell

CHAPTER FORTY

The Terms

Faith had not been diminished by her time in Phantasia. If anything, Charles thought as he watched her before the High Council, she was more radiant than ever. She had arrived at the appointed hour, not through one of the Towers of Doors, but through the main gates like visiting royalty. She had stood, poised and serene as the Council had asked her question after question. Some she answered openly, others he knew she demurred, for which Charles, and the Colonel he suspected, were grateful.

The Council had nodded sagely when she told them of the apple, and exchanged knowing glances when she had described biting it. When asked how she had come by such a source of Ink, she had replied, "By nature and by right." This bold assertion had not been received well. Certain of the Council had become animated at her arrogance, but she remained cool and composed in the face of their reproach. When the High Council had retreated to confer among themselves, she wore a mysterious half-smile that suggested she found the whole affair quite amusing.

Charles wanted nothing more than to simply stand and look at Faith, but a rustle and shuffle in the entry arch forced his eyes away. The Council had returned from their deliberations. Charles' heart beat in his throat. The statues on the corbels up above seemed to lean closer, intent to hear the outcome. The Council retook their seats; only the Council scribe remained standing to announce their judgment. He cleared his throat and began to speak in a voice that rang throughout the Hall.

"It is the Council's determination that Guild Master Trumbull's daughter has most likely discovered a novel source of Ink. This Guild was established by a sacred trust to protect the Ink and guard it from misuse, regardless of its origin. We consequently assert our dominion over this new source. We further find that the Guild Master's daughter has used said source to create a number of dangerous beings and conditions within Phantasia, putting Masters of the Guild, herself, and potentially unwitting members of the public, in gravest danger. The Guild Master's daughter cannot therefore be entrusted with the keeping of said source, or further use of the Ink. We hereby demand that the Guild Master's daughter surrender the Ink which she has discovered to the Guild for safekeeping and she herself be separated from all sources of Ink for now and forever."

When the scribe's words faded, the Hall was silent. Charles' eyes flew to Faith, searching for her reaction. He was surprised to see her smiling. And then, Faith tossed her head back and laughed. The sound reverberated off the dome of the ceiling like bells ringing. When it ended, there was another silence. The Council was slack jawed with shock.

When Faith spoke, it was not loud but carried clearly from ear to ear.

"You speak with authority and yet you are mistaken about a great many things. The first of these is your belief that you can and should keep Phantasia free of dark or disturbing thoughts. That is like creating a painting that is all light and no shadow! You are artists here. You know it is the contrast that makes the picture. And who alive possesses an imagination that pure? I challenge each of you to say with clear conscience before your god, whichever that may be, that there is nothing dangerous or untoward in your own worlds. How comfortable would you be for us all to take a tour?" She fixed them each in turn with a penetrating stare. They shifted in their seats, examined the table before them, anything but meet her gaze.

"As I thought." Faith said with a knowing smile. "No one is immune to dangerous and disconcerting thoughts; to deny them is to deny our humanity. They are a necessary evil to be tolerated, perhaps even cherished. Only by confronting the shadow in myself have I been able to master it. Left hidden, it grows wild and unchecked, and that is what is truly dangerous."

Faith took a step toward the assembled Council who collectively leaned away. "Your greatest mistake, however, is about the Ink itself. It is not something I discovered, a prize to be handed over. I am the source. To surrender it to you would be to surrender my body and soul, neither of which will I do. I believe that if you were to give your imaginations free rein, inside each of you, you might find a source as well."

Faith paused, letting her words sink in. When she resumed, her voice was stronger, commanding. "Your final mistake today is the belief that I am here to surrender to your judgment or even to negotiate. You have no leverage over me, no position of strength. You cannot take what I do not wish to surrender. I have come here today to do two things: to satisfy your curiosity and to give you my terms of peace."

There was an angry rumble from the Council but they were muted by her raised hand. Charles wondered if their silence was voluntary.

"It is my belief that no one should be denied the Ink who has the Talent to use it. I have considered taking down this Guild and putting an end to your self-righteous machinations. I realized however, that daVinci, in wisdom or foolishness, has bequeathed his source to your care not just for the protection of the Ink but for training in its art, a service I would urge you to emphasize in the future. This Guild serves a purpose, even if it serves it imperfectly. I have no more right to take that from you, than you have to demand the Ink from me. And so, these are my terms: I will leave you your source to do with as your body dictates, and I will do the same with mine. I will not interfere with how you manage your source, and you will not interfere with how I choose to use or bestow my gifts. I offer this on one simple condition. No one, whether in body or mind, will enter my part of Phantasia without express permission or invitation. Should anyone associated with the Guild violate this term, your right to control daVinci's source is forfeit."

The Council erupted into angry protest, each piling loudly atop the last.

The last voice standing rang out clearly. "The Guild Master's daughter has no authority here! By what right does she threaten us?"

Faith's answer echoed in the chamber. "I am no longer the Guild Master's daughter. I am Faith. I am my own creation."

"What do you mean by that, precisely?" Guild Master West asked with knitted brow.

Faith shook her head with a small smile. "Gentlemen. Use your imaginations. After all, that is what qualifies you to sit here is it not? The only limitation to my power is what I believe to be impossible. I now believe nothing to be impossible."

"So, what you are saying is-"

Charles interrupted. He cleared his throat and stepped forward. "If I may address the Council..." He received no objection. He glanced at Faith and then back at the Council. "I think a demonstration of Faith's power would assist the Council's understanding better than words. If you agree."

"Absolument pas!" Guild Master David shouted, his eyes wide.

"Are you afraid?" Faith asked.

He frowned and straightened at this challenge. "Non! I am not afraid of a woman. She has no pen."

"I don't need one." Faith's answer sent a nervous titter through the gathering.

Faith's body, that had moments before seemed as solid and real as any other in the room, began to blur and spin. She became a whirlwind of light and color that stretched to fill the height of the central dome. The papers of the Council flew from beneath their hands and they grabbed at wigs that threatened to lift away. A few cowered behind the table and the Colonel looked as though he wished he could become one with the floor. And then, in the heights of the dome, the wind coalesced into bright flames of red and gold until they took on the form of a great firebird with a tail that stretched to the floor. The phoenix called out, the Council answered with frightened cries of their own. The bird raised its wings and contracted towards the dais until Faith was once again standing before the awed and silent Council.

It was Guild Master West who broke the silence as he righted his wig. "In light of the demonstration, I move that the High Council agree to the Guild- to Faith's demands."

"Before we consider the motion, I have one point of clarification," Guild Master Goya said. "You say we are to stay out of your world, but you have said nothing about staying out of ours."

"I promise to respect the privacy of any living world."

"Only the living?"

"Oh, I am quite keen to explore daVinci's world and you can expect to see me around the Hall. I promised not to interfere. I am not promising not to be present."

"That's hardly equitable."

"It's not meant to be. Do we have an accord?"

The motion was passed with varied levels of reluctance. Charles breathed a sigh of relief. As they waited for the scribe to draw up an official document, Charles approached Faith timidly. She was so changed. He was as infatuated as he was afraid.

Faith greeted him with an open smile and his heart thudded wildly. "Thank you Charles for all of your support. I have not deserved it, but I hope to make up for it yet."

"Does that mean I will have an invitation to visit?"

Faith laughed and gave him a mischievous wink. "You are welcome for tea anytime."

When Faith had signed the accord with a flourish of her empty hand, she turned to the Council with a sly smile and said, "this is my sign to you." Her image stretched and thinned once again, but this time it formed an arc of colored light that rose into the shadows of the ceiling and then disappeared.

Yonder is the sea, great and wide...
There go the ships
and Leviathan that you formed to sport in it.

- Psalm 104

CHAPTER FORTY-ONE

Faith

The ginger tabby leapt onto Faith's writing desk. Purring loudly, it insinuated itself between her and the guest list she had been working on. With a fond reprimand, she extracted the paper and held it up before her. The cat batted it lazily as she considered who to invite to her next dinner party. Contrary to what Charles had warned, Phantasia was far from lonely even if she did not create a single soul to populate it.

Of the living, Mr. Blake had become a fixture. He never ceased to fascinate her with his unusual insights, and if he brought a Devil as his guest, so much the better. Between Mr. Blake and Jarvis, there would never be a dull moment. Faith had also made connections with the few women of the Guild, and those who should have been among its members. In particular, she hoped Madame Le Brun and Ms. Cosway would be able to attend. She wanted to consult with them on how best to encourage young women in the arts. Not only were there those whose current Talent should be fostered, but there were several promising young girls who could be the force that turned the tides when they came of age. Perhaps in a year or so, as her skills improved, Faith's mother might be able to join as well.

Among the deceased, the possibilities for intriguing guests was endless. Faith did not know if there was a separate soul that went to heaven, but she had been delighted to find that genius left an indelible mark on Phantasia, and it was not limited to visual artists. She could have Gentileschi and

Ruysch, Beethoven and Mozart, Nannerl preferably, Shakespeare and the recently departed - or should she say arrived? - Ms. Austen.

But what to do about Master daVinci? Faith had made it a regular habit to invite him, after making his shade's acquaintance, out of curiosity and then respect. He was as much a genius as reputed, but he pursued his inspirations in a probing and methodical way that tried Faith's patience. He also had an irritating habit of wandering off in pursuit of some line of thought. He did not make the best guest.

Faith tapped her cheek with the end of her pen, a diamond stylus wound 'round with gold and silver vines, as she counted up her guests. Satisfied that she had included enough men, she found a spot on the desk the cat had not commandeered and crossed daVinci from the list. Of course, she could have simply dismissed the thought of him, but Faith had discovered she found the ritual of writing deeply satisfying.

Glancing at the shadows on the wall, Faith put her pen back on its filigree holder. She would send the invitations later. With an affectionate scratch behind the tabby's ears, she pushed back from the desk. Headed for the northwest tower, Faith crossed through the center of her pleasure dome.

Faith had struggled to decide what, other than gardens, a pleasure palace should contain, until she realized that gardens alone were sufficient so long as they were shared. What purpose did their beauty serve if she alone enjoyed them? And so she had built her pleasure dome around her garden courtyard and invited the better part of Phantasia to join her there in celebration. The fountain, now a phoenix and a serpent instead of nymphs and dolphins, still spilled both water and fire. It was surrounded by a broad plaza where guests could dance to the music of the sirens and the singing stars. Beneath the vine draped arcades that circled the perimeter were small, intimate courtyards for quiet conversation, lit with bowls of fire. The great tree stood at the center, basking in the soft light and prismatic color of the crystalline dome, offering any fruit a heart could desire, save one.

Faith walked along the white stone paths, past planters filled with palms and citrus twined with jasmine, and up the spiraling steps to the room at the peak of the tallest tower. Next to an oaken door with a Celtic shield carved on its face was a marble pedestal and a narrow table along the wall. On the pedestal was a single apple, perfect in every way but for the bite taken from it. On the table was a silver tea tray. In front of the teapot patterned with blue roses was a brightly hued butterfly resting on a sprig of fresh picked violets.

The butterfly flitted away as Faith picked up the flowers and held them to her nose with a smile.

"Wait at the Summerhouse," she said to the dancing butterfly. She gently blew across its wings and it disappeared from sight.

Faith crossed the room to the balcony, passing gauzy curtains that blew in the breeze through wide open doors. The sky above was cloudless, the sea below, no longer icy and slate gray, was warm, serene, and turquoise bright. The weather was clear now, but there would be rain tonight. She just had time for a flight before the storm, and Charles, would arrive.

Faith leapt onto and then past the balcony rail, far out into open sky. She fell, arms spread wide, past the palace and the island's edge, past the silver ribbon of the cascading river and through its mist. As she fell her arms became great scarlet wings, her legs a trailing tail of fire.

Just before she reached the ocean's surface, she leveled out and glided. Her reflection skimmed and bounced as though over rippled glass, like glints and sparks of sunset gathered into a swift river of molten gold.

A horned head with dawn-lit eyes and metallic scales, glimmering with all the pearlescent hues of depths and ice, broke the surface and scattered her reflection. The serpent raced along in the shadow of her outspread wings, its sinuous body rising and falling, twisting and turning, in graceful curves that left shimmering eddies in its wake. Faith banked and dipped, her wingtips kissing the surface to trace their own delicate arabesques of foam. No longer foes, the phoenix and the serpent danced across the blue sea to a misty far horizon.

Faith had been lost in a world of pure imagination. Through fire and water, hope and fear, it had been restored.

If you enjoyed this book, please consider reviewing it on Amazon, Goodreads, or wherever you like to discover new books

Forthcoming Titles:

The Shard and the Scale
Book One of the Chromaeria Series

Joined with the White Crown
Mistress of the Banks
The Warrior Queen Duology

Historical Notes

The kernel of this story was originally inspired by the children's book, *Harold and the Purple Crayon* by Crockett Johnson. This is a charming book in which Harold has an adventure in a world he creates with his favorite crayon. He draws an apple tree only to scare himself with the dragon he draws to guard it. He creates a boat when he ends up in water and a hot air balloon to save himself when he falls from a mountain top because he forgot to draw the other side. The end of the book is concerned with his search for home, and what home really is, so that he can go to bed. I love Harold's resourcefulness and creativity as much as I love the closing pun. I was further inspired by other favorite moments where art comes to life, such as the chalk pavement pictures in *Mary Poppins*, the chase scene that runs into and through the art in *Night at the Museum: Battle of the Smithsonian*, and even aspects of the *Matrix*. From these sources, the Ink was born.

The original concept for this book was about modern teenagers who had (re)discovered this mysterious Ink. In addition to learning its powers, they would also be challenged within the imaginary world by the shade of a disgruntled artist intent on revenge. The development of this antagonist is what drove me back in time to the early 1800's. Before then, particularly in the Renaissance, women were not excluded as professional artists, regardless of what their current state of recognition might suggest. Later in the 1800's many talented and bold women were once again gaining some traction, uphill as it might have been, but during the Regency era the art world was nearly devoid of professional female artists. Who could possibly be more disgruntled than an artistically gifted woman who did not aspire to society's expectations for that time? Thus, Faith's story began as a villain origin backstory. Alas, the original book with alternating time lies was too long, the baby was cut in half, and Faith's story ended up being the more compelling of the two.

Although Faith was fictional, as mentioned in the opening note about the characters, I wanted to embed her in an historically accurate world. The search was on for an historical artist who was renowned enough to be a Master of the Guild, but whose personal life lent itself to a fictional, but theoretically plausible, conflict with an imaginary daughter. When I read Trumbull's autobiography as edited by Theodore Sizer (Yale University Press, 1953), I knew I had found my man. I'm not sure I could have made up what Trumbull's real life offered. Even the name Faith, his mother's name, turned out to be the perfect double entendre for the theme that emerged. From that point on, the story practically wrote itself.

In addition to a plot which is built around his actual circumstances, I have used many of Trumbull's own words and expressed opinions in the development of his character. I have also employed the perspectives of his contemporaries which are available in the appendices provided by the editor Sizer, as well as the writings of William Dunlap, the real life, gossip-prone curator of the Academy, who wrote *History of the Rise and Progress of the Arts of Design in the United States* (now that's a catchy title) and in his *Diary*. However, I think it is important to differentiate between the real Trumbull and the fictional villain.

Anyone who has ever seen the back of a two dollar bill, toured the US Capitol Rotunda, taken US History in middle school, or driven through Connecticut has a passing familiarity with John Trumbull. His father, Johnathan Trumbull, was the governor of Connecticut both before *and after* the Revolution (no small feat), lending the family name to a host of roads and landmarks. Trumbull himself ultimately retired to New Haven and was buried beneath the art Gallery at Yale that bore his name. He was the painter who created the four enormous canvases in the National Rotunda, including the Signing of the Declaration of Independence, an engraving of which is on the currency. He was involved in the "André affair" during the Revolution and was on the Jay Treaty Commission following the war. He was indeed (briefly) an Aid du Camp to General Washington, was asked by Jefferson to be his secretary (but turned him down), and witnessed the storming of the Bastille, carrying home from the Marquis de Lafayette a message and warning to the US President about the imminent French Revolution. Trumbull's autobiography is a fascinating, if somewhat dry, tour through the major events of the times, for a surprising number of which he was physically present.

As someone who was, in fact, obsessed with leaving a lasting legacy, he would be pleased to have made this kind of mark. While he is justifiably proud to have been witness to history, it is apparent he was more of a leaf caught up in the whirlwind of the times rather than a moving force itself. As anyone would in their autobiography, Trumbull shows himself to best advantage, reproducing at length the evidence of his triumphs and glossing over his failures, if he mentions them at all. (We will get to what he doesn't mention in a moment). In the best light, the Colonel was religiously faithful, noble in aspiration, industrious, intelligent, courteous, and urbane, these last a result of intense status consciousness and the propriety that went with it. In a more negative light, even accounting for the bias of his self-presentation, he is aristocratic, condescending to those below him, sycophantic to those above him, excessively proud to the point of spite, and his efforts at self-effacement come off as false humility. His contemporaries, even in eulogy, noted his "passionate" (read: easily offended) and dictatorial nature. But, was he the misogynistic, patriarchal jerk that I have portrayed?

Jerk, maybe. I will let you be the judge of that. Misogynistic, probably not. At least, not any more so than his contemporaries. An accomplished woman of the time, as Mr. Bingley noted with amazement in *Pride and Prejudice*, was expected to have some competence in singing, dancing, embroidery, and drawing. This latter was expected to be confined to the lower forms of art, namely fruits, flowers, and miniature portraits. The higher forms of art such as historical, allegorical, etc., required a careful study of the human form which was strictly off limits to proper women. When the British Royal Academy was founded in 1768, there were two female members, Angelica Kauffman and Mary Moser. Kauffman subsequently brought Maria Cosway in, but she was the last female artist admitted to the associated art school until 1861 and no woman was an Academy member until 1936. The Academie des Beaux Arts in France stopped admitting women in the late 1700's, before which only 15 out of 450 members were women. Women were not again admitted until 1897.

During these times, the only avenue of art instruction for women was private, and even that presented problems socially and, often, maritally. In the mid-1800's, the sisters Edma and Berthe Morisot took lessons from famous French artist Joseph Guichard. In a letter to the girl's mother,

Guichard warned that if they became painters, it could be catastrophic for their social standing. Essentially, becoming a painter was the social equivalent of eloping or other scandalous behavior. Edma capitulated and married, a choice she seems to have regretted later. Berthe went on to become a well respected painter, only later marrying the brother of artist Edouard Manet. The point of this exposition is that female artists were not encouraged by society at large in any way. A woman like Faith would have met with resistance at every turn.

If I owe the Colonel an apology, however, it is with regard to his attitude towards women in art. This is one place where I have veered away from the factual evidence for the sake of conflict and plot, channeling through him the misogyny of the time as opposed to what he personally seems to have espoused. He cites his own sister's oil paintings, two portraits and a landscape hung proudly in the family parlor, as early inspiration for his art career. He also praises without reserve the work of Madame LeBrun, Maria Cosway, and Angelica Kauffman in the autobiography. The catalog for the first American Academy exhibit in October of 1816 included a couple of still lifes painted by Sarah Trumbull. Admittedly, he actually may have been more tolerant of female artists than many of his contemporaries.

As for the rest of his actions...

Let's begin with what the Colonel included in his memoir. Trumbull suffered an injury to his left eye falling down a flight of stairs as a child. In spite of this disability which only got worse as he grew older, he aspired to become an artist at an early age, particularly after a visit to Mr. Copley in Boston. Interestingly, it was Mr. Copley's rich manner of dress and apparent wealth that inspired him, not so much the pictures. Trumbull's father did try to disabuse him of the notion that art was the way to wealth and immortality, and Trumbull did attend Harvard, but he remained convinced that art was the way. And then the Revolution began.

Trumbull was in the military for a total of one and a half years out of a seven year conflict. The words I put in Vanderlyn's mouth while complaining to Dunlap about their very real rivalry, sum up the discrepancies between Trumbull's image, both personal and public, as a war hero and the reality of his service. Strangely, all of these circumstances are clearly laid out by Trumbull who seems unaware of the contradictions. For example, Trumbull notes with pride that he was made a Colonel on June 28, 1776 by General Gates. However, when Congress approved his change in rank officially, the date was recorded as September 12, 1776. When Trumbull learned of this in February the following year, he immediately began a letter writing campaign which he has reproduced verbatim in the memoir, expressing his deep offense at this misdating. He resigned his commission entirely, rather than tolerate such a discrepancy in his record, unless Congress both apologized and rectified it. He presents this information as though the insult is plainly obvious to the reader.

It is not just time and distance that makes this temper tantrum mystifying. The responses he received, which he also included, show that the recipients of his letters were equally put off by his attitude and demands. Congress in its turn was insulted and refused. So Trumbull, in the midst of an ongoing war abandoned duty and service in a fit of pique. If Congress would not meet his demands, they would be denied his enlightened contributions (which he positions as critical to several of the Army's successes even though he never saw actual combat) until they realized the depth of their mistake and implored him to return. And yet, he self-identified as a "patriot-artist," uniquely suited to be the official raconteur of the nation's birth, and clung to the disputed rank for the rest of his life.

After resigning his commission, he went to the enemy country to pursue his career as an artist.

With an introduction from Benjamin Franklin in hand, Trumbull sought out Benjamin West, an expat American who had become royal painter to the King and founded the Royal Academy. Trumbull was only one of many American artists who studied under West and went on to great success. Trumbull did struggle on account of his eyesight and was advised by West to stick to smaller paintings, as larger compositions exacerbated his problems with perspective. Consequently, West discouraged Trumbull from pursuing the large rotunda paintings, and a panorama of Niagara Falls (a project which Vanderlyn had received West's support for), contributing to their falling out many years later. Trumbull studied with West for a very short time before he was arrested, surprise!, in connection with the ongoing war. The Americans had hanged two British officers, including Major John André, as accused spies. Britain responded by imprisoning a (former) American officer who conveniently happened to be hanging out in London. Although Trumbull was theoretically under threat of execution as retribution, he was allowed to pick his prison and was well fed and visited with ample time to stroll the prison grounds. He was also free to pursue his art.

When the war was over, he returned to the States and, leaning fully into his patriot-artist vision, pursued a lofty project to document the birth of the nation in several historical paintings. To this end, he traveled the entire country to capture the likenesses of the original Signers of the Declaration. If they were deceased, he used relatives who, by consensus, were deemed good stand-ins. It was about this time that he painted the scenes, in smaller scale, that would one day decorate the Rotunda, and which garnered him the most acclaim. Sadly, the large scale versions that are his most obvious legacy were universally regarded inferior to the originals. He also painted a number of scenes that were sympathetic to the British side, which he exhibited when he was again in Britain some years later. This further undermined his *bona fides* as patriot in his detractors's minds.

In addition to painting, Trumbull embarked on several commercial ventures, all of which failed. His painting career likewise vacillated, but as noted, he always seemed to be an extra on the scene of history's most critical events. He relates these stories with evident self-satisfaction in his autobiography, apparently unaware, as with the resignation of his commission, at how prickly and pretentious he sometimes paints himself (if you'll pardon the pun).

However, it is what he left out of his memoir that is most intriguing. To me, it was practically an engraved invitation to cast him as a villain in this story.

The least shocking, but still strange, omission was his position with the American Academy. Not only was he a founder, but he was President of the Academy between 1817 and 1827. By then, a faction of younger artists had become fed up with his traditional and inflexible attitudes about art and broke away to form the National Academy of Design in 1825. When Trumbull finally stepped down from the American Academy, his resignation was accepted without fanfare or thanks. It seems he had made more enemies than friends by that time. The conflict with Vanderlyn over his exhibit at the Academy was real. According to Dunlap, Trumbull did engineer Vanderlyn's eviction and other difficulties, although Vanderlyn's conviction on this score is less clear. Ingham was one of the earliest associates of the newly reformed American Academy in 1816, but he too moved to the new National Academy and became a leading member there.

Although Trumbull did not think his tenure at the Academy merited mention in his life story, it is what first recommended him as the Master of the Guild that I was looking for.

Far and away the most interesting of Trumbull's omissions from his biography are his romantic interests. He makes no mention at all of his first love, Harriet Wadsworth, nor (understandably) his child out of wedlock, but he also fails to document his marriage to Sarah Trumbull. In his entire biography, she is mentioned only three times. The first is tangentially in a reproduced letter from 1818, eight years after their marriage. The last is her death. All information about these women come from outside sources.

The Trumbull and Wadsworth families were closely intertwined as several Trumbulls seem to have married several Wadsworths. Harriet was John's niece or cousin. He was thirteen years her senior and held her as an infant. When he returned to the States after the War, she was 20 years old and he became infatuated, as evidenced by his letters. For some unknown reason, these stopped in 1791. Frail and in poor health, Harriet went to Bermuda in 1793 where the sea air was expected to help, but she died. Trumbull painted two miniature portraits of her posthumously, keeping one for himself.

About the time his correspondence with Harriet ceased, Trumbull was tempted by and succumbed to the amorous advances of a servant in his brother's household in 1792. He claimed there were several other potential candidates for the resulting paternity, but believed that the woman pinned it on him because he was best able to pay. It probably helped that by the time she had the child, he was out of the country and unable to address the issue privately. A legal judgment was entered against him, he paid his fine, and otherwise forgot about the incident, which he referred to as an "accident that befel" him when he was "a little too intimate with a Girl." All those who met Ray, and were aware of his possible relation to Trumbull, remarked on how much he resembled the Colonel.

It wasn't until Trumbull was engaged to marry Sarah, some seven years later and at her behest, that he was moved to see to the boy's welfare. In the letter to James Wadsworth, the confidant he tasked with finding and settling the boy, he laments that Ray was not provided "with a more probable Father", and the woman with a husband, simply because Trumbull was "the more able bodied man." In closing the letter, he declares that "It is bad enough to be called the Father of a Child whose Mother is little worth; — but, to be called the Father of a worthless, illiterate, profligate wretch (as He may prove if let uneducated) is a disgrace to which it is criminal to expose oneself, when it may be avoided by a little Care and Expence." Following on this warm sentiment, Trumbull did make an effort over the succeeding years to provide a living to John Ray Trumbull as a farmer, but did not provide his name directly. He maintained the fiction that Ray was his nephew, going into one his odd fits of offense when Ray had the temerity to refer to Trumbull and Sarah as his Mother and Father in a later letter. Ray ultimately rejected the life of a farmer and joined the British Army against Trumbull's wishes and advice. Their relationship deteriorated over the years, particularly when Ray married, again without approval, and Trumbull eventually seems to have rescinded his support.

In 1794, after Ray had been born and Harriet had died, Trumbull went to England again as part of the Jay Treaty Commission. In July of 1799, Trumbull wrote the just referenced letter regarding Ray. In a later letter to a different recipient, Trumbull says that he told Sarah of his past indiscretion as something she was entitled to know upon proposing marriage to her. In return, it was she who insisted that he care for the boy. Thus, the Colonel must already have proposed to Sarah Hope Harvey by July of 1799. In October of 1799, he rented a room for her use, for exactly one year ending on the date of their unusual wedding on October 1, 1800. This was a bizarre arrangement for an unmarried couple. Combined with Trumbull's refusal to identify Sarah other than "Mrs. Trumbull" to his closest friends who attended this wedding, including Rufus King who gave the bride away because she had no family to stand for her, there is more than a whiff of impropriety.

Even if these facts were not widely known, the mere idea that the "emphatically well-bred" Colonel, as Dunlap called him, would marry an English orphan of low status and upbringing, eighteen years his junior, with appalling manners to boot, was enough to engender rampant speculation and gossip. The Colonel defended Sarah in a letter as a woman of practical accomplishment, as a way of preparing the recipient not to expect a fine lady when they met. It is from that letter, and a few others, that we know she was an orphan, having lost her mother, brother and sister at a young enough age that she did not remember them, followed closely by her father, William Hope. There was no explanation of the name Harvey (her mother's maiden name was West). Even with this preparation,

Trumbull's own family was not thrilled to meet her. It is impossible to say what exactly transpired, but there is one letter from Trumbull to a cousin expressing his deep offense at the way Sarah was treated and his indignation that the family would question his judgment in selecting a mate. In typical fashion, such an insult prompted him to cut off further relations with the offending parties.

It is fair to assume that Sarah was just too hard to swallow. From other letters, we know that she was indeed carried home drunk from Mrs. Primes, that her manners were exaggerated, her dress and toilet poorly executed such that she looked like a washwoman on occasion, and that she got drunk and abusive in public. The Colonel was generally stoic about such instances, stating once that he was atoning for a sin.

Adding to the mystery, there is not one surviving letter from Sarah herself. Trumbull kept copies of all of his letters, even the salacious ones regarding Ray. He painted Sarah's portrait on numerous occasions, including on her deathbed (creepy), and used her as a model in some paintings. We know she was literate because he wrote many letters to her, and also remarked that her education was sound. So, where is her correspondence? Did he destroy it? What could possibly have been in those letters that he could not bear to leave a record? For what sin was the Colonel atoning?

As Dunlap relates in the story, there were a number of theories about poor Sarah's origins. Even if I had not been looking for a place to insert a fictional daughter, my bet is that the Colonel and Sarah had an affair, not necessarily an adulterous one, and she became pregnant. (Sarah's brief but intensely happy marriage to Mr. Harvey was fictionalized for her benefit. I felt she deserved at least a short moment in the sun). For whatever reason, perhaps because there were no other contenders for paternity this time, or an accumulation of guilt over the first, Trumbull decided to marry her. The deal would have been struck shortly after learning she was pregnant and the child would have been born sometime in the next six to seven months while she was staying in the room provided to her by Trumbull. The fact that no real child is ever mentioned would suggest that it did not survive, or was adopted out. Or, maybe, just maybe, there was a girl named Faith who disappeared into a world of pure imagination and all record of her existence on this side of reality was expunged by her shamed and overly sensitive father. Just sayin'.

As for the other characters, Jarvis was every bit the wild card depicted and deserves a story of his own. The Astors did have a house in the city close to where the Trumbulls lived. That, and their wealth, made them a good target for Trumbull's (fictional) ambitions. Though surely not the dullard I portray, William Backhouse Astor, for such a notable family, was surprisingly nondescript. He didn't accumulate more wealth, nor did he lose it. Besides some charity and investment in the arts, he did nothing remarkable, which suited my purposes perfectly. I did not want a marriage to a brute as a conflict in the story. I preferred the more subtle threat of a dull existence for which sympathy would be hard to find. It would be a quiet kind of torture.

Then there is Mr. Ingham. He was of the right age, in the right place, at the right time. Faith's physical appearance is based on two of his paintings: *Flower Girl* and the *White Plume,* which to my eye, employ the same model. The latter is only preserved in an engraving print, but it was described in a New York Mirror article (Volume VIII, Number 44) about an exhibit at the National Academy of Design. "By [William Tell by Inman's] side is the White Plume. Ingham. A face to be gazed on bended knee. It is a seducing vision of female loveliness, as soft and soothing as the other is vehement and ferocious. The shadow of a graceful bonnet never fell on a countenance more radiant and beautiful. How perfectly unclouded the features; how lightly the tresses repose on the soft shoulder; what a brilliancy of complexion; a mouth which you wish to fold your arms and gaze at forever, instead of going back to business and bargaining; and the eyes, blue and beaming — Oh! He who knows his heart is weak, of heaven should pray to guard him from such eyes as those!" High praise indeed. Mr. Ingham was well liked, well respected and, intriguingly, never married. Perhaps his heart had already been claimed by Faith.

Lastly, there is the Guild of Athena, which is, of course, entirely fictional. Or is it?

About the Author

Geneva Price has had more of a careen than a career. Although she has been talking about writing books since she was in elementary school, she has taken the twisty path getting there. She has been a lawyer, an archaeologist, an Egyptologist, a stay at home mom, an art teacher and, finally a full time artist and author. Geneva is a second generation native Southern Californian, but now lives in North Carolina where there is plenty of water and just enough seasons to be cute. She is a gardener who dabbles in landscape design, a tea drinker and dark chocolate connoisseur, a crazy dog lady who likes big mutts and urges you to adopt, not shop, a list maker, a dragon fanatic and, if it comes in purple, she's likely to buy it.

Printed in the USA
CPSIA information can be obtained
at www.ICGtesting.com
JSHW022355180124
55444JS00001B/1